A Death For Adonis

...

A Death for a Darling

Robert Forsythe 1 and 2

DUET

A Death For Adonis

...

A Death for a Darling

E. X. Giroux

Felony & Mayhem Press • New York

All the characters and events portrayed in this work are fictitious.

A DEATH FOR ADONIS/A DEATH FOR A DARLING

Robert Forsythe 1 and 2

PRINTING HISTORY
A Death for Adonis
First edition (St. Martin's): 1984
A Death for a Darling
First edition (St. Martin's): 1985

Felony & Mayhem Duet edition: 2023

The icon above says you're holding a book in the Felony & Mayhem "British" category. These books are set in or around the UK, and feature the highly literate, often witty prose that fans of British mystery demand. If you enjoy this book, you may well like other "British" titles from Felony & Mayhem Press.

———◆———

For information about British titles or to learn more about Felony & Mayhem Press, please visit us online at:

www.FelonyAndMayhem.com

Other "British" titles from

FELONY&MAYHEM

Who Killed Adonis?

VANESSA CALVERT

Calvert's bewitching wife,
a woman who craved the
young man for herself?

ELINOR ATLIN

Vanessa's devoted cousin, willing
to do anything for her relative?

MELISSA CALVERT

Sebastian's sister,
a woman obsessed by the
honor of the family name?

ROSEMARY CALVERT

His niece, at the time
a headstrong teenager
dangerously devoted to
her uncle?

JOHN HORNER

Calvert's secretary, intoxicated
by Vanessa and jealous of
David Mersey's affect on her?

This book is for Russell Gordon Paterson.

A Death For Adonis

Chapter One

The words that had been spoken had no place in the tranquil room. Sunlight filtered through floor-length windows, settling in a pool on a fine Aubusson carpet and leaving the book-lined walls shadowed and indistinct. The man sat with his back to the windows. The woman faced him across the expanse of his polished desk. Neither looked directly at the other. He appeared engrossed in a slim sheaf of papers neatly arranged on the green blotter. The woman steadily watched the toe of her shoe tracing a pattern on the dim colors of the rug. Almost tangibly between them hovered the words, alien, infinitely distasteful, and faintly frightening.

Finally the man moved, pushing the papers away from him. The woman's eyes, brilliant and lizardlike, darted from her shoes and brushed across his face. He hesitated, as though groping among the words for one he wished to isolate.

"This murder and the rest of it...how long ago did it all happen?"

"Twenty-five years ago. At least," she hesitated, "in two weeks, twenty-five years."

"That would make it August twenty-fifth, 1944."

1

She didn't speak. Her eyes were busy with the tip of her shoe again. He waited a moment and then continued, "The accused was tried, found guilty, and sentenced. Now you wish the case to be investigated and if new evidence is found you hope to reopen the whole affair. Is that correct, Miss Pennell?"

"That is correct." This time she lifted her head and their eyes met. "Please don't call me Miss, it sounds so cold. I prefer Elizabeth."

"Very well, Elizabeth. To be blunt I can't see anything to be gained by an investigation. In the first place I no longer practice law and I am certainly not what you Americans call a private eye." Glancing down, he flicked one of the papers with a finger. "I assume the lady who recommended me mentioned both these facts."

Her lips quivered and she smiled, her eyes traveling from his slenderly elegant figure to the window and the sweep of turf that ended at the banks of a placid pool. "Amelia didn't accuse you of being a private eye." Her smile vanished. "She merely said that you had been an enormous help to her in a highly private matter and that you might consent to help me. As I told you, the accused as you call him is my father and I must find out once and for all whether there is any possibility of his innocence. This may sound dramatic, but the balance of my life, or perhaps I should say normal life, depends on it. You see, Mr. Forsythe..." she hesitated.

"Robert," he offered in answer to the question in her eyes.

She accepted it. "Robert. I might be able to live with the knowledge that in the heat of anger my father could kill, but this butchery—"

Forsythe interrupted. His expression was gentler and his manner a trifle lest formal. "The second point I was going to make was that it is not likely after this length of time that any new evidence can be uncovered. But we'll leave that for the moment. Do you mind telling me when you heard about your background? Your uncle adopted you, changed your last name. Did he conceal the crime your father was convicted of from you?"

She shook her head. "No, he never tried. My mother died when I was born. By the time I was three months old my aunt and uncle were homeward bound with me to Boston. When I was old enough to understand, about seven I suppose, Uncle Howard told me that my aunt and he were not my parents. When I was twelve he told me some facts about my parents. That was the first time I knew that Sebastian Calvert was my father. I was told that he was a convicted murderer. I was also told my father didn't receive the death penalty for his crime, but is still alive if you can call being catatonic living. My uncle wanted me to hear that from him, not from someone else. But the actual details, I guess the newspapers would call them the gory details, I didn't learn until I was sixteen."

She shot a look at Forsythe, her eyes penetrating. "I think I know what you're driving at. My adopted parents died at the same time, an automobile accident, when I was twenty-two. I inherited a sizable estate. I'm also in control of two separate businesses, an interior decorating firm and a women's clothing factory. All the Calverts are talented people. I am too. I'm an excellent clothing designer. That's what you want to know, isn't it?"

"You're very direct. Yes, that's it. You were well aware of your heritage; you had plenty of money to investigate it. You also mentioned that you were six at the time of your father's trial, which would place you over thirty now. For almost a decade you could have acted, but didn't. Why now?"

Fumbling in her purse, Elizabeth Pennell found a cigarette case and removed a gold-tipped tube. Forsythe rose and moved around the desk. He offered her his lighter and then perched on the corner of the desk.

Exhaling gray smoke, she gazed up at him. "From the time I was very young my life was conditioned, I suppose by me. I learned to accept the fact that I am Sebastian Calvert's daughter. I never learned to accept the fact that he'd killed the way they said he had. How was it put? Oh yes, 'the most brutal, bizarre, and perverted in England's bloody history'—"

Forsythe broke in. "He is also considered one of England's foremost artists."

She brushed this aside as though it was of no consequence. "Save your platitudes, Robert. Quite frankly I don't give a damn about his work. Don't expect me to be a dutiful daughter pretending and mouthing dutiful remarks about him. My father had time to raise my cousin Rosemary; he had time to remarry; but he had no time for me. He didn't want me; my mother's brother could have me. Fine, I'm interested in me too. My whole life has been built around my father's actions. No life for Elizabeth. She had her work and her friends. She even had a number of casual sexual affairs."

Breaking off, the woman looked up at Forsythe. His face was expressionless. She reached past him and stubbed her cigarette in an ashtray.

"I may sound cold and hard, but it's the truth. I could never trust myself to have any real intimacy, not after what happened to my father's love. Emotion was forbidden to me. Then a few months ago I fell hopelessly, madly, passionately in love. I use these adjectives deliberately. The daughter of Sebastian Calvert can't afford to indulge herself this way. Think where his madness and passion is supposed to have led."

Breaking off, she sat silently for a minute, one hand pleating the soft silk of her dress. The hand was large for her size, almost ugly with powerful, spatulate fingers.

Forsythe regarded her closely. He admitted wryly to himself that his first impression of Elizabeth Pennell had vanished like most first impressions into limbo. When she had entered his study, one hand extended to him, the other grasping the letter of introduction, he had seen a small compact woman with magnificent dark eyes, a slightly sallow complexion, and a large nose. The eyes remained magnificent but now the nose was revealed as perfect for her features, thin, high-bridged, and arrogant. He sensed behind her composure, conflict and a tightly leashed power. She disturbed him, filled him with a sense of unease. Reaching for his pipe, he started to fill it, patiently waiting for her to continue.

As though suddenly noticing what her hand was doing, she stopped her nervous pleating and folded both hands quietly in her lap.

"So you see why I feel I must do *something*. All I ask of you is to give it a try. If you're unsuccessful, I'll have to give up this attachment. But if you do turn up something that points to my father's innocence, I will feel free to live as others live, to love as others love."

It was her turn to wait. He returned to his leather chair behind the desk and sank into it. "You've been most candid; now it appears to be my turn. There are many excellent investigators in England. I can recommend several. I'm afraid, Elizabeth, that I'm the very worst choice you could have made to deal with this matter. My own past—"

"I know about your past." Her voice was low-pitched but forceful. "One of these investigators you are so fond of mentioning got the full rundown on it for me. I'm not a babe in the woods. I happen to be a hardheaded businesswoman. I know all about Robert Forsythe, barrister from a long line of barristers, something of a child prodigy, passed the bar exams at an extremely early age and started to make good predictions of a brilliant career, gave up said career suddenly in his twenty-seventh year and returned to the family home in Sussex, where he has lived as something of a recluse for six years."

Forsythe kept his face impassive. "Then you know the reason why the so-called brilliant career was given up, why I voluntarily retired from my practice."

A small smile drew her heavy brows together. "Yes, at least I know the rumors. Reportedly, you got out just before the legal profession could start disbarring actions." Her eyes flicked quickly toward his face again. "And I have heard about Virginia Telser."

He couldn't keep the bitterness out of his voice. "After this, you still wish to engage me, a barrister who betrayed his profession and banished himself to avoid a charge of misconduct?"

Her voice was lower. He had to strain to hear her. "Possibly that was what decided me. You are a pariah too. I don't know whether you're innocent or guilty, but you live in the shadows,

6 E. X. Giroux

watching life. I thought you might be able to understand how I feel, why this is so important to me." Her eyes didn't flick toward his face this time; she caught his eyes and held them steadily, relentlessly. "Are you afraid?"

He didn't flinch. "Of course I'm afraid. I'd be a fool not to be. If I do undertake this dredging into the past, a nasty case at the time, and swelled into a monstrous legend now, I'll be forced to come into contact with, to interview some of the very people I've been more or less avoiding."

Her eyes were still locked with his. "Will you do it?"

If she had shown any signs of weakness, any tears, any pleading, he might have been able to have given her a flat no. She didn't. Her eyes contained only a challenge and a hint of derision. The gauntlet was in front of him. He picked it up.

"Where can I contact you?"

She named an address in London. "I've taken a small service flat. About your fee…"

It was his opportunity to throw the derision back at her. "We'll discuss money later. If I'm lucky, you may name your own amount. If not, I'll present a bill for expenses."

Rising briskly, she smoothed the dark silk over her hips. Forsythe was on his feet, his finger pressing the button on the edge of his desk.

The door swung open and Miss Sanderson appeared. She arched her brows inquiringly at him.

"Please show Miss Pennell out. Good day, Elizabeth."

Throwing him a cool smile, she followed his secretary's spare figure into the hall. Forsythe had one final glimpse of her as the door closed. Turning, he flung open the long window behind him and leaned against the frame, gazing unseeingly down the green slope to the waters of the pool.

A russet-coated cat stepped daintily over the sill and rubbed against his leg, huge emerald eyes glowing like green coals. Absently he bent and lifted it, holding it against his side, one hand fondling its fur. It flexed claws gently against his hand and then settled back, eyes closed, a husky purr beginning far down in its throat.

Forsythe didn't hear his secretary return. He stood in the same position until gradually he became aware of her. She was softly but urgently clearing her throat. He turned slowly, the beginning of a smile on his lips.

"Well?" he asked.

"That," she said, "is my line."

He regarded her fondly. She was almost his height, a thin, quick-moving woman with fine bones and a disciplined, almost austere face—a deceptively austere face.

"Give," she demanded.

Placing the cat on his chair, he leaned against the back of it. His smile broadened. "Elizabeth Calvert Pennell. Does the name ring any bell in that cross-index mind of yours?"

"Pennell doesn't. Hey, wait a minute, Robby; you said Calvert." She lifted her hand and began to click her thumbnail in an audible tattoo against her front teeth.

Forsythe sighed. "Sandy, can't you find some other way to stimulate your thinking processes without that infernal racket? I suggest biting your nails. It would be quieter, you know."

"You've suggested that before." Then her hand fell away from her face. "She wouldn't by any chance be a relative of Sebastian Calvert?"

"You win again. His daughter, adopted in her infancy by Howard Pennell, her mother's brother." His glance was admiring. "I don't know how you do it."

Miss Sanderson flashed a grin at him. "It wasn't hard. The Calvert mess gets a large go-round by the yellow rags every time they're stuck for some nice gooey sensational stuff. You'd think it would have died years ago, but the weird circumstances around the whole deal and the group of people involved still make it a best-seller." Her face grew thoughtful and she slid into the chair that Elizabeth had occupied. "Sit down, Robby; I hate looking up at anyone."

Obediently, Forsythe circled the chair where the russet cat was sleeping and sat down next to his secretary. She looked at him closely, her eyes matching the pale blue sweater she wore.

"Just what did Sebastian Calvert's daughter want with you?"

"She wishes to reopen her father's case."

"For what purpose?"

"To establish his innocence."

Miss Sanderson gave a most inelegant, not austere snort. "Innocence! Blimey, that would be in the same league as attempting to prove that the Marquis de Sade was only a decent, fun-loving boy."

"Do you remember the case?"

"Well now, I was just a slip of a girl at the time…" Without looking directly at him, she seemed to sense his grin. "Anyway, I wasn't even close to thirty and doing my best to put up with your dad's idiosyncrasies the way I'm trying to put up with yours now. I remember the trial. It was a rushed affair, closed to the public, and in record time Calvert was judged guilty but insane and hustled off to someplace in the Midlands, Grey something…"

Forsythe reached for one of the papers on the desk and muttered, "Friar, Grey Friar."

"Right. A plush sort of place with maximum security. Funny thing was that at the time not too much public attention was given to the whole affair. Of course, the war was in its fifth year and I suppose that death had become commonplace. What was one murder more or less? Then again, the Calverts were very wealthy. There were still great fortunes. Sebastian was a prominent figure in the arts, so I guess that it was hushed up a certain amount."

Reaching in the pocket of her baggy tweed skirt, she pulled out a crumpled package of cigarettes. Forsythe lighted one for her.

"Knowing you, Sandy, I'm sure that you made it your business to learn all the lurid details. What was your opinion of the murder, and do you think there's any chance they might have gotten the wrong person? Calvert was never able to speak in his own defense, you know."

"My opinion…" She stopped and quoted solemnly, "'Murder most foul, as in the best it is.'" Cocking one brow at her companion, she waited.

"My memory for the Bard isn't so bad either. Next sentence—
'But this most foul, strange and unnatural.'"

"Very good, Robby. That pretty well sums it up. The world
was younger then, less ready to accept the motive for the murder
than it would be now. I can remember that even I was shocked
at the time."

"You! I can't quite swallow that."

"You wouldn't have any idea of what a delicate shrinking
maiden I was then. You were a mere broth of a boy staying with
your mother's family in Scotland. Remember the lovely pack-
ages I sent you?"

"Black-market chocolates, among other things."

"It wasn't black-market, came directly from my own
meager rations," she said indignantly.

"Seriously, what about Sebastian? Was it all that airtight?"

"Couldn't have been more so. There were no actual eyewit-
nesses, but Calvert had the only motive and was caught literally
red-handed." She blew a smoke ring and regarded it. "What did
Miss Pennell say when you turned her down?"

"I didn't."

She almost dropped her cigarette. Turning sideways in her
chair, she stared at him. "You can't mean you're taking this on!
Raking up a bunch of mud and muck that should be over and
forgotten."

"I'm taking it on, Sandy. As for the muck, as you said, it's
raked regularly in the mags."

"This will be different." Her face was set and stern, all
traces of levity had vanished. "You'll be working with the people
closest to Calvert, the ones who have every right to try and forget.
Besides, some of the mud that will be raked may be your own."

Forsythe's face remained adamant. She continued, an
octave higher. "What right has Elizabeth Pennell to ask you to
do this? She's no child, must be almost your own age. Why the
sudden desire to clear a father she doesn't even know?"

His tone was level. "I rather think she's doing it for herself.
Apparently she'd like to get married and doesn't dare expose the

person she loves to the daughter of a man who is supposed to have killed horribly the one *he* loved. The point is, Sandy, I've agreed. Even you can't change my mind now. So," he reached over and plucked one of the slips of paper from the blotter, "here is a list of names. Write a nice polite note to each one and request an interview, mentioning Elizabeth's name and her relationship to Calvert. Be certain to stress that I'm doing this in a private capacity. Follow them up with phone calls wherever possible and ask for a date when I can speak with them. You can also make reservations for both of us at a hotel in London, someplace quiet."

Miss Sanderson glanced down the list of names. Her tone was as level as his. "Which one would you like to see first?"

"Might as well start with the solicitor who handled the defense."

"Firm of Meredith, Fuller, Meredith." She looked up. "Charles Meredith died last year. You'll have to consult with his son Peter. May run into some stickiness there. The old chap was a decent sort but his son…"

"I know. Went to school with him. We called him Porky. Suited him. But it can't be helped."

Forsythe rose, stretched, and moved to the chair behind the desk. Lifting the cat, he put it on the floor. It yawned, pink tongue curling out of the tiny red mouth, and stared up at him, its eyes wide and unblinking. After a moment it curled up on the carpet and resumed its nap.

"How did Miss Pennell get onto you in the first place?"

He handed her another sheet, this one heavy, cream-colored, embossed in gold. "Courtesy of Amelia St. Clair, reward for personal services."

Ruffling her short gray hair, Miss Sanderson gave another unladylike snort. "If you can call buying indiscreet letters from a slimy little blackmailer personal services, I guess she's right. Though it didn't save our Amelia in the long run, did it? Her husband ended up divorcing her anyway. I'll say one thing. She certainly can write love letters, didn't spare any details. They practically smoked."

Forsythe reached for a book and opened it. He glanced up from the pages and smiled at his secretary. "You do have lurid tastes, Sandy."

Shrugging one shoulder, she headed toward the door. "Perhaps. I will now go and make arrangements for Daniel to enter the lion's den."

Pausing, she stood with her back to him, her thumbnail beating its rhythm against her teeth. "Would you say your client was attractive?"

His face was puzzled. "Not in the ordinary sense of the word, but there's something about her—some quality. You might say she's a bewitching young lady."

The nail continued its drumming. "Did you know, Robby, in the seventeenth century there were covens of witches in England who actually offered human sacrifices?"

"Stop that racket, Sandy," he said impatiently. "Just what are you trying to say?"

She opened the door. Over her shoulder she threw one parting remark. "The majority of English witches bore the first name Elizabeth."

The door shut softly behind her.

Chapter Two

Forsythe tried to relax on the hard stone bench. Sandy had offered, almost insisted, on accompanying him for his interview with Meredith, but her offer had been refused.

Forsythe was glad he'd come alone. For the first time in six long years he'd walked the worn pavements of the Temple, gazed with nostalgic eyes at the smooth lawns, the Queen Anne and Georgian homes, felt the spray of the fountains against his face, and traced with lingering fingers the partially obliterated inscriptions on the sundials.

In a way it was a homecoming. The young law students passing him carrying beneath their arms sheaves of papers tied with traditional red ribbons reminded him of himself as he had been many years before, tall, serious, with a long narrow head and fine brown hair, a very young man in love with his mistress—the law.

There was a crowd in the Inner Temple today, tourists, employees from the offices on the Strand munching their lunches and enjoying the tranquility of the ancient seat of law. He watched a young girl on the next bench. She was pretty in a pale way, dressed in bright, shoddy clothes. Solemnly she crumbled bread from her sandwich for a sparrow watching her alertly a few feet away. A strident voice frightened the bird and it winged away. Both the girl and Forsythe glanced toward the owner of the voice.

She was indubitably a tourist directing her smaller male companion's attention to a sundial. Much amused, Forsythe watched the tableau. The lady stationed herself in front of the sundial, nearly hiding it from view as the man readied his camera. He apparently wasn't handling the whole thing properly as he got a great deal of advice right up to the minute that he snapped the picture.

It had to be her husband, Forsythe decided; no one else could possibly maintain the forbearance he was showing. Forsythe wondered how the picture with the large woman in the foreground poised with a kittenish smile, one foot daintily turned out, and what appeared to be an outsize miniskirt straining across her bulging hips would look to the folks back home.

After several shots, they gave up the picture-taking and strolled toward Forsythe. The woman was busily reading aloud from a pamphlet.

"Says here, Henry, that even the Lord Mayor of London can be refused permission to enter here if he appears accompanied by his Sword and Mace Bearers." She stopped in front of Forsythe's bench, looked him over thoroughly, and demanded, "Is that true, young man?"

Courteously, Forsythe rose. She was even more intimidating at close quarters. "That is correct, madam. In fact, a Lord Mayor did violate that rule in the seventeenth century and was met by a group of students who demanded that he lower the City sword before entering the Hall. He refused and it ended in violence during which the Sword Bearer was injured. When Charles the Second was told about the riot, he asked the Lord Mayor to leave the Temple."

While his wife considered this morsel, Henry said timidly, "I understand a great deal of damage was done here during the last war."

"That's true, sir. Repairs have been made, of course, but many of the things destroyed can never be replaced. The Inner Temple Hall was gutted completely and the adjoining Library was destroyed, with a loss of forty thousand books."

The man nodded sympathetically but his wife decided to take a more militant attitude.

"Talking about books and buildings being destroyed! Think of the lads who lost their lives—"

"Madam," said Forsythe coldly, "think about the men, many of whom died trying to protect those books and buildings. Many things were destroyed but many others were saved. The people who offered their lives to protect them must have felt they had value or they wouldn't have done it."

Her mouth snapped open but the expression on Forsythe's face silenced her. With a toss of her head, she stalked off. Her small husband followed her. Behind her back he threw Forsythe a delighted grin and raised his hand in the V for victory sign.

Waving a hand at him, Forsythe sank back on the bench. He wondered when Meredith would condescend to see him. His clerk had informed Forsythe that his master was sorry to be late but he hoped to be free in an hour. Forsythe wondered whether it was only a way to humiliate him before the interview. Pushing up his sleeve, he glanced at his watch. The hour was nearly up.

He rose and began to retrace his steps. He was halfway there when he saw the clerk hurrying toward him.

"Mr. Meredith can see you now, sir, if you'll follow me."

"Is he waiting in his chambers?"

"No, sir; he has another trial starting in two hours so he's resting in an anteroom."

The clerk set off at a brisk pace. Forsythe followed his bent, black-clad figure across a stretch of lawn, through one paved court that led to another mulberry-colored one. The building they entered seemed eminently suited for the law. It was full of nooks and crannies, twisting passages, and unaired corridors. Forsythe breathed in deeply with a feeling of pleasure. The distinctive odor hadn't changed. It was impossible to define, consisting of hints of ancient parchment, ink, old leather, all overlaid with a mixture of dust and tobacco.

The clerk stopped so suddenly that Forsythe nearly walked up his heels. He opened a door softly, mentioned Forsythe's name, and then stood aside. Forsythe stepped into the room, aware that the door was closing just as softly behind him.

Meredith rose behind the deal table but didn't extend his hand. He looked warm and a trifle tired. His robe and wig were tossed over a chair and he wore a gray suit and a rumpled shirt.

"Well, Forsythe, it's been a while, hasn't it? Sit down, man, sit down."

He gestured with one hand and Forsythe sank into the chair opposite him. The table in front of Meredith was covered with law books and briefs, the remains of a lunch pushed to one side.

Forsythe studied his old schoolmate. Not much of the young Porky Meredith was left. The rolls of loose fat that had helped give him his nickname were missing. He was lean to the point of emaciation, but his nose was still the same, snoutlike with dark cavernous nostrils that faced the world squarely.

"I dug out the stuff your secretary said you wanted. How is Miss Sanderson anyway? Still as bright as ever, I'll wager. The full transcript of the trial is here and I threw in dad's notes on it. They may be of some help. Looked it over last night. I knew most of the details; bit of an obsession my dad had over it. Didn't want to take it on in the first place but had no choice. Our firm handled the legal affairs for the Calvert family for three generations, you know."

Meredith was speaking rapidly, disjointedly, and Forsythe realized that he was nervous, unsure of what to say.

"Good of you to go to all this trouble, Meredith."

"I feel I should ask you one thing. What does Calvert's daughter hope to gain by this investigation?" He didn't wait for an answer. "I think she should keep clear of it. Her father had a fair trial. Dad called in one of the best criminal barristers he could get. Jacob Seburg, remember him? Died last year, a couple of months after dad's death. Supposed to be a boating accident."

Forsythe broke in. "Supposed to be?"

"Common knowledge Seburg did himself in. Got involved with a girl young enough to be his granddaughter. She was going to spill the beans to his wife and Seburg couldn't take it. Can't for the life of me understand how a levelheaded man can lose his head over a bit of fluff—" Meredith broke off, avoided his companion's eyes as a flood of hot color inched up his face.

Forsythe ignored his last remark and said coolly, "You said your father was obsessed with this case. Do you think he had any reservations about Calvert's guilt?"

"Not the slightest. Used the only defense possible, insanity. No argument about that, Sebastian was crackers. The whole affair sounds a trifle like one of those classical novels that were written in the thirties. Old manse, chock-full of relatives and guests, and then a murder. That's about the only similarity. Nothing of a drawing room, tea, and good taste about this one. Smelly affair. No, dad was upset because of Melissa Calvert and her young niece. She wasn't much more than a child at the time and dad did his best to keep her off the stand, but of course he couldn't."

Neither man spoke for a moment. Meredith seemed to be studying the dust motes floating in the band of sunlight that spilled across the table. When he did speak his voice had slowed. "Sorry to see you getting mixed up in this, Forsythe. You don't *have* to do this sort of thing, do you? I mean I always understood you were all right financially, a fair income…"

He glanced up at Forsythe's set features. The tide of color that had receded came flooding back and he stuttered, "I'm deucedly sorry, old man, none of my ruddy business. Here," he rose and extended a cardboard folder, "keep these as long as you want."

"Thank you." Forsythe rose and accepted the folder, his movements a little stiff. He turned toward the door.

Meredith spoke behind him. "I wanted to tell you, Robert. Dad never did believe that scandal about you and the Telser woman. I think he'd have wanted you to know that."

Swinging back, Forsythe studied him. He asked softly, "And you, Peter, how do you feel?"

Meredith's eyes fell. "She was a most attractive woman. In fact, deucedly attractive. And you—well you were young and impressionable."

"Thanks for your faith." Forsythe bit off the words. Swinging open the door, he forced himself to close it gently. He stood quietly for a minute, fighting the tide of anger that was sweeping over him. Meredith's clerk scurried up, his hands full of papers. When he saw Forsythe he stopped, surprise on his face.

"You're finished, sir?"

"All finished." Forsythe brushed past him and strode down the corridor. He'd reached the entrance to the building when he heard his name called. Turning, he felt tense muscles relaxing. Hurrying across the stone floor was a familiar figure, a wide smile lighting his face, his hand outstretched.

Forsythe clasped the hand warmly. "Good to see you, Gene."

"I can't tell you how good it is to see you. Couldn't believe my eyes for a minute. So you have come back. I always knew you would."

"Sorry to disappoint you, but I'm only visiting."

"Visiting?" The man's face fell and he eyed the folder under Forsythe's arm.

"Picked it up from Porky Meredith, a personal matter."

"Well, when are you coming back? I mean for good."

Forsythe grinned. "What makes you think I have any choice?"

"Don't give me that stuff, Robert." He jerked his head at the corridor behind him. "The old school nicknames were always apt. Meredith is still a pig and you're still Foxy Forsythe. Someone did do some dirty work in the Telser case, but it damn well wasn't you."

Forsythe's smile broadened. "I'm glad I saw you, Gene. If you're ever in Sussex, look me up."

"How about lunch?"

"Already have a date with a gorgeous lady."

"Not Miss Sanderson, by any chance?" Forsythe nodded and his companion continued, "Will you be in London for a while?"

"A few days."

"Give me a ring and perhaps we can go out on a bash. Be like old times. Oh yes, give my love to Sandy."

"Righto."

With a flip of his hand, the other man headed down the corridor. Forsythe strolled through the mulberry court. A feeling of warmth and well-being filled him. The first hurdle had been taken. He strode through the Temple, crossed the Strand, and entered the restaurant where Miss Sanderson was waiting.

She was sitting at a corner table working methodically on a tall glass of amber fluid. This was a much different person from the Sussex Miss Sanderson. Her short gray hair was exquisitely coiffed and she wore a beautifully cut linen dress.

Forsythe slid into the seat opposite her and gestured at her glass. "I could use one of those myself."

At the same moment that she said, "Already taken care of," the waiter set a similar glass in front of Forsythe.

He took a long swallow of his whiskey and soda. "Most efficient. Have you ordered?"

"Lamb chops, a baked potato, and tossed salad. All right?"

"Fine." He glanced at her gleaming hair. "You made good use of your morning."

"That I did. First the hairdresser, and then some shopping." She fingered the sleeve of her dress complacently. "And how was your morning?"

"Better than I thought it would be. Porky managed to jab a few tender spots, but I think he was more embarrassed than I was. He gave me the impression he didn't quite know how to handle the situation, nothing in his books to cover it. Anyway, I have what we need. By the way, I ran into Eugene Emory. He wanted me to give you his love."

"Nice boy." Miss Sanderson glanced up as their orders arrived. They consumed the meal in silence. Over coffee she spoke again. "I managed to get onto Sir Hilary, at least to his man. He'll see you tomorrow morning. I also got in touch with Rosemary Horner." She stirred cream into her coffee. "I find I'm rather looking forward to seeing the terror of the courts again. Quite a man, Sir Hilary."

"One of the best minds in criminal law that this century produced. Good Lord, he must be close to a century himself."

"In his nineties and still clear as a bell mentally. He's in poor shape physically, had several strokes. His man, you must remember Hooper, asked me to make our interview as brief as possible. It seems strange to think of Sir Hilary as an invalid, he was so vital. What a life he had, three wives and countless mistresses."

Forsythe leered at his secretary. "Better watch yourself, Sandy; the old gentleman is or was a notorious rump pincher."

"Patter, and probably is rather than was," she said. "What about the balance of the day?"

"We will hie ourselves back to the hotel and spend the afternoon and possibly the evening going over the transcript of the trial and Charles Meredith's notes with a fine-tooth comb."

"Exactly what will we be looking for?"

"Well, to acquaint ourselves with it. After that—God knows. Anything, a word, something that doesn't jibe."

She looked at the cardboard folder at his elbow. It was discolored with age and the ribbon tying it that had originally been red was now a faded pink. "Blimey, I feel like an archaeologist, about to dig among relics of the past."

Forsythe chuckled as he got to his feet and picked up the folder. "Come on, Sandy, let's have a go at opening the Pharaoh's tomb."

"With my luck," she said gloomily, "this is probably one that has an ancient curse attached to it."

Chapter Three

It all matched, the old house, the furnishings from another, gentler century, and the ancient man. The room was small, dark despite the early morning sunshine that peeked forlornly through the two tiny windows, and stuffy.

An electric heater glowed near Sir Hilary Putham's chair and a wool blanket was draped over his knees. Forsythe could feel his collar wilting and dampness gathering in the middle of his back. Even Miss Sanderson, clad in a light dress and holding a shorthand pad and pen at the ready, had a light film of perspiration dewing her forehead.

Sadly, Forsythe studied the old barrister. The big, virile figure that had dominated so many courtrooms was shrunken and wasted. All that remained were the bristling brows, snow-white now, that formed a bar over his deep-set eyes, and the voice, still deep and resonant.

The famous voice boomed out now. "I won't have time for polite amenities. Hooper is quite capable of interrupting at any minute. He seems to do it as soon as things get interesting. I think he's in a conspiracy with the damn doctor. Hooper always was something of a mother hen but now he's insufferable. However, I would like to mention that Abigail is as lovely as ever." He smiled at her. "And you, Robert, seem very fit. Country living must agree with you."

He braced his elbows on the arm of his chair, lifted his waxen fingers, and made a temple of them. "But you didn't come here to listen to this sort of thing. You're interested in the Calvert case. There's no use in going through it bit by bit; you've read the entire transcript, you say?"

Forsythe nodded. "Went through it yesterday, sir."

"Then what Miss Pennell wants and what you're looking for is a loophole, anything that might point to a miscarriage of justice. I'm afraid I can be of limited assistance there. Sebastian Calvert was the only person at the Hall who could wish Mersey dead. He had the opportunity and threatened the boy's life within hearing of all the witnesses. Above all, he was discovered by his publisher friend Deveraux with Mersey, or what was left of him, clutched in his arms. Horrible bit there. The local sergeant—good man he is too—managed to get pictures of Calvert and Mersey before they moved them. Ghastly things. I remember we had a long recess after the jury was shown the photographs. It must have been too soon after lunch and several of them went green."

Miss Sanderson shifted slightly. "You have a marvelous memory, Sir Hilary."

"Cheated a bit, my dear. Boned up on the case after I got your letter. But it's amazing how many of the details are clear. Of course, for me personally it was perhaps the most difficult case I ever had to prosecute. I knew Calvert slightly and I admired him. Tremendously talented chap, versatile. Wrote, painted, and sculpted. He wrote competently, was a good painter, but he excelled at sculpture."

Sir Hilary paused and gestured toward a decanter. "I'll have a small spot of brandy. Do you care to join me?"

Forsythe poured the drinks and handed each of his companions a glass. Sir Hilary sipped slowly, seemingly lost in his own thoughts. After a moment, without raising his eyes, he continued.

"But it was more than Calvert that bothered me. His sister Melissa and I had once been very close. She's a great deal younger than I, but I've never considered age a detriment. There was a time I wanted to make her my wife. It was one-sided; Melissa couldn't take me seriously. In fact, she considered me a philanderer." Lifting his eyes, he slanted a smile at Miss Sanderson. "It may have been an apt term, but I've remained very fond of her. At the time of the trial I was forced to prosecute her only surviving brother. The older one, Allan, had been killed in the early years of the war. I think during the trial Melissa learned to hate me."

"Surely," this was Miss Sanderson, "she understood that you had to do it, that you had no choice."

"Melissa did understand that. What she hated me for was putting her niece, Rosemary Calvert, on the stand. Defense counsel did their best to keep her off, but her testimony was essential. I hated myself for doing it. Rosemary was only sixteen and at what I would suppose was the awkward age. A big, chunky child with that deplorable adolescent skin condition—"

"Acne?" Forsythe suggested.

"That's the one. The child was devoted to her uncle. A brilliant girl, sensitive and high-strung. She'd been in one mess in school after another. I must admit she stood up well under cross-examination. I had to tear every sentence from her bodily. It was a brutal job. I didn't blame Melissa."

He stopped, drew a deep breath, and lowered his voice. "Strange, as one gets older it's always the ones who got away that are remembered clearly. I can hardly recall what my first wife looked like and yet I remember Melissa Calvert well. She was the only woman I was ever attracted to who wasn't good-looking. An unattractive child and a plain woman. Yet I saw her a few years ago and she's one of those rare women who improve with age. She's quite stunning now. In the end, I suppose my taste was still operating."

"Your taste," said Miss Sanderson, "was always impeccable."

Sir Hilary placed one hand over hers for a moment. "Thank you, Abigail. But I digress. Old people are guilty of that frequently, I fear. To get back to the trial. You are both asking me the same question with your eyes. Was Sebastian Calvert guilty? Speaking only with logic, I'd have to say definitely. But two points have disturbed me for nearly a quarter of a century."

Forsythe had forgotten his discomfort from the heat. He leaned forward alertly. "What are these, sir?"

"The actual crime, its damn inconsistency. You know the details, of course?"

"By heart," Forsythe said. "David Mersey was killed from an overdose of morphine administered by hypodermic. At the time of the injection he was in bed, unconscious from the same barbiturate that the rest of the household had been fed. He was carried from his room to Sebastian's studio on the main floor, where his corpse was hacked to pieces with one of the swords from a display hanging on the wall, a scimitar. The following morning—"

"Right," said Sir Hilary. "And the hypodermic needle and the case that both the morphine and barbiturates were kept in were wiped clean of fingerprints. First the boy was drugged, then killed with morphine. He could just as easily have been carried down alive but unconscious and then killed with the scimitar. Now think of this, the first part of the crime executed in a quiet, painstaking way to avoid discovery of the murderer's identity. After all these precautions, Calvert lugs the body downstairs, across the hall, through the drawing room to his studio, and deposits it at the foot of the statue. There he carves the body up and throws down the scimitar covered with his fingerprints."

The old man shook his shaggy white head. "I have no idea why Meredith and Seburg didn't stress these facts at the trial. It was macabre, almost as though two murderers had been loose that night."

Forsythe smiled faintly. "If defense counsel had, what would the able prosecutor have flung back at them?"

Sir Hilary smiled also. "True. I would have insisted that after the first part of the crime Calvert's mind gave, and he was certainly mad, and the rest of it was the work of a maniac." His smile faded. "Yet it has always bothered me." He put his glass on the table beside him and adjusted the plaid blanket. "However, it was the only explanation. The most damning thing in the whole trial was that the evidence that convicted Calvert came from the people who were valiantly trying to protect him— Melissa, his niece Rosemary, his secretary, his friend, and even his wife's cousin and companion—what was her name?"

Miss Sanderson's hand was flying over her notebook. "Atlin," she murmured, "Elinor Atlin."

"That's the one, a nice young woman, quiet, nothing like Vanessa."

"Vanessa Calvert," Forsythe said. "She was the only witness hostile to Sebastian, wasn't she? What was she like?"

Putham's expression changed. Suddenly he looked years younger. "Vanessa! A woman to weave dreams of, a memory to warm a man's heart when he's too old to warm it any other way. All the big, dramatic adjectives should be used to describe her because she was truly larger than life."

"Was she beautiful?" Miss Sanderson broke in.

"Beautiful, no. She was much too large to be beautiful or pretty or lovely. I said the big adjectives—*stupendous, marvelous, fantastic.* Vanessa must have been close to six feet tall and built to scale. Not one of your skimpy boy-women with no hips and breasts. Words can't describe Calvert's second wife. I think the closest I've ever seen was the other day in one of those sordid little books, an article rehashing the Calvert case, titled 'Why Did Davey Have to Die?' The title suited the writing—trashy stuff. But in one place, the author said that Vanessa had played Aphrodite to David Mersey's Adonis. I found that pleasing, suitable. Aphrodite, goddess of love. That *was* Vanessa, a goddess walking among mere mortals, one of the ancient goddesses terrible in her wrath—"

"I hate to interrupt," Miss Sanderson interjected dryly, "but from the transcript I'd say your goddess sounded more like a fishwife."

Sir Hilary regarded her quizzically. "You *are* very feminine, aren't you, Abigail? Cold words—and mere words on paper are cold—couldn't possibly give you any idea of Vanessa in the courtroom. She was aflame with vengeance, wouldn't believe for one moment that her husband was insane. She wanted Calvert dead and if we weren't willing to oblige, she was ready to draw and quarter him herself. I said terrible in her wrath. She was frightening, but at the same time I'll lay you odds there were few men present who wouldn't have sold their souls to possess her."

Miss Sanderson's jaw set stubbornly. "I still think—"

Forsythe stirred impatiently. "Before you start debating goddess versus fishwife, let me put a word in. I believe you said there were two points that disturbed you. You explained one. What was the other?"

Sir Hilary swung his eyes to Forsythe. "The first point was nebulous. The second is even more so. Have you seen the work that Calvert completed the day of Mersey's murder, his *Adonis*?"

Both his listeners shook their heads. "I thought not. Melissa wouldn't allow it to be shown for years. She was afraid of public reaction. I suppose she was right; the nature of the statue and the relationship between the sculptor and model would be enough to create a great deal of...shall I say, sordid speculation. However, about two years ago Melissa was finally persuaded to give permission for it to be shown at a small art gallery sponsored by private donations. Timed to be released at the same moment was another of those scurvy attacks on Calvert and his relatives, digging the same dirt up and rolling in it again. A close friend of mine was in the gallery when the public started to arrive. He said they flooded in, mobs of them, all walks of life. Apparently a lot of them had come to nudge each other in the ribs, the ''ey, 'arry, fancy bloke, wasn't 'e' type of people. There was none of that. They saw the statue; they kept their filthy mouths closed; and they left rather stunned. You'd have to see it yourself to understand. I suggest you do." He handed Forsythe a slip of paper. "This is the address."

"But what—" Forsythe started to ask.

Sir Hilary lifted a hand. "I won't say any more. Just go, look at it, and arrive at your own conclusions. Now," he turned to Miss Sanderson, "would you indulge an old fellow and hold Hooper at bay for a few more minutes? He's due to come bursting in and there's something I'd like to say to Robert."

She was dismissed, however gently. Rising, she tugged her slim skirt down and closed her notebook. Smiling up at her, Sir Hilary maneuvered one arm behind her. Forsythe saw it move in a patting motion. He held his breath, waiting for Sandy's ever-ready temper to explode. She turned a bit pink but looked as though it was more in pleasure than in anger. Stooping, she brushed Putham's wrinkled cheek with her lips.

Putham's eyes followed her to the door. As it closed, he spoke to Forsythe without removing his gaze from the heavy oaken panel.

"You're a lucky man, Robert, and so was your father. There goes the most competent legal secretary in London. Just how are both of you making out in Sussex? How do you fill your time?"

"Reading, a certain amount of sports to keep in shape, and then there's a fair amount of social life. We've been working on the treatise on criminal law that father started. I have all his notes and it's shaping up fairly—"

"Great! A wonderful existence for two people like you." The eyes under the bristling brows looked directly at Forsythe. "A worthwhile project for you and Abigail."

Forsythe flushed. "Sandy came with me at her own insistence. I tried to dissuade her—"

Sir Hilary cut him off again. "Loyal, my dear boy, as many of your other friends have been loyal, waiting for you to come to your senses. I'm very old, near the end of the road, and I'm going to tell you a few truths other people have been afraid to spill out. If you think I'm taking advantage of the fact that I was a close friend of both your father and grandfather, you're absolutely right. I'll take any advantage I can get."

"I know what you're going to say—"

"Then sit and listen without interrupting. At the time of the Telser scandal, I was the person responsible for calling the wolves off your trail. By exercising my influence—and I had a fair amount—I was able to effect a gentleman's agreement. You'd left your practice. Fine, if you stayed away from professional life, our fellow members of the bar agreed to leave you alone. At the first indication that you intend to return to your practice, they'll be on you. You'll have to clear yourself. I've been patient. I've hoped that long before now you'd have tired of your hopeless chivalry and decided to become a useful member of society."

The color had receded from Forsythe's fine features and his face was pale. "At the risk of sounding ungrateful, sir, this is my decision, my life."

"Your *life*, Robert? What kind of a life? You've buried yourself in the country and you're engaged in an old man's life, or I should say existence. You're trying to tell me to mind my own business."

The booming voice faltered and he glanced down at his hands folded on the plaid blanket. "You have a right to, my boy, but can't you see that it's many people's business when a man like you lies fallow? Give up this exile of yours, bring Abigail back to London, and pick up your practice. Clear yourself, I know you can."

"I'm going to use an old-fashioned word, Sir Hilary. My honor, I gave my word."

The elderly man threw up his hands. "Honor, misplaced chivalry. What about the fair maiden you rode forth to defend? I understand she remarried shortly after the trial and now has a young son. Her life goes on—"

Forsythe was on his feet. "I believe you presume, sir."

Sir Hilary sighed and laid his head against the chair back. He looked exhausted. "I believe I do, Robert. I was trying to tell you that knighthood is no longer in flower. The last of the knights-errant died many centuries ago. It's sad there isn't someplace in this modern world for them but, alas, there isn't. Abigail and yourself—that's a terrible loss. The people you could have helped…Believe me, Robert, you're acting more like Don Quixote than Sir Lancelot and you're forcing Abigail to be your Sancho Panza. There, I've said it all and I'm very weary."

The icy anger faded from Forsythe's face. He put his hand on Sir Hilary's shoulder and then turned toward the door. Sir Hilary spoke once more.

"If you uncover anything in the Calvert affair, will you let me know?"

His hand on the knob, Forsythe turned to face him. "I certainly will, sir; you'll be kept informed. Thank you."

Outside the door, Hooper was waiting. His wrinkled face was anxious.

"How is he, sir?"

"Very tired, Hooper, best you go in to him."

"I'll see Miss Sanderson and you out first."

"We'll find our way. How…how long do they give him?"

Anguish twisted in the faded eyes. "A few weeks, months. They can't really say."

Forsythe nodded. The smell of death had been in the small hot room. It had looked at him from the old man's eyes. As Hooper opened the study door, Forsythe walked slowly down the hall. In the foyer Miss Sanderson was bending over a strange object set in the middle of it. As he approached, she glanced up.

"I noticed this on our way in and couldn't believe my eyes. I still can't."

Forsythe stopped beside her. "It does shake you a little, doesn't it? Not very often you see a sundial in a house."

"Who put it here?"

"I have no idea. It's been here as long as I can remember."

"Why do you suppose Sir Hilary's kept it?"

Forsythe shrugged. "I've always thought it might be the inscription."

Bending over, she read the carved words. "'The Wine of Life keeps oozing drop by drop. The Leaves of Life keep falling one by one.'" She raised her eyes. "*The Rubáiyát?*"

He nodded. "One of the lesser-known quotations. If there's one person who doesn't believe in missing one of those drops or leaves, it's our host."

Alertly, Miss Sanderson scanned his face. "He gave you a bad time." It was a statement, not a question.

"You know me too well, Sandy, or does the blood show?" He tried to grin. "There'll be time later to lick my wounds. Now I think we'd better get moving." He swung the heavy door open for her.

At the bottom of the steps, she looked over her shoulder at him. "Where away?"

"Where else but to see *Adonis* and try and figure out what Sir Hilary was driving at?" Under his breath he muttered, "Or to find one more windmill to tilt at."

Adonis stood in an alcove, a soft light shining on his marble form. Midnight blue silk fell gently behind him and a small metal plaque at his feet said simply: *Adonis*—Sebastian Calvert.

Forsythe and Miss Sanderson stood with their eyes riveted on Calvert's creation. The quintessence of male beauty lived in his face, his form. Somewhere Forsythe had read that this statue was often compared to Michelangelo's *David*. It shouldn't have been. This was no stripling, but a man in his prime, glorying in his strength and beauty. Marble was the material used by the sculptor, but under his hands marble had turned to living flesh, veins and muscular structure molding its surface. So lifelike was *Adonis* that Forsythe felt that at any moment the raised arm might lower and the figure would step off its pedestal.

Miss Sanderson was gazing at the face, the features serenely noble, a blend of intelligence and compassion. Her pale blue eyes were misted, and Forsythe had to strain to hear her words.

"'O weep for Adonis—he is dead.'"

Her companion squeezed her arm in understanding and quoted from the same poem, "'Peace, he is not dead, he doth not sleep—he hath wakened from the dream of life.'"

Digging in her handbag, Miss Sanderson found a crisp square of linen, and touched it to her eyes. "I feel such a fool, Robby."

Still gripping her arm he turned her away from the alcove. "Don't, Sandy; if it wasn't considered unmanly, I'd shed a few tears myself."

"Sir Hilary was right."

"He was right. Whatever Sebastian Calvert was…well, he was no destroyer."

The attendant was waiting close to the street door. He was discreetly dressed in morning coat and striped trousers. Just as discreet was a silver salver on a background of black velvet close to his elbow. Forsythe placed a folded note on it.

The attendant carefully avoided looking at the donation. Clearing his throat, he murmured, "What do you think, sir?" One hand delicately gestured toward the alcove.

Forsythe murmured back, "Not guilty." He raised his voice. "Definitely not guilty!"

Tugging at his sleeve, Miss Sanderson urged him through the door, onto the pavement. "The man thinks you mad. His mouth is falling open."

"Let him," said Forsythe grandly.

"This feeling we both have that we share with Sir Hilary, it's wonderful; but how do you think it will stand up in court?"

Forsythe eyed the vehicles moving by, the lumbering double-decked buses, the compact cars, an occasional chauffeur-driven limousine, with motorbikes darting erratic paths through them.

"The main thing is that now we are sure of our objective, which God knows we weren't before. Sir Hilary is a sly old devil; he's pointed the way. Now it's up to us to find proof. I'm going to put you into a cab and send you back to the hotel."

"But what about our lunch? I made arrangements at the hotel for a most scrumptious—"

"You eat it like a good girl. I'll pick up a sandwich on my way. This afternoon I want you to transcribe the notes you took this morning." He flagged a cab. "I'll go on and see Rosemary Horner." He noticed Miss Sanderson's wistful look. "If she'll consent, I'll tape her and you can hear the interview this evening."

The cab drew to the curb and Forsythe opened the door for his secretary.

"What if she refuses to be taped? I could come along and take notes."

"Uh-uh. I think she'll talk more freely if there's only one person listening. If she won't consent, I'll remember the pertinent points and dictate them to you later."

Reluctantly, his companion got into the cab. Sticking her head out the window, she cautioned, "Take it easy with her husband. He's supposed to be something of a firebrand and he's a most important man in his profession."

Forsythe watched the cab drive off. He was lucky. In a few minutes he'd located another one and was headed in the opposite direction.

Leaning back against the cushions, he started to pack the bowl of his pipe.

"'Weep not for Adonis,'" he mumbled.

He didn't realize he'd spoken aloud until the driver half turned and asked, "What's that, guvnor, say something to me?"

Forsythe's eyes traced his craggy profile, the lines of a greasy leather cap pulled low on his forehead.

"No," he said to the driver, "not really."

Chapter Four

John Horner's home didn't look like the house of an important man. It was a small villa, well-kept, cheerful but hardly pretentious.

Forsythe liked the looks of it and he liked the looks of the woman leading him into a rose-walled lounge. Rosemary Horner had made the transition from a chunky child with deplorable skin to an attractive matron with taffy hair hugging a finely shaped head. She was ten years older than her cousin Elizabeth, but looked younger. Turning, she smiled warmly at Forsythe.

"I was just thinking of having a gin and 'it.' Would you care for one?"

Placing his briefcase on the cretonne-covered divan, Forsythe smiled back. "That sounds fine, Mrs. Horner."

"Rosemary, please. I'll only be a moment."

Approvingly, Forsythe watched her leave the room. He was about to sink onto the divan when the photographs lined up on the chimneypiece caught his eye. Wandering over, he looked at them.

The one in the middle was a wedding picture. A radiant Rosemary smiled from the photo. Beside her, a short stocky man also smiled, although his was the forced grimace so many bridegrooms direct toward the camera in their nuptial pictures. The most striking of Horner's features was his jaw, hard and jutting and pugnacious.

Against the frame was propped a small snap of two boys dressed for cricket. The taller had a look of Rosemary about the eyes; the shorter was a smaller and younger replica of Horner.

"Our sons, Allan and John, Junior."

Forsythe swung around. He hadn't heard Rosemary enter the room. Her hands were empty.

"I thought we might sit in the garden. It's such a beautiful afternoon and the house seems stuffy."

Nodding, Forsythe picked up his briefcase. Patting it, he asked her, "Do you mind if I use a tape recorder? It's much more accurate than notes or relying on memory."

"Of course not, if it will help."

It was pleasant in the garden. Under a large flowering tree, their drinks waited on a white iron table. Wicker chairs with bright cushions were arranged around it. Gesturing at one chair, Rosemary sank into another.

"I can't tell you how glad I was to get your letter. The mere thought that someone cared enough to look into my uncle's case was heartening. My cousin must be a wonderful person."

Forsythe looked up from the machine he was adjusting. "Have you not seen her?"

She shook her blonde head. "Of course, Elizabeth may have tried to contact Aunt Melissa. My aunt's in Scotland. She took our boys with her for a short trip. So Elizabeth is probably waiting for her return."

Remembering the look on Elizabeth's face as she'd spoken of her father raising Rosemary, Forsythe mentally shook his own head.

"Now," he said, settling back in the chair and lifting his glass, "I know that this will be difficult for you, but I'd like to have you tell me what you remember. Any detail, no matter how insignificant, may help. I'll ask you one question. Do you believe your uncle guilty?"

"No." The wide-set eyes, more gray than blue, met his. "I never have and I never shall."

"The evidence against him was overwhelming."

"I realize that. You'd have to have known Sebastian as I did to be convinced that he was incapable, not of violence, but of that type of murder. He was temperamental at times, but basically he was gentle, understanding. My father was Allan, his older brother. Father divorced my mother when I was seven. She remarried in record time and my father gained custody of me. He was a professional soldier, stationed in India at the time. Father found he was not able to raise a child by himself, so he sent me back to England, to Aunt Melissa and Sebastian. My aunt was competent; she was the one who chose my schools and looked after my needs, but it was Sebastian who gave me all the attention I ever got."

Breaking off, she gazed down into her glass, swirling it so the pink bitters lanced through the icy silver of the gin. "My childhood was most unsettled and I didn't help any. I was in scrapes at school continually. It was always Sebastian who came to the rescue and bailed me out."

Forsythe interrupted. "Could you tell me something of your uncle's background?"

"Well, as you may know, he gained an international reputation in the art field as a very young man. Sebastian married fairly young, when he was twenty-four. His first wife, Mary Ellen Pennell, was one of those milk-and-water females. You know the type—loved being the wife of a famous artist and playing lady of the manor. I never had the impression she liked anything else that went with it. She struck me as the kind who would consider the nuptial couch an instrument of torture."

Forsythe felt his lips twitching. "You must have been a most precocious child, Rosemary."

She gave him a gamine grin. "That I was, a holy terror. Anyway, when I was nine Mary Ellen became pregnant and her whole world went topsy-turvy. She treated poor Sebastian as though he alone was responsible for it and lay around as though she was about to die at any minute. The damndest part of the whole business was that she did die when Elizabeth was born. My uncle was desolate, more with guilt than grief, I would imagine. He wanted no part of the baby and as Mary Ellen's brother and his wife were childless, it worked out well.

"Sebastian seemed much calmer after they left for America. He went to work with a vengeance and did several good things in that period. All was fairly serene until war broke out. Sebastian couldn't get into the forces. His left leg had been injured when he was a boy and he walked with a slight limp. Then in forty-one, he met and married Vanessa. It was a whirlwind courtship and I didn't meet her at that time.

"Vanessa and Sebastian went to Ireland for their honeymoon and stayed there for nearly a year. For that year I was inconsolable. I guess that Sebastian was a symbol, the only security I'd ever known, and he had left my life. He wrote me a couple of letters during the first month and then he didn't write anymore. I reacted like a pint-sized demon and Melissa was just about at the end of her tether with me.

"Then my aunt wrote that Sebastian had returned to the Hall alone. I went home even though it was the middle of the term, took French leave and just walked out. Sebastian looked like death. He had no interest in me or anyone else. My aunt forced me to go back to school, but promised she would let me know how he was. Sebastian improved physically, but he'd lost all desire to work. His work was important to my aunt. I imagine even then that Aunt Melissa knew that Sebastian would never have a son to carry on the name and the name was an obsession with her."

Forsythe leaned forward. "Your aunt wished Sebastian's fame to compensate for the end of the family line?"

"Exactly. A type of immortality you could call it. I believe she did everything in her power to rouse him from his—what would you call it?—depression, resignation. In September of forty-three, Sebastian went to London to visit Richard Deveraux and he returned with David."

"Adonis," said Forsythe.

The bright head nodded. "Adonis. From then on Sebastian worked like a madman—" She stopped and the clear eyes clouded. "The terms we use."

"We all do," Forsythe said gently.

"We shouldn't. But to continue. Sebastian came back to life. Melissa was delighted. She was pushing herself too hard trying to run that huge house with practically no help and was involved in war work up to her ears. Next to Sebastian's work, she was obsessed with patriotism. She literally drove the villagers into every type of civil defense you could think of. Of the three Calverts, Aunt Melissa had the strongest will. Neither my father nor Sebastian had her willpower."

Rosemary paused. "Is all this what you want, Robert?"

He chose his words carefully. "It's necessary. The data from the trial isn't enough. I have to sift through the lives of these people. Somewhere in the strands there may be a clue. Please continue."

He'd spoken sincerely. From cardboard cutouts the people involved in the murder were beginning to take shape, to assume flesh and blood.

He prompted. "In May of forty-four you returned home."

"In disgrace, or I should say that without Sebastian it would have been disgrace. As I mentioned, my school record was vile; I had a frightful temper. This was my last and worst mess.

"We had this games mistress, a great muscular woman. I always suspected she had too many male hormones and her actions bore this theory out. Always with her hands on one of the girls, you know.

"Early in the term I'd shown her it was hands off with me and from there on she had it 'in for me' as we used to say. The morning it happened she asked me a question and I answered. I don't really remember what it was all about. The upshot was that she called me a liar and struck me in front of the whole class.

"The next thing I remember two of the teachers were pulling me off her. She was sprawled on the ground, quite red in the face, holding her throat. I'd gone berserk and knocked her down. Then I'd grabbed her head and banged it on the ground.

"They hauled me away and locked me in my room. Then they phoned my uncle and told him I'd become homicidal. Sebastian arrived like a knight on a white charger." Forsythe winced at the words, but Rosemary didn't notice. "In record time he cleared the whole thing up, forced the teacher to confess there had been provocation, and extracted an apology from the headmistress. She even wanted me to stay on in school, but Sebastian grandly announced that his niece would never return to a school that employed teachers of poor caliber."

Rosemary had been speaking rapidly; now she paused to catch her breath. She continued more slowly. "We went home. Aunt Melissa reluctantly agreed that I was to stay until the fall term and the next few months were a utopian time in my life. There were five of us at the Hall—Sebastian, Aunt Melissa, David, and, of course," she smiled, "John."

"You met your husband at Calvert Hall?"

"I met a young poet whom Sebastian had taken under his wing. John had been invalided out of the army and was acting as his secretary. I don't think John knew I existed, and as far as I was concerned—well, he was a weird young man who reminded me of a bantam rooster running around with his hands full of papers. We met later in London, years after the trial. I was in art school...but we don't have to go into that, do we?"

"Tell me a little about it, Rosemary."

"It was the turning point of my life. I was twenty-five and had never considered marriage, children. The murder, the trial, all those people staring at Sebastian's niece. Can you understand what I'm trying to say?"

Across Forsythe's mind flashed another woman's face, a dark face with brilliant black eyes. "A normal life," those were Elizabeth's words.

Rosemary read the understanding in his face. "John changed all that. We married; Allan and Johnny were born; and yet...I don't think I'll ever really lose the apprehension. I hold my breath when either of the boys get annoyed, even boyish anger. It's foolish but to me it's real." She straightened in her chair. "But I've learned to live with it."

Forsythe wondered if she had. Her composure was not as perfect as it had been. He could see the strain on her face.

"If you'd prefer, Rosemary, we can finish this later…"

"No, let's go on. Back to forty-four. Strange the scattered impressions I get looking back at that summer. I can see David, the sun gilding his body as he dived into the lake; Sebastian at the end of the day coming out of his studio with a smile on his face—I waited for him every night. I remember the meals, the dreadful meals. Aunt Melissa was a stickler for using only our rations. Not that I'm advocating for the black market, but she could have gotten extra eggs and milk from the tenant farmers. Not Aunt Melissa; you would have thought an egg would sabotage the entire war effort. I was always hungry. I'm making my aunt something of a monster, aren't I? She wasn't, just—"

Rosemary broke off abruptly and laughed. "I'm becoming disjointed. Could you help me back on the track?"

"Vanessa and Elinor Atlin arrived in August. Fill in the months between."

"The months between." She drew a deep breath. "As I said, it was a wonderful time. Sebastian worked hard but he was so happy. Aunt Melissa was wrapped up in her auxiliaries but she found enough time to involve me as much as she could. I helped in the local hospital as an aide. Much of my spare time was spent with David Mersey. He enjoyed the same things I did. Between us we cleaned up the tennis court; it hadn't been used in years. And we swam and hiked; went down to Meads Green quite often. That sort of thing." She looked at Forsythe. "Those were the months before Vanessa arrived."

"You say you spent a great deal of time with Mersey. Did you have any idea about your uncle and him?"

"You mean," Rosemary said quietly, "did I know they were lovers? You said I must have been precocious. I was. Years in a girl's public school only made me more so. I knew about that sort of thing, all the grubby names. Yes, I was aware they were homosexuals."

"It didn't bother you?"

"Bother me? No. You must realize, Robert, I idealized Sebastian. I never really reasoned it out. I suppose I felt that whatever was good for him had to be right. David definitely was. They were different from my notions of…well, 'fags.' David was incredibly handsome and very masculine, and there was nothing overt. Whatever happened privately between them had no part in our day-to-day life. If you knew Aunt Melissa you'd be certain that if it had, she never would have allowed me to return."

"And Melissa, did she know?"

"She must have, but she never let on."

"Let's get back to Mersey. What was he like?"

"Handsome, but I've said that. Very physical. He had gym equipment in the basement and worked out regularly. Mentally, rather slow. He'd been brought up in Limehouse. I think he'd been a dockworker, and you'd expect him to be crude. He wasn't. Aunt Melissa said he was much like a chameleon. He aped superbly—dress, manners—he even spoke fairly well. You could see him watching us, trying to do things the same way as we did, speak the same way. I'm not being very helpful, am I?" She rose. "I'd forgotten. I have something that might help. Excuse me."

Forsythe watched her walk up the flagstone path to the house. She moved well, with a balanced grace. Flicking off the recorder, he rose and paced back and forth, a slight frown pulling his brows together. Rosemary was trying hard, too hard, and it was taking its toll.

She was gone only a short time. When she returned, she opened a large sketchbook and gestured to Forsythe.

"These are the sketches I made that spring and summer. Not terribly professional, but I feel I've caught many of them."

Forsythe bent over the table and examined them with interest. The first one was labeled "Sebastian." Elizabeth was very much her father's daughter. Sebastian had the same dark eyes, the high-bridged nose. There was a hint of her arrogance, but her father lacked the strength around the mouth and chin that his daughter had.

Forsythe turned the page. A dark-eyed woman gazed from it, the same features, her hair neatly waved back from her brow. This time the resemblance to Elizabeth was startling. There was no name on this one.

"Aunt Melissa," Rosemary murmured.

The next face he recognized. He was younger but the chin was the same. The mouth was more vulnerable. Forsythe spoke before Rosemary could.

"Your husband."

"Yes, and this is David."

Rosemary had been modest. This one was professional. Without asking, Forsythe knew that the thick wavy hair was blond, the large, long-lashed eyes blue. This was the face of the statue, but there was some difference. Rosemary was watching him.

"It's the expression," she said.

"Are you a mind reader as well as an artist?"

"Not much of either, I'm afraid. You mentioned when you arrived that you'd just been to see Sebastian's *Adonis*. I have no doubt my uncle did see in David's face the qualities he gave *Adonis*. But David was not Adonis. He was merely a very beautiful male animal with an expression of good nature, nothing else."

Forsythe started to turn the page. Rosemary put her hand on it. "Not yet, please. We'll get to the last two."

They returned to their chairs and Forsythe started the tape. She looked questioningly at him. He prompted her again.

"August and Vanessa."

She gave him a lopsided grin. "Or should we say, enter the serpent into the garden of Eden? Paradise doesn't last forever. Ours didn't. On the twelfth of August, without any warning, Vanessa arrived. She came like a bolt from the blue with mounds of luggage and Elinor Atlin.

"I wasn't at the house when they got there. David and I were swimming in the lake. Melissa was still treating me like a small child, and I wasn't allowed to go down alone. When we got back to the Hall, we entered through the side door, still wearing our swimsuits. We heard voices from the drawing room. I wandered in and there Vanessa sat, her shoes kicked off, smoking a cigarette and looking amused. Aunt Melissa looked like death. But there was nothing she could do. Vanessa was Sebastian's wife and had as much right there as any of us."

Rosemary paused, felt in the pocket of her skirt, and asked her companion, "Do you have a cigarette?"

He offered her his case and a light. Sitting back, she inhaled deeply. Then she continued. "I'm trying to remember who was there. Sebastian had already seen Vanessa; I heard that later. Oh yes, Elinor was standing beside Vanessa's chair, very awkward and ill at ease. John was watching Vanessa. He couldn't see anyone else from the moment she arrived. When I came in, Aunt Melissa started to introduce me but Vanessa wasn't paying any attention. She was staring past me. I looked around and David was behind me, still in his bathing trunks. And—" She broke off and the gamine grin touched her lips again. "David in trunks was something to see. Melissa introduced David to the two women. Then she spoke sharply to David and me, told us to get upstairs and get some dry clothes on.

"Vanessa got up and stretched, slowly, you know. She said she might as well get settled. It ended up with her leading the way and David, Elinor, and me carrying all her luggage. Vanessa allowed me to stay while they unpacked; at that point I don't think she could have driven me out.

"Her clothes! Mounds of beautiful, yummy things. Real silk stockings, piles of lingerie. Everything was color-coordinated, shoes and hats for each suit and dress. It nearly took my breath away. You must remember, I was used to wartime England, everyone slightly shabby and drab. Where Vanessa got this wealth of goodies from, I still don't know.

"Vanessa pumped me about David—who he was and why he was there, why he wasn't in the services. I couldn't answer that. When she had all I knew, she gave me a pair of stockings and a tiny bottle of scent and got rid of me. Aunt Melissa, of course, made me give them back later."

Forsythe broke in. "What was your impression of Vanessa? Do you have a sketch of her?" His hand moved toward the book.

"No. I did ever so many but tore them all up. I couldn't get her. Her features came out fine but not...well, her. As for Vanessa, I don't know how anyone could describe her. After what she did to my uncle I suppose I should have hated her. But just walking into the room and seeing her, dressed all in white, a great mass of hair resting on her shoulders, one was impressed. She wore it in the style so popular in the forties. A high pompadour and a roll on the shoulders. Her hair was very long when it was down, nearly to her waist, flaming hair, a true red-gold. I could describe her appearance but it wouldn't help."

"You didn't hate her."

Rosemary spread her hands expressively. "How could I? It would be much like trying to hate a natural force, a typhoon, a hurricane. You might hate what they *did*, the havoc they wreaked, but you couldn't hate them."

"And she did start to wreak havoc."

"It started the minute she arrived. The little group that had been so placid was gone and was replaced by...Well, John was mad for Vanessa. He followed her around and scribbled poems about her. Aunt Melissa was all nerves; she acted terrified of what Vanessa would do to Sebastian. I couldn't do anything right. Clumsy, within the first week I'd sat on and smashed my aunt's glasses—and she was lost without them; my kitten and I managed to ruin a batch of knitting she was working on; and, oh yes, I broke a kitchen window. I suppose Aunt Melissa had good reason to be snappish with me and she was. In the meantime, Vanessa was in pursuit of David, had her hands on him at every opportunity."

"How did Mersey react to that?"

"He seemed dreadfully embarrassed and avoided her as much as possible. David, Elinor, and I spent a great deal of time together. Elinor was as athletic as we were. We went swimming, played tennis, hiked into Meads Green. Anything to keep away from Vanessa."

"What about Elinor?"

Rosemary turned a page in the book. "Here she is, or was then. A big woman like her cousin. Her parents were missionaries and she certainly looked the part. She wore steel-rimmed glasses, flat shoes, dowdy clothes, and had her gingery hair pulled straight back in a bun. She was Vanessa's age, about twenty-eight. Elinor was quiet, devoted to Vanessa but appalled by her at the same time. A nice woman."

Turning the page, Rosemary said, "And here is the last one, Richard Deveraux, Sebastian's good friend."

Richard Deveraux looked from the page with humorously sardonic eyes. He had a good face, firm mouth and chin, aquiline nose. Thick hair was brushed back from a perfect widow's peak.

"A fine-looking man."

"And a fine man, Robert. Aunt Melissa sent out an SOS for him during the first week of Vanessa's stay. Richard arrived the following Sunday. Vanessa was away that weekend visiting friends a few miles away. She returned the next morning—Monday."

"About Sebastian, how did he react to Vanessa's attentions to Mersey?"

Rosemary pushed a strand of hair from her forehead. "Of all of us Sebastian seemed the least affected. Of course, he was working on his *Adonis* and he carefully avoided his estranged wife. He even took most of his meals in his study or studio. Perhaps he didn't realize the extent of Vanessa's infatuation, or maybe he felt too sure of David. Whatever the reason, Sebastian was the calm in the middle of the hurricane."

Taking a small notebook from his pocket, Forsythe consulted it. Rosemary watched him silently.

"Wednesday night the hurricane began to gain force, didn't it?"

"For Aunt Melissa and me, yes. That would be on record in my testimony at the trial, wouldn't it?"

"The outline is. Could you fill it in?"

"I was starved Wednesday night. When we went to bed—my aunt and I were sharing the same bedroom—all I could think of was the remains of a cold chicken in the icebox. I drifted off to sleep but awakened around three, famished. Aunt Melissa seemed sound asleep so I crept out of bed and headed down to the kitchen. She must have had a mental alarm. No sooner was my hand in the icebox when I heard her voice behind me. She said something like, 'Get to bed!' and stalked into the hall ahead of me.

"Both of us were used to the layout of the house and she didn't turn on the lights. We padded up the stairs; I was in bare feet and she wore soft slippers. We were near the top when I heard a man's voice and a woman laughed, a deep, throaty laugh. There was a dim light in the upper hall and I had a glimpse of Vanessa leaving David's room. Then I was pushed back against the wall by my aunt. I stood there holding my breath—"

"Let me get this straight, Rosemary. Mersey's room was the first one, closest to the stairs."

"That's right. When Aunt Melissa figured the coast was clear, we returned to our room. I crawled into bed and lay there shaking. My aunt paced up and down for a moment, not really wringing her hands, but very close to it. Then she told me to go to sleep. She left the room. When she came back, I pretended I was asleep and I heard her crying. That really shattered me. My aunt is not the sobbing type of woman."

"And the next day David was still pretending to avoid Vanessa?"

"He acted just the same. I remember looking at him and wondering what kind of an actor he was. Yet there was Vanessa coming out of his room. I can still see her, her long hair falling down her back, one of her negligees, a pale blue one, flowing around her. Both Aunt Melissa and I knew that she had won."

"Did either of you let on to Sebastian?"

"I felt he should be told, but Aunt Melissa ordered me not to mention it. The following night, Thursday, Richard—"

"Yes, I know what Richard saw and did."

Rosemary was pale and drawn now. Lines showed around her eyes and mouth that Forsythe hadn't noticed before. He made a move to turn off the recorder. She stopped him, her fingers cold against his hand.

"Please, I'd like to finish."

"Wouldn't it be easier at another time? You look exhausted."

"It will never be any easier. Friday, the twenty-fifth of August, was the last day. It marked the end of one life, the beginning of another.

"I was helping Aunt Melissa prepare breakfast. Our old cook was not well and the only other help we had, a girl from the village, wasn't there. The morning was so beautiful that my aunt decided to serve breakfast on the terrace. It runs right along the west side of the Hall. Everyone but Sebastian and Vanessa was at the table. I didn't think anything of their absence. Vanessa usually slept late and Sebastian's meal hours were irregular."

"Your aunt didn't tell you that Sebastian knew about Mersey and Vanessa?"

"She didn't say a word. The first thing I knew about it was when we heard voices from the sunken garden, just below the terrace. They became louder and louder until we could hear every word. It was Sebastian and Vanessa. They were quarrelling violently about David.

"Sebastian was bringing up dreadful things that had happened during their marriage and Vanessa was throwing insults back at him. I was sent upstairs just after they got started, but I went into Richard's room; it was right over the terrace. From there I could not only hear them, I could see them. Sebastian was flushed and furious and Vanessa looked as though she was enjoying herself. She seemed to thrive on violence."

Forsythe checked his notes again. "This was when Sebastian made his threat."

"Vanessa was taunting him. She said, 'What can you do to stop me? I may even leave and take David with me.' My uncle just roared, 'I'll stop you. You'll never have a chance to do to that boy what you did to me!' She laughed. I can still see her laughing, her head thrown back, the sunlight on her face. She said something awful about David preferring a real woman to a fag like Sebastian. I thought for a moment he was going to strike her. He raised his arm, then he lowered it slowly and said, 'I'll see him dead first.'"

"The most damning piece of evidence at his trial."

"Everyone heard that. The next part, the reason I was forced to testify at the trial, came later. I remained upstairs, just lying across the window seat in Richard's room. In some ways I was a woman, in some still a child. The child came out when I looked out of the window and saw David heading for the lake in his swimming trunks. Badly as I felt, I went to my room, changed into my bathing suit, and followed him—very cautiously and quietly. I didn't want Aunt Melissa to catch me. I knew she had meant me to stay in our room."

"Elinor Atlin followed Mersey too."

"She was there first. I'd just about reached the lake when the loose lace on my sneaker tripped me. I knelt down to tie it. I wasn't trying to eavesdrop. At the time I didn't know Sebastian had already taken David into his study for a talk. When I approached the lake, I found that Elinor had followed David and they were talking. I heard a few words and then I listened."

"Can you remember the exact words?"

"I should be able to; I had to go over and over it at the trial. 'Then you've made your choice?' Elinor asked David. He said, 'I have.' She asked him, 'Did you tell Sebastian?' David said, 'I did. I'm sick of being pulled two ways. I'm my own man and I'll do as I damn well please.' Then Elinor said something about ruining his life and he didn't say anything for a minute. I couldn't catch the next few words, but then he mentioned Vanessa's name. Elinor made a sound like a short laugh and said, 'Don't worry about me. I've been deserted before by Vanessa—when she married Sebastian.'"

"Did you understand what Elinor was alluding to?"

"Not at that time. Later I learned that the only time the cousins had been parted was the year of Vanessa's marriage to Sebastian, when they remained in Ireland. But to get back to the lake. The next thing Elinor said was, 'You don't seem to realize what this will do to your life.' David muttered that it was his own affair, and Elinor started down the path toward me. She called back, 'You may regret it.' I was busy getting out of the way. I needn't have worried. Elinor went right past and didn't see me."

"Adonis," said Forsythe, "had chosen Aphrodite."

Rosemary said somberly, "He'd also chosen death. I went back to the house. I was so worked up I found Aunt Melissa and blurted the whole thing out. She took me up and put me to bed. I was nearly hysterical. My aunt was very gentle and kind. I didn't see any of them until evening. Aunt Melissa brought my dinner up on a tray. She was trying to make me feel better and had put a glass of cream soda on it. I drank that, but I couldn't eat a bite of food. After they'd dined she came up and got me. Sebastian wanted—"

Rosemary's voice had been rising. Concerned, Forsythe looked up from his notebook. Tears glazed her eyes and were trickling down her ashen face. She was groping blindly in her pocket. He rose and handed her his own handkerchief.

She sobbed. "I thought I was going to be such a brick, get through the whole thing." Groping for the handkerchief, she dabbed at her eyes. "I saw them. Sebastian clutching that awful thing in his arms. David had been disemboweled. His neck was nearly severed. Sebastian's clothes, his hands were covered with—"

"Don't. Let it go." Gently, Forsythe pulled her to her feet, put one arm around her shaking shoulders. "I've been a ruddy ass. I should have had more sense."

A voice spoke behind Forsythe, grinding the words out.

"You're damn right you should! What do you think you're doing to my wife?"

Without releasing Rosemary, Forsythe glanced around. John Horner was watching them, his eyes far from friendly.

Rosemary wiped her face and pulled away from Forsythe's arm. "Don't be a ninny, John. Robert's not the ass; I am. I'm acting like a neurotic."

Her husband's expression relaxed a trifle. He slid an arm around her waist. "Neurotic or not, my dear, you're all through for today. I'm going to take you to the house and you're going to rest for a bit."

She didn't protest. She only looked searchingly at her husband and asked, "Will you talk to Robert?"

"I'll talk to him." He led her away. Over his shoulder he flung at Forsythe, "Wait for me in the shed. The door isn't locked."

Gathering up his recorder and briefcase, Forsythe looked in the direction Horner had pointed. Almost hidden by an arbor was a good-sized shed. It looked like a tool or potting shed. One end of it had been torn out and a large pane of glass installed. Inside he found that the center of the splintery floor had been covered with a piece of garish linoleum and someone had tacked green wallboard over the studs. Other than that it was still very rough. A discarded kitchen table sat squarely in the middle of the floor with two straight chairs near it. Arranged on the table was a typewriter, a bottle of scotch, and two glasses. The floor was littered with untidy piles of books, magazines, and paper.

He was setting up his tape recorder beside the typewriter when Horner returned and stood straddle-legged beside the door.

"You might just as well pack that stuff up." Horner gestured toward the recorder. "I've spent most of the day trying to head you off. They said at your hotel that you were expected back for lunch. Your secretary arrived alone, so I knew you'd reach my wife before I could stop you. Since then I've been walking around trying to cool off." He didn't look like he had succeeded. "I'm going to give you some advice. For your own good I'd suggest you take it."

Forsythe kept his voice friendly. "If it's sound, I certainly will try."

"It's sound. Drop it. Drop the whole business and clear off. Don't ever approach my wife again and leave her aunt alone."

"Why?"

"I checked you out when we got your letter. Found out you had gotten involved in an unsavory affair a few years back. No discredited shyster is going to put my family through this hell. Raising hopes in a couple of poor women who have had all they can take of this, for some shoddy little scheme of your own."

"Hardly my own, Horner. I was retained by your wife's cousin."

"I don't give one damn for some cousin my wife's never even seen. Now get your junk and get out."

"How do you think your wife will feel when she finds you wouldn't even try to clear her uncle?"

"Blackmail now, by God! You'd better leave before I throw you out."

Forsythe could feel his own temper snapping. "Would you like to try? I'll leave in a minute, but before I go I'm going to tell *you* something. I've had quite a day and I'm in the mood. In the first place I didn't want to get involved in this. But Elizabeth Pennell deserves this much and, although I thought it hopeless, I agreed to try. Do you think I enjoyed your wife reliving the whole damn nightmare again? You must know what is at the back of her mind. Looking at her two boys, wondering—"

"That's bloody nonsense. My boys are not their great uncle. The chances of them being like him are so remote it's ridiculous."

"I agree with you, but I don't think Rosemary does. If there's any chance of giving her peace, wouldn't it be worth it?"

Horner seemed to have simmered down a bit. He thought for a minute. "You said yourself it's hopeless."

"I thought that at the beginning. This morning I took the advice of a man who knows what he's talking about and went to see the *Adonis.*"

Horner looked puzzled. Slowly he closed the door and walked over to the table. "And?"

"You're a creative person yourself. Any writer with your following has to be. Can you really believe that the man who expressed the love that Calvert did in that chunk of marble could kill the boy who inspired it in the *way* he did? He would be as incapable of an act like that as of smashing the marble *Adonis* to bits."

"Calvert was tried and convicted. All the evidence, the motive—"

Forsythe cut him off curtly. "He was tried as much for his sexual behavior as for his supposed crime. Sebastian Calvert's mind was gone. He was a pervert in the eyes of the world. Just how thoroughly did they sift to try and find motives for the rest of you?"

"Motives?" Horner ran his hand through his shock of graying hair. "Who else would have wanted to see the boy dead?"

"That," said Forsythe shortly, "is what this discredited shyster is trying to find out."

All heat had left the other man's face. Pulling out a chair, he slumped on it, waving Forsythe to the other.

"Sit down. You have an apology coming. I fire off too fast, always have, and you're entirely different than I pictured you. Very well, I'll cooperate. Turn your tape on but," he shot a piercing look at Forsythe, "remember I'm doing this not because of your threat about Rosemary but because I owe it to her and to Sebastian Calvert."

His brow furrowed and he looked past Forsythe. "I owe a lot to Calvert. In the fall of forty-three, I was invalided out of the army. I'd been in the North African campaign and got badly shot up. When I wrote Calvert I was a mess. Most of my money was gone; I had to help my parents and I was down to my last few pounds. I still wasn't recovered physically and my nerves were in worse shape than my body. I couldn't hold an ordinary job.

"I'd met Calvert some time before and he'd expressed interest in my work. I wasn't a novelist then; I was working in poetry." He broke off and grinned, his face suddenly charming.

"It's a good thing my prose is better than my verse. Calvert saw something in me even then. He sent me a ticket to Meads Green, and I went to live at the Hall. He made a job for me that wasn't too demanding so I wouldn't feel a charity case."

"David Mersey was already there when you entered the picture."

"Yes, Mersey and Calvert were right in the middle of a hot little love affair. As a real man's man straight out of the army I

52 E. X. Giroux

was pretty disgusted, but I couldn't afford to show it. Anyway, Mersey was an inoffensive chap and Calvert was a genius. I suppose I decided that you couldn't expect normal behavior from a man of his ilk.

"Gradually I got used to it, and the life was good for me. I did what I could to ease the burden on Melissa, took care of Calvert's correspondence, and the rest of the time I concentrated on my own work—god-awful stuff it was too. I looked at some of it the other day, all about mortars and blood and guts. Just what you would expect from someone as unstable as I was at the time."

"What did you think of the people at the Hall?"

"As I said, Mersey was completely inoffensive. All brawn-and-looks type, but not conceited. I was fond of Melissa; she bore the brunt of everything. Calvert, well I was grateful to him but I never liked him. He was such a weak sister. You take Rosemary, for instance. Melissa made all the effort there and Calvert took all the credit. Rosemary needed the discipline that Melissa gave her, but every time she kicked up her heels there was Calvert to play the hero and tell her it was fine. Then his sister could hunt around, find another school, and try to make it fine. That was Calvert all over."

Forsythe considered for a moment. "Rosemary came home in May, didn't she?"

"Yes, her devoted uncle instead of smacking her bottom brought her home. She did just about as she wanted, spent most of her time with Mersey. Melissa did her best to get her into a routine, interest her in war work. She did force Rosemary to help at the hospital, but Calvert kept interfering. If it hadn't been for her aunt, the girl would have been ruined."

"This is an entirely different look at Calvert," Forsythe said thoughtfully.

"Every person has many sides. However, to get back. Everything went smoothly until Vanessa Calvert decided to come back and stir things up bit. I'd heard about Vanessa in London. The artists' colony seemed to find her affair with

Calvert amusing. General idea was that after his first wife he found Vanessa too much of a challenge.

"She came to the Hall and the first time I saw her I just flipped. I'd never seen anything like her before. How Calvert could ever walk out on a woman like that—" He broke off, grinned, and reached for the bottle. "I think a drink is in order." He poured a couple of inches in both glasses and handed one to Forsythe.

"Vanessa I can describe in one word. She was a lion. Not a lioness. She was completely feminine and still a lion. Shaggy mane of red hair, slightly flattened nose, and great amber eyes. She even moved like a lion. Swung her full weight from one foot to the other with those great shapely haunches swaying…"

"She seems to have made quite an impression. Would you say she was oversexed?"

Horner looked quite serious. "No. Vanessa was warm-blooded, but I think it was the effect she had on men that made people think that. Turned any man around her into a sex fiend. She turned me into one. I lusted after her. My poetry veered from battlefields to feverish works on Vanessa's thighs and breasts. I'd swear if she hadn't been four inches taller and twenty pounds heavier than I, I'd have tried to assault her."

"Did she know how you felt about her?"

"She couldn't have helped. Every time she turned around I was panting along behind."

"What about Elinor Atlin?"

"She faded into the background. I thought at first it was just her cousin's overwhelming attraction that did it, but even when Vanessa wasn't around she was—how would you put it? Bland. But as luck would have it Vanessa wasn't interested in me. She was working on Mersey and seemed to be making no headway at all. Every time she touched him he blushed like a girl and moved away."

"Rosemary said that Calvert didn't seem to realize what was going on, that he was the calmest one of the group."

"If he did, it certainly didn't appear to bother him. He was a thorough egotist. He adored Mersey, therefore he thought Mersey would be true to him. Calvert hadn't counted on Vanessa's charms. She didn't appear to be making much headway publicly, but she most certainly was privately.

"I know I'm not much help, Forsythe, but to be honest I must admit that except for Vanessa I didn't know another soul was alive. Maybe I'd better qualify that. I knew Melissa was going through hell. She had enough on her hands without Vanessa. Besides her war work, she had the house and Rosemary, both big jobs. There was a maid who came in from the village and an ancient crone of a cook, but most of it fell on Melissa. She'd established a rule that the members of the household and guests must tidy their own rooms. The women were fine at this and I looked after mine army style. But you should have seen Sebastian's and Richard's. I don't think they ever did more than pull the bedspreads over their crumpled sheets and blankets."

"Did you know that Mersey and Vanessa had become lovers?"

"I certainly didn't. After the murder I found that Rosemary and Melissa had tumbled, and of course Richard set the whole thing off when he saw them. The night that he did see all was also the night that my love or lust or whatever you'd call it for the fair Vanessa vanished and was replaced by loathing."

Forsythe leaned forward, his eyes hard on Horner's face. "There was no mention of this in your testimony at the trial."

The other man's lips quirked into an ironical grin. "I'm baring my breast for you. Not much use repeating the small amount I did give at the trial. It was Thursday night, fairly late in the evening. Vanessa was in her room alone. I knew that. I'd seen Elinor talking to Melissa and Richard in the drawing room. I hunted Vanessa down in her lair, determined to throw myself bodily on her if necessary. I was really at a fever pitch and clutched a bunch of poems about her in one hot hand. Vanessa called for me to come in and there she was in one of those transparent nightgown things, brushing her hair at the dressing table.

"I can see her now, the purple chiffon not hiding one curve of her body, the brush striking sparks from that long, gorgeous hair. I more or less collapsed in a chair by the door and devoured her with my eyes. She was pretty short with me, must have been getting ready for her assignation with Mersey then.

"I got right to the point. I don't remember what I said. Probably the usual things about not being able to live without her. She just kept brushing away. Finally she lifted her head, threw back that mane of hair from her face, and yawned. Yawned, by God, like a bloody cat. Not covering her mouth or anything, just that moist red tongue curling back on her teeth.

"I must have gone wild. The next thing I knew I was behind her, my hands on her, doing my best to tear off her nightie. Vanessa was strong and had no trouble fending me off. I fell back breathing like a frustrated bull, and she calmly started to adjust a purple velvet band in her hair.

"She looked…amused. Finally she met my eyes in the mirror and drawled, 'Go sit in your corner, little Jack Horner. Come back when you get your full growth.'

"I backed away, picked up the poems I'd thrown around, and left. I guess Vanessa always knew a person's weakest spot. She'd hit mine. I was ashamed, sensitive about my size at that time. She couldn't have found a better way to humiliate me. Anyway, I got back to my room somehow. I was close to weeping from rage. I hated her then and it was many years before I did anything else.

"I didn't sleep much that night. The following morning I intended to go and see Calvert and make some excuse to leave. But the next day, in the midst of breakfast, Calvert and Vanessa cut loose, and I figured she'd be leaving soon.

"They were really going at it, hauling all their dirty linen out, and we had to sit there and pretend we couldn't hear them. Mersey was sitting next to me. I couldn't see his face but his hands were knotted into fists. Melissa sent Rosemary upstairs and then she sat there as though turned to stone. Richard Deveraux put his hand out to pat hers and Melissa pulled her hand away in a hurry and just stared at him. Richard blushed. I didn't know he was the one who spilled the beans to Calvert. Poor Elinor kept lifting her cup but she never drank a drop. Finally it slipped out of her hand

and broke on the flagstones, but nobody paid any attention. At last they finished and Calvert shouted his threat."

"He did say, 'I'll see him dead first.'"

"That's what he said, Forsythe. Then Calvert stormed up the steps to the terrace. As he passed the table he ordered Mersey to come along to his study. They left together and then Vanessa sauntered up cool as a cucumber, sat down, and helped herself to bacon and eggs. I left the table and went to a little room off the kitchen that I used as an office and tried to work."

"You didn't see any of the others for the rest of the day?"

Horner gestured toward the bottle. Shaking his head, Forsythe watched the other man refill his glass.

"I damn well didn't. I sneaked into the kitchen and got some milk and a sandwich and stayed in my room. But I couldn't get out of dinner. It was at eight as usual and Calvert joined us, which he didn't do too often. The last bit of work had been finished on his statue."

"All of you were there but Rosemary?" Horner nodded. "How did Calvert appear?"

Horner thought. "Exhilarated, almost manic. His eyes—he has the dark Calvert eyes—were glittering and he was flushed. He talked a lot and too high. Deveraux and Melissa tried to keep their end up, but the rest of us just sat there, pushing our food around on out plates. At least, all of us but Vanessa. She had a good appetite and looked like a cat lapping up cream, those amber eyes of hers sliding from Mersey's face to Calvert's.

"When Calvert dined with us we usually gathered in the drawing room later for brandy and conversation. That night we were only too eager to get away from each other. Calvert wouldn't hear of it. He asked Melissa to go up and get Rosemary and sent me down to the cellar for his most treasured wine. He had only half a dozen bottles left. I left everyone but Melissa in the dining room—she'd gone up to get Rosemary—and I went downstairs. The rest of it is in my testimony."

Forsythe consulted his notebook. "You testified that you went down, got the wine, stopped in the kitchen to open it and wipe the dust off the bottle. Then you arranged a tray, goblets and wine bottle, and carried it to the drawing room."

Taking a sip of his scotch, Horner nodded. "Right. When I got there the whole clan was gathered. I put the tray on the table near the fireplace and Calvert poured the wine. We waited for him to hand the glasses around but he didn't.

"During dinner a storm had broken, one of those fast summer storms with jagged lightning and cracks of thunder. Calvert picked up a goblet, walked to the front of the room, and pulled the drapes back. Then he started to talk. None of it made sense. He spoke in quotations about the ancient gods, the gods of thunder and lightning. We more or less milled around the table, anxious to drink up and get out. Finally Vanessa said something like, 'Well, I'm not standing here all night,' and Calvert said, 'Serve the wine.'

"Elinor was closest to the table so she handed the tray around. Sebastian gave her time to do it and when she picked up her goblet, he struck a pose in front of the window. I can still see the lightning flashing behind him. He announced he was going to propose a toast. Lifting his goblet, he called, 'To Adonis.' We all looked at Mersey. He flushed cherry red and we drank."

"You didn't notice anything odd about the taste of the wine?"

"I certainly didn't. We all more or less bolted it, anxious to have it done with and get out of there. The only ones who had any left in their goblets were Calvert and Vanessa. She stood there smiling at Calvert and then she raised her glass. 'I have another toast,' she said, 'to the victor.' Nobody moved and Vanessa raised her goblet and drained it. Calvert startled all of us. He flung his goblet and the wine in it at the fireplace. He missed and it splintered against the wall. The wine looked like spatters of blood against the ivory.

"Then Calvert turned toward Vanessa and said, 'Tomorrow I want you out of my house. Take everything you brought and go.' She was standing near Mersey. She walked over to him with that heavy, deliberate tread of hers and took his arm. She smiled at Calvert and said, 'Do you mind if I take a little more than I brought?'

"He didn't answer her, just turned on his heel and went upstairs. I was glad to see him go. It meant we could all get to our own rooms. And there was something in that room that night, a kind of...malevolence. You could have cut the atmosphere with a knife. Mersey went upstairs next, then Vanessa and Elinor. Melissa always locked up. She was leaning against the back of a chair and she looked ghastly, shrunken and old. She said something about locking up and Deveraux told her to go along, he'd take care of it.

"Melissa didn't argue, in fact, Rosemary had to help her up the stairs. The drug must have been taking hold. I felt dreadful, worn. It was no wonder. When the police analyzed the dregs in the wine goblets, they found we'd been fed enough barbiturates to knock out a horse.

"Deveraux was banking the fire. He looked up at me and said not to bother trying to help him, he'd look after it himself. He said I looked like hell, almost as badly as Melissa. I said something about it being no wonder after the day we'd all had.

"I left Deveraux there and went up to my room. I can't even remember getting my clothes off and falling into bed. The next morning around six—"

Forsythe leaned over and touched Horner's arm, gesturing him to silence. Then he rose, quietly covering the few feet that separated him from the door. He flung it open. Rosemary was standing there. For a moment her face was blank. Then her lips parted and she smiled up at him. She looked much better. She'd changed her dress and put on fresh makeup.

"Oh, Robert, I was about to knock. I didn't want to interrupt you, but will you be able to stay and have tea with us? It's almost ready."

"I think not; my secretary will be waiting for me, but it was kind of you."

He started to gather up his equipment. Getting up, Horner stretched.

"Don't you want me to finish, Forsythe? It will only take a few more minutes. Rosemary can hold tea for that long."

"I don't think it necessary. You've given me what I need. The rest is covered pretty well in your testimony. We can take it from there."

The Horners walked with him to the gate. He glanced back as he left. They were standing close together, not touching. Rosemary was looking after Forsythe. Her husband's eyes were fixed on her face. Vaguely troubled, Forsythe walked toward the cab stand.

He left tired, drained. Two things were disturbing him. He had heard Rosemary outside the shed door long before he'd moved. She'd had lots of time to knock. She wouldn't have stood there unless she was eavesdropping. And her husband's eyes had reflected an emotion that looked very much like fear.

Chapter Five

Forsythe's depression and weariness had vanished during the night. The following morning he worked with Miss Sanderson in their suite on the tapes of his interviews with Rosemary and John Horner. So engrossed was he that it was several minutes after one when he arrived at the Gourmet's Club. The steward directed him to a reading room and it was there that he found Richard Deveraux.

There was only one person in the room, a big man sunk in the depths of an ancient Morris chair. As Forsythe introduced himself, he was conscious of a sharp stab of disbelief. He'd expected changes in the years since a young Rosemary had sketched Deveraux, but he hadn't been prepared for the gross figure that faced him. In the bloated ruin of Deveraux's face only his eyes and hairline remained the same. The aquiline nose, firm mouth, and decisive chin had disappeared into a mass of pink flesh.

With an obvious effort, Deveraux heaved himself out of the chair.

"Do you mind if we talk after lunch, Forsythe? I've taken a lifetime membership in this club for only one reason. Come along and you'll see what I mean."

Forsythe followed him into the dining room. It was dim, paneled in dark wood. Most of the tables were occupied, but there was none of the hum of conversation that one would expect with so many diners. They seemed to be concerned only with their plates.

Lowering his bulk on a chair, Deveraux grinned at his companion. "See what I mean? The food is the whole thing. Will you have a drink before we get to it?"

"If you'll join me."

"Sorry, don't indulge anymore. My doctor's made me a promise. Unless I give up alcohol, tobacco, and cut down on food I'm not long for this world. I met him two-thirds of the way. Food, well, that's too much to expect. By the way, I've taken the liberty of ordering for you."

Their lunch arrived, served by an elderly waiter who seemed to hold his breath until he received Deveraux's nod of approval. They ate in complete silence. Forsythe could see what Deveraux meant. The cuisine was superb. He tried to avoid watching the man opposite him but at times found himself staring in fascination. Deveraux consumed literally mountains of food. His knife and fork moved like surgical instruments as he dissected lobster tails, carved pink curling slices of ham, spread sweet butter on smoking garlic bread.

After the coffee had been served, he raised his eyes to Forsythe. "Ah, that's better. Now we can get on to business. I've a couple of rooms here; gave up my house several years ago. We'll go up and do our talking in private."

A creaking lift took them to the second floor. Deveraux's living quarters were simple, a combination living and study area with a bedroom opening off it. They made themselves comfortable and Forsythe, with his host's permission, set up the recorder.

Deveraux massaged his jowl with one pudgy hand. "Now to go back, way back. I never thought I'd have to travel that road again. When I heard that Sebastian's daughter was having some digging done, I couldn't refuse to help her. But Elizabeth's wasting her time and yours."

"A few days ago, I'd have agreed with you heartily. Now, I'm not so sure. But anyway, I've taken the job on."

Deveraux looked at him quizzically, his eyes containing the touch of sardonic humor that Rosemary had caught in charcoal. "If I ask you where to start, you'll probably say the beginning. Very well. The beginning goes back to my boyhood. Don't look so alarmed, Forsythe; I'm not going to go on for hours about my youth. I only wanted to mention that Sebastian and I grew up together, went to school together. Regular Damon and Pythias relationship. We were still close in manhood. I suffered through his first marriage with him. Mary Ellen, bless her virginal little heart. Cold as ice was Mary Ellen."

Forsythe felt his lips twitch in a grin. "You sound like Rosemary. Even as a child she must have had her aunt figured."

"Rosemary was a very special child. Completely unattractive physically but with a mind like a honed razor. She learned the facts of life early. Her mother was the toast of the officers' club and the girl saw lots of action before Allan divorced his wife.

"To get back to Sebastian. We'd shared everything up to his marriage to Vanessa. Melissa was the only one who had a chance to meet Vanessa before the lovers left for Ireland. I could tell from Sebastian's infrequent letters that the woman he'd married in haste was giving him trouble. When he returned to England, he wired me to meet him at Plymouth. What a wreck got off that ship. I doubt if he could have made it to Meads Green by himself."

"Everyone has been talking around this Irish episode. Exactly what did Vanessa do to Calvert?"

Shrugging his shoulders, Deveraux said, "God knows. Sebastian was almost delirious when he arrived, raved on about the woman consuming him body and soul. Afterwards he never mentioned her again."

"But surely as his closest friend you had some idea."

"That I did. I was never under any illusions about Sebastian. I was as fond of him as one man can be of another, but I knew him. He was a man of small appetites. He complained about Mary Ellen's coldness, about every bit of love ending up in a rape scene, but I always suspected that she was an ideal wife for him. I have no idea why Sebastian was attracted to a woman like Vanessa. She had strong drives. The demands she made on Sebastian must have seemed unnatural to him. His energies were directed toward his art. I don't think he had enough left to satisfy her, so in his eyes she was a monster. A man-eating, consuming great chunk of female flesh."

"So he left her."

"Cold, and came home. He hoped never to see her again. He was like a zombie. Melissa and I were worried about him. We couldn't interest him in anything—working, recreation—nothing. Then I forced him to come to London, took him down to Limehouse to see an amateur wrestling deal. Mersey was one of the wrestlers. Sebastian sat and watched him and his eyes began to glow with the first enthusiasm I'd seen in months. When Sebastian went back to Calvert Hall, Mersey went with him."

"Did you know at that time that Mersey was a homosexual?"

"No, I didn't have a clue." Deveraux frowned. "I don't really believe at that point he was, perhaps latent but certainly not active. Mersey was a nice lad, beautifully built, a golden boy. He talked a fair amount to me about his background. Sordid business, son of a patient Griselda of a mother and a big, brawny dockworker who got drunk with great regularity and beat up his drab wife. Mersey quite obviously was devoted to his mother, loathed and feared his father. I suppose a psychologist would say that's where his tendencies came from, that he tended to identify with his mother."

Fumbling in his pocket, Forsythe located his pipe and started to fill it. "When did you tumble to the relationship between Calvert and his model?"

"My first trip to Meads Green after Mersey settled there. He'd been there about three months and the statue was really taking shape. I was delighted to see Sebastian working away with his old fervor, but I wasn't so delighted when I found out how he felt about the boy. I wasn't disgusted. Sebastian and I were in our late thirties, and I considered myself a man of the world. But I was disturbed."

"Did you try to talk to Calvert about it?"

"I did. He closed right up. Wouldn't discuss it. Said it was his business, and it was. I let it go. My hands were full at the time. My publishing business was just getting off the ground and I was involved in civil defense up to my neck."

Forsythe struck a match and held it to the pipe bowl. After a moment, he removed it from his mouth and blew out a cloud of smoke. Through it he regarded his companion's fleshy face. "Melissa asked you to help after Vanessa arrived, didn't she?"

"She phoned and told me that Vanessa had come to the Hall and she feared that Sebastian might be hurt by her again. Melissa didn't come right out and ask for me to intervene, but I knew she wanted me for moral support and also for bait."

Forsythe raised his brows. "Bait?"

"You probably wouldn't believe it to look at me now, but at that time I was considered a catch, a most eligible bachelor. A man on his way up. I wouldn't say women were falling in my path, but I had any number of chances to marry well. Melissa is a shrewd woman. She wanted Vanessa's attention diverted from Mersey and hoped I might turn the trick.

"I got to Meads Green as fast as I could. Vanessa wasn't due back until the following morning, so I had a chance to see what she had already done. Melissa was a bundle of nerves; young Horner was living in a world of his own; and Rosemary was almost out of control. Sebastian seemed glad to see me. Much to my relief, he appeared to be taking Vanessa in stride. He discussed it a bit with me and said he felt that as soon as his wife realized he wanted no more of her, she'd leave.

"I must admit that I was curious about Vanessa, looked forward to meeting her. On Monday she returned. I had never believed in love at first sight, figured it only existed in romantic novels. I changed my mind. I looked at Vanessa and knew why

I had never married. My entire life must have been a waiting period for a woman like my friend's wife."

Forsythe bit down hard on his pipe. "You mean Vanessa got to you too?"

Deveraux shifted his bulk and smiled ruefully. "Got to me and stayed with me. It wasn't like John Horner's infatuation. I'm not going to say that sex wasn't connected with my feeling for her, but it was deeper than that. As you can see, it's lasted. I never married.

"Vanessa Calvert to me was a living example of the famous women who changed the course of history. For the first time I knew how Napoleon's Josephine, Cleopatra, and Helen of Troy must have appeared in the flesh. I'm not going to tell you that I couldn't see Vanessa's destructive side. She wanted to hurt Sebastian, she loved to needle him. But I believed that all she needed was the right man, someone who could handle her. I felt I was that man."

"Did Vanessa respond to you?"

An old anger moved in the depths of the other man's eyes. "She looked right through me. In a way it had the makings of a black comedy. Vanessa was in hot pursuit of Mersey; Horner was making a bloody fool of himself, sniffing after her like a fox terrier after a female Great Dane; and I was watching the whole affair, brim-up with unrequited love."

Forsythe shook his head. "She *must* be quite a woman!"

"Understatement, Forsythe. Well, that was the situation. Something was bound to give, and it did. The days passed and Thursday night arrived. I couldn't sleep. To be frank with you, I was half starved. Melissa's idea of food was pathetic. Knowing about this, I'd smuggled in my own supplies. About twelve o'clock I broke down, got out of bed, and started foraging. I had some biscuits and canned meat, so I made a rough sandwich and wandered around eating it.

"I stood by the window and looked out. It was a cloudy night, one of those nights when thick gray clouds go scudding across the moon. I glanced down into the sunken garden and at that instant the moon came popping out and I could see two people directly below. For a moment it was as clear as day. The man was Mersey and in his arms was Vanessa. They were involved in a passionate embrace. She was dressed in this sheer garment, her body was quite visible through it, and he was moving his hands over her.

"As luck would have it, clouds closed in across the moon again, and they were gone. I stood there like an idiot, my mouth full of food, not able to chew let alone swallow. I suppose I shouldn't have been hit that hard, but seeing the only woman I'd ever loved making love with another man rocked me. Even knowing it was Vanessa who had pushed the whole thing didn't help. I was wild with jealous fury, and my fury was directed at Mersey. At that moment I could have killed Adonis myself."

Deveraux paused and rubbed his eyes. "Since that night I've tried to remember exactly why I decided to face Sebastian with the truth. I couldn't sleep, in fact I didn't even go to bed. I don't think I told him for spite. I know I was wondering what would happen to his fragile balance if he stumbled over this sort of scene unwarned, whether it would be best for me to break it to him."

"So you told Calvert."

"The next morning. I went to his room. I tried to break it to him gently. Never in all the years I'd known Sebastian had I seen the look I saw that August morning. He went white and his eyes looked inhuman. He spoke calmly, even thanked me, and asked me to tell Vanessa to meet him in his study.

"I left him and headed toward Vanessa's room. I couldn't do it. I couldn't face her. I went down to the kitchen. Melissa was preparing breakfast and I told her what I'd seen, what I'd done. She stared at me. Her eyes were chips of granite. Then she said, 'I've known this, Richard, and I've been concealing it from my brother. Between Vanessa and David they've ruined him. He'll never work again.'"

Forsythe broke in. "A cold reaction from a devoted sister."

"Rather more dedicated than devoted. You must understand Melissa had carried the whole burden of the Calvert family. First Allan, then Sebastian, were the nominal heads of the family, in financial control. They never lifted a hand to look after the estate. Melissa ran it all, saw to the farms, the villagers. She'd banked all her hopes on Sebastian's genius. Even though the family ended with him, the Calvert name would be remembered." He added bitterly, "It has been remembered, but not in the way she'd hoped."

"Vanessa and Calvert didn't meet in his study, did they?"

"No. Melissa went up to Vanessa, and at first Vanessa flatly refused to get out of bed. Then she did agree to see Sebastian, but in the garden. Perhaps she wanted an audience. She loved scenes.

"While we were having breakfast, they met, and the whole thing was out in the open. I left the terrace as soon as I could, went to the drawing room and tried to read. I felt dreadfully responsible. I knew that Melissa blamed me. Time passed, and then Rosemary came running in the front door, dressed for bathing. I caught a glimpse of her face and followed her. When I got to the kitchen, she was telling Melissa about the conversation she'd overheard when Elinor Atlin was trying to persuade David not to leave Sebastian. It was clear to us that Sebastian had lost and Vanessa had won.

"Elinor came in a few minutes later and told us that Rosemary was right; it was all over. Melissa got the girl upstairs and Elinor and I persuaded Melissa to lie down in Elinor's room for a while. Melissa's iron control had given and she was close to collapse.

"The rest of the day passed in a blur. I made plans to leave the next day. I felt like a coward, but I couldn't stand any more. We managed to get through dinner and then there was the scene in the drawing room when Sebastian drugged us—"

"Just a moment." Forsythe consulted his notebook. "The drug that was used and the morphine—it was proved that everyone in the house knew of their existence and had access to them, wasn't it?"

"It was no secret. They were kept in a metal box in the medicine chest of the main bathroom. They were a carryover from Calvert's mother. She'd died several years before of a long, painful illness. Melissa had nursed her, and they'd never disposed of the drugs that remained. Melissa, at lunch on Monday, had discussed them with her brother. She wanted to get rid of them, give them to the hospital. Sebastian agreed. We were all there."

Forsythe flipped a page in his notebook. "You were the last person downstairs on Friday night."

"I volunteered to lock up. I felt queer, but figured it was the result of the emotional binge we'd been on plus my sleeplessness the previous night. I sent Melissa to bed. Horner offered to help me, but he was looking rotten himself so I told him to turn in. I went through the house, checking the doors and windows, turning out the lights.

"By the time I got back to the drawing room, I was stumbling. I sat down on the sofa, one of those stiff formal pieces covered in scratchy brocade. I figured I'd rest for a moment before I went upstairs. That's the last I remember. I passed out. The next morning…" He stopped and looked at his companion. "You know the layout of the house, don't you?"

Forsythe nodded. "I studied a sketch of it."

"The side the drawing room is on consists of two rooms. Sebastian's studio opens directly off it. Originally the studio had been a conservatory, paved in tile, with a lot of glass. Double doors, solid wood, were at the far end of the drawing room. They were closed when I went to sleep.

"When I woke up, it was just after six; I lay there trying to figure where I was. I felt as though I'd been on a six-week bash. The top of my head was coming off; my mouth tasted like a sewer; and I was stiff and sore. Then I realized that I was still in the drawing room, sprawled on the sofa. There was something over me, an afghan that generally was folded over a chesterfield at the other end of the room. Under my head was a satin cushion that was always with the afghan."

Forsythe was staring at him. "You said you passed out. If you only sat down for a minute, why did you bother with the cushion and the cover?"

Deveraux stared back. Something moved in the depths of his eyes. "I didn't. When I slumped down on the sofa both of them were in their usual place. In the night someone had put the cushion under my head and covered me up."

"This didn't," Forsythe said evenly, "come out at the trial."

"I withheld it. Only one person in that house would have been able to do it, the only person not drugged."

Without warning, Forsythe shivered. In his mind was the picture of that silent house, the occupants sleeping like the dead. Deveraux sprawled on the sofa with someone's hands lifting his head, drawing a cover over his still form.

The other man nodded with understanding. Forsythe now recognized the expression in Deveraux's eyes. As the anger had been old, so was the fear. But it was still there. "Not a pretty thought is it, old man? A murderer stopping in the middle of his bloody work to make an unconscious man more comfortable. That's why I never mentioned it until now. It's another piece of evidence that points directly to Sebastian Calvert.

"But anyway, I came to, pushed back the afghan, and sat up, my aching head in my hands. I must have sat there for a while before I lifted my head. When I did, I saw the open doors of the studio. The weather had cleared through the night and morning sunshine slanted across the studio. *Adonis* was standing bathed in it, his marble body turned to gilt. I didn't waste any time looking at his beauty. I realized I was not alone. At *Adonis*'s feet, Sebastian sat. He still wore his dinner jacket and in his arms he held something.

"I still wasn't alarmed. Getting up, I walked toward him, and then I saw what he was holding. I saw Mersey's head. It was half severed from his neck, just kind of dangling over Sebastian's arm. The body was nude and badly mutilated. Sebastian looked directly at me. Our eyes met. I saw no recognition in his. I said something, probably like, 'My God, what have you done?' He just sat there staring."

Deveraux took a deep breath. "I blanked out; I didn't know what to do. Finally I started to snap out of it. I knew I had to have help. I went up and wakened Horner. I had a devil of a time getting him conscious enough to understand me. He got up and came quietly down with me. We didn't want the women in on it.

"The little chap had a lot of guts. He took charge. He went up to Sebastian, waved his hand in front of his face. Sebastian didn't move or even blink. Horner said, 'I've seen something like this before. He won't give us any trouble; he's out of it. Better get onto the police.' Then there was this gasp behind us. It was Melissa, hanging on to the studio door. Her own eyes looked half mad. Horner managed to grab her before she collapsed. He was holding her when Rosemary started to scream. She'd followed her aunt down and saw the whole hellish thing, poor ruddy kid. Melissa pulled herself together; she had to for the girl's sake. I helped her get Rosemary out into the hall.

"They headed up the stairs and I went to the telephone. The only one in the house was in the hall, near the front door. I was talking to Sergeant Hennessy when Vanessa came downstairs, wrapped in a yellow robe. She went into the drawing room, and I finished the call. As I put down the receiver, I heard sounds of a struggle from the drawing room and Horner gasped, 'For Christ's sake, come and help.'

"I ran in, and he was wrestling Vanessa. She was trying to get to Sebastian, had this poker in her hand. Horner couldn't begin to handle her. She was throwing him around. I grabbed her arm, but even the two of us couldn't control her. Then Elinor came from nowhere and took over. She got a hold on Vanessa and shook her. Vanessa came to her senses and started to cry. All the fight went out of her. Elinor got her into a chair and stood beside her. A few minutes later, the police and doctor got there.

"They wanted to get Sebastian out of there, someplace he could be looked after. He needed a change of clothes. The ones he had on were—well, covered. I went up to his room to get them. I was near the breaking point myself. When I opened his door all I could see was a portrait he'd done of David, a head and shoulders, in oils—magnificent. I sat down on his bed and broke right up. Gradually I pulled myself together, got up, and started automatically to straighten the bedspread again. Funny the things we do under stress. There was my best friend, directly below me, covered with the blood of an innocent boy, and what was I doing? Housework on a bed that Sebastian never slept in again."

Deveraux gestured with one hand. "That was actually the end of it. Calvert was put temporarily into a nursing home. The doctors judged him unfit to turn up at his own trial. The evidence was weighed; Sebastian was found guilty and has spent the last twenty-five years at Grey Friar as a human vegetable. And me, well, I suppose I am eating myself to death, as my doctor says. Compensation, he calls it, a form of death wish. Sebastian killed David Mersey, but I'm just as guilty. If I'd minded my own business—"

"Calvert would have found out eventually, Deveraux. You can't blame yourself."

Deveraux didn't speak. He seemed sunk in his own thoughts.

Forsythe started to pack his recorder. Curiously, he glanced at the older man. "You weren't in the forces either. Do you mind telling me why?"

With a visible effort, Deveraux came back to the present. He touched his massive chest. "Had rheumatic fever as a lad. Left me with a wonky heart. Wasn't serious when I was younger; wouldn't be yet if I dropped some weight." He managed a grin. "We were a pretty stove-up crew at the Hall. Sebastian had a stiff knee he'd picked up in a cricket game when we were in prep school. The war had done for John Horner, and I had a heart murmur."

Snapping the lock on his case, Forsythe asked, "What about Mersey? Neither Horner nor Rosemary knew the reason he wasn't in one of the services. I suppose it was the homosexuality business that kept him out."

"Not at all. As I said earlier, I doubt whether he'd shown those tendencies until he met Sebastian. No, Mersey had a good sound medical reason. He was a diabetic."

Forsythe was on his feet, his slender form towering over the man in the chair. He shouted, "A diabetic. Do you know what you're saying, Deveraux?"

Chapter Six

"I don't believe it," Miss Sanderson said flatly.

Handing Forsythe a cup of tea, she shoved the plate of sandwiches closer to him. He stretched his legs toward the flickering warmth of the gas fireplace. The warmth was welcome. The sun had disappeared earlier and the late afternoon was overcast and chill.

Miss Sanderson had been working. A stack of neatly typed pages was piled on her work table beside two tapes labeled Rosemary and John Horner.

Shaking his head, Forsythe pushed the sandwich plate away. "Not after Deveraux's idea of a light lunch. You don't believe what, Sandy? No reason why Deveraux would lie about Mersey's disability."

"That's not what I meant. I don't believe a man of Deveraux's intelligence—he is intelligent, you know. He built a publishing empire that's top-rate. Surely he must have realized what Mersey's condition would have done for defense counsel. There was nothing about it in the transcript. I went over and over it."

Forsythe sipped his tea. "I suppose he didn't grasp the significance. The only people who knew that Mersey was a diabetic were Calvert and Deveraux. He said Mersey was sensitive about it, didn't want it known."

"But surely Melissa must have known. The boy would have needed a special diet, wouldn't he?"

"Deveraux vetoed that; he said Mersey just picked out what he could eat. He wasn't a large eater anyway. Melissa was much too rushed to worry about what people ate or didn't eat. As for Deveraux's intelligence—look at it fairly. It wasn't diabetes that killed the boy; it was morphine."

Miss Sanderson's jaw was set. "But the autopsy. Surely that would have disclosed it."

"Not necessarily, Sandy. If the doctors had any reason to look for it…certainly. But they didn't. As for the injections Mersey gave himself, well, the body was so badly mutilated they probably wouldn't show."

His companion was gently tapping her front teeth with her thumbnail. "A diabetic can die so quickly, Robby. All Calvert had to do was wait until Deveraux went back to London, empty out Mersey's insulin, and replace it with water. Sebastian could have covered the coma easily—just kept the boy in bed until he was dead. It would have looked like a natural death. No earthly reason for all the elaborate hocus pocus with barbiturates, morphine, and a scimitar." Dropping her hand, she stared at Forsythe. "Do you think that fact is enough to go on?"

Staring down into his cup, Forsythe answered slowly. "Legally, you mean, to have the case reopened? It certainly is a step in the right direction, but we'll come up against she old claim again. Calvert wasn't thinking sanely. To all intents he was a madman when he killed his model."

"Balderdash." She snorted the word. "The actual method of murder, the morphine, was not the work of a mad mind. Wiping all the surfaces clean, does that sound like anything but a sane, logical mind? It would have been just as logical, or more so, to have let the boy die from lack of insulin."

She thought for a minute and then added, "You're right about the legal aspects. But as far as I'm concerned, this establishes Calvert's innocence. I would suppose we can also eliminate Deveraux. He could have killed Mersey the same way."

Forsythe sat up. "I disagree. Deveraux was a guest in the house. He wouldn't have had the same chance to cover Mersey's death. And Calvert was there, close to the boy. He knew all about the body's condition. No, Deveraux is still very much in the running."

"Well..." She sighed deeply, pulled herself from her chair, and walked over to her work table. "I guess we might as well continue digging. Oh." She stopped suddenly and turned toward Forsythe. "There are two messages for you. Our client must be becoming impatient. Wants you to meet her this evening. Here it is, time and place." She handed him a slip of paper. "She picks a queer spot for a business appointment, doesn't she?"

Forsythe glanced at the address. "That she does, but she's paying the bills. I'll have to humor her." He looked up at his secretary "You said two, what's the other?"

Miss Sanderson's face was cold. "Better brace yourself. After all these years, the lily maid of Astolat wants to see you. She's staying at the Stewart Arms."

Sticking the slip of paper into his pocket, Forsythe reached for the telephone. Her eyes bleak, his secretary watched.

"Are you actually going to contact her?"

"Why not?"

She sat down in front of her typewriter and began to roll a sheet of paper into it. "Indeed, why not?" She added, "She has the pound of flesh, why not the blood?"

Forsythe was dialing. He didn't appear to hear her. Miss Sanderson started pounding the keys as though she was punishing the machine.

When he stepped through the door of the cocktail lounge, Virginia was the first person he saw. She sat at a small corner table, the light from the centerpiece illuminating her face.

She hadn't changed. Sandy's nickname, "the lily maid of Astolat," suited her. Virginia's beauty was pastel, all pale gilt hair and cameo face. Her figure was curved and faintly sensual. Forsythe waited for the familiar leap of his heart. It didn't come.

When he reached her side, she raised her head. Her voice was the same also, low and husky. "It was good of you to come, Robert. You haven't changed."

"I was just thinking the same about you. It's been a long time."

She nodded, sheaves of pale hair swinging against her face. "Five and a half years. I've never tried to see you. Guilty feelings, I guess, for what I've done to you."

"You did nothing to me, Virginia. Anything that happened was my own decision."

Her eyes dropped. He studied the shadow the fringe of lashes cast on her cheeks. A waitress in a brief skirt and low-cut blouse took their order. When it was delivered, Virginia lifted her eyes and her glass.

"Perhaps I phrased it badly. I meant I feel responsible. I did a foolish, panicky thing. Bribing Jennings to change his testimony. But I was young, Robert, and afraid. All I could see was the mound of evidence against me and the death penalty if I was found guilty."

Forsythe put his glass down. "So young, so frightened, so lacking in faith. I would have got you off. I could have proved that a prowler entered your house that night. With the witnesses I had lined up to show your husband's wild temper, it's probable they would have found the shooting a result of the entry."

Virginia shuddered. "Frank was a terrible man. I can't believe I actually lived three years with him."

"And now, are you happy?"

"Very. We have a son, three years old. I know I should have told you before our wedding, but Douglas wanted no one to know. There was so much publicity because of the trial."

"I can see what he meant." Fishing in his pocket, Forsythe's fingers touched his pipe and then fell away from it. "Graham's name had been linked with yours."

Her eyes met his. They were glittering, luminous, as though with unshed tears. "Douglas and I owe you so much, Robert. You were the only one who seemed to believe in my innocence."

"Much more," he said gently, "than you believed in my ability."

"You protected me. When the rumors started circulating, you left your practice so they wouldn't know it was—"

"I loved you."

Her expression was distressed. "I know. I wish I had loved you. I couldn't, even after all you did for me."

"You can't control love. However, enough about the past. What did you wish to see me for?"

"Just to see you. I was in London and heard that you were here too. You never seem to leave your home. I was wondering…" Her voice trailed off.

There was compassion in his eyes. "I haven't come to resume my practice. It's an entirely private matter that brought me here."

She tossed the gilt hair back from her face. "I'm incredibly selfish, Robert. It's Douglas and my son. I don't know how I could face any more."

Pushing back his chair, he answered the question in her eyes. "I gave you my word."

She put one slim hand over his. "Would you care to have dinner with me?"

He glanced at his watch and rose. "I'm sorry. I won't even have time for a sandwich. I've an appointment and I'll be late if I don't hurry."

"Perhaps we can see each other before I leave. You could ring me."

"I'll try." He touched her shoulder. "Goodbye, Virginia."

He was conscious of her eyes following him as he left. He didn't look back.

It was twilight when Forsythe turned onto Fish Hill Street. He hadn't been wholly truthful with Virginia. He'd not been late. There had been time to walk from Steward Arms to the Monument.

He saw it looming ahead of him against the darkening sky. The silhouette of the vase of flames at the very top caught the last weak rays of light. He cast only a glance at the bas-relief of the City of London as he passed it. For almost three hundred years the mournful woman representing London after the Great Fire had drooped in the same position, ignoring the other figures attempting to raise her.

Forsythe gave the guardian a good evening and his sixpence and started up the winding black marble steps. He blessed the sports that had kept his wind sound as he reached the two hundredth step. At step three hundred, he began to wonder whether he *had* kept himself in good shape.

All this was forgotten as he stepped into the iron-grilled cage at the Monument's top. For a moment he glanced down at the sweeping view of domes, roof tops, chimney pots, and winding streets.

After a moment, he realized he wasn't alone. At the east end a small figure dressed in cloak and hood stood silently.

"Elizabeth?" he called.

Without turning her head, she spoke. "The view is worth that awful climb, isn't it? This is the first time I've been up here. Uncle Howard said my mother loved this view when she was a young girl."

Joining her, he looked down at the Tower and the Thames, wide and silver, running beneath its many bridges toward Westminster. Mist was rolling in eerie gray billows from the river.

"It looks as though we may be in for a spot of fog. A bit unseasonal." He looked at his companion. All he could see was her profile, the thin proud nose, her eyes veiled by her lashes.

"I've been waiting," she said abruptly. "Sitting around that dreadful little apartment waiting. Do you have anything yet?"

"I've been able to speak with the prosecutor, Sir Hilary Putham, and I've managed to get the full brief from Peter

Meredith. Three of the witnesses, Deveraux, Rosemary, and John Horner, have been interviewed."

"Were they willing to be interviewed?"

"Yes. Rosemary and Deveraux did their best. Horner, well, he came around. By the way, Elizabeth, your cousin said you hadn't contacted her."

"I haven't. Have you uncovered anything, Robert, that will help?"

He shifted his position, trying to see her face more clearly. "There are a couple of things," he said cautiously. "Nothing concrete, but something to start with. I think I can safely say that my secretary and I have no doubt that there was a miscarriage of justice. We feel your father is innocent."

"Will it stand up in court?" He shook his head. Her voice rose slightly, "If Sebastian Calvert is innocent, one of the other six must be guilty. Have you any idea which one?"

Again his head moved in a negative gesture. "It's still too early. I have the other three to talk with—Vanessa, Melissa, and Elinor. This is a matter of patience. A murderer who has managed to stay concealed for all these years is not going to be easy to flush out in the open."

She wheeled to face him. In the dark shadow of her hood he could see the glitter of her eyes, the set of her mouth. "I'm expecting too much, too soon, but it seems so—hopeless. How can you force a confession from a person who would hide the truth, allow me to suffer the way I've suffered?"

He spoke mildly. "Your cousin has suffered and so, I imagine, has your Aunt Melissa."

"To hell with their suffering. They had a part of him, a share of his life. They've earned their suffering. I haven't. One of them might even have killed Mersey."

He walked away from her to a point where he could see the dome of St Paul's. Her voice followed him.

"I'm sorry, Robert. I'm afraid I don't make a good waiter. I'm on edge tonight. You're doing well, at least you feel there is a chance. Where do you go from here?"

"To Rome. Vanessa has lived there for a number of years. I leave in the morning."

He hadn't heard her move but he felt her hand on his arm. "Please keep me informed. If it's a matter of money—"

"I don't think there's anyone or anything we can buy, Elizabeth."

Her hand fell away and she turned back to her study of London.

He regarded her steadily. The feeling of unease she seemed to induce troubled him. After a moment he moved away from her, toward the steps.

"Are you coming down now, Elizabeth? I'll see you back to your apartment."

"No." Her voice was muffled. "I think I'll stay here a little longer. You go along."

He went down the corkscrewing steps past the guardian. Crossing King William Street, he halted in front of Monument station. Vainly he tried to hail a cab. It was cold now and dark. The fog he had predicted was rolling in. Finally, he shrugged, turned up his coat collar, and prepared to walk back to his hotel.

It was an eerie walk. There weren't many pedestrians and they loomed suddenly from the fog, upon him before he realized they were there. He strode along swiftly. A few blocks from the hotel, Forsythe decided to leave the main thoroughfare and shorten his time by cutting down a quiet, cobblestoned street. The fog seemed lighter here, drifting in swirls. He passed the shop fronts, most of them shuttered for the night.

Toward the end of the street he could make out the street light on the corner where he would turn. He lengthened his stride, eager to be out of the clammy fog. He'd almost reached the corner when he stumbled. As he fought for his balance he heard it. The soft rush of footsteps behind him and then a sharp crack. At the same instant, he felt the blow, searing pain along the left side of his head.

Breaking into a run, he covered the distance left and fell into the side door of his hotel. Pulling himself to a stop, he stood there panting. In the mirror over the desk he could see himself. His face was white and tense. A dribble of blood was running down his cheek.

His shock was mirrored in the face of the man behind the desk.

"Mr. Forsythe. You've been hurt."

The desk clerk hurried around the desk, his hand out. Forsythe waved him away. Pulling out his handkerchief, he pressed it against the side of his head.

"Just a scratch. Ran into a lamppost in the fog. Clumsy."

"Think you should have it looked at, sir? I could ring up a doctor. There's one just around the corner."

Forsythe managed a reassuring smile. "It's not that serious. I'll go up and dab something on it. Good night."

He was aware of the man's worried eyes on him as the lift door closed.

Miss Sanderson's eyes were on her work. She was typing, a cigarette held in her mouth, one eye closed against the smoke. She looked tired.

"Back so soon, Robby? There's coffee on the table. It's still hot." She glanced up. The cigarette fell from her lips unheeded. "My God! You're covered with blood."

She was on her feet. Forsythe allowed her to push him into a chair. She tilted his head up to the light. "Looks worse than it is. Just a shallow groove along your skull. What in hell have you been doing?"

"Minding my own business. Walking along and someone took a shot at me. Just outside the hotel. Luckily I stumbled over a cobblestone at the same time."

She straightened. "Are you sure?"

He dabbed at his face. "I know a gun when I hear one. Better get something and clean me up a bit."

She was only gone a minute. The tin box she brought back had a small red cross on one side. Her hands were deft.

"This will sting."

He winced. It did. She stood back and surveyed her work.

"You look piratelike with that sticking plaster on your head. Quite dashing."

Forsythe grinned up at her, but her concerned expression didn't change.

"Looks as though the digging you're doing has upset someone. You've received your warning."

"If I hadn't stumbled, old dear, I'd be out there with a neat hole in the middle of my head. That was no warning. Whoever dislikes me meant it for keeps."

Gently her nail flicked her tooth. "But what for? We haven't anything definite." She lowered her hand and started to count on her fingers. "Rosemary Horner listening at a door she could just have opened and entered. A look that you swear was fear in John Horner's eyes. Deveraux's claim that the murderer took time to cover him up. The knowledge that Mersey was a diabetic. Just a bunch of unconnected facts."

"Apparently someone is afraid we'll connect them, Sandy. Even after all these years we must be on a hot trail. Maybe someone said too much and didn't realize it at the time. Perhaps one of the people we haven't yet interviewed fears something that John, Rosemary, or Richard could have told us."

"The burning question right now is—do you continue?"

His mouth was suddenly grim. "Nothing could stop me now."

She returned his look. "A bullet might."

"Let it go for now, Sandy. Do you have my reservation for Rome tomorrow?"

Her hands were busy with the coffee pot. Handing her companion a steaming cup, she flicked the gas fire up a notch and sank into a chair opposite him.

"All in order. You must be looking forward to meeting Vanessa Calvert. From those comments on the tapes, she's something of a puzzle. The effect she made on the people who knew her is confusing. How can one woman be all those things?"

"I know what you mean, Sandy. Goddess, natural force, lion. Definitely a woman of many parts."

Miss Sanderson grinned. "You've forgotten Deveraux. Blimey, Helen of Troy and Josephine wrapped up in one package. However, Robby, twenty-five years is a long time. Don't be disappointed if Vanessa is no longer the package she once was."

He smiled back at her. "Goddesses and natural forces know no age."

"Lions do, my boy. They get mangy hides and lose all their teeth. Then," she looked gloomily into the fire, "the hyenas gather to finish them off."

They sat in silence for a while. Finally Miss Sanderson lifted her eyes and looked hopefully at her companion. "Any chance of changing that single reservation into a double? I could go along as a kind of bodyguard."

He chuckled. "Guarding me from what—bullets or Vanessa?" He said to Miss Sanderson, "I'm sorry."

Chapter Seven

Forsythe said to Vanessa Calvert, "I'm sorry."

"You should be. You were *staring*. But don't look so abashed, Mr. Forsythe; I should be used to it by now. In a way I suppose I even like it. I would far rather be stared at than ignored. Tell me, do you find me a disappointment?"

Forsythe would have liked to have avoided that question. He'd felt a sharp stab of regret when he'd first seen her. She was sitting under a peppermint-striped awning at a tiny glass-topped table. The Italian sunlight was merciless. Vanessa was still impressive, but the flesh on her upper arms was loose and the breasts that John Horner had immortalized in poetry were pendulous. Under the broad brim of a white hat, her hair was an improbable shade of red, quite frankly dyed. Huge sunglasses obscured her eyes and features. It was when she had removed them that Forsythe had stared. The essence of the Vanessa he'd heard about still lived, mirrored in huge amber eyes.

He saw the same amusement that the people he'd talked with had remembered.

"Don't bother answering that question. You'll probably try to be tactful and I loathe tact." She sipped her liqueur. "I must admit that after the trial many of the stares directed at me were unfriendly. They say one can't touch pitch without being dirtied with it. It's true. The most unholy rumors have come to my ears through the years. Not only about myself. I could understand that. But the gossips spared no one. Poor Melissa was painted as some sort of middle-aged monster who procured innocent young men for her depraved brother. Sebastian's relationship with his niece, Rosemary, was bandied about. Even his friendship with Richard was hinted at being unnatural. They decided that John Horner, one of the most masculine men I've ever known, was another of Sebastian's lovers. Bloody nonsense, all of it."

"What did you hear about yourself?"

She moved one white-clad shoulder. "Another monster, crazed with sex, who had nearly driven Sebastian mad during our marriage and finished the job by luring David away from him. In my case they did have some grounds, though I never considered that Sebastian had to be driven to it. He was always unbalanced, couldn't quite stand women."

"He did marry twice."

"And both were flaming successes, weren't they?"

Forsythe tried another tack. "Do you mind me coming here, rehashing past history?"

"Mind? No, I'd say the reverse. It's been a deadly dull season. If you wish to waste your money, or I suppose I should say Sebastian's daughter's money, it's fine with me."

"There's no use of asking you how you feel about your husband's guilt, is there?"

"Not the slightest. You said you've read my testimony. It still stands. Sebastian couldn't face the fact that David preferred a woman to him. I think I might have understood him killing the boy, but I couldn't understand how he could chop that magnificent body to bits. What a build the lad had. Now the battle lines are drawn, Mr. Forsythe. You understand I have nothing to contribute to clear my dear husband's name. Do you have any questions?"

Forsythe signaled the waiter for another drink. He was a good-looking chap, hirsute, but with fine eyes. His manner was a blend of contempt and servility. Forsythe noticed he managed to brush against Vanessa. She didn't draw away.

"Questions, yes. Why did you return to your husband's home if you disliked him so intensely?"

"Not disliked. I don't like; I adore. I don't dislike; I hate. I hated Sebastian. Not at first. I think I fell in love with his work, with the fine, passionate things he created. I confused the art with the man. It wasn't long before I found that he was a spineless mass with ice water in his veins. But in my own way I did everything possibly to make our marriage work. Sebastian was unique. Not only was he the only man I ever married but also the only one to walk out on *me*. It wasn't with any thoughts of patching our marriage up that I came to the Hall. It was a simple matter of money."

Forsythe raised his brows. "I understood that you were wealthy in your own right."

"On paper I was. At that time the principal was still in trust and I had only an allowance to live on. It was generous, but I lived on rather an exalted scale. What I wanted I bought. On the black market you could get anything you desired. But it was expensive. I was stony broke. I'd never asked anything from Sebastian, so I decided he might as well divvy up."

"Calvert wasn't a mean man. Why didn't you write and ask him for some help?"

She lifted her glass in a large, shapely hand. "You don't know me. I wanted him to ask me to accept it. I thought after a few days in his peaceful home he'd be willing to bribe me to leave. I didn't have the faintest idea about David. The moment I saw him all idea of money was gone. I'd have wanted him even if he hadn't belonged to Sebastian. That only added spice to the chase."

"And you won first prize, Mrs. Calvert?"

"Won and lost. David chose me and Sebastian killed him. It's as simple as that."

"Did you know that David Mersey was a diabetic?"

She frowned. "No, I didn't. Was he really?" She looked at Forsythe sharply. "What is this supposed to mean to me?"

"Calvert knew. Doesn't it seem strange that he killed the boy the way he did?"

"Not at all. It's the old story of Salome all over again. She wanted John the Baptist's head. Calvert wanted me to have David served up like a butchered carcass of beef. The man was mad, Mr. Forsythe, mad. At the trial I'll admit I thought he was faking, trying to escape punishment. I know better now."

"I see." Forsythe's eyes moved from Vanessa's face to the people sauntering along the street. Many of the girls were lovely, moving with a sensuous grace. His dark suit felt out of place. In the brassy sunlight of Rome, among its bright colors, he felt stiff, very English, and depressed. He'd wasted his time. Vanessa had nothing for him.

Vanessa's voice called him back. "I am what I am. I'm not going to say I'm a perfect human being. I'm merely human. I didn't seek Sebastian out to do him harm. I loved David, wanted him. The loss of that beautiful, bright creature was painful. You've seen the *Adonis*?"

"I've seen it. I've also seen the love that Calvert put into it."

"Love of one man for another. What kind of love is that?"

"I don't sit in judgment, Mrs. Calvert, and try to decide what is right and what is wrong. All I know is that the emotion in that piece of stone is as pure as any emotion that the human beings you were mentioning are capable of. That's why it will outlive our lives, our time. Long after Mersey's death is forgotten, Sebastian Calvert's love will immortalize his *Adonis*."

"A pretty sentiment, but only empty words. The model is dead."

Forsythe started to rise. Then he sank back into his chair. "I almost forgot. Neither Elizabeth's investigator or my own bloodhound, Miss Sanderson, was able to trace your cousin. Can you tell me where I can find her?"

Vanessa looked directly at him. He couldn't read the expression in the golden eyes. "Lin? I suppose they might have drawn a blank. Yes, I can tell you where she is, but it won't help you."

"Will she not be willing to speak with me?"

"No, Lin will not speak with you. There's a tiny village in the Swiss Alps called by the unbelievably trite name of Edelweiss. On the mountain behind the village there's a deep crevasse. At the bottom of it is Lin. She's been there for twenty years."

"But we couldn't find any record of her death."

"The record is there in the little town hall, all spelled out neatly on a brass plaque. It mentions such words as gallantry, bravery. It doesn't say anything about stupidity. It should."

"How did she die?"

"Lin left me shortly after the trial. We'd been together as long as I can remember. Her parents died when she was young, of some type of jungle fever in a godforsaken outpost. They were medical missionaries. I was an only child, and my parents raised Lin as my sister. She was much like her parents, an idealist, very religious. I don't know how she stood me. She disapproved of me completely. But there was a bond, a strong one, between us. The only time we were ever apart was the year I spent in Ireland.

"Lin didn't want me to go to the Hall, but she never could stop me. She was a bit of a martyr. I said she needn't come, but she tagged along anyway. When we got there and the ruckus started over David, she sided with Melissa and the rest. After the first few days, she gave up trying to reform me. But even at the end, the Friday when Sebastian had it out with me, Lin went to David and tried to convince him he'd be better of with Sebastian. She told him I'd give him a rotten time."

"After the trial Miss Atlin left you."

"Couldn't bear the sight of me. Lin blamed me for the whole grisly business. I never realized until she was gone how much I depended on her. I've missed her. But to get to her death. Lin had no money of her own; her parents left her nothing. As the saying goes, they were as poor as church mice. She took a job as a governess; a Swiss banker hired her. She was on vacation when she died, a skiing holiday. A boy had fallen in the crevasse. Only his father and brother were on the mountain-side. They didn't know what to do. The child had been caught partway down on an outjutting of ice. He was hanging there, unconscious. Lin knew there was no time to get more help; the ice might collapse at any moment. She roped herself up and went down after him. There was only one rope. She tried to make a noose, get it around him. She found the rope wouldn't support both their weights.

"So Lin got a toehold on the ice, got the rope off herself and around him. They got the boy up all right. They were just lowering it to her when the ice gave. They said she didn't make a sound as she fell."

Forsythe stared at the woman. "You call that stupid."

She waved a hand wearily. "The boy died that afternoon in the hospital of internal injuries. She'd given her life for a child who was to all intents already dead."

"She never knew that."

"No, Lin never knew."

There was a pause. Then Forsythe did get up.

Vanessa raised mocking amber eyes. "I wasn't any help to you, was I?"

His voice was even. "You never intended to be."

She gave him a smile, her lips curling back from even white teeth. "Goodbye, Mr. Forsythe, I shan't wish you good luck."

He strode away. His shoulders, under the dark jacket, were erect. She watched his slim figure vanish in the crowds. The waiter was back, one hand on her shoulder.

"Tonight, Signora? The usual place."

She glanced at his hand, her eyes icy. "Haven't you learned yet, Giulio? I do the touching."

He withdrew his hand but didn't move away. After a moment she snapped her sunglasses into place. Behind them her eyes traveled up the column of his throat to his heavy jaw.

She shrugged and reached for her glass. "Tonight, Giulio. Why not?"

Chapter Eight

Shifting slightly, Melissa Calvert paused, her hands hovering over the tea tray.

"Milk or lemon? Yes, here you are. Do have a scone; they're delicious. I can say that honestly as I didn't bake them. I've always been a poor cook and now I rely mainly on bake-shops for this sort of thing." She took a tiny sip of her own tea and regarded her guest. "I must admit, Mr. Forsythe, I was surprised to hear that you'd met Vanessa only two days ago. You don't wear that dazed expression that Vanessa usually induces in males."

"It's been a long time since you've seen her. She's aged but I could still see a hint of the magic she once must have had."

"I've never been able to picture her as any different than she was in forty-four. Other people, yes, I have no trouble associating them with age. Not poor Vanessa."

Forsythe raised his brows and studied his companion. Sir Hilary had been correct. The plain woman was not stunning. Her dark hair had turned into silver plaits, drawn around features softened and beautified by time. Only her eyes, dark and flashing behind heavy-rimmed glasses, reminded him of the sketch made by Rosemary Horner. He questioned Melissa. "Poor?"

She smiled faintly. "It must sound strange to you when I use a word of that type with Vanessa's name. But I've never really disliked her even though I know that she was directly responsible for my brother's ruin. I've always pictured Vanessa as something of, now what is the word? The mischievous ghosts who rattle and bang—"

"Poltergeist," Forsythe suggested.

"That's the word. A big troublemaking child in a woman's attractive body."

"A dangerous combination."

"Perhaps not to the average man. To my brother, yes. He should never have married at all." She smiled at the expression on Forsythe's face. "Spinsters are reputed to be innocent, dried up creatures with no comprehension of life. I'm afraid that's a fallacy. The mere fact that they have no life of their own, live in other people's lives, makes them see more accurately than the people involved.

"Sebastian was not masculine. His first marriage to Mary Ellen Pennell was the result of my interference. Good intentions do pave the way to hell. I very much wanted an heir, a son to carry on the Calvert line. Allan was no help. He had a daughter, Rosemary, but his marriage was breaking up. So I forced my younger brother into a marriage he didn't wish.

"I thought Mary Ellen would be ideal for Sebastian. She came from a fine background and seemed a quiet, competent girl. I was being selfish to an extent. The estate had been my responsibility for so long that I hoped she might be able to take over. I was over thirty and felt time slipping away from me."

"His marriage didn't work out as you had hoped."

"Not in any way. I only gained another burden. Sebastian was unhappy and as for Mary Ellen...she did put in an appearance at social gatherings, garden parties and fêtes, posing in flowered chiffon and large floppy hats. Other than that she did nothing. Mary Ellen was much addicted to lounges and people waiting on her. She became pregnant, and I was overjoyed. But her conduct became worse. I sometimes have felt if she had moved around a bit she might still be alive."

"She wasn't a delicate woman?"

Melissa snorted. It reminded Forsythe of Sandy's derisive sound. "Far from it. The doctor tried to make her exercise, but she actually died of complications that could happen to any woman in childbirth. Sebastian was, I think, inwardly relieved. He set about getting rid of the baby as fast as possible. I wanted to keep Elizabeth, raise her as my own child, but he wouldn't hear of it. He wanted no reminder of his wife. So Howie and Anne Pennell took her. It worked out better for the child. At least she was spared a certain amount. I'd hoped she would never have to know about her father. But Howie must have decided otherwise."

"A wise decision, Miss Calvert. Elizabeth was bound to have learned sometime, the shock..."

Melissa didn't appear to be listening. She was looking down at her knee. Her composure was much better than Rosemary's had been. Any disturbance she felt was betrayed by her hands. One of them was nervously pleating the silk of her dress, Elizabeth's gesture.

"Knowing Sebastian as I did, I was amazed to learn that he planned to remarry. He met Vanessa in London, at a cocktail party, and within a month they were married. He did bring her to the Hall first to meet me. I was dismayed when I saw her, saw that robust, demanding nature of hers. I tried to persuade both of them to wait, at least for a short while. This was one time I couldn't sway Sebastian. He wouldn't even wait for Richard Deveraux to meet her. Well, you must know about that. When Sebastian returned, I tried to build him up, get him back to work..."

She looked up at Forsythe, met his eyes squarely. "Many close friends feel I was interested in Sebastian the artist to the exclusion of Sebastian the brother. At one time I would have denied this. But as one gets older one has a tendency to lose self-illusions. My brother was not an admirable man. He was weak, vain, and unbelievably selfish. But he was also a great artist. I was glad when he brought David home even though I sensed immediately that Sebastian's interest in him was homosexual. If anyone was corrupted, it was young David. But he was easily corrupted. His parents had died a short time before—"

"Deveraux told me," Forsythe interrupted, "that Mersey came from a sticky home, wife beating and all that."

"He did. His father had beaten his mother once too often. She died of her injuries. In drunken remorse the man killed himself. David considered his mother a saint. But, as I said, he was alone, no education, a slum product. Sebastian changed all that and David liked the changes. He was a protégé of a rich and famous man, living at the Hall. His future was assured. I have called him a chameleon. He was. When he found what Sebastian wanted from him, he went along with it. And, God forgive me, so did I. If David had been a true homosexual I doubt whether Vanessa would ever have swayed him."

Forsythe looked at his notebook. "Rosemary returned in the spring and then in August Vanessa and Elinor Atlin arrived."

"Yes, Rosemary came home. I'd accepted David and although I wasn't happy about Rosemary being at the Hall, I accepted that also. David and Sebastian were discreet. I never believed that the child would understand what their true relationship was. Rosemary was clever. She hid her knowledge from me and life went on.

"I was overworked. I suppose you've heard about that. It was my own fault, but I felt it necessary. Our country was at war. You've probably also heard about my stand on our rations. I was teased about it, but I felt this necessary too. Thousands of others were getting by and we would also. Rosemary still complains about it. The truth is that it was good for her. Her skin was bad and she was overweight."

She paused. "If you don't mind waiting, I'll make some fresh tea. I find it soothing. Excuse me."

Forsythe watched her leave the room. He liked Melissa Calvert. There was a physical resemblance to Elizabeth, and Melissa used the same pleating motion. Other than that, he noticed no similarity to her niece. Melissa was a strong woman, honest and possibly ruthless, but she made no effort to spare herself. In a way she reminded him of Sandy.

He looked around the room. It was a compact flat, modern and comfortably arranged, but looking more like a hotel suite than a home. The only touch that indicated Melissa's background was a delicate Sheraton desk near the window. There were few ornaments and no photographs.

She wasn't gone long. Pouring out hot tea, she started to speak.

"When Vanessa and Elinor arrived, I knew immediately what was going to happen between my sister-in-law and David. I saw her eyes when he came into the drawing room in his bathing suit. Even knowing didn't help. I was powerless to stop her. For a time I had hopes; David seemed to be fending Vanessa off. But I felt her undoubted appeal would eventually break him down. In desperation I called Richard. Women liked him. I thought Vanessa might take to him."

"Just the opposite happened, Miss Calvert."

"Richard fell in love with her. I couldn't believe it. He'd had a great deal of experience with women, but I'd never seen him lose his head. Even Richard was no help.

"Then the Wednesday night before the tragedy, my fears were confirmed. I saw Vanessa leaving David's room. I pushed Rosemary behind me, hoping vainly that she wouldn't see. Then I closed my eyes and stood there wondering what I could do. Rosemary was upset, so I took her to our bedroom and told her to go to sleep.

"I waited a moment to see that she was all right and then I went to Vanessa's room. I was in a rage. I didn't bother knocking, just flung open the door and marched right in. Vanessa was in bed, propped up on her pillows. The upper part of her body was wrapped in her spare blanket. She always had her window wide open. She was calmly reading a novel and eating chocolates. Black-market, no doubt."

Forsythe stifled a grin at this point. Melissa didn't notice. Her hand was busily pleating again.

"Vanessa looked up and asked me why I had come at that ungodly hour and couldn't I knock. I said to her, 'Don't play games with me, Vanessa; you know why I'm here. I saw you coming from your rendezvous with David. My niece saw you too. This is too much. This is as much my home as Sebastian's. I want you to leave.'

"She did have grace enough to drop her eyes. When she looked up, they were glowing with unholy amusement. The woman had no shame, no decency. She did look lovely. That mass of hair, held back with a green satin ribbon, was spilling over the blanket.

"She said quite softly, 'Would you rather that Rosemary caught her beloved uncle coming out of David's room?' I didn't answer. I couldn't. I was choked with rage." Melissa stopped abruptly and looked at Forsythe. "I have never understood why David was killed and not Vanessa. If ever a woman could inspire murder, it was her. But to get back. She threw her hair back and smiled at me. 'Very well,' she said, 'I know when I'm not welcome. I'll leave quietly, but of course I'll have to tell Sebastian the reason.'

"Vanessa knew she had the upper hand. At that time I had no idea how close Sebastian's statue was to completion. I needed time. She read my face and laughed. 'We'll be fellow conspirators, Melissa. You keep my secret and I'll keep it too.' She'd won. All I could do was swing on my heel and leave."

"You didn't gain much time, Miss Calvert."

"I blamed Richard for years. But it would only have postponed it if he hadn't told Sebastian. My brother would have found out. Vanessa loved to torture him; she'd have told him herself.

"Friday morning Richard told me my secret was no longer a secret, that Sebastian knew and wanted to see Vanessa. I went up to her. She wouldn't agree to go to Sebastian's study. She said he might have everyone else on a string but she'd broken hers. They met in the sunken garden. I suppose you know exactly what happened."

"Yes, that's been well covered. Could you tell me something about the rest of the day? Where was everyone and what were they doing? I know it's expecting a lot from your memory—"

"My memory is clear, Mr. Forsythe. I've often wished it wasn't. After breakfast Rosemary came bolting in and told me that David had chosen Vanessa. She was overwrought. It was hard enough for an adult in that house, but a child exposed to the tension...Well, I put her to bed, and Richard and Elinor insisted I rest in Elinor's room so I wouldn't disturb Rosemary. As I started upstairs, David was just returning from the lake. He came in the front door, brushed past me without a word, and went up to his room. As I passed his door, I heard the lock click. He stayed there until dinner time.

"I couldn't stay still. In a short time I got up and went downstairs. All was quiet. Richard was in the drawing room reading. John Horner was in a little room at the back of the house where he worked. Rosemary, of course, remained in our room. The cause of all the trouble was on the terrace. Vanessa was stretched out in a chaise lounge, sleeping quite peacefully in the sun. Sebastian was in his studio."

"Was that the situation until dinner time?"

"That was it. I went down to the kitchen and Elinor joined me there. We did housework; we didn't bother with lunch. Everyone was busy staying as far away from the others as possible. I don't know how I would have gotten through the day without Elinor."

"What was your opinion of Elinor, Miss Calvert?"

"I think perhaps I tended to identify with her. She was in somewhat the same position as I. Elinor saw her cousin with harsh realism. She knew that Vanessa was completely amoral, but Elinor was devoted to her. Their separation during my brother's marriage had been a sore blow for Elinor. I think that Elinor feared that Vanessa and David would have no room in their lives for her. I believe that was the reason she entreated David to stay with Sebastian. None of our actions are wholly selfless. But whatever the reason, Elinor was one note of sanity in that dreadful August."

"Can you tell me about dinner that night?"

"Elinor cooked it. I puttered around in the kitchen, made the coffee. It was even worse than usual. We arranged a tray for Rosemary and I took it up to her while Elinor put the dinner on the table. Dinner itself was awful. Richard and I did our best to act as though nothing had happened. The rest, except for Sebastian, didn't try."

"How did Sebastian strike you, his behavior at dinner?"

"Frankly, he frightened me. He was excited, spots of color on his cheekbones and his eyes flashing. He seemed frightfully keyed up."

"You hadn't expected this reaction."

"With Sebastian, of course, you could never be certain. But I had thought he would be quiet, draw in on himself. He was the opposite." Her fingers were working at her skirt again. "I suppose he was breaking down even then, nerving himself to do the horrible thing he did later that night."

"There is no doubt in your mind that your brother did kill Mersey?"

"I've struggled through the years to believe otherwise. It's been an impossibility. I was there, you see; it could have been no one else. You think me a poor sister not to share Rosemary's belief in Sebastian's innocence? Well, there was the matter of the drugged wine—"

"Just one moment, Miss Calvert." This time Forsythe didn't check his notebook. "John Horner brought the wine from the cellar. He opened the bottle in the kitchen. Surely he had the same opportunity."

"There was no trace of mother's barbiturate in the bottle. The only traces they found were in the goblets. We all put them down just anywhere when we went to bed."

"I know that. But Horner could have put the drug in the goblets *before* the wine was poured. He arranged the goblets on the tray."

"It wasn't brought out at the trial, Mr. Forsythe, but the drug itself was a liquid, pale brown. The goblets were clear crystal. Even a small amount would have shown. Someone would have noticed it."

"After Sebastian poured it, he didn't serve it immediately. I see the rest of you were 'milling around the table.'"

"We were. Most of the others were watching Sebastian. I wasn't. I couldn't bear to look at him because he disturbed me to such a degree. I was close to the table. I'd swear that no one had a chance to pour the liquid into the wine in the goblets. Elinor handed it around. But she just walked over, picked up the tray, and carried it around. She had no chance to drug it.

"No, Mr. Forsythe, the only time the wine could have been drugged was when my brother was pouring it, when his body shielded the table from our eyes. When the police analyzed the dregs of the wine, every intact goblet showed traces of the drug. The goblet that Sebastian had broken still had enough wine on the shards to show no drug was in his goblet. And he had selected his own goblet, carried it away with him before the others were served."

"I had hoped, Miss Calvert, that you could give me some encouragement."

"I wish I could, but I can't very well lie, can I? There was too much evidence against Sebastian. He hadn't slept in his bed that night. He was still wearing the dinner jacket he'd worn the previous evening. The only one of us who was not drugged and helpless was my brother. I'm truly sorry. I would have liked to help. As far as Sebastian is concerned, proof of his innocence would accomplish nothing for him. Two people died that night, David and my brother. But for Elizabeth, for Rosemary and her sons, I wish I could change it."

Gently, Forsythe asked, "Have you seen your brother since—"

"Since they took him away? Yes, I went once. I hoped he might improve. The attendants tried to break through to him. They put pencils, crayons, paints on the table where he sat. He just sat there and stared. Then they tried modeling clay. He liked that. He picked only two colors, bright red and a grayish-blue. The day I was there, he sat there rolling it in his clumsy fingers." Forsythe had a fleeting thought of the hands that had fashioned the *Adonis*.

"Then I saw what he was doing. He was building a little figure, like children build snowmen, balls of clay piled one on the other. When he was finished, he lifted his hand, tightened it into a fist, and smashed the figure. The red and blue material oozed out between his fingers. His expression didn't change. Mine must have. His hands looked as they did that morning when Richard found him. I never went back. No, Mr. Forsythe, do what you wish, but in the end Elizabeth must accept the tragic fact that her father killed."

Forsythe quietly began to repack his case. "Nevertheless, it was good of you to trust me, to speak so frankly."

Melissa smiled slightly "I phoned Sir Hilary. I haven't contacted him since the trial, but I still respect his opinion. He's the one who inspired the trust. He told me that you, despite the rumors I'd heard, deserved all the help I could give you. If anyone could uncover evidence to help my brother, he believes it will be you. Sir Hilary has a high opinion of your ability, says you have a devious mind, more suited to a detective than a barrister."

Forsythe rose. "He's very kind and so are you. I hope I deserve his faith and your confidences. Good day, Miss Calvert."

Melissa saw him out and then returned to her chair. She spread her hands on her lap. There was a tremor in the fingers. She stared down at them.

Chapter Nine

Abigail Sanderson settled more comfortably against the leather seat. Turning the hood of the small car northward, Forsythe darted a glance at his companion.

"You're looking chipper today, Sandy. Are you looking forward to seeing Meads Green?"

"Partly. Mainly, I'm just glad to be out of that hotel suite. It was fine for you racing around meeting people, but it did get a bit tiresome for old faithful holding the fort with nothing but a tape recorder and typewriter for company."

"How did ex-Sergeant Hennessy strike you when you rang him up?"

"Exceedingly cordial, the hearty type. I could almost draw you a picture of him from his voice."

"Draw away."

"Over sixty, but of course we know that. Short, stocky, florid, and probably bald. I imagine a great floppy mustache. Polite but not the forelock-tugging kind."

Forsythe threw back his head and laughed. "Pretty difficult to tug a forelock with no hair."

"Come now, Robby; you know what I mean."

"I know what you're doing. Typing the poor chap. Your description fits every rural sergeant who ever appeared in novels or on telly."

"Very well, well make a bet. I'll give you five to-one. One of your shillings to five of mine."

"With those odds I can't refuse. I don't mind taking your money at all."

They'd turned off the main road and were coasting down a gentle hill. Near the bottom, the car rumbled over a stone bridge and into a small village.

"There's the police station." Forsythe waved toward a green and white building.

"Keep going. The good sergeant lives on the next side street. Turn right, third house."

Obeying her instructions, Forsythe pulled up in front of a neat detached house. A box hedge surrounded it and the garden was a riot of color.

"Nice place to retire, Robby. Look, someone's coming now."

A tall man, lean and gray, strode down the walk toward them. With mirth in his eyes, Forsythe turned to his companion.

"Short, stocky, and florid, eh? Pay up."

Looking faintly downcast, Miss Sanderson climbed out of the car and waited for the man to open the gate. He no more than glanced at her as he brushed by and started briskly up the worn pavement. Another man was hurrying down the walk.

"Miss Sanderson, hello there; you're prompt. I suppose this is Mr. Forsythe. Do come in."

Forsythe shrugged his shoulders as his secretary threw a triumphant glance at him. Except that this man had a thick head of graying hair, her description fitted perfectly.

She managed to mutter in her employer's ear as they followed the stocky figure into the house, "Typecast, do I? You owe me."

"Come into the lounge. The wife's out; she'll be home soon. Imagine you'll want to talk to her too. I can make us some tea or perhaps a small spot of brandy?"

They followed him into a small, crowded room. He waited for them to be seated. Miss Sanderson smiled up at him and said expansively, "Brandy sounds like an excellent idea." Forsythe nodded, and their host poured three generous drinks.

"Now"—Hennessy sank into a shabby leather chair—"Sir Hilary Putham has been in touch, asked me to give you all the cooperation I can. Not that I wouldn't have anyway, seeing as how Mr. Sebastian's daughter is involved. I went over to the station and had a chat with the active sergeant. He was my constable when the murder was committed. We compared notes so's I wouldn't forget anything. Talked a bit to my wife about it too."

Miss Sanderson was looking perplexed. "You mentioned your wife before. Has she some connection with the case?"

"That she has. Meg—she was Meg Brady then—was helping at the Hall when this happened. We were thinking of marriage. I wanted her to chuck her job, but she wouldn't. Miss Melissa needed her, and Meg was fond of her. Meg became Mrs. Hennessy shortly after the trial."

"In that case," said Forsythe, "we certainly will want to talk with her."

"Where would you like me to start? The morning of the murder—"

"Before that, if you will. Did you or any of the people of the village have any idea of what was going on at the Hall?"

Hennessy nodded at Forsythe and settled more comfortably in his chair. "You mean Mr. Sebastian and the Mersey boy? No, we had no idea. Didn't know anything about it until after the murder. Couldn't believe it. Of course Mr. Sebastian never had anything to do with Meads Green. He was either at the Hall or in London. Same with his older brother, always away. When their father died, Miss Melissa took over. Good job she did too. Most of us have something to be grateful for. She saw nobody came to any harm. If money was scarce she was always there—sickness, education for a lot of bright youngsters. Yes, she did well.

"After the trial when the newspapers and magazines sent their people around, the villagers wouldn't have anything to do with them. Figured it was none of their business. Can't say we liked what Mr. Sebastian had been up to but he was a Calvert. Been a Calvert at the Hall as long as there's been a Meads Green. Not anymore, last one was Miss Melissa and she left in forty-four. Closed up the house and went to London. She still helps, though she hasn't much income now herself. Once in a while I let her know if someone's in real trouble and she scrapes up some money and sends it down for them."

Forsythe finished his brandy and set the glass to one side. "What did you think of the other people at the Hall?"

"Well, young Mersey came down to the village often. Nice young fellow, turned the girl's heads, you know; he was such a good-looking chap. But he was quiet, no airs. After Rosemary came home she was here a lot too. Regular scamp, Rosemary, tomboyish as they come. We all liked her. Abby Temple kept as much stuff for her as she could, sweet buns and toffee, that sort of thing. The secretary, Horner, he came down to the stationers, picked up paper and books. Wild-eyed young man, he'd been badly stove up in North Africa. Pretty short and brusque, but he was a poet, you know."

Miss Sanderson' s hand was flying over her shorthand pad. At this remark, she lifted her eyes and grinned at Forsythe.

Avoiding her eyes, he asked Hennessy, "When Miss Atlin and Mrs. Calvert arrived, were they in Meads Green at all?"

"Mrs. Calvert passed through a couple of times." His mouth under the heavy mustache moved in a smile. "Every man, regardless of age, saw *her*. A lot different from the first Mrs. Calvert. Noticed her myself. Got in a little trouble with Meg about it. Too enthusiastic, I guess. Miss Atlin, she came down quite often too, with young Mersey and Rosemary. Picked up embroidery stuff and books from the lending library. Always stopped to pass the time with Clara Ben, she runs the bookstore. Seemed a decent enough person."

Hennessy struggled out of his chair and picked up the brandy bottle. "Little more for you?" Both his guests shook their heads and their host poured himself another drink. Forsythe waited until he was seated.

"Then there was nothing to lead up to the morning of the murder, no warning that all wasn't going well at the Hall?"

Hennessy shook his head. "Not a thing. Meg said that Miss Melissa was all nerves, didn't like Mrs. Calvert being there. But I had no idea what was going on. On the morning that Mersey was found dead, I got a call from Mr. Deveraux. It was early, at 6:46 A.M. Deveraux was pretty upset; I could tell that. He said Mersey was dead, murdered. Asked me to bring a doctor and come up fast as we could get there. I routed out my constable, Baines—we both slept in quarters behind the station—and I put in a call for Doctor Jarvis. He was an elderly man then. Been dead a good thirteen years. Doctor Jarvis said he'd meet us at the Hall.

"Baines and I went right up. Miss Melissa and Rosemary were upstairs. The rest of them were waiting in the drawing room. They'd partially closed the doors that led to the studio. Horner took us in, and there they both were. Baines had brought a camera, but he didn't take the pictures. He headed for the back door after one look. I could hear him outside." Hennessy slanted a look at Miss Sanderson. "It was bad, very bad, and Baines was just a young fellow. Never saw anything like it. I took a couple of shots of Mr. Sebastian and Mersey. Then Doctor Jarvis arrived.

"Mr. Sebastian was gone; his mind was finished. He just sat there holding that thing, staring straight ahead. Well, we got him cleaned up and took him to the hospital. I knew I was out of my depth, the people involved and all. So I requested assistance from the Yard. I was glad to see them take over. Feeling as I did about the Calverts, it would have been rugged to have had to dig the truth out of poor Miss Melissa and the girl."

Forsythe eyed the other man. "You never had any reservations about Sebastian Calvert's guilt?"

Slowly, Hennessy's big head moved from side to side. "No doubt about it. He'd cracked up and did for the boy. I didn't like to believe it but…" He spread his hands.

"Your wife. How did she feel? She was closer to the people involved."

"Meg, well she—" Hennessy broke off and cocked his head. "Here she is now. She can tell you herself."

Hennessy had keen hearing. Both Forsythe and Miss Sanderson looked up. The woman who was entering the room was much younger than her husband. She was plump and neatly dressed, with a gentle, plain face.

Rising, her husband took her arm. "This is Miss Sanderson and Mr. Forsythe, my dear. They want to hear about the Hall and the people—"

She broke in, looking slightly flustered. "It was all so long ago, Henry. I don't know how I can help."

Her husband soothed her. "Just you sit down here, Meg. You do your best now; you know Mr. Sebastian's daughter is the one who wants to know how it was. We owe her that."

"Poor child. How dreadful it must be for her. How can I help, Mr. Forsythe?"

"Your husband said you didn't have any suspicion of what was going on between…any of the people at the Hall."

"That I didn't. I wouldn't have stayed on there even for Miss Melissa if I had. But Mr. Sebastian and Mr. Mersey, well, they didn't show anything. All I knew was that Mr. Mersey was posing for the statue. Never saw that either. I wasn't allowed in the studio. As for the rest of them, well, Miss Melissa was terribly put upon. She'd everything to do."

Miss Sanderson glanced up from her notebook. "It must have been awfully hard on you with such a small staff in a house the size of the Hall."

"Impossible. We did all we could. Old Hannah, the cook, did her best in the kitchen though she was poorly most of the time. Miss Melissa and me, we gave the first floor a lick and a promise. Kept the rooms as clean as we could. The bedrooms we never touched, or hardly ever. Miss Melissa laid it down; everyone must do their part. And some of them—you wouldn't believe it. After Miss Atlin come she helped us; took care of Mrs. Calvert's room as well as her own. More like a maid she was to that woman than a cousin, always fetching and carrying. I'd be upstairs once in a while, cleaning the hall or putting linen in the linen room, and I'd tidy up after Mr. Sebastian and Mr. Deveraux when he was down. Poor men, no idea even where to start."

"About Mrs. Calvert—" Forsythe began.

He'd touched a sore point. Mrs. Hennessy's gentle expression hardened. "Her! I've said it before and I'll say it again. Worthless trash, no better than a fancy trollop. Letting poor Miss Atlin wait on her hand and foot. Chasing after Mr. Mersey. No shame. Right in front of Miss Melissa and Rosemary."

"Now, now, Meg." Her husband leaned over and touched her hand.

She drew it away indignantly. "And you, Henry Hennessy, no better than the rest. Gawking at her when she come through the village."

Miss Sanderson's eyes were twinkling. Forsythe said softly, "Can you tell me about the last week, after Mr. Deveraux arrived?"

Mrs. Hennessy tore her eyes from her husband's face and looked at Forsythe. "I wasn't there. Left the Friday night before Mr. Deveraux come. My sister, she was having her first child, and Miss Melissa said to go to her. Said things couldn't get in a worse mess than they already was. Afterward I was glad I went. It was a horrible thing."

They were all silent for a moment. Then Mrs. Hennessy added, "I'm sorry. I'd like to help Mr. Sebastian's girl. It's just that there's nothing I can say."

Forsythe rose. "You've tried. That's the main thing; you've tried." He looked at her husband. "Do you suppose we could go up and have a look at the Hall?"

The older man pulled himself out of the depths of the leather chair. "You certainly can. I'll get the keys and take you right up."

"Henry."

Hennessy paused at the sound of his wife's voice.

"Have you forgotten the christening party?" She looked apologetically at Forsythe. "Our grandson, we have three now, the latest one is being christened today. He's named after my husband. Our daughter will be heartbroken if we don't come."

Hennessy looked at her with a harassed expression. "That's right. I'd clean forgotten."

"Perhaps Miss Sanderson and I can go up alone," Forsythe offered. "That is, if you think it would be all right."

Hennessy beamed with relief. "Certainly. Sorry, but that's how it is with a family. I'll get the keys."

Snapping her notebook closed, Miss Sanderson returned her pen to her handbag. She looked up at Mrs. Hennessy. "Has the Hall been unoccupied all these years?"

"Never been a soul living in it. Miss Melissa just locked it up and gave Henry the keys. We look after it as best we can. Henry gets a couple of the lads and chops at the grounds once in a while. I do my best inside. We keep some heat going in the winter." She sighed. "Seems a terrible shame. Such a place, and a happy home it once was."

"No trouble with vandalism?" asked Forsythe.

"The villagers would never go near it. As for the day trippers and the reporters," her lips curled slightly, "Henry soon sets them right. All the looking they do is through the bars on the gates and they can hardly see the house from there."

Henry had returned. He handed Forsythe a ring of keys. "They're labeled. You won't have any trouble finding the place. Go along to the end of the main street, turn right on White Rose Lane, and keep going. It's near the top of the hill. Big iron gates. Are you planning to stay over tonight?"

Forsythe nodded. "It will be a little late to start back to London."

"I thought you might. I spread the word. There'll be rooms for you at the Inn. Stan and Bea will see you're comfortable." He noticed Miss Sanderson's baffled look. "The villagers don't take well to strangers, specially ones wondering about the Calverts and the Hall. But they know who you are and who you're working for and they don't mind that."

Forsythe nodded his appreciation. "Fine. Thank you, Sergeant Hennessy and Mrs. Hennessy. We'll get the keys back to you."

Beside their car, Miss Sanderson paused. "How about walking, Robby? After a week vegetating, I can use the exercise."

"Good idea." He took her arm. "We can work up an appetite for Bea's tea. With our sergeant recommending us, I have a hunch it may be formidable."

White Rose Lane had only a few scattered cottages along it. They were set back from the lane and looked drowsy and peaceful. They'd seen only one person, a very old man, dozing under the shade of a plane tree. The scents from the gardens floated to them, spicy and sweet, carnations and roses. Somewhere in the distance a dog rattled its chain and barked.

Beyond the last cottage, the road wound upward, steadily but gently. Partway up, Miss Sanderson laid a hand on her companion's arm. They stopped and looked back at the valley and the village streets.

"Looks a haven of peace, doesn't it? Impossible to believe, looking at it, that violence ever happened here."

Forsythe leaned against a wooden stile set into a low stone wall. "People create the violence, Sandy, not the place. In even the most civilized of us is still that seed of violence. It requires only the right set of circumstances to bring it out."

Climbing onto the stile, Miss Sanderson sat down. She plucked a long tuft of grass and nibbled on it. "Even in thou and I, old philosopher." She gazed thoughtfully down on Meads Green. "Speaking of violence, you don't seem to be overly disturbed about someone taking a shot at you."

"As you may have noticed, I haven't been taking any chances. I've been rather careful where I go and how."

"You also had an eye on the rearview mirror all the way from London. Expecting company?"

"Just checking, that's all."

She cast a glance at his profile. "I have noticed one thing. For the last couple of days, you've had the same smug look around the mouth that I've learned to recognize. Your father had that expression when he'd found a hole in the prosecution's case and was getting set to blow it to bits. I've plowed through the same stuff you have and I can't see a ray of light. Like to share what you're thinking?"

"There's a pattern emerging. I even thought for a short time that I could name the murderer. But there's something wrong with my theory, something that still doesn't fit. Haven't you any idea yet?"

"Scads. That's what's wrong, just too damn many. The Freudian slips in those tapes have me grasping at one person, then another. Take Melissa, for instance. One minute she announces she doesn't even dislike Vanessa. The next minute she gets all worked up and states she can't understand why Vanessa wasn't killed instead of Mersey. Confusing. But the original evidence against Sebastian—as far as I can see—it still stands."

Forsythe held out his hand to her. "Jump down, old girl; you've rested long enough. I can see the gates that the sergeant mentioned from here." They started up the hill. "You're mistaken, Sandy; the evidence against Calvert has holes all through it. But enough of surmising. As they say in the shilling shockers, let's get on to the scene of the crime."

Forsythe ignored the huge iron gates. Selecting a key, he opened a small grilled door set to one side. As soon as they were though it, he carefully relocked it. The remains of a gardener's cottage stood beside the gate. Then the driveway twisted away between huge oaks toward a corner of a house. They could see it more clearly as they turned the first curve.

Miss Sanderson was looking critically at the grounds. "Blimey, it's been a while since Hennessy and his lads have been up here chopping. Look at the undergrowth."

"Forget the grounds and have a look at the house. Smasher, isn't it?"

"Perfectly lovely."

It was. The long sprawling building had graceful proportions. Even the neglect in its surroundings couldn't detract from the lines. Wooden shutters were closed over the upper windows, but the lower ones were uncovered. The front door was hand-carved and had an ancient knocker shaped in the form of a dragon. Forsythe checked the key ring and opened the door.

Standing on the green and white tile of the foyer, Miss Sanderson gazed up the long sweeping flight of stairs. "Where do we start?"

His eyes followed hers. "Might as well go straight up. Just a minute. I have the floor plan." He stopped two-thirds of the way up. "You go on, Sandy; Mersey's room was the first on the right. Open the door, stand in front of it for a minute, and then saunter down the hall."

She obeyed. Forsythe stood where he was, his eyes on her.

"I'm right down at the end, where the hall branches toward the servant's wing. Is that far enough?"

"Fine." He climbed the rest of the stairs and walked down the hall toward her. It was dim and the air was stale. "Let's check the room Deveraux used. It's two rooms down from Mersey's."

She rejoined him. The room was quite dark, heavy furniture looming out from the walls. Forsythe threw up the window sash and unbolted the shutters. He heard his secretary's sigh of satisfaction as the sun came streaming in.

"Ruddy mausoleum," she muttered as she stepped up beside him.

They both leaned over the sill, their eyes sweeping the area directly below them. Forsythe leaned out further. "There's the terrace and the steps leading down."

"The garden must have been beautiful when this happened, Robby. It's a tangle now, but you can still see traces. Look at the roses. What a sight they must have been when they were properly tended."

He pulled the shutters closed and bolted them. "Let's have a look at the lower floor."

At the foot of the stairs, Miss Sanderson started to turn left. Forsythe touched her arm.

"This side first. Let me see." He swung open the first door. "Sebastian's study, nothing for us there."

"Mrs. Hennessy hasn't done badly, Robby. Lots of dust, but no signs of cobwebs, and the furniture is carefully covered. All the pictures and ornaments are gone. Melissa must have either sold them or had them stored."

Forsythe opened the second door. "Probably sold them. She needs the money. I'm surprised she hasn't sold the whole property. Ah, the dining room, and beyond, the terrace. Let's have a closer look at that garden you were admiring."

He opened the French door and they stepped out. Forsythe leaned against one of the stone pillars at the edge of the terrace. The rough surface was warm under his hand. His companion wandered down the shallow steps into the garden. Picking her way through the tangled growth, she headed toward a clump of rosebushes. Selecting a large yellow bloom, she pinned it carefully to her jacket. Forsythe wasn't watching her. He appeared to be gazing into space.

She retraced her steps. "Damn shame, letting a beautiful place like this stand empty." She looked sharply up at Forsythe. "Hey, wake up. What are you thinking about?"

He started. "Nothing, Sandy. Come along; we'll have a quick look at the other side of the house."

The drawing room opened directly off the foyer. It was an enormous room. Rose velvet covered long, mullioned windows. Miss Sanderson drew them back from the front window. She stood with her back to it, gazing around.

"Look at the way the colors have been blended, Robby. Whoever decorated this room had taste. Everything perfectly coordinated. These drapes are finished; the velvet's rotted clear through. But look at their color against the deeper rose of the rug. And the furniture," she pulled a dust cover off the chair nearest her, "ah, just as I hoped, rose brocade picked out with the same ivory as the walls." She bent closer and inspected the arm of the chair. "The brocade's rotted too. How could anyone let this happen?"

Forsythe was walking toward the double doors at the other end of the room. "I suppose Melissa just couldn't stand it. She loved this place, everything it stood for. Her dreams turned into a nightmare, and she's letting the house crumble away."

He swung the doors wide. Joining him, Miss Sanderson looked into the studio. It was as large as the drawing room. It was empty. Two walls were paned with glass and the floor was worn stone tile. The sun was streaming across the room. It should have been warm. It wasn't. She shivered and moved closer to her companion. He was looking with interest at the inside wall. Dust-coated daggers and medieval swords were arranged down its length.

"That's where the scimitar must have hung."

Miss Sanderson followed his eyes and then turned back to the drawing room. She slipped and nearly fell. Moving quickly, Forsythe steadied her.

"Take it easy, Sandy. There's moss growing on the stone in places. You could break your neck."

They both looked down at the gray-green fungus clinging damply to the stone.

"Let's get out of here, Robby." She pulled her arm from his grasp and walked swiftly across the rose-colored rug toward the foyer.

"What's the matter with you?" Forsythe called after her. "Wait for just a minute. I want to check the lock on the French door in the dining room."

His secretary paused by the front door. One hand brushed at the neck of her sweater. Her sleeve caught the yellow rose. Slowly, several petals drifted to the floor.

"Check away. I'll wait for you outside."

When he came out a few minutes later, Forsythe found her standing in the middle of the driveway. She was staring up at the gray stone bulk of the Hall. Her face was grave, almost cold.

Forsythe grinned. "What spooked you, my intrepid friend? One minute you're going on about how lovely the house is; the next you take off like a scalded cat."

She didn't smile back. Forsythe looked more closely at her. Then he took her arm and turned her away from the house, toward the gates. The old trees closed off the sun. They moved through shadows.

When Miss Sanderson spoke, her voice was muffled. Forsythe had to strain to hear her.

"Don't laugh, Robby. Do you believe in ghosts?"

"I certainly don't and neither do you."

"Well, do you believe that sometimes houses have auras, that you can sense something waiting?"

He squeezed her arm. "No to that too."

She looked directly into his eyes. "I don't like this place. I'll be glad to get out of it." She hastened her step. They were nearing the gates.

"Look, Sandy, you're not a fanciful woman. Be sensible. You knew the history of that house. You were fine until you stepped into the studio, the spot you've heard so much about. Then your imagination took over. Houses don't have auras. People's minds supply them."

Her pale eyes were wide. "I could almost see someone pulling a cover over Deveraux, then stepping into that damn stone-floored room and lifting a scimitar over David's body. But there's no sense in trying to explain to you. At times you're revoltingly logical." She tried for a grin. "You're also probably right. Let's get back to Meads Green and have tea. On second thought, I may skip the tea and have something stronger. Anyway, I'll be glad to get back to London tomorrow."

Forsythe closed the grilled door behind them and relocked it. Without looking at her he said, "We won't be going back to London tomorrow."

She waited for him to turn to face her. "Just what will we be doing?"

"No matter how you feel about the Hall, we'll have to go back to it one more time. That's where it started. It seems a fitting place for it to end. I want you to get in touch with the five people connected with this case. Wire Vanessa in Rome, and let them know we're having a get-together party."

Her voice was level. "When and why?"

He pulled out his pipe and tobacco pouch. "In three days, it will be the twenty-fifth of August, exactly twenty-five years since the death of Adonis. You may have seen ghosts at the Hall. I saw the face of a murderer. A quarter of a century is a long time to go blameless while another man has to take the guilt. It's time the killer was unmasked. Elizabeth is most impatient. Ring her first."

"Do you think all of them will consent to come? We can't force them, you know."

"They have no choice," he said grimly. "They've all tried to show Sebastian either guilty as hell or innocent. If one of them is afraid to turn up now, what would that prove?"

Miss Sanderson was tapping her nail against her front tooth. It was the only sound on the quiet road. After a moment, she dropped her hand to her lapel. The remains of the rose she unpinned and held in her hand. They both stared down at it.

She said quietly, "The only one who would fear this meeting is the murderer. You're right; they'll all be here." Her fingers loosened and the rose fell to the road. "Including our killer."

Chapter Ten

The rose-shaded lamplight and the flickering glow from the fireplace were kind to the room. They disguised the rents in the velvet hangings, the tears in the rich brocade, the worn spots on the rug. The drawing room of Calvert Hall looked as it must have twenty-five years earlier. The furniture was uncovered, ashtrays now dotted the low tables, and on a chest at the end of the room an assortment of glasses and bottles were arrayed.

Forsythe stood with his back to the fire, his feet slightly apart, his hands clasped behind him. His face was relaxed, any tension within him was carefully concealed. At the left of the fireplace, on a long table that years before had held a tray of wine goblets, Sandy had set herself up. In front of her were neatly arranged a tape recorder, a pile of boxed tapes, and a number of cardboard folders. At the end of the table, ex-Sergeant Hennessy relaxed in the room's largest chair.

Forsythe looked at the rest of the gathering. The chairs in which they were seated were arranged in a semicircle around him, each chair placed a good distance from the next. All but one of the witnesses from the trial of Sebastian Calvert were present.

To his right was Elizabeth Calvert Pennell, clad in a dark suit that blended with the shadowed corner she had selected. Her eyes were flipping from face to face, settling on none but seeing all. Near her, Melissa Calvert sat, her feet close together, her thin shoulders erect. Richard Deveraux was beside his friend's sister. He wasn't watching Forsythe. His eyes ranged past Rosemary Horner, who sat on his other side, to Vanessa Calvert. Vanessa was very much at her ease. The soft lighting was as kind to her as it was to the room. She wore a high-necked amber gown and a tiny matching hat clinging precariously to her red curls. Against the back of her chair was tossed a honey mink stole. The last member of the group, John Horner, was seated between Vanessa and Sandy's table. His eyes were hard on Forsythe and had been since he'd entered the room.

Horner spoke now, a forced lightness in his voice. "This looks much like the setting of one of my early novels. All the suspects seated with their faces in a good light. The famous detective, or in this case barrister, facing them. The stolid policeman quietly waiting to make the arrest." He jerked his head toward Hennessy.

"Ex-policeman, sir, and not here in an official capacity. Mr. Forsythe was kind enough to invite me to sit in, simply because I was here at the beginning."

Forsythe smiled at Horner. "That's correct. We're all here for a purpose. I'm here to disprove the charges against Sebastian Calvert and you're here for your own private reasons. For a time, I may sound more like a teacher than a detective, but bear with me—and I'd appreciate it if none of you interrupt. There'll be time to question later.

"Elizabeth Pennell, as you are all aware, came to me for help. I began to check the old case out, not with any real hopes for success, but I determined to treat it as I would a case I was defending in court. Sebastian is my client. To prove him innocent, I had to suspect each of you in turn.

"I soon found a sound basis to support Sebastian's innocence. David Mersey was not the perfect physical specimen he appeared to be. Like many of us, he had a weakness. He was a diabetic. Sebastian, if he had been capable of organizing Mersey's death in the way he was accused of, would have been capable of killing him simply by using this weakness for his own means.

"There was also Sebastian's temperament to take into account. Sebastian was far from a strong person. He'd allowed his sister to push him into his first marriage. He was shattered by his second and came home to let his relatives and friends pick up the pieces for him.

"Are we to believe that Sebastian would deliberately and for the first time make a decisive move and kill Mersey? Then there was his attachment to the boy. After two disastrous marriages, he turned his back on the female sex and chose this boy as his love object. When Mersey decided to leave him, it would have been more in Sebastian's character to go to pieces again, but not to kill Mersey and butcher the body he worshipped.

"So I took the opposite tack. If Sebastian Calvert was innocent, he was not the one who had drugged a house full of people. He was drugged as they were. Only the murderer was conscious that night."

"But the wine. I told you my brother—" Melissa suddenly covered her mouth with her hand. "I'm sorry, you asked us not to interrupt."

Forsythe looked at her. "The wine is going to have to be overlooked at this point. Later, in its proper place, I will prove that your brother did not drug the wine."

His eyes left Melissa's face and swung around the circle of faces. "To continue. I proceeded to do the thing the police should have done at the time of the murder—look for motives. I didn't have to look far. As my right-hand girl, Miss Sanderson, will tell you, there was an embarrassment of motives."

"Motives?" This was Horner. "What motive could any of us have had?"

"Let's take you first, Horner. What was the general situation in forty-four? Not just at Calvert Hall, but all over England."

Horner looked puzzled. "It was wartime, the fifth year of a bloody horrible war."

"Exactly, a bloody horrible war. All of you had lived through the Blitz. Violence had become commonplace. Each of you was a strong, able person. Who did we have thrown together under this roof? A man who would later be a famous writer; an equally famous publisher; a decisive woman who not only ruled her own family but an entire estate; a brilliant and precocious girl; a woman who laid down her life in a daring rescue; and Vanessa. I don't think we'll argue about Vanessa. You all recognize her qualities.

"All of these people had personal problems of their own. Then they're thrown together in a set of circumstances that erupts into murder."

Horner had been lighting a cigarette. He gazed through the smoke at Forsythe. "Very well, barrister, the background was hardly normal. I'll give you that. Present your case against the famous writer."

"It's obvious, Horner. In your own words you were unstable, had a nasty case of war nerves. You certainly were no stranger to killing. You were straight from the battlefields of North Africa. Into your life comes Vanessa. Not only do you want her, you want her with every fiber of your being. Vanessa not only preferred Mersey to you, but humiliated you about your size. Little Jack Horner was quite capable of venting his rage against the big handsome man she wanted. Killing Mersey would be double-bladed revenge. Vanessa would be hurt badly."

Horner squinted through the cloud of gray smoke. "Not bad, Forsythe, proceed."

"Melissa is next. I don't have to outline her qualifications. You know her. Her obsession really was her brother's work. She was prepared to do anything for it. She managed Sebastian, drove him, forced him into a loveless marriage, and accepted a homosexual relationship she disapproved of to further his career. Melissa is a woman of rigid morals apart from her brother. Think of the shattering effect on her when she learned her sacrifices were in vain. At the apex of his career, her brother was, as she said to Richard Deveraux, 'finally ruined by David and Vanessa.' By killing David, Melissa would also have her revenge on both of them."

Richard Deveraux interrupted. "You're wrong there, Forsythe. Perhaps Melissa did have a motive, but do you actually think anyone her size could carry a big man like Mersey down a flight of stairs to the studio?"

Forsythe shifted slightly "This point, like the drugging of the wine, will have to wait. We aren't yet discussing the means, only the motives. Let's look at our next candidate for murderer. Elinor Atlin, the colorless one, the woman who always faded into the background—"

Vanessa spoke. It was the first time she had broken her silence. "Can't we leave Lin out of this? She's dead—"

"She was very much alive at the time of the murder. Here we have a repressed woman, devoted to her cousin, and capable of fast thinking and action. Her death proves that. Also possessed of enormous physical strength. Both Vanessa and Elinor were large women. Elinor was an athlete, able to handle Vanessa when Deveraux and Horner couldn't. Elinor depended on Vanessa financially as well as in every other way. She'd already been, in her own words, 'deserted by Vanessa' during her brief marriage to Sebastian. She did her best to talk Mersey out of this alliance. Elinor could have killed the boy to keep him away from Vanessa."

"That sounds pretty weak," Horner commented.

"Murders have been committed for weaker motives than that," Forsythe answered. He glanced down. Miss Sanderson was vigorously tugging at his jacket. "What do you want, Sandy?"

"But—"

"Are you going to start interrupting too?" Forsythe asked good-naturedly. She subsided in injured silence, and her employer continued. "We come to our fourth suspect—Richard Deveraux. Here we have a mature man, admired by women, but not captivated by any one of them. He finally meets the woman he always has wanted, Vanessa, his best friend's estranged wife. How strong his devotion is we can see before us. Deveraux claims his obesity is the result of compensation. He prefers to believe that it is guilt for Sebastian's crime that drives him toward the gluttony that slowly is killing him. Deveraux is deluding himself. I believe he accepted that guilt long since. He never accepted Vanessa's loss. He not only lost her, but saw her in a love scene with David. A man of Richard's caliber could quite easily plan and execute the crime. Again with two objectives, the destruction of a hated rival and the injury of Vanessa."

Vanessa stretched and smiled. "Wonderful! So far everyone wants to kill because they either adore me or hate my intestines. I had no idea I could inspire such feelings."

"I think you're being truthful, Mrs. Calvert," Forsythe said dryly. "Melissa's description of you is apt. You really are a poltergeist."

Her amber eyes widened. "A *what?*"

"Never mind. Let us go on. Number five—Rosemary Calvert Horner."

"Mr. Forsythe." It was Melissa. "My niece was a child at the time. I'd prefer we kept her out of this."

"As you would have preferred they'd kept her out of the actual trial? It can't be done. Rosemary also had a motive. You call her a child. She was not a child. She was a big, adolescent girl, strong and highly intelligent. Rosemary was capable of violence. Her attack on a teacher proves this. Furthermore, she idolized her uncle. Rosemary felt she'd almost lost him when he returned from Ireland. Here was the same woman, Vanessa, threatening him again. In the girl's eyes, David was a traitor, as guilty as Vanessa. It occurs to me that Rosemary might have killed Mersey."

Horner grunted. "I don't know about the rest of you, but I could use a drink."

Forsythe turned to his secretary. "Would you do the honors, Sandy?"

While she was fixing the drinks, they sat silently. They accepted their glasses just as silently and waited for Forsythe to continue.

"There are serious flaws in my reasoning. We'll take the one Deveraux mentioned. Melissa could have done the first part of the crime, the actual murder by morphine. So could Rosemary. She'd worked in the hospital and either given injections or seen hypodermic needles used. Rosemary was large for her age, but neither Melissa nor she had the strength to carry Mersey that far. The rest of the suspects, Elinor, Deveraux, Horner, could have done both parts. But there was the problem of Sebastian. To be innocent, he had to be drugged and helpless. How did he get down to the studio?"

"For a time I thought I had the answer. Deveraux had slept the night through in the drawing room, fully clothed. What if Sebastian hadn't been able to undress before the drug hit him? He might have collapsed on his bed. Drugs affect different people different ways. Very well, I tried picturing Sebastian waking first, going to David's room. The boy is on his bed, dead, the hypodermic needle and the case beside him. There would be only one reason for Sebastian to complete the pattern, carry the body downstairs, and disfigure it—an effort to divert suspicion from someone Sebastian cared for. For his sister or niece, a man, even one as weak as Sebastian, might have tried to cover up."

Horner leaned forward, his hands clenched on his knees, his jaw jutting. "Just one minute. Why couldn't Calvert have passed out fully dressed and instead of going to David's room when he came to, come directly down to the studio? He could have found the mutilated body, gathered it up in his arms, and gone quietly insane. That fits just as well."

"I agree, Horner; I considered that theory also. But there's one flaw that shoots holes in both those ideas. My mental efforts to get Sebastian fully dressed into the studio with the murdered man—well, I'll show you. Sandy, got the tapes ready?"

She nodded and pressed the button. They heard Horner's voice. "...the members of the household and guests must tidy their own rooms. The women were fine at this and I looked after mine army style. But you should have seen Sebastian's and Richard's. I don't think they ever did more than pull the bedspreads over their crumpled sheets and blankets."

Miss Sanderson depressed the switch and Horner's voice stopped abruptly.

Horner moved impatiently. "Okay, so Sebastian was a messy bedmaker, what in—"

Forsythe raised his hand. "The next tape is Deveraux's. He's telling me about the morning of the murder, just before Sebastian was taken away. Sandy."

She arranged another tape and Deveraux's rich baritone echoed through the room. "I sat down on his bed and broke right up. Gradually I pulled myself together, got up, and started automatically to straighten the bedspread again. Funny the things we do under stress. There—"

Horner still looked baffled, but sick comprehension was looking from Richard Deveraux's eyes. Forsythe asked the big man, "Why did you say 'again'?"

"I'd rumpled it where I sat. And the bed was neat, the spread pulled tautly over it, perfectly made." Deveraux rubbed one hand across his eyes. "All these years," he muttered, "it was right in front of me and I never saw it. Sebastian never made that bed. Someone else did."

Forsythe repeated slowly. "Sebastian never made the bed. The only other person who ever touched his room was Meg Brady, and she was away that week. Now we know that Sebastian went to bed that night and slept the same way the rest of you did, a deeply drugged sleep. Deep enough for the murderer to dress him in his dinner jacket, carry him downstairs, and leave him in the studio with the corpse of David Mersey in his arms. Then the killer went up and methodically made up Sebastian's bed. The killer slipped there by making it neatly. But in the state the rest of you were in afterward, nobody noticed it. When Sebastian roused from his drugged slumber that morning, think what he saw, what he held in his arms. Does anyone wonder that his mind gave?"

"Why?" It was only a whisper from Melissa's pale lips.

"Because," said Forsythe, "this was a crime of passion. The passion was hate. You said yourself, Miss Calvert, that two men died that night. I don't think the murderer counted on Sebastian losing his mind, but it served just as well. The idea was that Sebastian would be accused of the crime, be tried, and executed. We can see that Sebastian was supposed to suffer more than David Mersey. This explains why David was killed painlessly with morphine before the scimitar was used. The murderer couldn't bear to cut into his living body."

Forsythe paused and looked at Horner. "You were right about the malevolence in the drawing room that night, but it didn't emanate from Sebastian. It came from another mind, coolly waiting for the drug to take effect to cover the sounds of two heavy bodies, one unconscious, the other dead, being carried down the stairs."

Rosemary shuddered. Her taffy hair was bright against the pallor of her face. "Who could hate that much?"

Horner looked at his wife. Then he rose and stood behind her chair, his hands gripping her shoulders.

Forsythe continued. "I lost all my suspects at one fell go. Rosemary, Melissa, Deveraux would never deliberately implicate Sebastian. Horner didn't like his employer, but he respected him as an artist and was grateful for his help. Elinor Atlin might kill to keep her cousin, but she most certainly wouldn't have any reason to pull Sebastian in on it."

Vanessa touched her lighter to a cigarette. "I could have shot that theory down when you outlined it. Lin didn't stay with me after the trial. If she'd thought enough of me to kill, she certainly wouldn't have left me and gone to Switzerland."

"That's what I was trying to say, Robby, when I was pulling at your jacket," observed Miss Sanderson.

Horner spoke from behind his wife's chair. "You've talked yourself out of suspects, Forsythe."

"Not quite. There's still one left." Forsythe's hands fell from behind his back. They were clenched into fists. He looked directly at the woman on the chair next to Rosemary. Her head was tilted back and her eyes were narrowed through the smoke of her cigarette.

"What about Vanessa Calvert?"

Chapter Eleven

Vanessa leaned over and butted her cigarette. She smiled brilliantly at Forsythe. "Hurrah! What *about* Vanessa Calvert? Now I don't feel so left out."

"You were never left out," Forsythe said grimly. "When I realized hate, directed mainly toward Sebastian, was the motive, you were the one I concentrated on."

Horner broke in. "You know you almost had me hypnotized for a while. Figured you should be the writer, not me. But your plot failed. I'm only too willing to pin this on Vanessa and I'll agree that the way she felt about her husband might have inspired part of the crime. But my mind boggles at the thought of Vanessa sacrificing a boy she was infatuated with and wanted to take with her just for the fun of seeing her husband executed. Vanessa is too much of a connoisseur of male flesh for that. Of all of us she was the only one with nothing to gain from David's death."

Forsythe hadn't moved his eyes from Vanessa's face. "What they don't realize, Vanessa, is that Mersey never had any intention of leaving Sebastian. He wasn't going anywhere with you, was he?"

Everyone was talking at once. Forsythe held up his hand and their voices stilled one by one.

"You were all there; you kept saying it. But you couldn't see what was happening the day of the twenty-fifth. Just what proof did you have that David, in his showdown with Sebastian, had actually decided to throw in his lot with Vanessa?"

Deveraux spoke. "Elinor's testimony at the trial, and Rosemary overheard the conversation by the lake."

Forsythe turned to Miss Sanderson. "Give us the gist of Elinor Atlin's testimony, not word for word."

Flipping open a folder, Miss Sanderson started to speak, her voice dry and precise. "Elinor Atlin testified under oath that she approached David Mersey on the morning of August twenty-fifth, 1944. Mersey had just spoken with Sebastian Calvert. David Mersey told her that Calvert had tried to persuade him to give up his estranged wife. Calvert pointed out to Mersey the many advantages he would have if he stayed on at the Hall. Mersey felt that Vanessa Calvert was also wealthy and could give him the same things. Miss Atlin said she tried to tell the boy what Vanessa was like, that she would drop him like a toy when she tired of him. She asked Mersey whether his decision was definite. He answered it was. Then she asked whether Mersey had told Calvert of his decision. He again answered yes. She told him he would be ruining his life. Then—"

"That will do, Sandy." Forsythe swung back to the rest. "From there on Rosemary was listening. She didn't hear the entire conversation, only the end of it. And even that part was not all audible. In Rosemary's testimony there is no real evidence of *whom* David had chosen. Think back carefully."

Rosemary moved restlessly. "But that one sentence. I heard it clearly. Elinor knew that Vanessa would leave her again. She said—"

"We'll get to that sentence. Let's consider this. If David Mersey told Elinor that he intended to remain with Sebastian, do you think she would have betrayed her cousin? Would Elinor have given testimony that would have given *Vanessa* the only motive to kill the boy? Elinor could no longer help Sebastian. He was hopelessly insane.

"Now think back to what happened directly after the meeting at the lake. David did not seek out Vanessa. She was on the terrace. He came in the front door, went straight up to his room, and remained there. Does that sound like a young man so madly in love that he had just renounced Sebastian and the security he offered? No. All any of you had to go on was Elinor's story and the little that Rosemary heard that seemed to bear it out.

"Now we come to dinner, the only time that day you were together. Here we have Sebastian Calvert, a man who crumbles under hurt. Yet at dinner, you say he's almost manic, talkative, his eyes bright, his color high—not crushed but exhilarated. You didn't see a man who had lost. You saw a man who not only had finished his greatest work, the *Adonis*, but also received Mersey's word that he would remain with him."

"You're right," Horner muttered, "by God, you're right. Then Vanessa drugged the wine. I have no idea how, but I think you can explain that. She waited until we were all unconscious and proceeded to kill Mersey and arrange the scene. Think of it, the two men who had rejected her destroyed at one go."

Everyone but Deveraux nodded their heads. They were silent. It was a stony, frightening silence. Vanessa looked only at Deveraux. Her mouth was suddenly younger, more vulnerable.

"I know you have no reason to believe me. But I swear to you that I never killed anyone. I didn't." Her eyes dropped away from whatever she read in the man's face.

Forsythe moved from the hearth to Vanessa's side. He stood there, one hand hovering over her shoulder. Slowly he moved it and rested it on the back of her chair.

"I know you didn't *kill*, Vanessa. But you are guilty, guilty of protecting the murderer all these years. To do it, you've taken the scorn from these people and the world."

Horner left his wife to face Forsythe. "Are you mad?"

Forsythe waved him back. "Totally sane. Vanessa was the one I believed guilty until the other day in this room. Sandy said something and the whole thing fell into place. All the bits and pieces that wouldn't fit were complete."

Miss Sanderson was staring at him, her mouth slightly open. "I said something? Do you mean in the studio?"

"I mean right here."

His secretary looked around the drawing room. "All I said in here was that I admired the way the colors had been blended. The various shades of rose so beautifully coordinated."

"That's all you said, Sandy. Then I heard Melissa's voice again. I heard her say three little words, vital words, and I knew that Vanessa couldn't be the killer. She had no reason to kill Mersey."

He looked around the intent circle of faces. "We've ignored the one person who was most important—David Mersey. Who was David Mersey? All your memories told me that he was an ordinary young man with an extraordinary amount of good looks. Aside from his beauty, he was good-natured, not bright, a chameleon who was able to ape manners and speech. But was he capable of dissembling the way he seemed to?

"Mersey's outward reaction to Vanessa was dislike and embarrassment. He avoided her. He avoided her because he *really* didn't like her; she repulsed him. All any of you could see was Vanessa. You couldn't see the forest for the trees. Just who did Mersey spend his time with besides young Rosemary? Who did he swim, play tennis, go to the village with? Who sought him out to learn his decision about Sebastian?"

Melissa looked at him, understanding flashing across her face. "Elinor Atlin."

"Elinor Atlin, the colorless one. David worshipped his mother. You've called her a patient Griselda, drab, a saint. Who fits that description better than Elinor?"

"Wait a minute." Rosemary was leaning forward, her gray eyes wide. "I saw Vanessa coming out of David's room. So did my aunt."

"And I," echoed Deveraux, "saw them in the garden. Or are you going to say that some other man was holding Vanessa?"

Forsythe nodded. "It was David. But the woman in his arms was not Vanessa." He moved slightly. "You, Deveraux, had a quick look at the scene below in moonlight. Rosemary only had a glimpse of a tall woman in a long negligee walking down a dimly lit hall. She mentioned long reddish hair. Elinor was built much like her cousin; her hair was gingery; she wore it long, 'strained back in a bun.' The woman you both saw was Elinor Atlin. The only person who had a close look at her was Melissa."

Melissa's fingers were pleating the silk of her skirt. "Are you saying I lied, Mr. Forsythe?"

"No, I say you told the truth about what you *thought* you saw. If I remember correctly, Rosemary had broken your glasses the previous week. You needed those glasses. I checked and found that it would not be likely you'd have them back the following Wednesday. They had to be sent from London."

Melissa was staring at him. "I didn't have them. And I closed my eyes. I didn't see which room Vanessa, or the woman I was positive was Vanessa, went into. But when I went to Vanessa's room a few minutes after—"

"How long after?" Forsythe broke in.

"Not long. I put Rosemary to bed, perhaps ten minutes."

"Ten minutes later you found Vanessa in bed, reading a novel and eating chocolates—strange behavior for a passionate woman who was supposed to have just come from her lover's embrace. But that wasn't all. Vanessa was wrapped in a blanket. You said the upper part of her body was covered by it. You couldn't see the color of her nightgown, but she wore in her hair—these are the three vital words—a *green satin ribbon*."

He paused and gestured toward the woman sitting quietly beside Rosemary. "Look at Vanessa. What is she wearing, Rosemary?"

"Why, a golden or amber dress, matching hat, shoes, and bag."

Forsythe touched the mink stole. "Even her fur is honey-colored. Color-coordinated, that is Vanessa's trademark. The morning of her arrival at the Hall, we have Vanessa all in white. Rosemary sees her wardrobe. Shoes, dresses, hats, all in matching colors. The night Horner went to Vanessa's room to plead his case, what was she wearing?—a purple gown and headband.

"Can you imagine a woman so sensitive to color going to meet her lover wearing a green ribbon in her hair and," he turned to Rosemary, "what color was the woman who came out of David's room wearing?"

"Pale blue."

"You've hit it, by God." Horner was excited. "But why would Vanessa let Melissa believe it was her that night?"

"Right in character for her, Horner. No one has ever accused Vanessa of being a small person. She knew at once it had to be her cousin, her *quiet* cousin, having an affair with Mersey. Vanessa was amused. She loves mischief. If she couldn't get to David, very well, let Elinor have him. Vanessa covered for Elinor gladly and diverted your attention from the lovers.

"Vanessa let Sebastian think the same thing. She enjoyed every moment of their meeting in the garden. She knew Sebastian would find out the truth from David, but in the meantime she was having a wonderful time baiting her husband.

"David did tell Sebastian, but they must have struck a gentleman's agreement. David liked his position at the Hall. He wasn't going to give it up for a penniless woman. But the two men did protect Elinor, letting the rest of you still believe it was Vanessa. David must have told Elinor that her name would be concealed, that she could leave with no embarrassment. She saw her chance. Elinor knew Vanessa would protect her. So Elinor deliberately misled Melissa and Deveraux."

Rosemary broke in. "I'll agree that most of the conversation by the lake—well, Elinor could very well have been talking about herself. But I remember the exact words in that one statement. She laughed and said, 'Don't worry about me. I've been deserted before by Vanessa. When she married Sebastian.'"

"Those were the words, Rosemary. What Elinor actually said was 'Don't worry about me. I've been deserted before. By

Vanessa when she married Sebastian.' Sometimes we hear words the way we *think* they should sound.

"When Elinor left David that morning, she voiced the real threat on his life. She said, 'You may regret this.' Then she went ahead to make him regret it.

"David Mersey was Elinor's one chance at love. She had a strong, repressed nature. I would say for the balance of the day she was far from sane. Elinor was driven wild with jealousy, with hate. David had betrayed her, taken her body and discarded her. How would she have felt about Sebastian? He bought with his money and fame the one man she'd loved. Calmly, coldly, horribly, she plotted the murder."

"I can see all this," said Deveraux slowly. "But how did she get the drug into the wine? I know she had no chance, no chance at all."

"Very simple, she didn't. You were not drugged by the wine. Elinor had plenty of time later that night to put a few drops in all the wine goblets but Sebastian's. Didn't any of you ever wonder at the speed with which the drug took effect? You'd hardly downed the wine before you were showing signs of the drug.

"I knew from the beginning there was something wrong with the time element. Melissa told me exactly how Elinor did it."

"She helped me with dinner," Melissa said dully. "It must have been in the coffee, the horrible coffee."

"Yes, the drug was in the coffee."

"I wasn't at dinner." Rosemary's voice was loud; it startled all of them. "I had no coffee and yet I was drugged too."

Forsythe looked at her. "You were indeed. Your aunt put on your dinner tray something Elinor knew you would drink—a glass of cream soda. Elinor knew all about your sweet tooth. She put the drug in the cream soda and you drank it.

"As soon as everyone was asleep, Elinor moved through the quiet house carrying out her plan. Deveraux was asleep in the drawing room, sprawled on an uncomfortable sofa. She took time to cover him, put a pillow under his head. Elinor did the most vicious deed I've ever heard of, but she was basically just what you thought her, a decent human being—a woman pushed to the breaking point, and she broke. The seed of violence erupted—one man died; the other was driven mad."

Forsythe placed his hand on Vanessa's shoulder. "Don't you think the time has come to break your silence? You can't shield your cousin any longer."

Vanessa tilted her head back and looked up at him. Her eyes were amused, but this time it was a bitter amusement. "I knew from the moment I saw you in Rome that you would never stop digging until you found Lin. I did my best to put you off the track, but it was no use. Very well, you've won.

"Lin was guilty. She killed David and did everything else the way you said. I didn't know at the time that David decided against her. It was something I couldn't have understood. I thought he had chosen Elinor. The night in the drawing room that I proposed the toast to the victor, I was speaking of my cousin. Sebastian told me to get out and take everything I'd brought, meaning Lin, with me. I touched David and told Sebastian I might take something else with me. I really thought David would come with Lin.

"The following morning when I saw Sebastian and David in the studio, I went wild. I believed that Sebastian had killed the boy to keep Elinor from having him. At the trial, I took the part of the villainess that I'm apparently cut out to be. I saw no purpose in exposing Lin to the pointing fingers and sneering mouths. The world believed that David was my lover, very well, let it.

"After the trial, I began to wonder. I was thinking more clearly. Many things started to bother me. Why had Lin taken David's death so calmly? I found out. My cousin was only too eager to confess to me. She wanted expiation. Lin was ready to go to the police. She had a ghastly conscience. Lin said she wanted to clear Sebastian so she could have peace. I talked her out of it."

"You talked her out of it." For the first time Elizabeth Pennell spoke. In her shadowy corner, her features were indistinct.

"You could have solved the murder. Instead, you let me grow up believing my father did that terrible thing. Didn't you care?"

Vanessa shrugged. "About you or your relatives? No. I cared only for my cousin. I told Lin there was nothing to be gained. It would make no difference to Sebastian. Finally, I persuaded her to remain silent. She left me shortly afterward and went to Switzerland and her death."

Vanessa looked around, her eyes challenging. "Lin suffered for her crime—far more than any of you believe. Forsythe was right. She was a good woman. She paid."

The red-haired woman opened her handbag and removed a long envelope and a slim book bound in faded green. "After Lin's death, I was sent her personal effects. She didn't have many. A few clothes, some books, that was all. Among them was this book of poetry." She glanced around. "Are any of you familiar with Wilde's 'Ballad of Reading Gaol'?"

Several of them nodded. Vanessa turned the book over in her large shapely hands. "It's worn. There are marks on some pages that look very much like tear stains. There's one verse heavily underscored. Lin went through her own private hell."

She flipped the pages over and began to read. Her voice was level. A strange dignity about the woman held their attention.

And there till Christ call forth the dead,
In silence let him lie:
No need to waste the foolish tear,
Or heave the windy sigh:
The man had killed the thing he loved,
And so he had to die.

They sat quietly when her voice had stilled, all of them lost in their own thoughts.

Vanessa's voice broke the silence. "In this book was an envelope. The contents had been written two days before her death. It's a full confession, duly witnessed. Lin intended to clear Sebastian. If she'd lived, she would have."

Elizabeth was no longer in the shadow. She was on her feet facing Vanessa. "And you...you've held on to this more than twenty years while I thought—What kind of woman are you? Have you no pity?"

"Pity?" Vanessa raised a mocking brow. "Not for you. I don't think you require it. You have quite enough of your own. As for Rosemary and Melissa—yes, I now wish I'd turned the confession in. But it's too late."

Vanessa rose in one smooth motion, picked up her handbag and fur. Elizabeth backed away from her, her eyes blazing. Handing the envelope to Forsythe, Vanessa turned to Deveraux.

"It's too late for many things. One of my regrets will always be that I didn't notice you twenty-five years ago. Perhaps if I had, Richard, both our lives would have been different."

He struggled to his feet and extended one massive arm. "They say, Vanessa, that it's never too late. Shall we find out? I'll drive you back to London."

Vanessa took his arm and smiled up at him. Her amber eyes were luminous. Without a glance at anyone else, they left the room.

"Well!" Elizabeth was close to spitting. "Very pretty. And they lived happily ever after. What a grotesque pair!"

"Don't," said her aunt. "Please don't, Elizabeth. We've had enough of hate. Both Richard and Vanessa are unhappy people. They may have a chance for a life together."

Turning toward her own chair, Elizabeth gathered up her coat and handbag. She looked at Forsythe, quietly standing with the envelope in his hand.

"You'll know what to do with that. Thank you, Robert; you've been wonderful. May I see you later about your fee?"

"Of course. At your convenience. You can find me at my home in Sussex."

Melissa had risen. She put one hand on Elizabeth's arm. "Before you go home, my dear, will you come and see me? I'd so like to get to know you."

Elizabeth flinched away from her touch. She looked at her aunt. "I'm not a hypocrite. My father tossed me away like a piece of garbage and you allowed him to. I have no desire to know you. We're strangers now. Let it remain that way."

Nodding at Forsythe and Miss Sanderson, Elizabeth walked across the rose rug to the foyer. Forsythe returned the nod. Miss Sanderson didn't.

Rosemary hurried over to Melissa and put one arm around her waist. "The bitch! The cold, inhuman bitch!"

Behind the heavy glasses, her aunt's eyes looked damp, but her voice was firm. "No, Elizabeth's right. We're strangers. She'll never forgive me."

Melissa extended her hand to Forsythe. He clasped it in both of his. It was warm and dry; the skin felt like crushed rose petals. "There are no words. You've done so much for us. Sebastian's name will be cleared; Rosemary and Elizabeth will be free of fear. And you've given an old woman peace." She glanced around the big room. "This house, so many times I've been asked to sell it. I shall now. It knew happiness, laughter. Calvert Hall will have the chance to know these things again."

Melissa and Rosemary smiled their goodbyes at Forsythe before they turned away. Hennessy scrambled to open the door for them. He followed them through the foyer while Forsythe sank into a chair.

His feet parted, Horner had silently been watching. He spoke now. "I'm very much in your debt. You hit the nail on the head when you were talking about my wife's motive. For years, nightmares have haunted me. Remembering the type of girl she was, the way she felt about Calvert. Well—"

Forsythe finished for him. "You wondered whether Rosemary might have killed Mersey and Sebastian covered for her."

"Only with one part of my mind. I love my wife deeply but, damn it all, the way she felt about our boys, always watching them. I couldn't believe she worried about a great-uncle's violence. It seemed closer."

"More like a mother's violence?" Forsythe asked. "The day I interviewed you in the shed, you knew Rosemary was listening, didn't you?"

Horner grinned. "She was listening, all right. Rosemary knows my beastly temper. She was trying to find out whether I was giving you a bad time. God, what suspicion can do. Say, how do you know all this?"

"I saw the fear in your eyes. You're not the sort to feel it for yourself."

Horner stuck out his hand, grasped Forsythe's warmly. "You'll never see it again." He turned to follow his wife and her aunt. Horner flung a parting remark over his shoulder. "Anytime you want anything, Forsythe, yell. I'll come running."

Pulling herself out of her chair, Miss Sanderson stretched. "I'm bushed. But that wraps it up." She glanced sideways at Forsythe. "I'm also starved. Do you suppose when we get back to the Inn, Bea might cut us a couple of sandwiches from that delicious pot roast we had tonight?"

Hennessy spoke behind them. "After what you did here, I'd guess that Bea will open her kitchen and make you a hot meal. You two go along now. I'll straighten up here."

Forsythe rose and wearily wandered the length of the room. He opened the doors that led to the studio. Miss Sanderson followed him and stood at his elbow. The moonlight was pouring through the glass walls.

"Do you notice, Robby, it feels warmer in here now?"

He grinned tiredly. "We have had a good fire going, you know."

"Not hot enough to penetrate this far."

"Now don't start talking about ghosts and auras again. These things don't exist. It's just that you're looking at this room in a different way. There never was anything waiting here."

She was watching the moonlight falling in silver ribbons across the stone floor. "I have a question, Robby. I know you're exhausted, but there's one thing you didn't explain and it's important."

"No more questions tonight. I know what you're thinking about. Later, old girl, much later."

Taking her elbow, he turned her away from the door.

"Have I laid to rest all your ghosts and goblins for you?"

She took a last look at Sebastian Calvert's studio. "Perhaps," she said, "perhaps."

Chapter Twelve

The pond at the end of the garden no longer reflected blue August skies. A cold November wind driving icy rain before it turned the water into foaming steel gray.

Rain pounded against the long windows of Forsythe's study. Inside it was warm and cozy. The only sounds in the room were the scratch of a pen and the crackle of a wood fire. The russet cat sprawled full length on the carpet in front of the hearth, its eyes half closed.

Forsythe wrote steadily, copying in longhand from his father's closely written notes. When his secretary entered the room, he didn't look up.

"Visitors for you, Robby. Miss Pennell and a friend."

He pushed his work away. "Show them in, Sandy."

Elizabeth entered swiftly. Taking Forsythe's outstretched hand, she smiled at him. "I would imagine after all this time you thought I'd forgotten you."

"Not at all. You're looking well, Elizabeth."

She was. Her cherry wool suit was matched exactly by the tiny Robin Hood hat that perched on her dark hair. Under it, her eyes were bright and her expression vivacious.

Behind and to one side of her, a young girl waited. Forsythe looked at her with admiration. She was a beauty, gold and white with enormous blue eyes. Elizabeth made the introductions.

"This is my secretary, Darlee West. She joined me the first part of September and we've been making a tour of the continent."

Smiling at Elizabeth's companion, Forsythe said, "You must have had a chance to see many countries. Which did you prefer?"

Her voice was disappointing, high and nasal, with a midwestern twang. "I liked the south of France and some of Spain. We saw a bullfight in Madrid and—ugh!"

"No, they aren't very pleasant. Will you be seated?"

Darlee West daintily perched on the chair opposite the desk. Elizabeth stood behind it. Fishing in her handbag, she located and extended to Forsythe a small pink slip.

"Here is your fee, Robert; you said I could put my own value on your services."

He looked at the check. "But this is enormous. Far out of proportion to—"

"Not at all. I can well afford it, and you did do the impossible."

He placed it on his desk. "I must admit, Elizabeth, I'm surprised to see you in England. I thought you might have returned home to choose your trousseau and make plans for your wedding."

The beautiful little blonde swung around and looked up at her employer. "What's he talking about? What wedding?"

Placing one hand on the girl's shoulder, Elizabeth flicked her eyes across Forsythe's face. "You're mistaken, Robert; I have no intention of marrying."

"But when you came to see me, you said you were in love, that it was necessary to clear your father—"

He stopped abruptly. Elizabeth's large, spatulate hand was gently caressing the girl's shoulder. His face became cold and stern. "You deceived me."

Her eyes flashed with derision. "I didn't lie to you. All I said was that I'd fallen in love. You see, I am my father's daughter." She smiled. "Would you have taken the case if I'd told you my exact reason?"

"I damn well wouldn't have."

"There, you see? You're an old-fashioned man, Robert; it was necessary not to be too frank." She laughed, a brittle, tinkling sound. "Come now, don't look so forbidding. This is the latter part of the twentieth century, you know." She looked down at her secretary. "Come, Darlee; I have a feeling we're no longer welcome."

Forsythe had already pressed the button on the corner of his desk. Miss Sanderson opened the door as Darlee rose. His secretary waited.

"Show Miss Pennell and Miss West out, Sandy."

Stony-faced, he waited until the door closed behind them. He glanced down at the check. Then his lips began to quiver. He started to laugh, helplessly guffawing, holding on to the edge of the desk.

Miss Sanderson's voice broke across his laughter. "Share the joke, Robby."

She'd returned and was standing beside the desk staring at him. Helplessly he pointed to the pink slip. She picked it up, her eyes widening.

"Just when has a small fortune been funny?"

He struggled to control himself and sank breathless back into his chair.

"I think...I think we should have a drink to celebrate. Break out a bottle."

Her face still puzzled, she turned toward the door. He called after her, "Bring in the files on the Calvert case, everything you have."

When Miss Sanderson nudged the door open, she was holding a large sheaf of manila folders with a tray precariously balanced on top.

Lifting off the tray, Forsythe proceeded to remove the cork from the green bottle. "Very good choice," he said, "champagne is suitable."

"You did say we were going to celebrate," she grunted, dumping the folders on the desk. "May I ask what the occasion is?"

"The emancipation of slaves," he said gaily, "the overthrow of tyranny and the death of a knight errant."

She accepted the brimming glass and looked suspiciously at him. "Are you sure you need this? I have a hunch you may have a snootful now."

He laughed and drank half his glass. "Sit down, Sandy, and prepare to take notes."

While she located her book and found a pen, Forsythe strode back and forth. The cat lifted a sleepy head and stared at him. He bent to pat it. "Now, make a list. I want my books crated"—he waved one hand expansively around him—"arrange to have the house closed. Meeks and his wife may as well stay on as caretakers. I want my chambers opened and cleaned. Get an ad in the *Times* for a couple of good clerks..."

Abigail Sanderson wasn't writing. She was staring at him, her mouth agape. He replenished his glass and waved the bottle at her. She shook her head. "One of us had better stay sober. Are you trying to tell me you intend to return to your practice?"

"That's exactly it, old girl. We're going back where both of us belong. We're going to begin living again. Close your mouth, Sandy; you're managing to look like an idiot."

Spots of color glowed high on her cheeks. "I can't believe it! What in the devil changed your mind?"

Forsythe picked up a manila envelope and began to lay the loose sheets of paper on the fire. "An old cliché, Sandy, but true. Elizabeth Pennell finally broke this camel's back. I saw her in her true colors and, at the same time, I saw myself." His eyes moved from the burning paper to Sandy's flushed face. "Have you any idea what was the real object of our earnest quest to prove the innocence of Sebastian Calvert?"

"You said Elizabeth was in love, wanted to—"

"In love, yes, much in love. In love with none other than her lovely young companion, Miss Darlee West." He groped for his glass and tipped it up.

Miss Sanderson held out her own glass. "On second thought, I'll have a touch more bubbly. I think I need it." She was smiling. After a moment her face became serious. "But this couldn't have changed your mind."

"It helped. I've been considering going back to work for some time. This did it. Sir Hilary was right and so, in a way, was the estimable Miss Pennell. This is the twentieth century and it's high time I came up to date. Now is the time to ask your question, Sandy, the one you wanted answered that night in Calvert Hall."

She twirled the stem of her goblet. "Very well. I've had a tough time trying not to force an answer from you. Your reasoning was sound. Elinor Atlin killed David Mersey. Her confession clinched it. But—if she was the murderess—who the devil took a shot at you? The only person who tried to protect Elinor was Vanessa Calvert. And Vanessa was in Rome. She might have hired a killer to stop you, but I can't believe it. I feel Vanessa would do her own killing. Anyway, a professional assassin would have been thorough. I can't see one giving up after a solitary try."

"Sound reasoning, Sandy. I believed that one of our suspects was out to finish me off until I knew definitely the identity of Mersey's killer. Then I suddenly realized who my assailant had been. Think, Sandy, what else had I done the day that I was nicked?"

For a moment, there was only the sound of the soft tapping of Miss Sanderson's nail against her tooth. "Well," she softly, "we worked through the forenoon in our suite. You had lunch with Richard Deveraux and came back to the hotel. Then you went out to meet Elizabeth. On your way back the shot was fired." She stared at him. "Not Elizabeth."

"Hardly. No possible reason why she'd want her sleuth dead. No, I met someone else that evening. You must have a mental block about her. You should remember."

"I certainly should. I loathe her. Virginia, Virginia Telser."

"Now Mrs. Douglas Graham. Yes, little Virginia. I never discussed our meeting with you. The old magic was gone. The moment I saw her I knew she was merely another man's wife. Whatever I'd felt for her was over. I suppose a woman always knows. Another thing I know now is that Virginia was guilty. She blew Frank Telser's brains out and planted fake evidence to blame a prowler."

"I always knew *that*. You would have too if you'd been able to think clearly. The woman was besotted with Graham. She'd have done anything to get him."

"And she'll do anything to keep him. I looked dangerous to her. She was afraid I'd blow her paradise to pieces. So Virginia followed me to the Monument, then to the hotel, and tried to ensure her safety by killing me." He ripped some pages out viciously and threw them on the flames. "The poor fool, she didn't understand she had my word. No matter how I felt about her, I'd have kept it." The cat moved; it was rubbing against his knee. One of his hands brushed its bright, thick fur.

"What Virginia doesn't know is that I have some insurance myself. Murdering me would only have exposed her. I took a statement from Albert Jennings that will stand up in court. It's in my safety box in London, and would have been opened after my death."

His secretary leaned forward. "What will happen to you? In a way you've been concealing evidence."

"I'll have my fingers rapped. But it was privileged information. Virginia is the one they'll roast. The case will either be reopened or they'll try her on a charge of bribing a key witness. Either way, she'll be out of circulation for a long time."

"Her son, Robby, how do you feel about him?"

"Badly," Forsythe admitted. "But my promise has been canceled out. Now that Virginia has tried to kill me once, she may have another go. I don't really fancy setting myself up for target practice."

Miss Sanderson looked dazed. "I'm finding it hard to believe." Her eyes sharpened. "What was that about the death of a knight errant and Sir Hilary?"

"He compared me to Don Quixote. As usual, Sir Hilary was brutally accurate. I can hardly see Sir Lancelot riding out to battle wearing the colors I did—one gallant banner for a cold-blooded murderess, the other for a lesbian heiress."

"You must remember, Robby, that your last ride did a great deal of good for a nice group of people. What about Melissa Calvert and Rosemary?"

"Agreed. But the good was purely coincidental. No, Robert Forsythe has ridden that trail for the last time. The next time we don armor, Sandy, it will be in a court of law, for someone who really needs our help." He rose from the hearth. "Finish burning these, will you? I feel restless. I'm going for a walk before tea."

Picking up the check, she held it delicately by one corner between her thumb and forefinger. "What about this?"

"Burn it—" he stopped abruptly. "On second thought, that sounds like the old Robert Forsythe. No, deposit it in our business account. We've earned it and, as Elizabeth said, she can afford it." He grinned at his secretary. "It may help provide funds for someone who can't afford our services."

Flinging open the window, he stepped over the sill. She watched him as he strode across the wet turf. His shoulders moved easily and his step was brisk and young.

With a smile, she turned to the hearth. Kneeling in front of the fire, she laid the rest of the papers on the flames. They flared up and burned briskly. In a short time all that remained of the Calvert case was gray ashes.

This book is for Terry Fidgeon, my doctor and my friend.

A Death for a Darling

Chapter One

Robert Forsythe felt a deep contentment. It was his favorite hour, early evening, his favorite month, May, and he was in his favorite sanctuary, the library of his home in Sussex. It had been far too long, he was thinking, since he'd had time to drive from London and spend a weekend here.

He sat at his desk, his long fingers sorting fishing flies into two piles, one lot to return to the metal box, the other to take with him. Dropping the last one, this a particularly fine specimen of lilac and orange, he shoved back the chair and stepped to the long window overlooking a stretch of turf leading gently downward to the pond. Rays of sunset, as vividly colorful as the fishing flies, gleamed across the water and outlined the higher branches of the plane trees. Sunset...May...days stretching enticingly out before him, days to fill exactly as he wished. Inhaling hungrily, he drew in clean country air redolent with fresh-cut grass, blossoming fruit trees, and the sharper odor of lime recently spread around the roots of the lilac bushes.

Miss Sanderson had been on the right track as usual and Forsythe smiled as he remembered his reaction to her demand that they take a vacation. With no hesitation she'd pinpointed his feelings. "Robby, you're positively hostile to the idea of leaving this office. You take after your father and are turning into a workaholic."

Abigail Sanderson was an authority on his father. For a number of years, before Forsythe had inherited her, she'd been his father's secretary. The younger Forsythe told her, "A week, perhaps even two, yes. That I can see, but a month…Sandy, it's out of the question."

"Nonsense!" One capable hand made a wide circle of their chambers, encompassing not only Forsythe's office, but also the reception area, the cubicle where she held sway, the room shared by two juniors, and the cramped storage area piled nearly to the ceiling with boxes and file folders. "You're married to these chambers. Robby, how long is it since we returned to law practice?"

"Several years."

"And in those years we've had our shoulders to the wheel, our noses to the grindstone—"

"To say nothing of keeping our eyes on the ball."

Slowly and with dignity she rose, and bestowed on her employer a long, glacial look. "You have no intention of speaking seriously. I'm wasting my time."

"Now don't you get hostile. I simply dislike clichés. State your case."

"Very well. You're exhausted and so am I. The Dawes-Hinton trial drew out to improbable lengths—"

"We did get them off, Sandy."

"Don't interrupt. The point is—" she ticked off points on her fingers "—young Peters and Vincent are quite capable of handling the practice for a month. In case you have reservations Eugene Emory is willing to act as consultant—"

"So you've been after Gene too."

She sank back into the chair and Forsythe took a closer look at her. Gray hair framed a face composed and austere but there were dark smudges under her eyes and lines he'd never noticed before across the brow, around the mouth. "You are exhausted," he said. "You're also right. We both need a break. A month it is. Tell me, have you made plans?"

"For the first week, yes. Duty calls. My sister Teresa is enjoying yet another honeymoon and wants me to substitute for her annual visit to a friend in Norfolk. I'm not charmed with the idea but Honoria looks forward to seeing Teresa and apparently she's a lonely person so..." Miss Sanderson sighed. "After that I'll indulge myself. I may go to bed and read."

"Good Lord! Yet another honeymoon. What is Teresa's score to date? Is it five or six husbands?"

"I'm afraid I've lost track. But her business sense is still working. The latest bridegroom is not only ancient but owns a shipping company. Anyway, Teresa's conscience was bothering her and she made me promise to spend a few days with Honoria. She has a large house and is wretchedly poor—"

"Odd combination. If your Honoria is wretchedly poor, how does she maintain a large house?"

"With difficulty, no doubt. And she isn't *my* Honoria. She was a childhood friend of Teresa's and I hardly know her. I do remember her father, the colonel." Miss Sanderson smiled. "I always thought of him as an ogre."

"Ugly?"

"Not in appearance. In fact I suppose the colonel was handsome in a cold forbidding way but he was a tyrant. Kept poor Honoria virtually a prisoner, drove his only son away from home, and then died a year ago leaving the poor woman that house, two old retainers, and a starvation income. Odd..."

Forsythe raised his brows. "Do I scent a mystery?"

"No. It just seems strange that a man as money-conscious as the colonel should fritter away a substantial amount of lucre in the last years of his life. Teresa says she thinks the old devil did it for spite—simply to enjoy the idea of his daughter eking out the rest of her life in poverty."

"The colonel does sound like an ogre. Has Honoria no relatives to come to her aid?"

"None that I know of. Teresa would gladly help but she doesn't dare offer. Honoria is proud and pride may be the only thing she has left. But enough of me, Robby. I don't suppose you've had time to consider your holiday."

He closed the file on his desk, the final one on the Dawes-Hinton trial. "Scotland," he said firmly. "I'll ring up the MacDougal and then I'm off to trout streams and peat fires and long evenings by said fires."

"And long days wading about and doubtless falling into frigid water. Shivering and cleaning slimy fish. Not my idea of Heaven."

"But mine." He stretched luxuriously. "I'll have to drive to Sussex to pick up my fishing gear. The Meekses will be delighted to see me."

Miss Sanderson grinned. "Mrs. Meeks won't be delighted."

"Bosh. She'd like nothing better than to stuff me with home cooking."

"Mrs. Meeks is compulsively neat, Robby. And I've seen you prepare to visit the MacDougal. Looks like the sky rains fishing gear. Bet you."

"You're on. I win, you buy a drink our first day back at work."

Sticking her hat on at a jaunty angle, she opened the door. Over her shoulder she called, "Seeing you'll be paying, make mine a double."

Forsythe withdrew his gaze from the pond. The sun had set and he turned to switch on a lamp. The ginger-colored cat had taken over his chair and as he bent to dispossess it the door opened. On the threshold Mrs. Meeks stood with her hands planted on her hips. Never had a person been so misnamed. The housekeeper, her considerable jaw jutting, cast a disgusted look over the reels, cases, creels, and rubber boots littering the carpet. "I told you I could pack this...this stuff for you." And added, apparently as an afterthought, "sir."

"And I thought I told you much of the pleasure of a fishing trip is sorting over the gear."

Bending, she prodded a rubber boot. "I do believe dried mud has dropped all over the carpet."

"Hardly. They look as though you've put them through the washer. Was there something, Mrs. Meeks?"

She clapped a hand to her brow. "Clean forgot. Miss Sanderson for you on the telephone, sir." As she said the secretary's name a note of approval tinged her voice. Miss Sanderson would never be guilty of marring a fine Aubusson carpet with assorted trash.

She stood aside to allow him to enter the downstairs hall where the phone was located and then busied herself brushing imaginary dust from the banister, all the better to hear her employer's every word. As he picked up the receiver he wondered, as he frequently did, why he'd never bothered to put extensions in. There was no chance for privacy with this one. In his ear Miss Sanderson's crisp voice asked, "Do I buy or do you?"

"I owe you a double, but surely you didn't call to settle a bet. Are you having a good time?"

"Scrumptious. And I'm issuing an invitation for you to join us."

"You and Honoria."

"And a batch of houseguests."

Forsythe had a mental picture of those houseguests. Spinsters, perhaps widows…Sandy bored to tears and looking for some diversion. This time she wasn't going to manipulate him. "Nice of you to think of me, but tomorrow in the wee hours I head north to the MacDougal and that trout stream."

There was a pause and then Miss Sanderson asked sweetly, "Did you tell the MacDougal exactly when you were going to arrive?"

"I don't know myself. I'll travel in a leisurely way, pausing to drink in the scenery and partake of hospitality at picturesque inns."

"So, you see, no problem. You can drive up here tomorrow, do try to arrive for lunch, spend the weekend, and bright and early on Monday continue your trip."

"What are you up to now?"

Miss Sanderson was evasive. "Come along and see." She added, "It's seldom I ask you for a favor."

"It's seldom you don't." He glanced over his shoulder. Mrs. Meeks was practically breathing down his neck. "This is important to you?"

"Yes, and it is to you too."

Sandy was speaking as guardedly as he was. Perhaps she had an audience too. "I am not carting along a wardrobe that will be useless to me fishing."

"No worry. Come as you are. This is strictly informal. And Robby, I have a surprise for you."

"What?"

"If I told you it wouldn't be a surprise. I can promise you'll never regret this weekend."

Exasperated at his own weakness, Forsythe rang off. The redoubtable Miss Sanderson had an uncanny habit of being right, but there are exceptions to every rule. As it turned out, this weekend was to prove the exception.

Chapter Two

Forsythe made no effort to arrive at his destination for luncheon. The shadows were lengthening as he drove through the village of Bury-Sutton, stopped to ask directions from an elderly man walking a poodle, continued over a covered bridge, and turned into a winding road that followed the River Carey's capricious course. Finally he swung the Rover between gateposts, noted that the gates standing open needed repair, spotted a tumble-down gatehouse, and piloted the car up a gravel driveway that wound as much as the Carey. The grounds echoed the forlorn entrance to the estate, shaggy grass much in need of clipping and untrimmed plantings. Turning the last curve he was pleased to see that the manor house stood among neatly clipped lawns and well-tended flower beds. The house was Georgian, with clean lines and pleasant proportions. There seemed no evidence of neglect on its imposing façade, no broken tiles or peeling paint. But then, Forsythe remembered, the colonel or ogre had passed to his reward only a year ago.

He pulled the Rover to a halt before the portico, crawled out, and stamped his foot. His left leg, injured years before in a hotly contested soccer game, had stiffened up. Limping, he rounded the car and opened the trunk. As he lifted out his pigskin case, a low and ominous rumble sounded directly behind him. Glancing around he found the source of the sound. The mastiff was the size of a calf and brindled lips pulled back tautly from ivory fangs. "Nice boy," he said soothingly, and looked around for aid.

At that moment the door flew open and Miss Sanderson trotted to the top of the steps. "You're late," she told him tartly.

"Never mind that." Forsythe kept his voice low and soothing. "Do something about this monster."

The mastiff growled deep in his throat, small eyes appearing to be sizing up Forsythe's throat.

"Dratted animal. Would you believe he treed the milkman this morning?"

"Yes," Forsythe said faintly. "Call him off."

"No use. He won't pay attention to me. Look harmless. I'll get Potter."

Forsythe stood motionless, not daring to move a muscle, and tried to look harmless. Time passed, it seemed to stretch out into hours, then rescue arrived in the person of an ancient man attired in a threadbare butler's suit. He tottered down the steps and said sharply, "That's enough Heathcliff. Around to the back where you belong." Potter might have been old but he had good lungs. Heathcliff cast one last hungry look at Forsythe, backed away, and then reluctantly obeyed.

Miss Sanderson, who had prudently stayed behind Potter, joined them. "That animal should be chained, Potter."

"This is his job, miss; he's a watchdog and a good one." Rheumy eyes peered up at Forsythe. "Sorry about that, sir. Heathcliff's bark is worse than his bite. Your case, sir."

"He didn't bark," Forsythe pointed out, and surrendered his case.

"Perhaps, miss, you could show Mr. Forsythe to the drawing room while I take his case up."

Miss Sanderson linked arms with her employer. "Don't look so surprised, Robby. Haven't you seen a butler before?"

"Not for a number of years and never one quite that old. White side whiskers!"

"He's one of the retainers I mentioned. The other one is his wife, an inspired cook. The Potters practically raised Honoria. Her mother died when she was born and the colonel wouldn't allow her to attend school. Honoria had a succession of governesses but the butler and cook looked after her." Miss Sanderson paused to catch her breath and then said indignantly, "And the ogre made no provision in his will for the Potters."

"You seem to have made good use of your time, Sandy. Soaked up the family history."

"More than I really wanted to. The colonel was a heartless brute." As they entered the house her voice changed. "Isn't this charming?"

The hallway was as gracious as the exterior. It was spacious, with gleaming parquet, a magnificent flight of stairs, and a vaulted ceiling. It was also bare, furnished only with a side table bearing a telephone and a china urn of lilacs. A uniformed maid appeared from a doorway to the left, bobbed her head, gave Forsythe a shy smile, and ducked into another room. "It doesn't look as though Honoria is suffering financially," Forsythe muttered. "The grounds around the house are practically manicured and—"

"Honoria does most of the gardening herself. She has a boy in from the village to cut grass and that's all. As for the maids…that's part of the surprise."

Miss Sanderson led the way down the hall and as Forsythe followed, he wondered what the surprise was. Could Honoria have come into an inheritance? No, Sandy had mentioned she had no living relatives. Miss Sanderson swung open one panel of a set of double doors and turned to give him a wide smile. Warily he approached, bracing himself for a gaggle of middle-aged women. There was only one middle-aged woman and she was hurrying to meet them with both hands outstretched.

"So pleased, Mr. Forsythe. Abigail thought you'd be here much earlier. Did you have difficulty locating the house?"

"None," he told her.

Miss Sanderson made introductions while Honoria Farquson beamed up at him. She was as tall as his secretary but much heavier. She'd be handsome, he decided, if she were wearing something besides that shapeless flowered dress, those heavy oxfords, and if she had that amazing hair properly styled. At first glance he had thought her hair white but now he could see it was that rare shade of blonde that glints silver. Honoria's skin was delicate and highlighted with rose-pink. Taking his arm she led him toward the trio of men who had risen from around a low table.

"You must meet my guests," Honoria told him and proceeded to introduce him. Forsythe could see what Sandy had meant by informal. The men wore faded blue jeans, sweatshirts, and sandals. There any resemblance ceased. Samuel Cochrane was enormous, and reminded Forsythe a bit of the mastiff. With some trepidation he allowed his hand to be swallowed in a massive paw, but apparently this giant felt no need to emphasize his strength with a bone crusher. Cochrane merely gave a firm but gentle squeeze and relinquished his grip. Beside Cochrane, Melvin Borthwick looked like a terrier, if a terrier could be pictured as totally bald. As though to make up for the hairless skull, Borthwick had shaggy brows and had cultivated an equally shaggy mustache. The younger man was about Cochrane's height but he had a build that more resembled the greyhound lines of Sandy's figure. Funny, Forsythe thought, how his mind kept running along canine lines. Giles Eady, the greyhound, shook hands, gave a sudden and radiant smile that made his homely freckled face charming, and asked, "Did you by any chance make the acquaintance of Heathcliff?"

Forsythe smiled back. "I did; luckily the butler came to the rescue before he had a piece of me."

Waving them into chairs, Honoria said contritely, "I'm sorry Heathcliff startled you, Mr. Forsythe. I suppose he should be chained but actually he's a comfort in a place like this."

Giles transferred the charming smile to his hostess. "You may have to change his name. Mickey has a strong objection to it."

"That's a shame but Heathcliff had his name before Mr.—" Honoria clapped her hand over her mouth. Looking guiltily at Miss Sanderson, she murmured, "My tongue does run away with me. I nearly spoiled your surprise." Turning to her latest guest she told him, "We were hopeful you would arrive for luncheon but you are in time for tea. I've been holding off, hoping the young people would be with us."

"Might as well forget about them," Borthwick, the terrier, told her.

"Right," Giles agreed. "Young lovers, you know, and a day in May."

Honoria nodded and reached for a bellpull. "I suppose so. We'll have tea but there's Marcia too. She should have her tea. I'd hoped to have all the guests gathered when you arrived, Mr. Forsythe, but the young people went to Bury-Sutton and Marcia is feeling miserable. A head cold, you know, all stuffed up and can't breathe properly and so I told her directly after luncheon, 'you simply must go up and rest.' The only cure for a cold is rest—" Breaking off, she glanced over Forsythe's shoulder.

"Relax, Honoria, Marcia is here," a vibrant voice announced.

Honoria bobbed to her feet. "Do you feel better, dear?"

"I feel like death warmed over. My head's pounding like a trip hammer but I couldn't rest, just twisted around."

Wondering if this could be the surprise, Forsythe got to his feet and turned. This woman wasn't entering the drawing room; she was making an entrance. She'd paused, holding her tall body in the hipshot pose of a model. She was heavily and expertly made up, her dark brown hair expertly styled, a simple white suit of stunning elegance displaying every curve of a full and fine figure. She didn't wait for introductions but told him, "I'm Marcia Mather." Then she waited expectantly as if for applause.

Knowing some reaction was expected, Forsythe said, "Delighted, Miss Mather," and glanced at Miss Sanderson for enlightenment. The enlightenment came from Giles Eady. He hooted with laughter. "Don't look so puzzled, old man. Marcia's waiting for you to rave on about seeing everything she ever appeared in, assuring her you're a devoted fan."

"Don't be silly, Giles," Marcia said and finally moved, taking the chair Forsythe was holding for her. "One can't expect every person one meets to have seen one's films. Anyway—" bitterness tinged the vibrant voice—"I've never been a star, only a supporting actress."

Forsythe tried to make amends. "I'm sorry, Miss Mather. I know little about actors or films. I seldom attend the cinema."

"Except for one particular actress," Miss Sanderson said wickedly.

Forsythe shot a look at his secretary but Miss Sanderson was demurely watching Potter trot in, carrying in shaking hands a tray bearing a fine Georgian silver tea set. Everyone was watching the butler, collectively holding their breaths, wondering if he would reach the table safely. He did and lowered the tray shakily in front of Honoria. As she busied herself with the teapot, she told Forsythe, "Marcia is an old friend—"

"*Old.* You make me feel like Methuselah."

"I didn't mean it that way. I meant we've been friends since nursery days although in later years we've seen little of each other. That's another reason I was so happy about this weekend." Forsythe watched Honoria extending a cup to Marcia. Those hands, so close together, summed up his impression of the two women. Marcia's hands were the texture of the white silk of her suit, the oval nails flawlessly painted the same color as her lips. Honoria's hands were well shaped but with roughened skin over the knuckles, the nails clipped short. A capable hand, Forsythe thought, strong and tranquil. He found he preferred the pleasant dowdiness of his hostess to the actress's lacquered dark beauty.

Leaning back, Marcia smiled, a smile of remembrance. "My father called us the Three Musketeers. Remember, Honoria?"

"Three?" Borthwick's bald head turned from Marcia to Miss Sanderson. "Are you the third?"

"My sister Teresa is the third musketeer. There was an age difference, five years between us. It makes little difference now but when you're children it means two separate worlds, two separate sets of friends."

Briefly, Forsythe wondered which way the age difference went, but Miss Sanderson wasn't about to volunteer the information. Sandy's age was her carefully guarded secret.

"We were inseparable," Marcia continued. "Marcy, the doctor's daughter, Terry, the vicar's child, and Honey, daughter of the lord of the manor."

"Hardly a lord," Honoria murmured.

"Well, he certainly acted the part," Marcia retorted with a touch of asperity.

"I don't suppose the colonel was too popular; he was such a forceful man. Odd." Honoria brushed back a straying gilt lock from her brow. "I always called him father but I think of him as the colonel."

"Or ogre," Miss Sanderson muttered to Forsythe.

Touching a minute hankie to the slightly pinkened tip of her shapely nose, Marcia turned her attention on Miss Sanderson. "And Teresa has married again? Which number is this one, Abigail?"

"I've rather lost track."

"Let me see." Oval nails ticked off fingertips. "The first one was Howard...I do remember him. Teresa married for love and Howard was young and good-looking and penniless. She never made the same mistake again. Her other husbands have been creaking with age, not much to look at, and wealthy—"

"Mustn't be catty, Marcia." A deep voice chimed in with the thud of a bass drum and Forsythe jumped. It was the first time he'd heard Cochrane speak and the man's voice matched his size.

"I'm not being catty. As a matter of fact, Sam, I happen to agree with Teresa. This love stuff is for the birds."

"You should be an expert on that," Giles told her.

Marcia swung on him. "Now who's being catty? As for you, Giles, it's the pot calling the kettle black!"

"Break it up, children," Borthwick said sharply. "We've enough problems without bickering."

"Problems is putting it mildly." Giles slumped in his chair, his freckled face suddenly morose. "Want to bet the first thing Mickey asks when he gets back is whether I've rewritten that scene he was whining about?"

Slamming her cup down on the table with unnecessary force, Marcia told him, "He's got practically every line of dialogue now. And look at me. Five lines, for God's sake."

"You do tend to exaggerate," Giles told her.

"Well, six or seven." She turned an irate face on Borthwick. "You're supposed to be the director, Mel. Don't you have any control over that ass?"

Forsythe found he was sitting on the edge of his chair. "Pardon me, but is this a film company?"

In the shadow of the bristling brows Borthwick's tiny eyes glinted. "Part of one. Giles is the scriptwriter, as Marcia just made clear; I'm supposed to be the director, and—" he raised a hand. "No, Abigail, I'm not conspiring to keep this part a deep dark secret. Men must stick together, after all we're practically an endangered species."

Forsythe eyed Marcia. "And you've a role in it?"

"A cameo," Giles said.

The woman's painted lips curled. "A high-sounding term for a bit part. A few lines now and if Mickey has his way I'll be totally mute and with my back to the camera. *Cameo*."

Forsythe turned his attention to the huge man beside the director. Cochrane was slow spoken and slow moving and gave an initial impression of bovine placidity. His eyes gave lie to this. They were wide-set, feverishly bright, and constantly in motion, flicking from one person to another, from one object to the next. "And you, Mr. Cochrane, you're an actor too?"

"Let's drop the misters. I'm Sam if you're Robert." Forsythe jerked his head in agreement and Cochrane continued, "I'm only a cameraman."

Borthwick gave a sharp bark of a laugh. "Modest old Sam. He happens to be the best cameraman in the British Isles. We're lucky to have him, Robert."

So...they were all on first-name basis, Forsythe thought. He didn't care much for the quick switch but when in Rome... Honoria was now offering homemade Madeira cake and talking in fast bursts. "You have no idea how excited I was when they chose my home for location, I think that's what it's called, for their film. A dream come true! From the time I can remember I've been stagestruck, Mr. Forsythe. We have a literary club in Bury-Sutton and since the colonel's death I've had time to join it and appeared in a play." The charming rose-pink heightened in her cheeks and she confided, "Mr. Borthwick has offered me a part in this film. Oh, not exactly a part. An extra they call it. All I have to do is stand around with a group of people with a shopping bag over my arm and—"

"Very much like my role," Marcia muttered.

Forsythe noticed with amusement that Honoria Farquson hadn't yet succumbed to informality and was still using misters. "May I ask the name of the film?"

"No," Miss Sanderson said flatly.

"Come now, Abigail," Borthwick chided. "I can see no harm in that. We're doing a remake of *Wuthering Heights*."

"Brontë." Forsythe glanced around the drawing room. A pleasantly shabby room with much-faded chintz. "No doubt I'm displaying ignorance but I can't see this as a suitable setting."

"How right you are." Giles pushed his cake plate back and grimaced. "When we finish this thing, if we ever do, it will bear little resemblance to that epic. This is what is called a contemporary treatment of a classic. Everything up-to-date in Kansas City and even the title has been discarded." He winked at the director. "I suggested *Heathcliff Goes to the Dogs* to our Mickey and he says I'm not funny."

"I think you are." Marcia chuckled. "It's perfect. My God! Mickey seems to think the role of a brooding Heathcliff should be acted like a poor man's Marquis de Sade."

"I know," Borthwick agreed dourly. "This morning when he was running through some lines he kept twisting his face as though he had a nervous affliction."

"There's only one possible thing that can pull this one through." Cochrane's deep voice turned all heads in his direction. Those restless eyes flickered over the articles on the tea tray and fastened on a point behind Forsythe's left shoulder. "Thank God Catherine—"

"Sam!" Miss Sanderson said sharply.

"Sorry, Abigail. Nearly let the cat out of the bag."

Forsythe had had enough. "I'm getting a bit tired of this talking in circles. Sandy, what is all of this about?"

"Patience, Robby, is a virtue." She glanced around. "Shall we change the subject?"

"Excellent idea," Marcia said. She patted a hair into place, examined her nails, and asked demurely, "That actress Abigail mentioned, the one you go to see—may I ask who she is?"

While Forsythe was trying to find a way of evading an answer, his secretary blurted, "Erika Von Farr. Robby's not only gone to see all her films but he's even seen some of them twice. Didn't you see that one...what was the name? Ah, yes, *Dark Decision*, at least three times, Robby?"

Forsythe could have twisted her neck. What was wrong with Sandy? Normally she was reticent not only about her own affairs but even more about his. This conversation made him feel foolish, having to confess to infatuation with an image on a screen. He mustered as much dignity as he could and said slowly, "I very much admire Miss Farr. She has tremendous talent, and yes, Sandy, I did see that film three times. I particularly liked the last scene."

"Moving, wasn't it?" Marcia smiled but it was only a jerk of the painted lips. "Let me see. Erika was mounting a staircase and her lover, who had betrayed her, was at the foot. He says something like 'Forgive me' and Erika says"—she deliberately flattened the vibrant voice—"'Forgiveness is impossible but I promise I'll do my best to forget you.'"

This parody of his favorite scene sent blood into Forsythe's face. He felt they were laughing at him but the other three men showed no signs of amusement. Giles Eady said cuttingly, "The words do seem trite, my little cat, but I agree with Robert. It wasn't the dialogue; it was Erika. Every line of her body showed grief and outrage, the way she stood, half-turned, her hair falling in a single fluid line down her back...no tears...dry eyes that made tears appear merciful—"

"Oh God! Do spare me, Giles." Marcia dabbed at the pinkened tip of her nose with a lacy scrap. "I'm sick as a dog and I can see not only you but Sam and Mel are ready to pounce on me as though I've defiled the Mona Lisa. I apologize. I agree Erika is a magnificent actress but"—malice crept into her voice—"it would appear not everyone is overwhelmed by her. Did you read that interview when Erika first arrived in England? It was written by a woman...Riverdell?"

"Roverdale," Cochrane corrected. "I read it. The writer was a witch."

"Truly a nasty woman," Honoria said indignantly. "I felt Miss Roverdale was consumed with envy."

"Nonetheless," Marcia said, "much of what she said was the truth. Erika *is* built like a boy. And that bit about her face..."

"Rather too much brow and too little chin," Giles said. "Knowing you I imagine you didn't bother reading the responses to Miss Roverdale's criticism." He sat forward, his hands knotted into fists. "One letter to the editor said that Miss Roverdale appears to equate udders like a cow and a pretty face with talent. The writer said there were quite enough curvaceous talentless actresses and too few with Erika Von Farr's genius."

"Another letter put the whole matter into a nutshell," Borthwick said.

Dreamily, Forsythe quoted, "'Magic is not a matter of face nor form. Magic is the ability to convince one that an actress is beautiful without beauty, ugly without ugliness, young without youth, or old without age. Magic is a quality Erika Von Farr is blessed with and because of this we are all blessed.'"

"Bravo!" Marcia clapped her hands. "Keep this up, Robert, and you may join Honoria as an extra in this immortal film."

Forsythe was crimson with embarrassment. Not only that but he had finally, and it was past time, put all the threads and innuendoes together. He knew what Sandy's surprise was, he knew what they had been talking around, and he was stricken with panic. He felt as he had before stepping onto the stage in a school play. The tea and Madeira cake felt leaden in his stomach. Stage fright! The barrister who had dominated many courtrooms had perspiration drenching his palms, knees that were shaking. Dimly he was aware that Sandy was regarding him with the indulgent concern of a mother about to watch her son eat too much rich dessert and become sick. Honoria and her distinguished guests were chatting and making rather too much of not looking at him.

Then Sandy stiffened, turning like a pointer toward the door—that damn dog simile again. Forsythe couldn't turn. He felt paralyzed. Please, he begged, don't let me make a fool of myself.

Then a voice resounded from the direction of the door. Forsythe paid no attention to the words, all he heard was the familiar voice that could vary in tones from the whisper of black satin to the silvery swish of a rapier blade.

The other men jumped to their feet. Slowly Forsythe pulled himself up and as slowly turned.

Chapter Three

Erika Von Farr wasn't making an entrance. She simply strolled in and Forsythe avidly drank her in. He couldn't argue about Miss Roverdale's remarks. Erika did have the build of a boy: tight jeans strained over narrow hips, a loose sweatshirt displayed only a hint of curves, and her shoulders were wide and thin. Long hair was pulled back and held with a bit of yellow yarn and her face, which perhaps did have a bit too much brow and not quite enough chin, was dominated by huge, luminous eyes.

Forgetting completely about the other people, he found himself irresistibly drawn to her. She extended a cool hand and he clasped it in both of his. He opened his mouth but before he could speak Marcia called from behind him, "What Robert's going to say, Erika dear, is that he's seen everything you've ever acted in and he's president of your English fan club."

"With the exception of being involved in a fan club, that is the truth," Forsythe confessed shamelessly. "This is an honor, Miss Farr."

"Erika, please, and it's my honor. I've heard so much about you."

Had Sandy been babbling on about him? Forsythe wondered. "I'm a barrister."

"And also a detective. The California papers picked up some of your cases—the one involving the sculptor, Sebastian Calvert, and that terrible one last year where the three school girls were murdered on the moors."

Forsythe found he was still clinging to her hand and released it. As he led her toward the tea table he assured her, "I'm not a detective, not in the actual sense of the word. I've more or less fallen into a few cases and been lucky." He tried to steer the young woman toward a chair beside his own but Giles was already holding a chair between his own and Honoria Farquson's.

"Wouldn't it be exciting if we were to have a nice juicy case for you to solve this weekend?" Marcia asked.

"Marcia, *really*," Honoria protested.

Reaching over, Marcia patted the other woman's hand. "Not blood and gore and bodies in the library, only something to demonstrate Robert's detective ability. Something mild...say the theft of a priceless diamond necklace."

"A thief in *my* house!"

Erika darted a look at the older actress and said with the swish of rapier steel in her voice, "This is Marcia's idea of a joke. Pay no attention to her, Aunt Honoria."

Forsythe looked from his hostess to the girl opposite him. "Aunt?"

"A carefully guarded secret," Marcia told him. "Apparently the only person Honoria confided in is Teresa and she's never breathed a word. Honoria, you might have told *me*."

"How could I, dear? I hadn't seen you since we were girls." Honoria turned placidly to Forsythe. "Yes, Erika is the only child of my brother. I'm terribly proud of her but to talk about it would have seemed like...well, boasting. My brother died and Erika's mother took her to California. Erika was only about six weeks old at that time and we only met again recently. As a matter of fact that's how I met the rest of my guests. I was chatting on about this house and Mr. Borthwick said he'd like to see it because it sounded like the setting they needed in their film and...well, here we are."

Miss Sanderson beamed at the barrister. "When I got down here and saw Erika I knew how surprised you would be to meet her, so—"

"You swore everyone to secrecy and lured me down here, Sandy."

"Are you sorry you came?"

"No, certainly I'm not sorry." Forsythe wasn't. His eyes drank in Erika. For a bad moment before she'd arrived he wondered if the magic the actress projected in the shadow land of films would disappear in the real world. It hadn't. Her pale skin was as flawless now as it was before the cameras and wisely was not even touched with cosmetics. The lashes framing those luminous brown eyes were luxuriant and her every move had an unconscious and amazing grace.

He realized he was staring and wrenched his gaze from Erika. Potter was entering the drawing room, bearing fresh tea and another plate of thinly cut sandwiches. Giles was talking to Erika. "Where's the wonder boy? Lost him along the way?"

"A nice dream," Marcia muttered and accepted another cup of tea.

"Mickey decided to run back from the village," Erika said. "Felt he needed exercise, so I drove his car back."

Giles's charming smile flickered. "Wonders will never cease. Mickey allowed you to drive his precious Ferrari. Love is a wonderful thing."

Honoria was glancing at her watch. "I do hope he gets back soon."

"He'll be a while yet," Borthwick told her. "Probably out in the garage wiping every speck of dust off that gleaming finish."

Everyone with the exception of Forsythe and Erika laughed. Rose-pink color, much like her aunt's, flooded into the girl's face and she said hotly, "You love making nasty remarks about Mickey, don't you? He enjoys quality goods and takes care of them. Would you prefer him to neglect his possessions?"

"Small chance." Borthwick was laughing. "Remember what happened to that little script girl who draped Mickey's leather jacket around her shoulders when we were on location in Spain? He had her fired on the spot."

"And what about that business when poor old Carruthers slipped into Mickey's dressing room and nipped a swallow out of his bottle of scotch? Pure murder!" Giles said.

"Stop it!" Erika was on her feet.

"Do sit down, dear," her aunt soothed. "I'm sure they're only joking."

Dividing a dark look between the director and the writer, Erika slid back into her chair. Forsythe tried to distract her. He asked, "Who is Mickey? Or is that a secret too?"

This time it was Cochrane who answered. "The famous Michael Dowling, known to multitudes of adoring females as Mickey Darling."

Erika was still irate. "Now you're doing it too, Sam. I expect this picking away from Mel and Giles, but you!"

The feverish eyes in the broad placid face flickered in the girl's direction. "It happens to be the truth, Erika."

"Oh, what's the use?" she muttered.

Marcia said brightly, "You must have seen our Mickey Darling, Robert. You said you'd seen all Erika's films and Mickey co-starred in her latest. What do you think of it?"

Forsythe was beginning to dislike Marcia Mather. Now she'd turned her malice toward him and was doing it gleefully. He *had* seen the film she'd mentioned and had been terribly disappointed. There had been a few moments when Erika had managed to inject life into it but mainly it had been dull and even vaguely funny. There had been rather too much of Dowling's profile and bare manly chest and he seemed to have most of the dialogue. The problem was, the man, despite his amazing good looks, was absolutely wooden. As Forsythe tried to think of something tactful to say he was saved by Giles Eady. The writer was echoing one of his thoughts. "If it had been billed as a comedy it might have gone over," Giles said lazily.

"It was a drama and you damn well know it," Erika said. "Mickey didn't have quite enough experience at that time. He hadn't ripened as an actor."

"I thought he was a bit overripe," Giles retorted.

Erika was on her feet again. "I'm not sitting here and listening to this another minute. It's unfair to Mickey and—"

"What's unfair to Mickey?"

The man they'd been discussing stepped over the low sill of one of the long windows leading to the garden. Michael Dowling, even in a loose exercise suit, was as handsome as he was on the screen. Drops of perspiration dotted his bronzed brow but every hair on his curly head was in place. The famous profile was presented to Forsythe, and when Honoria hastily made introductions it barely moved. Dowling lifted a negligent hand. "Hi, Robert. Now who's been taking my name in vain?" Without waiting for an answer he took a chair beside Honoria and bent forward to see the writer. "While I was dusting the Ferrari down I thought—"

His words were drowned out in a gale of laughter. Even Honoria was trying to turn a chuckle into a cough and Forsythe felt the corners of his own mouth twitching. Dowling looked puzzled and Erika told him, "Pay no attention to these oafs, darling. What were you going to say?"

"I was going to ask Giles if he'd rewritten that scene."

"As a matter of fact I didn't. Thought we'd better discuss it."

"Nothing to discuss. I gave you the notes I made on changes."

Giles wriggled around on his chair, pulling a rumpled batch of papers out of a pocket in the tight jeans. "I think you'd better reconsider. Mel and I kicked it around and if we do it your way we're going to lose the effectiveness—"

"What's wrong with my ideas?"

"In the original script Heathcliff chases Catherine down a winding road on his motorbike. She's running and every motion shows she's terrified, like a mouse with a cat on her heels. Sam says that will be good from the camera angles, very dramatic."

"So? I didn't put any changes in there."

"The changes start as soon as Heathcliff wheels the bike in front of her, narrowly missing her, and then jumps off, looming over her. In the original script Heathcliff simply looks down at her—"

"Through the face visor of a helmet. I told you when I get off that bike I take the thing off. You can't see my face and what people come to see is Michael Dowling, not a damned helmet."

"Keep your shirt on and let me explain. The outlines of your face through the plastic visor are glimpsed. This way gives an ominous, mysterious look to Heathcliff. Anyway, you leave on the helmet, pick Catherine up like a doll and throw her on the back of the bike. Then you roar away and the camera—you tell him, Sam."

Cochrane's restless eyes moved toward the writer and then returned to their scrutiny of the sandwich plate. "It would be a dandy shot. Catherine's profile outlined against that brutish helmet, her hair blowing over the lower part of her face...picture it, Mickey."

"I have and I don't like it. I want to take off that damned thing and—"

"And make that speech you've jotted down here," Giles snapped. "It sounds like a soliloquy. Along the same lines as Friends, Romans, countrymen...It doesn't read, Mickey. Heathcliff would never talk like that."

"This Heathcliff does and that's the way it's going to be."

Giles and Dowling were glaring at each other like two turkey cocks and Forsythe was wondering dismally how Emily Brontë would have reacted to Heathcliff roaring around on a motorbike chasing Catherine doubtlessly attired in blue jeans. He jerked his attention back to the two men and found that Borthwick was trying to act as peacemaker. "Be sensible, Mickey. Giles and Sam and I agree the scene should stay as written. Erika, speak up and say what you think."

"I think," she said placidly, "an actor has a sense of role and it's up to him to decide how he wants to act it."

Marcia examined her nails and muttered, "Love is *really* blind."

The famous Dowling profile swung on her. "You keep your trap shut! Mel, I could care less what you and Sam and Giles think. Erika agrees with me and we're the artists. Rewrite it, Giles."

"And if I won't?"

Forsythe waited for an explosion but Dowling merely touched the handsome column of his neck. "I need a drink."

"I've rung for fresh tea," Honoria told him. "Ah, here Potter is now."

Dowling waved the tea aside and told the butler, "Never mind that. I'll have a scotch and soda."

"There is no scotch, sir."

"I had scotch last night, Potter."

"You, ah, finished the bottle, sir. Would you care for brandy?"

Honoria's face flooded with color. "I'm so sorry, Mr. Dowling. I had no idea. I'd send down to the village but I'm afraid everything is closed now."

The handsome mouth appeared to be setting in a pout and Honoria looked on the verge of tears. It was Giles who told her gently, "Not to worry. If Mickey wants scotch he can get it from his room. He always has a good supply of Glenlivet. As a matter of fact I could use a drink." He winked at the director. "What about you, Mel, and Sam? Better bring down the bottle, Mickey."

"I'll settle for tea," Dowling said hastily. He prodded a sandwich. "What is this? Watercress? I loathe watercress."

Honoria turned the plate around. "There's fish paste on this side. You like that."

He scooped up a handful of dainty sandwiches and turned his attention on Giles again. "As for you, genius, if you don't want to do it my way you can get the hell out. No two-bit hack—"

"Giles happens to be the best scriptwriter in London," Borthwick told him crisply.

"I couldn't care less. Dozens of writers would jump at the chance of working with me." As an afterthought he added, "And Erika. Shape up or ship out, Giles."

Pulling his greyhound body from his chair, Giles glared down at the actor. His expression was murderous but he kept his voice mild. "Nothing would give me greater pleasure. Having my name on the credit list of this dog would be embarrassing. Get yourself another hack."

"Both of you cool off," Borthwick ordered. "You do have contracts."

"Contracts are made to be broken," Dowling said, around a mouthful of sandwich.

"I want Giles and I *do* happen to be the director. You stay, Giles."

The writer's mouth snapped open and Erika reached up and touched his arm. "Please. For me, Giles."

He looked down at her and Forsythe caught a glimpse of his expression. The naked emotion in Giles's face told the whole story. His shoulders slumped and he said, "Mel?"

Borthwick flung his hands up. "Rewrite it Mickey's way."

"Peace at any price, eh? Okay, I'll get started."

As the writer ambled toward the door Borthwick pulled his terrier body up and jerked a thumb at Cochrane. "Should have time before dinner to check the lighting in that upper hallway, Sam."

Honoria, murmuring something about dinner preparations, left close on their heels, and Erika, after dropping a kiss on Mickey's cheek, followed. Marcia made no move to leave and lit a cigarette, staring moodily at the spiral of gray smoke drifting up from it. Dowling had apparently forgotten the unpleasantness and was demolishing a thick slice of cake. For the first time since being introduced he acknowledged the barrister's presence. "Hear you're another one in love with Erika."

Forsythe stiffened but it was Miss Sanderson who said coldly, "I told you Robby is a fan of hers, not—"

"Same difference. Marvelous girl, of course, and she makes an adequate Catherine. Whole movie hinges around Heathcliff though and I'm having a devilish time seeing that role gets full exposure. Everyone fighting me—even Sam."

If he was waiting for Forsythe to commiserate with him he was to be disappointed. "I know nothing about filmmaking,"

Forsythe told him curtly. He was thinking of that word—adequate. *What* a term to use to describe Erika Von Farr. He changed the subject. "How did this house come to be selected for the film?"

"Erika's aunt came up to meet her in London. Funny, Erika's over thirty now and it's the first time she ever met her aunt. Of course, this is also the first time Erika's been in England. Did most of her work in Hollywood and some on the Continent but never England. Erika introduced her aunt around and auntie started dithering on about her house. Mel was sorry for the old girl—it was pretty plain she was broke so he offered to rent the place for the movie." Dowling added generously, "I had no objection. Kind of keeps it all in the family."

"You and Erika are to be married?" Forsythe asked faintly.

"As soon as auntie gives her blessings. If she doesn't I'll talk Erika around and we'll get married anyway, but in some ways Erika's pretty old-fashioned and her aunt is her only living relative." He eyed the last piece of cake and then lifted it onto his plate.

Forsythe was wondering how to break away. Neither Marcia nor Miss Sanderson seemed inclined to make conversation, so the barrister finally asked, "You're an American?"

"Sure am, Robert."

"God!" Marcia grunted and got to her feet. "I'm not sitting through another rerun of 'Yankee Doodle Dandy.'"

"Better watch that mouth or what went for Giles goes for you too," Dowling told her.

"I happen to have a contract too."

"Your part *can* be rewritten."

She shrugged an elegant silk shoulder. "So what? You have me down to about six lines now." She bent and butted her cigarette. "A word of advice for old time's sake, Mickey. If I were you I'd be padding my role, not paring it."

"Is that a threat?"

"Let me put it this way. We're overdue for a nice long chat."

"We've nothing to talk about."

"That's where you're mistaken. And don't leave it too long. Coming, Abigail?"

Miss Sanderson paused only long enough to pat Forsythe's shoulder. "See you at dinner, Robby."

Forsythe looked longingly after the two women, wondering how to break away from Dowling. He had no chance. Dowling was unleashing a flood of words that sounded rehearsed, and in a short time the barrister knew what Marcia meant when she'd said "rerun."

"Yes," Dowling drawled as though nothing had intervened, "I'm an American, a true blue son of Uncle Sam. Born and bred on a small farm in the Midwest..." Forsythe heard all about Dowling's early life and then perked his ears up: "—and I admit women have always helped me along the way. Never men. Take my chance to get off that godforsaken farm. I was seventeen and just about going nuts and then one of my high school teachers came to my rescue. Miss Pike had a face like her name but the fluttering heart of a girl. She put up the dough for me to go to Los Angeles. Said she was interested in my mind." Here Dowling closed one eye in an exaggerated wink and leered suggestively at the older man. "What Miss Pike expected was for me to send for her and she would 'share my life.' Fat chance!"

Forsythe was no longer bored. He was repelled. Hoping to wind up the confidences, he said hastily, "And I suppose when you got to Hollywood fame and fortune were waiting."

"No. A string of menial jobs was waiting. I did some of everything—working in fast food places, pumping gas, parking cars. Then another woman came along. This time it was Junie, who turned out to be an agent. Not one of the topflight ones but she was not doing badly. I parked her car for her and a couple of days later she moved me into her apartment. Said she was interested in my talent." Here Dowling went through the same wink and leer again and Forsythe fought off the impulse to drive his fist into that leer. "After Junie and I played house for a couple of weeks I got restless and told her to find me movie work or I was spreading my wings and flying out of her life. She managed to get me a few bit roles. It wasn't great but it was better than pumping gas or parking cars."

"Bit roles?"

"Parts where I only appeared once. For instance, in one monster movie I was the guy that pointed at the giant praying mantis about to devour a town and yelled, 'Hey, look!' That sort of crap. It was a drag but that was the way I met Marcia Mather. Her name doesn't carry much weight now but at that time Marcia was recognized as a damn good supporting actress. The movie she was appearing in was one of those beach sagas and Junie had got me a part as a lifeguard. Marcia was supposed to come wandering along the beach, spot me, and stop to see if I'd seen so-and-so. The old girl took one look at yours truly in bikini trunks and that was it. Must admit she didn't beat around the bush. Didn't pretend she was interested in talent or mind, just what Mickey had stuffed in those trunks."

Dowling paused and for a bad moment Forsythe thought they were going to go through the wink and leer routine. But the younger man was fishing out a gold cigarette case and matching lighter. He selected a cigarette, made no move to offer his companion one, and lit it. "So...Marcia and I set up housekeeping. Just about broke Junie's heart but what the hell. Marcia could do more for me than Junie. But Marcia had no intention of helping me; she just wanted to keep me on a leash like a poodle. I soon set her straight. Either she'd use her clout to get me a decent part or it was bye-bye doggie. Once she got the idea she did her best but couldn't come up with a thing. I had a couple of screen tests..." Dowling turned an astounded look on the barrister. "Would you believe the damn fools said I couldn't act my way out of a paper bag?"

Forsythe believed it devoutly but mercifully he was spared answering. Dowling rushed on. "I started getting restless and Marcia was at her wit's end. God, but she was infatuated! Jealous as hell. If I looked at another woman she went into a tantrum. I tightened the screws and then she had an idea. She'd always wanted a starring role so she figured she'd fix me up and herself too. She had a fair amount of money stashed away and she borrowed the rest and we produced our own movie. A romantic version of the Trojan Wars—"

"A contemporary treatment?" Forsythe asked, thinking of Emily Brontë and *Wuthering Heights*.

"No, a period piece. Togas and the whole business. I liked the idea. Look great in togas." The actor paused again, this time apparently to savor the picture of his magnificent body displayed in a toga. Then he sighed. "The movie turned out to be a disaster. I was Paris and Marcia was Helen. The reviewers cut the poor old girl to pieces. As one of them said, 'Marcia Mather as the immortal Helen couldn't possibly have launched a thousand ships. Mather would be lucky to launch a leaky canoe.' From that time on her career went steadily downhill while mine went up. I took the lead in a string of oaters." Dowling grinned at the barrister's perplexed expression. "Westerns. I look almost as good in cowboy clothes as I do in a toga and the girls went wild. Screamed and sobbed and tried to rip my clothes off for souvenirs. Fan clubs started and I was away."

"What about Miss Mather?"

"Had to leave her behind. From then on she would've been dead weight. Know it sounds cold but that's survival. I steered clear of Marcia and the first time I've been near her since is on this movie. Mel's a softhearted guy and he gave her a bit part because he felt sorry for her. Then we found out she was a childhood friend of Erika's auntie and I got stuck with her this weekend. All Marcia's done is make snide remarks."

Forsythe pondered. Did Dowling have any idea or did he care what kind of impression he'd just made? He'd exposed himself as the most selfish, unfeeling man Forsythe could remember meeting, and there he sat, looking complacent. "I suppose Erika Von Farr was the next woman to help you with your career."

"Didn't meet her right away. Had to struggle on by myself for a while, Robby—"

"My name is Robert," Forsythe said icily.

At his tone the actor looked up, examined the barrister's long head, light brown hair, and wandered down the elegant length clothed in well-cut tweeds. "Abigail calls you Robby."

"Miss Sanderson is the only one who does."

"Don't get huffy. What's in a name? I get Mickey Darling all the time and I'm not crazy about it, but it is good business. Anyway, after I starred with Erika I became hot property. From now on they're going to pay through their noses for the services of Mickey Darling." He glared at the silver teapot. "God, I wish I had a drink."

"Why didn't you take Giles's suggestion and bring down your Glenlivet?"

"And have those freeloaders gulp it down? I make a practice of not sharing booze. If I started offering drinks around they'd bankrupt me. Hey, Robert, what do you think of this house?"

Startled by the abrupt change of subject, Forsythe glanced around the drawing room. "I haven't seen much of it but it seems charming."

"Charming and imposing but I got a hunch it's a white elephant. Going to be tough to unload. Have to spend a fortune modernizing this place. It needs central heating and decent bathrooms and the hot water supply is crazy. Either comes boiling out of the tap or it's ice cold. And, Robert, believe it or not, there's only one telephone in the whole house. Out in the hall. Can't even have a private conversation. In my house in Hollywood there's a phone in every room, even in the bathrooms. What do you think of that?"

Not much, Forsythe thought. Aloud he said, "Sounds most convenient. Are you and Erika thinking of living here with Miss Farquson?"

Dowling flung back his head to laugh, exposing the bronze column of his throat. "Not this Yankee Doodle Dandy. No, our headquarters will be in Hollywood. Erika has some damn fool notion of keeping this place on, but that's just sentiment. The old family home and that sort of rot." He cast a dissatisfied look around the comfortable room. "We'll have to unload it and that's going to be tough."

"Perhaps the house would be difficult but the land is valuable."

Dowling's head swung around. "The land...what do you mean?"

Silently, Forsythe cursed his rash statement but it was too late. "Didn't you notice the housing estates on the other side of Bury-Sutton?"

"Housing estates? Oh, you mean subdivisions. Hey, I see what you mean. There's good money in that business. Lots of land around this house too. Wonder how many acres auntie has."

Forsythe again felt a sense of revulsion at the avarice in Dowling's expression and voice. Just what had he started? He pointed out, "I hardly think you need concern yourself. Miss Farquson is not old and she obviously loves this estate."

"Auntie will be better off in a smaller place. And so will those two servants. That butler can hardly creep around, although I must admit his wife is a great cook." Pulling his long frame up, he walked around the room. He paused by a superb piecrust table and drummed his knuckles against it. "Know anything about antiques, Robert?"

"Very little," Forsythe said hastily and untruthfully.

"Thought you would, you being English."

"Being English is scarcely synonymous with being an expert on antiques."

"Abigail was saying you have a country home yourself. Been in the family for centuries and full of old stuff." Plucking up a Dresden shepherdess from the mantle, he spun it around. "You must know something about values. What about things like this?"

Forsythe had had enough. He was on his feet and heading toward the hall. Over his shoulder he flung back a few words. "I'm *not* in the habit of evaluating my hostess's possessions."

There was no answer and as he threw open the door he noticed that Dowling had picked up the Georgian teapot and was engrossed in its silver luster. Whether he was admiring the reflection of his manly features or assessing its market value, Forsythe neither knew or cared.

Chapter Four

Forsythe slowly mounted the staircase to the first floor. He felt chilled, his leg was stiff and sore, and his head ached dully. This was shaping up as a trying weekend and, despite the presence of Erika Von Farr, he regretted letting Sandy talk him into it.

On the landing he found Potter, who took him in hand, introduced him to an upstairs maid who was an older edition of the pert little girl Forsythe had glimpsed on his arrival, and finally ushered him into a large comfortable bedroom.

"About dinner," the barrister queried, "I understand dress is informal."

"Extremely, sir. The, ah, gentlemen connected with films generally wear those denim trousers, although the ladies do make some effort. Miss Honoria always dresses, sir. I took the liberty of laying out your dark suit. The bathroom is located at the end of the hall and if you should require anything further, ring for Sarah."

"Are the maids related?"

"Sisters, sir, and newly arrived to help with the guests. Mrs. Potter and I are getting a bit beyond our prime."

A masterful understatement, Forsythe thought, as the butler made his laborious departure. He sought the bathroom, found the hot water supply as erratic as Dowling had predicted, and, taking Potter's gentle hint, donned the black suit that the officious Mrs. Meeks had slipped into his case.

When he answered the dinner bell he was glad he had dressed. Giles, Borthwick, and Cochrane had merely exchanged sweatshirts for sport shirts but Dowling had changed into designer jeans and a blue silk shirt with a matching scarf at his noble throat. The actor's clothes might have been casual but they were costly. Touches of gold accented his costume, a Patek watch on one wrist, a link bracelet on the other, a glint of gold plating on his belt buckle. To carry out the blue theme, Forsythe was amused to notice deeper blue points peeking from a silk breast pocket. The ladies had made notable efforts. Marcia had discarded her white suit and was wearing a peach dress of similar elegance; Miss Sanderson looked well in crisp green; and Honoria Farquson was resplendent in a vintage and fussy dinner dress that happily echoed the color of her cornflower eyes.

It was Erika who caught and held most of the attention. She was dressed simply in something black and filmy that reminded Forsythe of a modified harem costume. She wore no jewelry and her face was innocent of makeup but she'd loosened her hair and it fell around her face and shoulders as softly and darkly as the chiffon flowed around her body. Candlelight was kind to everyone, but for Erika it was a perfect setting and Forsythe had difficulty tearing his eyes from her. He noted that Giles Eady was having the same difficulty.

Dinner proved to be unexpectedly pleasant. Potter, with the assistance of the shy little maid, wavered about serving course after course of the most delicious food the barrister had ever tasted. He'd expected the strains and bickering of the afternoon to continue but harmony reigned. All the film company, including Marcia, exerted themselves to be pleasant. Dowling, seated on Honoria Farquson's right, turned his considerable charm on that lady.

Forsythe applied himself to lobster bisque and covert scrutiny of Erika. For a time conversation was general but in the lull while the soup plates were removed, Forsythe said, "I had always thought of you as an American, Erika, but I understand your parents were English."

"I suppose I'm a true cosmopolitan, Robert." Erika laughed. "I was conceived in England, born in Italy, raised in California."

"Italy?"

"Santa Vittoria," Dowling told Forsythe. "Picturesque little place but it seemed deadly dull."

"A quiet village," Honoria agreed. "You've been there, Mr. Dowling?"

"Passed through it. Last summer. I did stop to try and pick up a souvenir for Erika but everything was gimcrackery and ridiculously overpriced."

Erika turned toward her aunt. "I know so little about how my mother and father met and married, Aunt Honoria. By the time I was old enough to be curious about the past, mother was…well, reticent on the subject."

"My fault." Honoria sighed heavily. "Von—her name was Veronica but she was always called Von—we had a dreadful and foolish quarrel when I learned she intended to put you in that first film. You were so young, only eight, and I'm afraid I said unforgivable things. I wrote and accused Von of fulfilling her own ambitions in your life. I hesitate to say this but Von was never a really good actress, dear."

"She knew that. Mother always said she was barely competent and that her brother Erik had all the acting ability in their family."

Soft color glowed becomingly in Honoria's face. "He had. If Erik had lived he would have been a great actor. He had the depth, the passion, the courage…it was a great pity he died so young. For years I've bitterly regretted not making up the quarrel with your mother. Von refused to write and I would have liked to have gone to Los Angeles and…I'm sure if I had we would have made up. But I couldn't leave the colonel and by the time he'd passed on, Von was dead." She sighed again. "We should really make time for the people we love."

Sam Cochrane's bass chimed in. "We all do it, Honoria. All of us live with guilty memories of not making time when we should have."

His eyes, which had been darting from one object to another, suddenly steadied and focused on Michael Dowling. Those words and Cochrane's gaze had an immediate and rather surprising effect on the actor. The salad fork dropped from his hand and Forsythe could have sworn the younger man shivered.

Erika was speaking to her aunt again. "I'm sure mother loved you and was unhappy about your quarrel too."

"I had no business to interfere, dear, but I was concerned about the effect on a little girl. Child actresses sometimes have difficult lives."

"I can't really picture life as being any different, Aunt Honoria. I was truly a movie brat. From the time I was on pabulum I was on a set. Mother took me with her—"

"But who looked after you?"

"Anyone who was handy. Script girls, wardrobe women, makeup people, anyone who was handy. It was a colorful exciting life for a child and I've never regretted it." Erika looked pleadingly at the older woman. "Do tell me about mother and father and Uncle Erik."

"Later, my dear, perhaps after dinner. I shouldn't want to weary my other guests."

Surprisingly it was Dowling who told her warmly, "We'd be enchanted to hear about them, dear lady."

Honoria glanced doubtfully around the table and the other guests made murmurs of agreement. "Very well, but if I become too wordy do tell me. Where shall I start, Erika?"

"At the beginning, please."

"That's a long time ago but…My mother was a great deal younger than the colonel and she died at my birth. If she had lived I've often thought Charles and I might have been different people. I only know mother through other people's memories. Charles was four years older than I and he remembered a bit about her and, of course, the Potters were devoted to her."

"Did grandfather not tell you about your mother?"

"The colonel never mentioned her. I have often fantasized that he loved her deeply and that's why he was rather unkind to me—"

"Bosh!" Marcia Mather said. "My father was her doctor and he said all the colonel wanted from his wife was an heir and a housekeeper. The colonel was *naturally* unkind."

"*De mortuis*," Honoria chided gently. "Regardless of his reasons I'm afraid my childhood was a lonely one. There was my brother and the Potters and after a time Teresa and you, Marcia, but father refused to send me away to school and I took lessons in this house with a governess. I remember weeping when you and Teresa went to school. There were vacation times and those were happy days but then Charles and the other two musketeers would go back to school and I would be alone again. As I grew older it became lonelier. The young people had their own lives and when I was eighteen I found I'd lost them."

"Teresa had married husband number one," Marcia mused. "And I was touring with my first play." Candlelight and memory softened her features and her voice had no touch of its usual acerbity. "Charles...he'd had a row with the colonel and left, hadn't he?"

"My brother had always rebelled against the colonel, by fits and starts that is. Charles was as terrified of father as I was but he was a boy and that made a difference. This argument was the worst they'd ever had. The colonel threatened disinheritance and Charles fought back and it ended with my brother flinging out of the house and going to London. To make his fortune, he said."

"Just how did he propose to do that?" Marcia asked. "Charles certainly wasn't outstanding at school and he had no profession, did he?"

"No, Charles wasn't brainy and the quarrel with the colonel was about a profession. The colonel wanted my brother to follow in his own footsteps and take a military career. Charles refused. The colonel had also picked out a wife for my brother, a county girl who was a wonderful horsewoman. Charles insisted she should be, as she looked exactly like one of her mounts. So, they had a tearing row and my brother left."

Miss Sanderson had finished her salad and was regarding her hostess with interest. "Teresa said you spent some time in London, Honoria."

Honoria watched the dish of grilled trout being shakily handed around by the butler and then she confided, "A little over a month. That was Charles's doing. Father wouldn't allow my brother to see me or correspond with me but I arranged a mail drop—"

"Like the secret mail drop we had when we were children?" Marcia's long-lashed eyes looked into the past and a small smile tugged at the corners of her painted lips. "Do you remember, Honoria? We pledged ourselves to secrecy and the Three Musketeers signed a solemn vow in blood. Funny, I never have broken that vow."

"Neither have I, dear. And it wasn't in blood. Teresa wouldn't prick her finger and I believe we ended up signing in tomato paste. Charles arranged a simpler way of corresponding with me. He sent his letters to the Potters. He was fond of me and worried about me alone with the colonel so he'd spoken to our Aunt Maud—"

"I remember her. The colonel's only sister. She looked much like him."

"She did look like the colonel but she wasn't the least like him. Aunt Maud agreed to write her brother asking I be sent to her in London, pleading illness. She sent a lovely letter telling him she needed me, I'd be such a comfort and could read to her and so on. The colonel didn't want to let me go but he had to. And so—" Honoria's eyes shone like blue stars—"I left home and went to London."

"And there you met my mother and uncle," Erika breathed.

"Such an exciting time, dear. Here I was a country mouse and plunged straight into what the colonel would call bohemia. Charles had become enthralled with the stage and through it had met Veronica and Erik Larsen. He was living in their tiny flat and had fallen in love with Von. They made room for me and it was close quarters. Three tiny rooms and only one bedroom. Von and I slept there and Erik and Charles bedded down on a daybed in the sitting room." Honoria's laugh tinkled with remembered mirth. "What a wonderful world. How free! I had visions of becoming an actress and watched all their rehearsals. Both Erik and Von had small parts in a play and Charles was working as a stagehand with it."

"Mother and father were married," Erika said dreamily.

"Von was wild about my brother and although he loved her he was as vacillating as he was with the colonel. One moment Charles was all for marrying, the next he was worrying about being cut off without a penny and how he would make a living. But Von was decisive and she got all the licenses and made the arrangements and one day when we drank a great deal of wine she acted. Charles was tiddly and proposing again and before we knew it Erik and I were witnesses and they were married."

Erika's high brow crinkled in thought. "Do you think father regretted it?"

Her aunt took a sip of wine. "I must speak honestly. Perhaps Charles would have in time but there was no time. For two weeks the four of us were wild with happiness and then…then Charles and Erik were both dead. Charles had bought a motorbike and there was an accident. The colonel always insisted the boys had been intoxicated but they weren't. I was there and I know."

"After the accident—what did grandfather do?"

Honoria bent her bright head. "He came to London and brought me home. He refused to attend his son's funeral and he wouldn't even speak to Von. One should not speak ill of the dead but he was a bitter, unforgiving man."

Her niece gave her a searching look. "And you went with him?"

"I had no choice. I'd been raised and conditioned to absolute obedience. I no sooner would've disobeyed him at that point than I'd have disobeyed God. But then he went too far and for the first and last time in my life I rebelled."

"What did he do?"

"Von sent me a letter—again by the Potters—and told me she was pregnant. I took it immediately to the colonel. He was outraged that Charles had married an actress but he had a strong feeling for the family line. He'd thought it had ended when my brother died. Now he had a chance for a grandson. He went to Von, reconciled with her, and brought her back here. I was so happy to see her. I loved..." Honoria's voice broke.

Reaching past Borthwick, Erika patted her aunt's hand. "If it's too painful, don't go on."

Honoria dabbed at her eyes. "The pain should be past. This was over thirty years ago. No, I'll finish. The colonel started on Von, telling her what she could do, what she couldn't. He made plans for her and for her baby. He was dictatorial. But Von was not a Charles or an Honoria. She was a high-spirited, independent girl. Von fought back and the colonel threatened to disinherit both her and her child." She gave a shaky laugh. "Von made a most improper suggestion as to what the colonel could do with his money and he ordered her out. I went with her."

Erika beamed at the older woman. "You finally did rebel."

"A short rebellion. But, yes, Von and I went to the Continent. She'd had a little insurance from her brother Erik and I borrowed some money from Aunt Maud and we went. We lived cheaply in hostels and took buses and trains. Once in a while fellow travelers would give us rides in their cars. Although both of us mourned our dead we were young and Von's pregnancy didn't bother her. We were in Germany and France and Switzerland and then we went to Rome. It was frightfully expensive there and suffocatingly hot. A nice German couple offered us a ride and we went north with them. By that time Von was close to term and very heavy and uncomfortable. When we reached Santa Vittoria she wasn't feeling at all well and so we stayed there. At that time the only inn was terrible and the local doctor, who spoke fluent English, took pity on us and took us into his own house." Honoria looked fondly at Erika's vivid face. "And that was where you were born."

"And then mother took me to the States and you went back to grandfather. Why on earth did you return?"

"Von begged me to go with her to Los Angeles. She said we could get jobs in films and raise you. I was going to borrow more money from Aunt Maud and go and then a wire arrived about the colonel. He'd had a heart attack and it sounded as though he was at death's door. I *had* to return. It was my duty. When I got home I found he was not ill at all. But that was the end of my freedom."

"Aunt Honoria, grandfather lived for twenty-nine years. Why didn't you break away and come to mother and me?"

"I wanted to. Ever so many times I thought I'll go but then the colonel would become ill or pretend he was and I'd think, I'll go as soon as he's well enough to leave. Time passed and then Von and I had that silly quarrel about you, dear, and it was too late…"

Erika was resting her chin on her palm, misty dark hair falling forward across the classic lines of cheekbones. "Did the colonel—grandfather—never want to see me?"

Her aunt hesitated and then said slowly, "I'm afraid not. If you had been a boy the colonel would have struggled to take you away from your mother. But he didn't…he had little use for girls. But you were valued, my dear, by your mother, by me. You were most precious to both of us." Honoria glanced up at the butler, who was hovering over her chair. "Oh, Potter. Is it that time already? Yes, do have coffee served in the drawing room." She gave a little laugh. "I'm afraid people who are much alone tend to be garrulous when they have a chance to talk. You must forgive me. I've monopolized you."

Dowling sprang to help her up. "Dear lady, you've been absolutely enthralling." He offered an arm to Honoria, the other to her niece, and led the way to the drawing room. Forsythe and Miss Sanderson were the last to leave. In a low voice Miss Sanderson asked her employer, "What do you think of our hostess?"

"Reading between the lines of life with father I'd say she should receive a nomination for sainthood."

Coffee and brandy were being served but Dowling waved them away, took Honoria's arm and said jovially, "I was wondering, auntie—"

She pulled away and said sharply, "Don't call me that, Mr. Dowling."

"What *am* I to call you? Miss Farquson seems unsuitable." He flashed perfect teeth. "Let's take a turn in the garden and discuss it."

"If you wish." She paused to scoop up a cardigan, draped it around her shoulders, and beamed at her guests. "I know this is a working weekend for you but I do feel you should have a little relaxation. If the weather is fine tomorrow I've planned a treat. A picnic on the river. I can borrow a boat and—"

"I must decline," Giles said hastily. "I'll be working all day."

"Nonsense. All work and no play, Mr. Eady. We'll discuss it later."

The writer wandered to the window and looked up at the sky. "Seems to be clouding over. Maybe we'll get lucky and have a downpour. I'll offer up a small prayer."

"You don't care for picnics?" Miss Sanderson asked.

"Loathe them. Never could see why anyone would want to sit on the ground and share their food with insects." He took another glance out into the darkened garden. "Can't figure why Mickey Darling is showering our hostess with attention. Yesterday he hardly knew she was around."

Forsythe could have hazarded a guess but it was Marcia Mather who snapped, "Our boy doesn't do anything without a good reason."

The other actress had picked up a magazine and was leafing through it. She flung it down and whirled to face the older woman. "Must you always be suspicious? Mickey is simply being kind to my aunt."

"He'd have to look up the word 'kind' in the dictionary."

Hastily Borthwick asked the writer, "How did you get along with the rewrite, Giles?"

"Only had enough time to look it over. What you need is a magician, not a writer. Can you imagine Heathcliff raving on about his identity, his inner being? The audience is going to be rolling in the aisles." Giles slouched over and lowered his lanky body in a chair near Erika. "I think you'd better consider this carefully, love. If this film goes ahead on schedule you're in a fair way of having your career ruined. Your fans may have stood still for that first film with Mickey but with this one they'll be running for the exits. Even the devoted ones like Robert here will be—"

"I don't want to hear any more!" She presented her back squarely to him.

"I think you'd better listen," Cochrane's deep voice turned all eyes to the shadowed corner where he sat in a wing chair. "Keep in mind the only reason Mel and Giles and I are working on this film is because of you. Mel and I worked with you from the time you were a child. Giles…well he wrote his first script for you when you were eighteen or nineteen. Not only are we all fond of you but we respect your talent."

"Mickey and I are going to be married. You can't stop that, Sam."

"We're not trying to. Marry the boy, live with him, do anything you want, but for God's sake don't work with him. Keep your careers separate. You've been in this business for over twenty years. You know what the score is, how fickle the public can be. Now you're a big name but—"

"For God's sake knock off the father act!" Erika flung her head back, long hair swirling around her shoulders. "You haven't the track record for it. After what happened to Jenny—"

Erika stopped abruptly, the angry color draining from her features, leaving them pallid and stricken. Forsythe glanced around. All of the other people, including Miss Sanderson, looked appalled. He couldn't discern Cochrane's expression but lamplight fell across the huge hands. They were bunched into fists.

"Sam." The girl went to the cameraman's side and stood, every fluid line of her body whispering contriteness, the outstretched hand mutely imploring forgiveness. "Sam, I'm so ashamed...I didn't mean...Sam..."

For a moment the big man was immobile and then the fist relaxed and he reached out to pat the girl's hip. "You're right, little girl, I don't qualify as a father or even as an advisor. Do what you want. It's your life."

For moments no one moved or spoke. Marcia raised her handkerchief and it looked as if she were wiping her eyes. Then Mickey came bolting in through the window and Forsythe, this time, was glad to see him. The actor stood in a dramatic pose, pointing at the window, and when Honoria stepped into the room he scooped her up and hugged her to his side. "Pay attention, people; I have an announcement. Come here, Erika." Reaching out a long arm he pulled her against his other side. "This is the happiest moment of my life—"

"God," Marcia groaned, "he's going to make another speech."

"Not even you can rile me right now, Marcia. So shut up, you're wasting your time. On Monday when we get back to London Erika and I are going to be married. Aunt Honoria"— white teeth flashed down at Honoria and she smiled back—"has given her blessing. It will be a small wedding. No time to fuss and those big affairs are a waste of money but there'll be a reception and you're all invited. Even you, Marcia—"

"Thanks but no thanks."

The white smile faltered and then reappeared. "Suit yourself. There's more news. Not only has Aunt Honoria consented but she's giving us an unbelievable wedding present. Erika, this house and estate is to be ours!"

"No." Erika tore herself loose from his arm and went to her aunt. "We can't accept that. This is your home."

"Don't be a little ninny," her lover told her. "This is what your aunt wants."

Gently Honoria detached herself from Dowling's grasp and embraced her niece. "It's my wish, dear. I can't possibly keep this place on. I simply haven't the funds and the Potters are beyond heavy work. We'll be cozy in a little cottage. Besides, this was your father's home, and his father's and…way back to your ancestors. You will want to keep it on, Erika, and raise your children here?"

"Oh, yes," Erika breathed.

Perhaps she means it, Forsythe brooded, but as soon as Dowling has his hands on it the old family home will blossom into a housing estate. You *damn* fool, he berated himself, you're responsible for this. Your big heedless mouth!

"I'm so happy!" Erika cried and burst into tears.

"Women," Dowling said indulgently.

The girl put out her hand blindly. "Hankie, darling."

He fumbled through his pockets. "Sorry. Aunt Honoria, do you have one?"

She was searching through the pockets of her cardigan. Paper crinkled and she laughed. "Only a shopping list. Marcia?"

Marcia was blowing her nose. "She wouldn't want mine."

Uncoiling himself from his chair, Giles produced a crisp white square and stepped to the girl's side. He tilted her chin up and tenderly blotted tears from her cheeks. Still holding her face up, he murmured, "I'm going to be the first one to kiss the bride." He bent and pressed his lips to hers. It wasn't a fleeting kiss, it was prolonged. There was passion in that kiss and Erika was wriggling to free herself but Giles held her firmly.

Forsythe's attention snapped to Dowling. An unbecoming color mottled the bronzed features and his hands knotted into fists. He raised an arm and Forsythe thought, now we're going to have fisticuffs. Borthwick hastened to intervene. Tapping Giles's shoulder, he said lightly, "My turn," as though asking for a dance. The young man's hands dropped away and Borthwick lightly kissed Erika.

The girl whirled toward Cochrane. "Are you going to wish us well, Sam?"

Picking her up like a doll, the big man brushed his lips across her brow. "I wish you well, little girl; I wish you the best. You deserve it."

He didn't mention what Dowling deserved and none of the other men were offering to shake hands with the prospective groom. Ignoring the actor, Miss Sanderson hugged Erika and then Honoria. Marcia Mather hadn't moved and was staring steadily at the wall. To Forsythe's surprise, Erika ran over to him and brushed her lips over his cheek. It felt like being kissed by a flower, he thought, and that was what the girl smelled like. Fresh and innocent and fragrant. For moments after that kiss he noticed nothing and then he snapped back and heard Dowling demanding champagne.

"I'm afraid we don't have any, Mickey." Honoria told him. Mickey Darling's mouth was arranging itself into a pout. She hastened to add, "First thing tomorrow I'll send to the village for several bottles. For now, we'll have wine. Potter, will you get a bottle, please? The colonel kept a good cellar and we still have some excellent vintages."

Miss Sanderson said, "None for me. I'm afraid I had a bit much with dinner. I'm going to stretch my legs before bed. Robby?"

"I'll join you."

They stepped into the garden and a fresh, cool breeze greeted them. A full moon threw silvery light and grotesque shadows and there was a scattering of stars but Giles had been right. Clouds were piling up ominously in the west. For moments they walked silently and then Forsythe said, "Better get it off your chest."

"Is she out of her mind?" Miss Sanderson exploded.

"By she I suppose you mean the estimable Miss Farquson."

"All she has is this estate and she's going to hand it over to that...that colossal ass."

"I take it you're not one of the multitude of Mickey Darling fans."

"I detest him. He's like something that crawls out from under a stone. A cockroach!"

Forsythe grinned down at her. "I doubt whether cockroaches live under stones. Perhaps you're thinking of a beetle."

"How can you take it so lightly? Oh, I know you don't know any of them but you seem to like Honoria."

"I do and I'm not taking it lightly. Your big-mouthed employer is the one who put Mickey on the trail. Explained to him this afternoon that this would be a dandy place for a housing estate."

"Don't feel badly, Robby. In time he'd have figured that out himself. Funny, I got here when the film group was arriving—Marcia was the only one who came early—and I'd have sworn Honoria had the same reaction to Dowling that I did. Then she makes a complete swingaround and gives him everything she has."

It was Forsythe's turn to console. "Don't blame her. He was doing a job on her tonight that few women could have resisted and as he says himself, he has a way with the fair sex." He touched her elbow. "Over here. Let's sit and let the beauty of the night soothe our savage breasts."

She sank down on the stone bench and appeared to be studying the distorted shadow thrown by a hawthorn. "Dowling was telling you about his women? Did he mention Marcia Mather?"

"Chapter and verse."

"Any other?"

"A teacher he conned into funding his trip to Hollywood and a woman agent he used to get his start in films. A sordid tale but one he viewed with pride to say nothing of satisfaction."

"Completely immoral. I've heard people described that way but he's the first one I've ever met. All he cares about is his slimy skin. And money, of course. He likes expensive trinkets but he's unbelievably cheap."

"You sound as though you're an authority on Michael Dowling."

"I am. Marcia has told me all. Of course I suppose one should be cautious. She practically bubbles over with venom."

"Care to share the details?"

"No!" She softened her refusal. "Robby, some things are best left alone."

"As you wish." Knowing the best way to elicit information from his secretary, Forsythe took out his pipe and proceeded to fill it.

As usual, an appearance of disinterest worked. Miss Sanderson gave him a sidelong look, studied the long fingers deftly packing tobacco into the carved bowl of the pipe, and then asked, "Did you notice Dowling's reaction to Sam Cochrane?"

"Only one incident." He shielded a match and drew lustily on the pipe.

"Which was?" she prompted.

"At dinner. Cochrane made some platitude about people never taking time for the ones they love and looked at Dowling. Mickey had an odd reaction."

"Well, he should. Marcia told me—and bear in mind she hates him—that there's a possibility that Dowling was implicated in Sam's daughter's death. Her name was Jenny—"

"Ah, the name Erika blurted out and then wished she hadn't."

"She was sixteen, hooked on heroin, and pregnant. Marcia didn't seem eager to give details. For a woman of her type she seemed rather emotional about it. But she did say many people thought Dowling was responsible for the child's corruption."

Forsythe shook his head. "That I can't believe. I don't mean the child's death. That kind of tragedy is far from rare. But I can't picture Cochrane working with his daughter's corruptor."

"Neither can I. But Marcia said it's all rumor, no proof. Then there was Beth Borthwick—"

"The director's daughter?"

"His wife. And this isn't rumor, it's fact. Seems Mel was devoted to his wife, why Marcia couldn't see. Mel is surrounded by pretty actresses and it seems Beth was far from pretty. Marcia said she was a dumpy little woman, looked like a brown mouse."

"Doesn't sound like Mickey's type."

"She wasn't and apparently he didn't seem to know she was alive until she came into an inheritance from a grandmother. Then he noticed her and swept her off her feet. Marcia tells me

Dowling has a weird effect on even sensible women. Almost hypnotizes them. Little mouse Beth didn't have a chance."

"Was Borthwick aware of the affair?"

"Very much but he was tolerant about it. Theatrical people appear to take that sort of thing rather philosophically. Marcia said Mel thought it would wear off but then Dowling had to go to France on location for one of his films and Beth followed him without even leaving a note for her husband. A couple of months later Mel heard that Dowling had walked out on Beth, leaving her stranded in a hotel in Cannes. Mel went hotfooting over to retrieve his wife—" Miss Sanderson broke off and twisted a handkerchief in her hands. "When Mel got there he found Beth had chucked herself off her hotel balcony. This time she did leave a note. Told Mel how Mickey had treated her, draining her of her inheritance, and then walking out. She said she was so humiliated she no longer wanted to live."

Forsythe's pipe had gone out but he made no move to relight it. He stared at his secretary. "And Borthwick is working with Dowling, placating him...What kind of man *is* he?"

"Hotheaded, according to Marcia Mather. She said at that moment Mel would have killed Dowling if he could have gotten his hands on him. But that was four years ago. As for Borthwick working with Dowling—he's doing it for the same reason Sam and Giles are. They all have an emotional involvement with Erika Von Farr and Marcia said they're trying to get her to see reason and drop Dowling. Marcia says Giles is deeply in love with the girl and has been for years."

Forsythe remembered the agonized emotion on the writer's freckled face when the young actress had touched his arm. "I fear I'll never understand show business, Sandy. Here we have three people, four counting Marcia, who all have good reason to twist Dowling's neck and they're not only working closely with him but letting him call the shots. I really can't see Sam Cochrane doing this. He strikes me as a man who could be dangerous. How long ago did his daughter Jenny die?"

"Marcia didn't say. The way she spoke, it was only a few months ago."

"Curiouser and curiouser. Does Honoria Farquson know about Dowling's past?"

"Marcia said when she met Honoria in London she told all."

"And what was her reaction?"

"Honoria put it down to gossip and jealousy. And she might be right. As I said Marcia is so full of venom she could be exaggerating." Miss Sanderson shivered and tugged her sweater closer.

"Chilly, Sandy?"

"Uneasy and I've been that way since I arrived." She turned and impulsively squeezed his arm. "I'll admit I was glad to see you, Robby."

He sighed. "Going fey again?"

"You don't *go* fey. I simply get feelings. Remember the one I had in Calvert's studio."

"Vividly."

"And I was right that time." Her pale eyes sought the equally pale moon. "There are undercurrents here, Robby—"

"I'm not surprised. Considering the tangled relationships among this group it would be strange if there weren't."

"It's not just that. It's—" She broke off and got up abruptly. "What's the use? I am cold and I'm going in."

Forsythe grinned up at her. "Allow me to put your feelings into words. 'I could a tale unfold whose lightest word, Would harrow thy soul, freeze thy young blood—'"

"My blood isn't young," she snapped. "You and your quotations. Honestly, Robby, you'd think you had sole rights to *Hamlet*. Try this one and it isn't Shakespeare, so you'll never pin it.

Her lips were red, her looks were free
Her locks were yellow as gold:
Her skin was white as leprosy,
The Night-mare Life-in-Death was she,
Who thicks a man's blood with cold.

"What is that supposed to signify?"

She threw him an icy look. "You figure it out, detective."

"Let's see…who do I know with locks of yellow gold?"

"Don't be so damned literal." Turning on her heels, she strode toward the house.

The barrister called after her, "Got it, Sandy! Coleridge and the Ancient Mariner."

She muttered something that sounded suspiciously like "Get stuffed" and stepped over the threshold of the long window.

Chapter Five

Long after Miss Sanderson had left, the barrister remained in the garden, staring unseeingly at the play of shadows, his pipe clutched in his hand. Then he realized he was chilled and glanced up at the moon. It was almost veiled by a bank of clouds. He got to his feet and lurched, grasping at the back of the bench for support. That ruddy leg again, but it was his fault. The cement seat was too cold to have sat on for so long. Rubbing his thigh, he limped into the house. Only one lamp was lit, shedding barely enough light for him to circle around the furniture. When he opened the door to the hall he found stronger light, and his hostess, who was rounding a corner that he presumed led to the kitchen. She was carrying a loaded tray.

"Allow me," he said and took it from her.

"So kind of you. Did you enjoy your walk, Mr. Forsythe? I notice you're limping."

"An old injury and I managed to get chilled."

"I have a heating pad in my room if you'd care for it."

"No, by morning I'll be fine."

They'd reached the landing and Honoria led the way down the hall. The lighting was subdued here also and caught her hair with a nimbus. Idly Forsythe wondered if this could be the deadly lady from Coleridge's poem. No, Honoria's hair was more silver than gold. She paused at a door opposite his own and he noticed the door was ajar. She switched on lights. "Please put the tray over there. Yes, on the desk will be fine."

He set the tray down carefully and stood back to admire the desk. "Sheraton?"

"My great-grandmother's and a piece I'm fond of. I must make room for it in my cottage. I can't bear to leave it." She looked at the towering four-poster and sighed. "So few things will be able to go with us."

"Will you regret leaving here?"

"Yes and no. I can't say I've had a happy life in this house but it's all I know. I see you've discovered my table of memorabilia, Mr. Forsythe."

"I didn't mean to pry."

"You're certainly not. I'm proud of my souvenirs and I know you admire my niece. As you see I have eight portraits of Erika as a little girl. Von was very good about it." Tenderly the woman touched a small object. "These were Erika's first shoes. Her mother had them bronzed and sent them to me. On every birthday Von sent me a portrait of Erika and when the child was old enough she always encouraged Erika to send a small gift. I've always loved dogs and Erika selected these little china replicas all by herself. And speaking of dogs, here's my Ciara." A shaggy little animal had crawled out of a wicker basket and was rubbing against Honoria's ankles. She scooped the Cairn terrier up and hugged it.

Forsythe patted Ciara's head and the lips promptly pulled back from tiny sharp teeth. "Neither Heathcliff nor Ciara are friendly."

Honoria laughed. "When you get to know Heathcliff he's a powder puff. Ciara is quite old and inclined to be grouchy. I must admit she never has been fond of anyone but Potty—I call Mrs. Potter that—and me. She doesn't even like Potter and he's most kind to her." Honoria looked affectionately down at the dog and added, "In some ways Potty and Ciara are much alike. Both old and rather irritable but protective and devoted to me. Take that tray for instance. Ever since I can remember Potty's made up a tray for me each night. She seems to feel I don't get enough nourishment. However, it is nice to be fussed over even if one does feel like a child at times. I see you're looking at my favorite picture of Erika, Mr. Forsythe."

The barrister had drifted back to the table and was regarding an early picture of Erika. She had been an enchanting child. Dimpled hands clutched a large teddy bear and elf locks fell over huge solemn eyes. He spoke his thoughts aloud, "A lovely child."

"She was four in that portrait. I did so love the child. When we met again recently I was surprised at the initial lack of warmth I felt for her. Still, when one considers that Erika is now a woman and I know little about her I suppose it is understandable."

Honoria was looking distressed and Forsythe hastened to comfort her. "She must have seemed a stranger. In time affection will come."

"Yes, I believe it will. These last few days…I already feel much different. Ah, I see you've spotted my brother's wedding picture." One hand detached itself from the dog and she picked up a faded picture in a silver frame. "We couldn't afford a good photographer and this isn't too clear but here is my brother Charles."

Forsythe looked down at the young man with his arm around a slender dark girl. There was a strong resemblance to his sister but his chin and mouth were weaker. A young Honoria had been incredibly lovely, with a quality of dewy innocence. "Your brother looked so much like you."

"We both took after our mother. She was Danish, an au pair girl when the colonel met her. Charles and I inherited our coloring from her." Honoria smiled. "Charles hated his hair. At school the boys called him Whitey. Erika looks much like her mother, doesn't she?"

"And her uncle. This man is Erik Larsen, isn't he?"

"Yes, that's Erik. Sad he died so young. A splendid young man and what an actor he would have made." Replacing the silver-framed picture, Honoria lifted the one of Erika at four. "The child so resembles her father." She added, "Not in looks, in nature. Now, Mr. Forsythe, are you certain I can't lend you a heating pad for your leg?"

"I don't need it, Miss Farquson, but if you have any books I would like to borrow one. I have a case of books in the car but I don't really want to go out again. Anything would do. I read myself to sleep."

She was stooping to tuck the old dog back in its basket. "I'm sorry, I have no books here. I usually do my reading in the colonel's library. He was a great reader, mainly of military history, but there is a selection of classics and I've added some modern novels. Do help yourself." She straightened. "Please leave the door ajar. Ciara is so funny now, she hates the door closed. Becomes quite restless and nervous. And, Mr. Forsythe, I'd like to say how happy I am that you are able to be with us this weekend."

"And I," the barrister lied gallantly, "am delighted to be here."

As he made his way along the hall and down the stairs he told himself that wasn't wholly a lie. As far as his hostess and her fascinating niece were concerned he *was* delighted. As for the rest of the guests, particularly Michael Dowling, well, that was another matter.

The library was directly across from the dining room and when Forsythe opened the door he found Giles Eady behind the desk, pounding the keys of a portable. In the powerful light from the desk lamp his freckled face was drawn and weary.

"Sorry," Forsythe said. "Didn't realize you were still working."

"Time I knocked off." Giles pulled a sheet from the typewriter and put it on top of a pile of yellow sheets. "Beastly job. Hey, Robert, how do you like this bit of Dowling-inspired dialogue? 'I am a complex man and my love is twisted and devious. Catherine, you will find Heathcliff's love a curse.' I've a feeling Brontë is going to be spinning in her grave." He pulled his lanky frame up and stretched. "What do you think of the colonel's sanctum sanctorum?"

Forsythe had been looking around the square room. It was full of dark leather, heavy furniture, and dark velvet hangings. "I don't fancy it."

"Must have suited the master though. There he is, over the mantel, still brooding over his domain."

Colonel Farquson had been painted in uniform and Sandy's memory of him had been accurate. He was handsome in a cold way. The small dark eyes were like chips of ice and there was a touch of cruelty around the lips. Giles wandered over and stood, his hands clasped behind him, gazing up at the painting. "Genus Heathcliff," he mused. "The colonel would have been a natural for that part."

"I think not. Brontë's Heathcliff called for passion, dark and distorted granted, but definitely passion. There's not a trace of passion in that face."

"You're right. Odd I didn't spot that. You're a quick study on faces, Robert." Giles swung around to face the older man. "Is that the barrister or the detective speaking?"

"Neither. Simple observation."

"Let me put you to the test. You met our little group only today." Giles drummed his knuckles on the desk. "I won't give you the easy ones. Anyone could spot Marcia as shallow and vain and spiteful. I'll give you a tough one. Sam Cochrane."

Forsythe humored the writer. "When I first met Cochrane I compared him with Heathcliff, the four-legged one. But on closer study I'd say the man is more like a rhino, huge and slow, but if he ever charged I'd hate to be in the path."

"Excellent. Now, the golden boy, Mickey Darling."

Forsythe's recent conversation with Miss Sanderson compelled him to say, "Either he's incredibly brave or unbelievably stupid."

"You batted out. The lad is neither brave nor stupid. Dowling's shrewd, or at least, he has a type of low cunning. Try Mel Borthwick."

"The opposite of Cochrane. Quick-thinking, quick-moving. Probably competent."

"Good. The magical Miss Farr."

Forsythe tired of the game. "She's too complex for me."

A wide grin lighted Giles's tired face. "You batted out again. Erika's the simplest of the lot." He watched the barrister as he moved along the ranks of books. "Unless you like Napoleonic history you're wasting your time in that section. The Crimean War is right below it and the Second World War to the right. Over there are a bunch of light romances, our hostess's contribution I would imagine, and at the end are a scattering of classics. There're two copies of *Wuthering Heights* if you're in the mood."

"Not tonight. I want to rest and I'm afraid I might have nightmares of motorbikes and jeans to say nothing of helmets against a background of moors." Running a finger over the line of classics, Forsythe asked idly, "How do you read Miss Farquson's face?"

"She certainly is nothing like father."

"Her mother was Danish."

"Ah, that's where the Nordic coloring comes from. A descendant of the Vikings." Again the attractive grin flashed. "Let me put it this way. If I'd been around thirty years ago and the right age I'd have snapped that lady up. I don't believe in fairy tales but I've a hunch she would have given a man the happy ever after. Too bad she never married."

"See any trace of her in her niece?"

"Nary a one. Maybe Erika's the one who takes after grandfather. Ah, I see you've picked a book. What is it? *L'Assommoir?* Isn't Zola a bit horrific and oppressive for bedtime reading?"

"The horror and oppression was long ago. The only horror that concerns me is today's and tomorrow's."

"How true." Giles thumped the pile of yellow sheets. "Now here's complete horror. Care for a nightcap? All I have is brandy. If you hunger for whiskey you'll have to appeal to Mickey."

"From the little I've seen of him it would be a waste of time. Does he ever share?"

"Only with Erika and that's simply an investment. Goodnight, Robert, sleep tight."

Forsythe headed for bed, a brief session with Zola, and then a deep and dreamless sleep.

Chapter Six

In the morning Forsythe found Giles Eady's prayer had been answered and rain was pelting against the house. When he reached the morning room he found the household breakfasting and the writer, wearing a complacent smile, eating a huge breakfast. Their hostess stood with her back to the room, regarding the rain-drenched garden. Winking at Forsythe, Giles told her, "A shame the rain's spoiling your picnic, Miss Farquson."

"Don't be hypocritical, Mr. Eady. I know you're delighted. As a matter of fact I have an alternative plan. The weather can be uncertain in May, you know. Bright and warm one day and nasty the next."

Giles's smile faded. "Does this plan involve the river and a boat?"

"Of course not." She turned and beamed at them. "You all will enjoy this outing. Our old gardener's grandson has started a business on the family farm. Leslie was a brilliant boy, took all sorts of scholarships, and now has a commercial flower business going. He supplies a number of florist shops in London and—"

"I am not," Giles interrupted, "going to tramp around muddy daffodil fields in the rain."

"Me neither," Marcia said. Her voice was hoarse and the tip of her nose was red and raw. Her makeup was not as perfect as it had been the previous day and she wore a thick tweed skirt and a heavy sweater. "I had a simply dreadful night, feverish, and I could hardly breathe." She'd taken a chair close to the roaring fire and she pointed to the hearth. "Honoria, I'm going to stay right here and keep warm."

"Don't be silly, dear. You can bundle up and you'll be warm where we're going. Mr. Eady, you will not be required to be outdoors at all. As for daffodils, it's well past their season."

"I think it's a great idea," Dowling said warmly. He was at the sideboard heaping his plate from an assortment of silver-covered dishes on a hotplate.

Honoria said firmly, "I've already rung up Leslie Koster and he's delighted to show us through his greenhouse. The boy is tremendously excited, as Erika is his favorite film star."

"Really?" Dowling didn't sound as warm.

"And his wife Ann worships you, Mickey."

"In that case we can't disappoint the lady. I vote we all go."

Marcia sneezed. "Not me."

At that moment a short woman with the build and bearing of Queen Victoria swept into the room. She swept by Forsythe in a rustle of long black skirts and told her mistress imperiously, "You haven't had a bite of breakfast and you were out walking in that downpour before the day was even started. Sit down immediately, Miss Honoria." Honoria meekly obeyed and the cook selected a boiled egg, two rashers of bacon, a slice of toast, and plumped them down before her. "Now eat every scrap." Mrs. Potter calmly accepted compliments on her cooking, raves about the grilled kidney from Dowling, more subdued gratification from Cochrane and Borthwick, and then, with a last admonishment to Honoria, made her regal departure.

Honoria sighed and sliced the top from the egg. "Potty makes me feel about six but she means well."

"She's a marvelous cook," Miss Sanderson said.

"Potty was the only person who seemed to have no fear of the colonel. Remember that summer, Marcia, when we were nine or was it ten and the Three Musketeers had got up to some mischief and—"

"Ten, and the colonel decided Teresa and I were a bad influence on you. He wouldn't let you leave the grounds and we weren't supposed to step onto them. Teresa and I did our best to keep in touch. We sneaked notes to our mail drop telling you about parties and picnics and so on."

"And succeeded in making me feel even worse. I moped around and went off my food and Potty went to the colonel. She told him if I wasn't allowed a normal life and playtime with my friends, Potter and she were handing in their notice. The colonel wasn't worried about Potter but he was terrified of losing a good cook like Potty. He set great store by a good table, you know. So, he had to retract and the musketeers had a wonderful summer."

Erika smiled at her aunt. "Were you really walking in the rain this morning?"

"Before any of you were up. I love walking and rain doesn't bother me at all, in fact, I like it. Now, are we all agreed on our little outing?"

Everyone but Marcia Mather nodded. She stubbornly shook her dark head. Honoria said coaxingly, "I think you will want to come, dear. Leslie does raise flowers commercially but his hobby is experimentation. Would you believe he successfully grafted six different types of roses on one bush? Think of it, *six*."

"I've never cared for roses, Honoria."

"What about orchids?"

Marcia murmured, "Orchids," and looked interested.

She was, Forsythe thought, the perfect type to dote on that fleshy odorless flower.

"Orchids," Honoria repeated. "An entire room devoted to rare species."

"I suppose if I bundled up it would do me no harm. When will we be going?"

"Directly after luncheon," Honoria promised.

That afternoon three cars rolled down the winding driveway and left the Farquson estate. The lead vehicle was a vintage Bentley driven by Honoria with Marcia, muffled to her ears, at her side. In the rear seat were Borthwick and Cochrane. Dowling's sleek Ferrari was next in line and Erika Von Farr, wearing a red anorak that matched the car's color, was his passenger. Forsythe brought up the rear with Miss Sanderson at his side and Giles Eady lounging in the rear seat. Honoria Farquson set a slow pace through Bury-Sutton, where, despite the weather, a number of villagers were moving about. All of them respectfully saluted the Bentley and Honoria, and stared with open curiosity at the Ferrari and the two actors.

Giles chuckled. "Must have set the locals on their ears having two screen idols in their midst. Mickey has been down here soaking in the adulation and possibly charging for autographs. Hauled Erika, much against her will, along with him."

"You're disgustingly cynical," Miss Sanderson chided.

"An occupational hazard."

It was raining even harder. The windshield wipers could hardly keep up with the deluge of water. They passed one of the housing estates, dismal and looking rather squalid, and turned onto a road that, like the one that led to the Farquson house, followed the meandering path of the River Carey. Eventually it ended in a farmyard walled with gray rock, with an ancient stone cottage squarely facing a modern structure built mainly of glass.

"From the looks of this layout I'd say our host is doing pretty well," Giles observed. "Talk about a study in contrasts. The past and the present. I rather like the past. That must be Leslie now. Looks more like a doctor than a gardener."

The plump man greeting Honoria was wearing a spotless, high-necked white coat. He had receding hair and huge glasses the thickness of bottle glass. Through these lenses myopic eyes were peering ecstatically at Erika Von Farr. I wonder, Forsythe thought, whether I wore that expression of absolute idiocy when I met her. He decided he probably had. Leslie Koster hurried them into the modern structure and an entrance room provided with clothes hooks along one wall.

"You had better let me take your coats," he told them. "You'll find this building warm, and in the tropical areas uncomfortably so."

They divested themselves of anoraks, topcoats, and raincoats while he beamed at them. Forsythe could see the man was fairly quivering with excitement. "Ordinarily visitors aren't allowed on these premises but because of Miss Farquson and all…Anyway, the best way to handle your tour is for me to show you around and then you can wander about by yourselves. If you have any questions I would be delighted to answer them. This way, ladies and gentlemen. As you can see this is actually a complex of rooms. We'll start at this end. There is the rose room, the next is devoted to carnations, and here we have begonias and…" Leslie set a rapid pace and they trailed along behind him through a dazzling display of colors and textures and odors. It was hot enough that Forsythe was tempted to remove his suit coat and he envied Dowling and Erika in jeans and sleeveless tops. Their host had his hand on Erika's arm and appeared to be addressing his remarks solely to her. A scowling Marcia tugged at the white jacket. "Honoria tells me you have orchids."

Without removing his eyes from the other actress's profile, he said, "They're at the far end. Now this area is—"

"What's that?" Borthwick asked. "Some sort of laboratory?"

They clustered around the director. The room he was pointing at was a small but well-fitted laboratory. There was much stainless steel and porcelain and it was spotless. Over a counter was a long shelf bearing bottles with black printing on labels that were large enough to be easily read from the doorway. Glancing at the weak eyes behind the huge lenses, Forsythe decided the huge printing was perhaps necessary. "Looks like the lair of an alchemist," Cochrane said in his deep voice.

"Hardly." Leslie laughed. "I make up my own fertilizers and sprays. With some of the delicate plants it's necessary and it's also cheaper than buying them ready-made."

Marcia moved impatiently. "The orchids."

Their host took a few steps and opened a door. "Right in here, Miss Mather. What do you think of that? It's a particularly fine specimen of Phalaenopsis. Observe the color. This is a Vanya. Over here we have Miltonias and Lycastes."

Leslie continued proudly naming the blooms and Marcia was flitting from one plant to another ahhing and oohing. The blast of air from the room was stifling and Forsythe, who cared little for orchids, backed away. He noticed some of the others were retracing their steps. Pausing, he admired a magnificent hibiscus and noticed with some amusement that their host was in hot pursuit of Erika, who was just disappearing into the rose room. Forsythe lost all track of time in those rooms filled with the glory and perfume of blooms. Vaguely he was aware of other people. Cochrane seemed engrossed in variegated daisies, Miss Sanderson was hovering over enormous shaggy carnations, Dowling was in animated conversation with Leslie Koster, whose spectacles turned steadily toward Erika. Dowling seemed to be pumping their host, not about plants, but about the housing estate they'd recently viewed. "I have no interest in such things," Leslie was saying. "I did receive an offer for this property but turned it down."

Dowling cocked his head. "Seems to me there should be more money in selling than in holding on. After all, you could set up elsewhere."

"Kosters," Leslie snapped, "have farmed this land for generations."

Forsythe didn't wait to hear the argument, sentiment versus business, that ensued. He wandered on, glimpsing Honoria examining hanging fuchsias, and paused by Erika's side. She was touching the petals of a pink rose. He looked, not at the rose, but at her. As bad as Leslie Koster, he thought, but what a magical creature the girl is. Every movement she makes is touched with grace. Poetry, he thought dreamily, a poem in human form. Eyes like limpid pools in which a man could lose his soul. He longed to touch her, to feel poetry beneath his hand. She turned her head, misty hair swirling about her shoulders, and she smiled at him. Her words were prosaic. "You like roses too, Robert?"

"Very much," he told her and forced himself away, down another aisle, into another section.

Cochrane loomed up beside him. "I'm glad we came," he told the barrister and added simply, "This is...soothing," and drifted away.

Later, and Forsythe had no idea how much later, he heard Leslie calling their names. He found their host in the doorway of the entrance room. Erika and Honoria were with him and the others were approaching. "Have you seen your fill?" Leslie asked.

"I could never get my fill of orchids," Marcia told him dreamily.

"My wife has prepared tea. She's been excited ever since Miss Farquson rang up. Now, please don't say no. Ann's a fan of yours, Mr. Dowling." Weak eyes examined the actor wonderingly as though looking in vain for the reason for his wife's devotion.

"I never," Dowling told him gallantly, "disappoint a lady."

Coats and jackets were donned and they dashed through pelting rain across the cobbled yard to the cottage. There in a paneled, beamed lounge filled with chintz and copper and, incongruously, Swedish Modern, an elaborate tea was waiting. Waiting also, and completely unnerved by the proximity of her idol, was Ann Koster. She was a round bouncy woman with straight-cut bangs. While they feasted on scones, three different preserves, clotted cream, bread and butter slices, a plate of sausage and ham, and so many small cakes they couldn't be counted, Leslie and Ann produced publicity shots of Erika and Dowling. Marcia Mather ate little and watched morosely as the glossy pictures were autographed. Then Ann, blushing furiously, brought out two movie magazines and showed Dowling articles and pictures across which he indulgently scrawled signatures.

Finally a move was made by Honoria and all of them rose. Their host had disappeared and when they returned to the cars they found what his errand had been. He was carrying a wicker basket and was heedless of the rain flattening thinning hair to his head, drenching his white coat. "Lovely flowers for lovely ladies," he breathed and drank in his lovely lady—Erika.

For Honoria there was an enormous bouquet of long-stemmed roses. She accepted them graciously and as graciously thanked Koster for his time and trouble. Gratefully, Miss Sanderson took a bunch of pink and white carnations. Leslie extended to Marcia a cluster of moist violets in a bed of moss. She looked from her gift to the sheaf of orchids Leslie, with a courtly bow, was presenting to Erika, snorted, and without a word climbed into the Bentley, slamming the door behind her.

The cars rolled out of the yard in reverse order to that in which they'd arrived. The red Ferrari vanished with a cloud of mud and water spurting up from its tires; Forsythe's Rover followed more slowly; and finally, the Bentley, like an aged dowager, made a slow and dignified exit. Miss Sanderson had her long nose buried in the spicy petals of the carnations and Giles no longer lounged in the rear seat but sat bolt upright. "There's going to be hell to pay," he said glumly.

Miss Sanderson removed her nose from the flowers and glanced over her shoulder. "What about?"

"Orchids. Marcia's ready to bite."

"But that's silly. Such a little thing."

"You have yet to learn about artistic temperament, Abigail. Actors throw tantrums, knock their heads against walls, and go into hysterics over the tiniest imagined slight. They're not adults, you know, simply big kids."

Without removing his eyes from the road, Forsythe said, "It seems to me I've heard that expression used about writers too."

"Not this one. I haven't a touch of temperament. Fully adult, worst luck. But if you don't believe me, wait and see."

They didn't have long to wait. Forsythe piloted the Rover into a coach house now used as a garage and found the Ferrari was already in its place. Dowling was lovingly rubbing down its blazing flanks as one might groom a favorite mare. Erika, cradling the sheaf of orchids in her arms, stood close to him. Without looking up from his work Dowling was issuing orders. "Grab a rag; that's a good girl; get to work on the hubcaps."

The girl looked around for a place to deposit her flowers and Giles picked up a clean cloth and bent to the hubcaps. Dowling raised his brows. "Not like you to be helpful. What's got into you?"

"Probably the only chance I'll ever have for contact with your scarlet beast. Think rainwater is going to dissolve it?"

The actor transferred his attention and a dry cloth to the grill. "Ever hear of rust? Trouble with most people is they buy something and then neglect it. Know what I paid for this car?"

Nobody showed any interest in the price, but Dowling proceeded to tell them anyway. He'd worked into the price of leather seats when the ancient Bentley puffed its way into the garage and Marcia erupted from the passenger seat. She stood with her legs straddled, glaring at the exotic blooms glowing against Erika's anorak. Glancing up apprehensively, Giles made a move to get between the two women but he was too late. Marcia spat, "You bitch! You've got everything else, might as well have these!" She threw her violets at the girl, hitting her under one eye, burst into a storm of tears, and lunged out of the door.

Erika called after her and Dowling, without glancing away from a fender, laughed. "She used the right word anyway. If there ever was a green-eyed bitch, it's Marcia Mather. Pay no attention, Erika, she's doing the woman-scorned act."

Erika looked as though she were on the verge of tears and her aunt went to her and took the orchids. "I'll put these in your room, dear." Stooping, she retrieved the nosegay of violets. "They're a bit bruised but Potty loves violets. I'll give them to her."

"Perhaps if you give the orchids to Marcia, Aunt Honoria, she'll feel better."

"I think not. Probably incense her even more."

Borthwick and Cochrane were now out of the Bentley and the director said, "We'd better get in, Sam, and see if we can smooth her ruffled feathers down."

Huge shoulders moved in a shrug. "I suppose we can give it a try."

Cochrane didn't sound hopeful but he did follow Borthwick. Forsythe touched his secretary's arm and jerked his head. As they trotted through the rain Giles Eady caught up with them. Ignoring him, Miss Sanderson said contritely to Forsythe, "I'm sorry I got you into this, Robby."

Giles put a comradely arm around her damp shoulders. "Not to worry. By dinner time all will be sweetness and light."

This time the writer was mistaken. Dinner proved to be an uncomfortable meal. Despite excellent food, candlelight, and wine, most of the faces around the oval table were glum. Not only was Marcia's shapely nose red but so were her eyelids. She didn't say a word, not even to Honoria. As usual Cochrane was taciturn and the generally talkative Borthwick spoke only once, to ask for salt to be passed. Michael Dowling, at Honoria's right, paid little attention to his hostess. He talked incessantly, mainly about housing estates and how foolish Leslie Koster was to hold on to his farm.

"I happen to agree with the boy." Honoria told him. "Kosters have lived on that farm as long as Farqusons have lived here. Money would be a poor substitute."

"Let me tell you about money," Dowling said. "I grew up on a dirt farm in the Midwest and..."

Forsythe stopped listening. This he'd heard before. He was heartily sick of the entire business and was relieved when dinner was finally over and a general exodus began. Coffee and brandy were being served in the drawing room but Giles went in the direction of the library. Honoria was trying to interest her remaining guests in a table of bridge. Miss Sanderson, Borthwick, and Cochrane were persuaded and Potter brought in a card table and proceeded to set it up.

The barrister had every intention of going to his room and

escaping into the pages of a book, but Dowling followed him into the hall. "How about a game of billiards, Robert?"

"Can I play too?" Erika asked.

"You can watch. You're a lousy player but I've a hunch Robert may be pretty good."

Forsythe *was* good so he grimly decided he would play. Do no harm to take this conceited ass down a peg or two. The three of them went into the billiard room, located at the back of the house near the kitchen, and proceeded to play. To Forsythe's chagrin he found that Dowling, although he made unnecessary flourishes, was a splendid player, far out of the barrister's league. Erika proved impartial, applauding every good shot regardless of by whom it was made. Forsythe did his best but he knew what the outcome would be. Finally Dowling struck a pose and, with a flourish, made a brilliant bank shot. He stood back and grinned at the barrister. "That's it. Licked you. You're not bad, Robert, but out of your class."

Muttering a silent curse, Forsythe racked his cue. It was then he noticed the silent figure leaning against the doorjamb. Marcia had changed into a caftan of a rich ruby velvet. Makeup was applied with a lavish hand and she'd managed to almost hide the redness around her nostrils. He could catch the scent of strong perfume from where he stood. From behind him, Dowling asked sarcastically, "Decided to stop sulking, old girl? Care to have a game?"

"I don't play games. I'd like to have that overdue chat."

"Talk away."

She jerked her head. "Upstairs, Mickey Darling."

He was chalking his cue. "Anything you want to say, you'll have to say right here."

"I don't think you'd care for that."

At her tone he glanced up. "Why the change? You're looking like a cat full of cream."

She took his arm. "Come along, Mickey."

For a moment he seemed indecisive, then he shrugged. "Don't go away, Robert. I'll be back shortly for a rematch."

Erika was staring after them. "What is she up to now?" Turning her head she told Forsythe ingenuously, "Marcia doesn't like me."

"I rather gathered that. Would you care for a game while we're waiting?"

"I'm not good at it. I've played a few times with Mickey but he's such a wonderful player he makes me nervous. But I would like to try, Robert."

Forsythe set the table up and allowed the girl to take the first shot. He felt suddenly content and at peace. The quiet of the room was broken only by the thud of cue against ball, the rustle of Erika's long cotton skirt as she moved around the table. He paid little attention to his own game, content to watch the girl, the grace of her wrists as she handled the cue, the soft fall of her hair against her face, the shadows cast by lashes on high cheekbones. As she bent and straightened he could smell her odor, a perfume entirely different from Marcia Mather's, this one the innocent fragrance of growing things. This exquisite creature, he thought dismally, is soon going to be the wife of Mickey Darling.

He wondered whether Dowling did have any affection for her. Whether he'd been misjudged and did actually love the girl. Hopefully Forsythe considered the expression on the actor's face when Giles Eady had claimed his kiss, the fury and the anger. Perhaps...then Forsythe shook his head. He remembered a week he'd spent at a client's house in Kent. The client, an aging man named Smythe, had a consuming passion, the collection of antique lusterware. It was kept behind locked doors, in glass cases lining the walls. As a special favor he'd unlocked the doors and while Smythe proudly showed the barrister the objects in the cases, another guest, this a rather brash young man, wandered to a small table in the center of the room where the prize of the collection was standing under a glass dome. Lifting the dome, he picked up the tiny vase and was turning it in his hands. Smythe turned his head, saw what was going on, broke into a howling rage, and ordered the young man from the house. Smythe's expression had been exactly that of Dowling's when Giles had kissed his fiancée. So, Forsythe admitted, Erika was only another possession, the star of his collection. After Dowling drained her dry, took everything he could get, she'd doubtless join the other discarded young women in his past.

A tide of red rage swept over the barrister. He could understand how Borthwick, Cochrane, and Giles felt. Magic was rare and should be protected and cherished.

Erika's voice broke into his reverie. "I asked if you were letting me win, Robert."

Forsythe opened his mouth to deny this and then to his horror heard himself quoting from Euphues. "'So beautie allureth the chast minds to love, and the wisest witte to lust.'"

The girl was looking at him without comprehension and Forsythe didn't blame her. A dignified barrister, he thought, a man nearing middle years, bleating quotations like a lovesick calf!

"I don't—" Erika started to say.

"Mr. Forsythe!"

He spun around. Honoria stood in the doorway, a hand clasped to her breast. "Come quickly! Mickey is shouting something down the stairs. About Marcia. She must be hurt or ill."

Forsythe dropped his cue and ran past her. A group of people were standing at the foot of the stairs, their faces turned upward. On the landing Dowling was leaning against the banister for support. "Don't any of you understand? She's having a fit of some kind!"

Forsythe took the stairs two at a time with Miss Sanderson at his heels. Wordlessly Dowling pointed down the hall. A door stood open spilling light across the carpet. Forsythe pulled to a halt. In the middle of the bedroom was a round table covered with a lace cloth. On it sat a tray with a partially full bottle of whiskey and an unopened bottle of mineral water. Beside the tray a crystal glass lay on its side, amber liquid draining from it, puddling on the lace. A chair was lying on its side and near it, on the Turkish carpet, sprawled a figure in ruby velvet.

Miss Sanderson grabbed at his arm. "Watch the glass."

He circled around the splinters of glass and knelt. Marcia lay on her back. The caftan was twisted and hiked up over her long white legs. The skin of her face was mottled and empty eyes stared sightlessly at the ceiling. The horror was her mouth. Painted lips drew back from her teeth in a dreadful rictus, as though she were silently screaming. Forsythe's hands moved over her throat, over her wrists. He sniffed at her lips and then looked up at his secretary. "Keep them out, Sandy."

Miss Sanderson stretched out long arms, barring the doorway. From somewhere behind her, Honoria called, "I rang through to Doctor Blake's home but he's out on an emergency. Shall I—"

"No rush now, Miss Farquson." With difficulty Forsythe pulled himself up. He'd forgotten about his bad leg but it was making its presence known. "She's dead."

"What is it?" Borthwick demanded. "Heart attack, stroke?"

Dowling's handsome face poked over Miss Sanderson's shoulder. "She had a fit! When I got back from the bathroom with the glass she was jerking all over the floor." He added as though it mattered greatly, "I dropped the glass and it broke."

Forsythe limped toward the door. "Sandy, go down and ring up the police. The rest of you get out of here. I'm shutting this room up until they get here."

"Why? This is my room. I've got a perfect right—" Dowling broke off and the color drained from his face. The glowing bronze skin turned suddenly muddy. "What happened to her?"

"She's been poisoned."

Dowling let out a howl, not a shout, more a scream. He jerked Miss Sanderson's arm down and stepped in front of her. One sandal came squarely down on a shard of glass but he didn't seem to know it.

"She had a drink of *my* whiskey." He looked wildly around. "Don't you understand? *My* whiskey. Someone tried to kill *me*."

Then, incredibly, he broke into a high-pitched laugh, a laugh of pure hysteria.

Pushing the man from the room, Forsythe closed the door on his laughing face.

Chapter Seven

Forsythe woke slowly and with reluctance, feeling hardly up to the effort of opening his eyes. In the dim light his secretary's face hovered above him. Sandy looked as exhausted as he felt. Violet shadows encircled her eyes and her skin was ashen. Removing her hand from his shoulder, she pulled back the curtains and brilliant sunlight dazzled him.

He struggled up against the pillows. "Fine day."

"As far as weather is concerned, yes."

"What time is it? I feel as though I'd only just put my head down."

"After eleven. You can't have been in bed long. I didn't get to my room until four and you were still down with Chief Inspector Parker. I hated to waken you but your presence is urgently requested."

Pushing his legs over the side of the bed, he reached for his robe. "I rather thought Chief Inspector Parker had drained me dry last night, or I guess I should say this morning."

"Reinforcements have arrived from London."

"Parker didn't waste any time yelling for help. Anyone we know?"

"Chief Inspector Adam Kepesake and his man Friday, Detective Sergeant Brummell."

Forsythe stretched and looked at the napkin-covered tray. "Breakfast?"

"Coffee and rolls. The best I could do. Things are a bit hectic in the servants' quarters."

Forsythe sat down and poured coffee. "Potter and his wife seem unflappable."

"They are and the older maid, Sarah, is taking her cue from them but her sister Edie is in a dreadful state."

"How are our hostess and the other guests?"

"Honoria is in bad shape. I insisted she remain in bed this morning. Erika's hands are full with her fiancé. They're barricaded in the late colonel's bedroom and a password is needed to enter. Mickey Darling certainly made a spectacle of himself last night. As soon as you shut the door he proceeded to go into raving hysterics. Most of us just stood around embarrassed and helpless but Cochrane came to the rescue and batted the golden boy right across the face. After that Erika led him away sobbing."

Forsythe spread marmalade lavishly on a roll. "*That* I wish I could have seen. So the dynamic duo are with us. How are Kepesake and Beau Brummell?"

"The chief inspector still resembles a male model and as usual poor Beau looks as if he'd slept in his clothes. What an unlikely nickname for such a slovenly man."

"With that surname I suppose it was inevitable. But we could have drawn worse officers. Kepesake and Brummell are bright and competent. Are you and I on the list of suspects?"

"No. I had the impression the chief inspector was a bit disappointed about that. But seeing we only met this group of people a couple of days ago it's a little difficult to uncover a motive." Miss Sanderson perched on the foot of the bed. She looked disconsolate and her next remark bore that out. "To think, Robby, I was responsible for pushing this vacation. Right now I wish I was back in our chambers and my peaceful flat was waiting."

Draining his cup, he stood up. "Can't turn back the clock, Sandy. Have they decided the type of poison and its source?"

"You were bang on. Cyanide, and quite possibly from Leslie Koster's little lab."

"That's what I thought. The crystals, once they hit liquid, have quite a distinct odor and I remembered seeing a bottle boldly labeled 'cyanide' on Koster's shelf. Now, you'd better get out of here, Sandy. I have to shave and dress. Maybe I'll feel human when I do. Tell the gendarmes I'll be with them in half an hour."

"Better make it sooner. The chief inspector is champing at the bit."

When Forsythe arrived at the colonel's library he found Chief Inspector Kepesake looking impatient. The air was blue with smoke and Kepesake was inserting another cigarette into his jade holder. Miss Sanderson's assessment of his looks was dead accurate. He was a model of sartorial elegance and his hair looked as though he'd had it freshly styled. The hazel eyes were as deceptively kind as ever.

"Ah, Forsythe, come in. Do be seated. You have a habit of turning up, don't you?"

Forsythe took the chair across the desk from the chief inspector. "Do I detect the words 'like a bad penny' tickling your tongue?"

"Definitely not. I'm delighted you're here. Nothing like having a skilled observer. Now, you met Chief Inspector Parker of the County Constabulary last night." Forsythe nodded at Parker. He looked youthful for his rank, a trim young man with a pink boyish face. As though to counteract that look of dewy youth, Parker had cultivated a fledgling mustache that succeeded in making him look still younger. The jade holder moved. "Of course you know Sergeant Brummell and this is Police Constable Summer of the County Constabulary. Summer, open a window a crack; the smoke is making my eyes water." Kepesake's gold lighter flickered and he lit his cigarette.

Forsythe contemplated the remark about a skilled observer. Kepesake was not in the habit of buttering him up. "I don't know how I can be of assistance." He nodded at the stack of files on the desk in front of Parker. "I told Chief Inspector Parker all I know last night."

"Fully and concisely, and I appreciate it. But I must admit I seem to be out of my depth. I've never dealt with theatrical people before and, reading over those statements, I find I'm confused. And artistic temperaments! Mr. Dowling flatly refuses to come down for an interview. Sent a message if I wanted to see him I could damn well go up to him."

Forsythe grinned. "Probably terrified he'll be attacked on the stairs by an ax-wielding maniac. What do you find puzzling about the statements?"

"The way these people babble on and on. Volunteering every detail. With the exception of—what's his name?"

"Cochrane," Chief Inspector Parker said. "Samuel Cochrane. He's the head of the camera section and supposed to be top-notch in his profession. It was like pulling teeth to get anything out of him. All the rest told me their life histories. Made no bones about either hating Michael Dowling or, in Miss Farr's case, adoring him."

"Yes, they do speak freely," Forsythe agreed, thinking of Dowling's confidences the afternoon he'd arrived. "But you must remember they're not like people in other professions. Their entire lives revolve around drama."

Kepesake removed the butt from his holder, snubbed it out, and inserted a fresh cigarette. "You realize what we have here, Forsythe? With the exception of you and Miss Sanderson we have an entire household with the opportunity and the motives to want Michael Dowling dead. I've drawn up a list of people above suspicion. You and Miss Sanderson head it and other than you there are only two names. The maids—Sarah and Edith Perkins."

Parker was fingering his fledgling mustache. "I think Miss Farquson's name should be included on that list. I grew up in Bury-Sutton and I've known her all my life. She's a gentle old-fashioned lady."

"Gentle ladies have been known to murder before," Kepesake told him dryly.

"Not Miss Farquson. If there was an ounce of violence in her I tell you where it would have come out. She'd have murdered her father. If there ever was a candidate for a bloody murder it was that devil."

Kepesake shook his head. "Miss Farquson stays as a suspect. She had opportunity and a good motive."

Forsythe was loading his pipe. Might as well add to the smoky atmosphere. "Are you convinced *Dowling* was the target?"

"Not convinced but it doesn't seem likely the poison was meant for Miss Mather." Leaning over the desk, Kepesake tapped the file folders neatly arranged before his colleague. "In every one of these statements, including the butler's and cook's, it's evident the speaker was aware of Dowling's…ah, peculiarity in regard to his personal possessions. Mr. Eady states that 'Mickey Darling wouldn't give a man dying of thirst a drink from his water bottle.' Mr. Borthwick says that in all the years he has known Mr. Dowling he never offered a drink. Apparently the only person he ever shows generosity to is his fiancée, Miss Farr—"

"Erika," Forsythe stiffened. "Could the poison have been planned not only for Dowling but for Erika?"

"That thought occurred to me," Parker said. "But, again, all of them are aware that Miss Farr never touched whiskey. She hates it. All she drinks is wine and an occasional martini."

Kepesake nodded his head. "I can't see a murderer trying to kill either Miss Farr or Miss Mather by putting cyanide in Dowling's whiskey bottle. Referring again to the statements, no one was aware Miss Mather was in Mr. Dowling's room last evening. They claim they never went upstairs after dinner. Is that right, Forsythe?"

"Miss Farr and Dowling and I were in the billiard room. Miss Mather came to see us there, demanded that Dowling speak with her, and they left. Miss Farr and I were together until Miss Farquson came to sound the alarm. I can't tell you about the others."

"Miss Sanderson vouched for the bridge players. Said Mr. Cochrane, Mr. Borthwick, and Miss Farquson didn't leave the drawing room until they heard Dowling calling down the stairs. Mr. Eady says he was here in the library working."

Sergeant Brummell spoke for the first time. "Miss Mather might have told someone earlier that she was going to talk to Dowling last evening."

His superior swung around. "How would they know it would be in Dowling's room? It could have been anywhere in the house."

With a big hand Brummell rumpled his already untidy hair. "Miss Mather hated Dowling. Maybe she poisoned herself trying to get him convicted of her murder."

Kepesake turned back to the barrister. "You must have received some impression about the woman's character. What do you think, Forsythe?"

"She wasn't the type. Marcia Mather was vindictive and I believe would have gone to many lengths to avenge herself on Michael Dowling but…no, I can't see her sacrificing her own life."

Parker frowned. "If Miss Mather was the target only one person could have killed her. Michael Dowling."

Leaning back in his chair, Kepesake blew a perfect smoke ring, regarded it, and muttered, "That would have been an incredibly stupid move. Dowling would be the only suspect. Forsythe, is he a stupid man?"

Forsythe took his time answering. Chief Inspector Kepesake seemed to regard him as an expert on the film people. He put his thoughts into words. "I've only known these people for about forty-eight hours. Hardly long enough to be an expert on their characters. I was told that Dowling is quite shrewd; the actual words were 'he has a type of low cunning.' My impression of him, for what it's worth, is that although he's vain and arrogant and totally insensitive he's not stupid. He strikes me as a person who values his own hide."

Parker laughed and even his laugh was boyish. "Reminds me of what that writer, Eady, said to the same question. 'Mickey

Darling,' he said, 'would have slipped the poison in Marcia's glass, not the bottle. Wouldn't catch the golden boy ruining a bottle of good liquor.' The way these people talk!"

His colleague from the Central Bureau didn't seem to care for Parker's lightheartedness. Giving him an admonishing glance, Kepesake said sternly, "No matter how colorful they are, there's a murderer among them. But how to pick him or her out? That director, Borthwick, raved on about Dowling being responsible for his wife's suicide. Giles Eady admitted he hates Dowling's guts, fights with him constantly, has been in love with Miss Farr since he met her years ago—"

"I like the words he used," Parker broke in. Apparently his colleague's reprimand hadn't quenched him and he wore a broad smile. "He said Miss Farr 'couldn't even see him' and it had been 'love at first slight.'"

This time Kepesake didn't spare a glance in Parker's direction. "Take Samuel Cochrane—Forsythe, have you heard about his daughter?"

"A little. Not specific details."

"A sordid and horrible business. Cochrane admitted he'd heard rumors that Dowling was the man responsible and it wouldn't surprise me if there was a connection there. This is in strictest confidence, Forsythe, but Narcotics Division have had their eyes on Dowling for months. Seems they had an anonymous tip that the actor was smuggling drugs into the country—"

"A user?" Forsythe interrupted.

"A dealer. The tipster said he's supplying hard drugs to members of the theatrical community. Narcotics Division haven't been able to catch him at it. But to get back to Cochrane's daughter…Parker, perhaps you'd better fill Forsythe in."

Parker was now as serious as Kepesake. "Had to drag the information out of the poor chap. According to him his daughter Jenny was a good girl, never gave a bit of trouble. Her mother died when the child was four and Cochrane raised her with Jenny's godmother's help. Said he blames himself and Marcia Mather—"

"Marcia?" Forsythe blurted.

It was Kepesake's turn to smile broadly. "Ah! I see our sleuth didn't ferret that tidbit out. Shame on you, Forsythe! Yes, Marcia Mather was the girl's godmother. Carry on, Parker."

"Cochrane says he and Miss Mather were too busy to keep a proper eye on the girl. Jenny was left in the care of a housekeeper. The same old story. The girl pretended she was staying overnight at friends' houses and sneaked out on the sly to meet a man. He hooked her on drugs and got her with child. Four months ago the girl locked herself into her bedroom and took an overdose. At that time Miss Mather was on the Continent and Cochrane was in the States. Rumors reached Cochrane about Dowling, but he said there was no proof the actor was the monster who had done it."

For a time they sat quietly, the silence broken only by the tick of a mantel clock and the rustling as Parker leafed through a folder labeled with Samuel Cochrane's name. The constable stood practically at attention near the window; Brummell slouched with an elbow on the mantel, seeming to study the tips of his unpolished shoes; Kepesake was gazing off into space. Forsythe gazed past Brummell's shoulder at Colonel Farquson's narrow dark face. He fancied there was a gleam of sardonic amusement in the painted eyes.

Parker broke the silence. He cleared his throat. "I asked each of the men the same question—were they responsible for the attempt on Dowling's life. Here their answers are, Mr. Forsythe." Pages flipped over. "Cochrane—a blunt 'No.' I asked him what he would have done if he'd had proof Dowling was the man responsible for his daughter's suicide. Answer—'I wouldn't have poisoned him. I'd have torn him apart with my bare hands.' Melvin Borthwick spoke at some length. He said at the time of his wife's death he went looking for Michael Dowling with a revolver and if he could have found the man he'd have shot him." Parker glanced up at the barrister. "Damning statement, isn't it? But then he said Mrs. Borthwick died four years ago and Dowling had sense enough to keep clear until he—Borthwick—

had cooled down. Borthwick stated that he would never forgive Dowling but he had long realized nothing could bring his wife back and his children—he has three—have lost their mother and he can't deprive them of a father. Borthwick also said, and I quote, 'Four years is a long time to keep rage at a fever pitch. I'm not that type of man. I flare up and then simmer down. I also realize Beth was an adult and no one forced her to run after her lover. No, I did not try to poison Michael Dowling.'"

"Giles Eady?" Forsythe asked.

Parker flipped open another file and his lips twitched. "'I assure you I'm sorry poor Marcia was killed in Mickey Darling's stead. I also assure you if I'd made the attempt I wouldn't have gotten an innocent bystander. And, no, I did not try to poison the golden boy.'"

Tapping his pipe dottle out in a glass ashtray, Forsythe spoke to Chief Inspector Kepesake. "That list of the people you don't suspect…I notice Erika Von Farr's name isn't included."

"I haven't interviewed her yet. The only people I've had time to see are Miss Sanderson, briefly, and now you. But I've read over the information Parker got last night and yes, Miss Farr is still among the suspects. She had the same opportunity as the others to obtain and use the cyanide. Correct me if I'm wrong but any one of you could have slipped into Koster's laboratory and taken the cyanide. After you returned from your visit to the greenhouse any of you could have gone into Dowling's bedroom and put the poison in the whiskey bottle."

Forsythe closed his eyes, his mind running over the events of the previous day. "We didn't stay in a group at the greenhouse. All of us wandered around engrossed in the plants. It's not one large room, you know. It's a series of rooms. It would have been simple to get the cyanide without being observed and there the bottle was on the shelf, clearly labeled—"

"Leslie Koster's eyesight is poor," Parker broke in. "At school we called him 'the mole.'"

Forsythe's eyes snapped open. "What does Koster use cyanide for?"

"Fertilizer," Parker told him. "Koster gave me a long lecture on every type he makes up. Seems he uses"—he flipped through a notebook this time—"a combination of lime and carbon as well as other names I can't even pronounce. He's never worried about having the poison sitting on a shelf. He handles the mixing himself and says few people except staff are ever allowed in the greenhouse. Koster was reluctant to admit the poison could be his but did say the level seemed lower in the bottle than it was the last time he'd used it."

"Then he has no idea how much is missing?" Forsythe asked.

"None. All we know is there was enough poison in that whiskey bottle to finish off the entire household."

Forsythe focused his attention on Kepesake. "Very well. The poison was accessible to any one of us. Again, any one of us could have gone into Dowling's room before dinner. Let's get back to Erika Von Farr. Certainly she had the opportunity and could have gotten the means, but what motive could she have to want Dowling dead?"

"Haven't discovered any yet but I'm keeping an open mind."

"And Miss Farquson?"

"A good motive. She admitted Miss Mather had filled her in on Dowling's lurid past. Do you think she wants to see her niece, the only relative she has left, marrying a man like that?"

"Miss Farquson also stated that she didn't believe a word that Miss Mather said," Parker said stiffly. "She said Miss Mather obviously had a grudge against the actor and was trying to make trouble. Miss Farquson has also given her blessing to her niece and Dowling and is going to deed over this estate to them when they marry."

"That's what she *said*," Kepesake pointed out.

"Miss Farquson's word is inviolate. And what about the Potters? How can you possibly suspect those old people?" Parker demanded.

"It wouldn't take much strength to open a bottle and pour cyanide into it."

"How did they get the poison? They weren't at the green-house. And just what would be the motive? They're a fine old couple. I've known them all—"

"—your life," Kepesake finished for him. "I'm afraid, Chief Inspector Parker, you're allowing personal relationships to cloud your professional judgement. Miss Farquson could have given them the poison and from what you've told me about those old servants they'd cut off their arms for their mistress." The local inspector subsided grumbling and Kepesake appealed to Forsythe. "Now, you've got most of what we know. For God sake's clarify the picture for me."

"In what way?"

The chief inspector's hand moved along his hair as though he was tempted to run his fingers through it and then dropped away from its perfection. "These theatrical people, I can't make head or tail of them. Here we have three of them, four counting the dead woman, who have good reasons for loathing the ground Dowling walks on. And what do they do? Work closely with him. Spend a weekend cooped up in this house with a man who was responsible for one woman's suicide, and suspected of the horrible death of a girl little more than a child. Why?"

Before Forsythe could answer, Parker, who appeared to have his second wind, said slyly, "Giles Eady answered that already."

"I read it. 'Show biz.' Spare me any more of that man's pithy comments."

"Eady made sense. Said in the film business if you worked only with people you liked you wouldn't be working."

A brick-like color was sweeping across Kepesake's face and the hazel eyes no longer looked kind. Forsythe hastened to intervene. "Perhaps I can help there. I understand all of them, except Miss Mather, are involved emotionally as well as professionally with Miss Farr. They're working on this film because of her and are hoping to talk her out of appearing with Michael Dowling. Now, it might be helpful if you could fill me in on Dowling's description of his talk with Miss Mather."

Kepesake jerked his head at the younger inspector and turned his attention to another cigarette. The constable coughed and opened the window wider. Parker flipped through his papers and selected one. "Dowling wouldn't come downstairs last night. I had to go up to the room he'd locked himself into and Miss Farr was with him. Dowling refused to let her leave so I took both their statements there. He said when Miss Mather and he went upstairs they turned into his bedroom. Miss Mather's room was farther down the hall near the bathroom and they just automatically turned into his. They sat down at the table and Miss Mather proceeded to beg him for a larger part in the film, told him her career was in jeopardy and a larger role would make it easier to get other jobs. Dowling turned her down flat. He said the actress then became abusive, throwing up things from their past, claiming he had ruined her. To quiet her down he suggested they have a drink. As he had only one glass in his room he left her and went down to the bathroom, where he'd noticed a row of glasses on a shelf. The glass looked a bit dusty and so he took a moment to rinse it out. When he got back to his room he found Miss Mather hadn't waited. She'd poured whiskey in the glass and it was tipped over with its contents all over the table. Miss Mather was on the floor, jerking and twitching around. Dowling said he didn't dream of poison; he thought she was having a fit of some kind. He ran to the top of the stairs and called down for help."

Up to this point the young policeman had been brisk and businesslike. Now he grinned and said with relish, "My wife is a Mickey Darling fan. Drags me to every picture he's made. I wish she could have seen him last night. A bowl of jelly!"

Kepesake grimaced. "Mr. Dowling is coming down here to *me*. No way I'm going up to him. Well, you know all we do now, Forsythe. Any ideas?"

"You had one piece of information I didn't. I had no idea Miss Mather was Jenny Cochrane's godmother." Forsythe got up. His leg had stiffened up again.

"One moment. We do have another piece of information. I wasn't going to give it to you but—" He swiveled around. "What do you think, Beau?"

"I'd give it, sir. Mr. Forsythe's close as a clam."

"And we have reason to know that only too well, don't we? Very well. Before the County Constabulary arrived last evening, Miss Mather's room was given a hasty search."

Forsythe sat down again. "Are you certain?"

"The upstairs maid was. Beau and I took her into the room this morning shortly after we got down here. Her younger sister, Edith, is a mess. So scared she can hardly talk, but this older sister is a levelheaded woman. Sarah Perkins took one look and said someone had been rummaging around in the dead woman's room. Sarah said Miss Mather was meticulous, and when we entered the room the bottom drawer in the chest was ajar, with a sweater hanging out of it. The top drawer, where the woman kept her hankies and scarves, was a jumble. Sarah swore they were always perfectly piled, the edges aligned. Not only that but the bedspread had been hiked up and the lower sheet pulled out as though the mattress had been lifted. Sarah said she'd been in Miss Mather's room to turn down the bed during the dinner hour and all was in order at that time."

"Hmm." Forsythe gazed at the colonel's portrait without seeing it. "A small item. Nothing of any size could be hidden under a pile of hankies or scarves. You said before the county police arrived. Are you certain?"

"As soon as we got here Summer went to Miss Mather's room and locked it." It was Parker's turn to swivel toward his constable. "Isn't that right, Summer?"

"That's correct, sir. The butler gave me the key from a ring; seems there's only one key per room and they generally aren't used. I went directly to the victim's room and locked the door. Kept the key right here"—he patted the breast pocket on his tunic—"till Chief Inspector Kepesake arrived. Gave it into his hands, sir."

"In that case," Forsythe mused, "the search must have taken place after Marcia Mather's death. Between dinner time and the time of her death only Marcia Mather and Dowling were on the first floor. I closed myself into Dowling's room with the body and Sandy joined me as soon as she'd rung through the police. Let me see…the body was discovered at about eleven. Chief Inspector Parker and his constables arrived at—"

"Eleven thirty-seven, Mr, Forsythe," Parker told him. "We had to drive from Elleston. I know what you're going to ask. Which person could have gone to Miss Mather's room and searched it in that time span? The answer is everyone in the house."

"Not again?" Forsythe asked.

Parker's notebook snapped open again. "I've made a list of movements. After you closed yourself in the murder room the three men—Borthwick, Eady, Cochrane—came downstairs in a group. Eady offered the others a drink of brandy in this room." His eyes lifted and he pointed to a tray with an assortment of glasses and a decanter. "Cochrane declined and headed for the front door. When we got here he was pacing up and down the driveway in front of the house, soaked to the skin from the downpour. Borthwick went along with Eady. He gulped down a brandy and left Eady alone here. Says he went into the drawing room, built up the fire, and he was there when we arrived."

"Erika Von Farr?" the barrister asked.

The younger chief inspector said, "Had to take Dowling in hand. There was an unpleasantness after you closed them out in the hall and Dowling got completely out of hand. Cochrane slapped his face and Dowling broke down and started to cry." Looking rather pleased, Parker continued, "Miss Farr told her aunt she was taking Dowling to her own room, but Miss Farquson's a very proper lady and wouldn't hear of it. Ended up with Miss Farquson ordering her niece to take him to the only bedroom not in use, one that had been her father's, so they went to it. Dowling wanted to lock the door and there wasn't a key, so Miss Farr went downstairs, found the kitchen in an uproar with her aunt trying to quiet down Edith Perkins, and finally got the key from the butler. She went back to the colonel's room and it took some time to get in. Dowling had piled furniture in front of the door. The two of them spent the rest of the time there."

Parker paused to catch his breath and Forsythe prompted, "Miss Farquson?"

"She went downstairs and found Potter looking for her. Edith Perkins was in an awful state, figured she was going to be murdered at any minute, so Miss Farquson went to the kitchen where Sarah and Mrs. Potter were trying to calm the girl. Miss Farquson managed to quiet Edith a bit, got some tea in her, and then decided to go to the morning room. Miss Farquson said she needed time to compose herself. The Potters were all over the house. So, Mr. Forsythe, any of the people here could have made a hasty search of Miss Mather's room."

"Borthwick was in the drawing room," Forsythe pointed out. "Anyone using the stairs would have been spotted by him."

"The doors were shut. Borthwick said he wanted privacy."

This time Kepesake did run his fingers through his hair. "Damnedest thing I've ever seen. Like shadow boxing. Why couldn't you have kept an eye on these people until Parker got here, Forsythe?"

"Rather difficult to be in two places at one time. And I thought it was best to remain at the scene of the crime." He regarded Kepesake warily. "Why are you baring your breast like this?"

"As I said, I need any help I can get. The media is bombarding the gates. I have constables down there fending them off. Television crews, reporters, radio outfits…my neck is on the line. Going to be pressure from all directions."

"I have never," Forsythe said bluntly, "thought you had a high opinion of me."

"You're wrong." Kepesake flipped up a hand. "Tell him, Beau."

Sergeant Brummell flopped into a chair beside the barrister's. "The chief and I admire you. Sure, we've had our differences but take that case of the moor murders last year. If you hadn't spotted that those three schoolgirls weren't wearing undershirts, we'd never have caught up with their killer. I guess you've been lucky but you got an eye for little things, things nobody pays any mind to. That's what the chief is trying to tell you."

"Well said, Beau!" For a moment Forsythe thought Kepesake was going to applaud. "Little things, that's your forte. You and Miss Sanderson make quite a team. And you're right on the spot. Perhaps you'll notice something or maybe you already have and—"

"I don't suppose you'd consider letting Sandy and me leave. We're not on your suspect list."

Pulling himself up, Kepesake stretched. "You're both staying right here."

"One hell of a place to spend a vacation."

"Let's put it this way, Forsythe. The sooner this case is cracked, the sooner you can get on with your vacation. Now, get to work and spot those tiny details."

"It will be impossible to keep us here after the inquest."

"Ah, but when will that be?"

Indeed, Forsythe thought, when will the inquest be? It looked as though Chief Inspector Kepesake was determined to get as much help as he could from a lowly barrister and his secretary.

In the hall outside the library two people were waiting. One was Samuel Cochrane, who had time only to nod before Constable Summer ushered him into the room. The other was Miss Sanderson, an apron tied around her narrow waist and a feather duster clutched in one hand. She raised her brows and Forsythe told her, "Borders on police brutality. The chief inspector is intent on keeping us around. Feels out of his depth with this crowd and wants us to act as spies."

"Nothing but cheap blackmail!"

"Precisely. I'm feeling a trifle peckish. Is lunch laid on?"

"A buffet in the morning room, but I was thinking of packing a basket and we'll eat outside. There's a summer house at the foot of the garden."

"Fine idea. The walls do tend to close in. I'll wait for you there."

The barrister wandered out the front door, through the portico, and down the winding driveway. He reached the final curve and from there could see three stalwart constables, aided by Heathcliff, guarding the gates. Retreating, he strolled across rich turf toward the garden. Sunshine beamed warmly down, blossoms wafted their scent, and with the Georgian house well behind him, he began to feel more cheerful.

Chapter Eight

Aften a time, Forsythe found he'd lost his bearings. Directly ahead was a low hedge and as he drew level with it he spotted a kitchen garden. Near the hedge the full black moon of an ample behind was poised over a row of radishes. He cleared his throat and the black moon rose in stately motion until it assumed the proportions of a look-alike for the royal Victoria. Mrs. Potter, even with her skirt hiked up and a scarf hiding her topknot, bore an uncanny resemblance to that lady. She also wore an expression indicating that she too was not amused.

"Looking for something?" she rasped.

"The summer house."

"Go back to those lime trees. Follow them. An idiot couldn't miss it."

Forsythe thought of Adam Kepesake and decided he might as well get to work. He offered a small olive branch. "Nice garden."

"Should be. Miss Honoria works her fingers to the bone on it." Mrs. Potter bent to her work.

Digging his pipe from his pocket, Forsythe proceeded to load it. "You've been on the estate a long time."

"Over half a century. Potter and me come before Miss Honoria was born." The cook critically examined a radish and then dropped it into her basket. "Never had a child of our own."

An oblique way, Forsythe thought, of letting me know they regard Honoria as a daughter and are not about to gossip about her. He tried another tack. "Seem to be a lot of locals milling around by the gates."

"No doubt having the time of their lives." Mrs. Potter snorted and hoisted herself up with less dignity than the first time. "Telling everything they know and a sight they don't to get their pictures in the papers or see themselves on telly. All I can say is they got mighty short memories. Miss Honoria's done a lot for them. Just last winter spent money for her own coat on one for the Widow Clement. Told her she was a fool but she says she can stand the cold better than the old lady. Lot of thanks she'll be getting!"

Encouraged by this long speech, Forsythe sent out a feeler. "I suppose you knew Miss Mather when she was a child."

"Didn't take to her then and felt the same when she come down here last week. Naughty, sneaking brat Marcy Mather was. Always thinking up mischief and then laying it on Terry Sanderson or Miss Honoria." The withered lips seemed to be trembling on the verge of "good riddance," but then they firmed. She contented herself with saying, "Never came near Miss Honoria all these years. Must admit Miss Teresa did some better. Didn't mind her but liked her sister a sight better. Miss Sanderson dug in and helped this morning. Kept Miss Honoria in bed where she ought to be too."

Cupping his hands, Forsythe managed to get his pipe going. "Miss Mather didn't seem to like the colonel."

"Who could?" The cook gathered up her basket and appeared to be about to leave.

Forsythe used the same tactic on her as he did on Sandy when she was reluctant to confide. He gave all of his attention to the smoke trailing from the pipe bowl. It worked. "Killed his wife, he did. Cruel man! Made the kiddies' lives hell.

Drove Mister Charles away, and he died too. Spent all his life punishing Miss Honoria."

"I imagine he held her responsible for her mother's death."

"That and other things. Pray for him every night, I do."

Forsythe blinked. "For Colonel Farquson?"

"Get down on my knees and pray. Say to the Lord, Keep that sinner burning in hell! Fry him good!" Turning her back, she moved away like a small galleon breasting the sea. Black draperies wafted behind her. So did a few words. "Evil shall be punished, I always say."

Indeed it should, Forsythe thought, but the sad fact is that it seems to happen so infrequently. Punishment appears to be meted out, quite unfairly, to the good—to people like Honoria Farquson who gave up a winter coat so an old widow would be warm.

Leaving the kitchen garden, Forsythe set off toward the lime trees. When he reached them he found they'd been planted in a double line. The boy from the village had not been cutting here, and grass, high and lush and damp, was knee-high. Someone had come this way before him. In places the tall grass was tramped down into a tangled mat. When he came out in a sunny clearing he could see the summer house. It was whimsical and had a roof like a pagoda with heavy pillars supporting it. He mounted shallow steps and found Honoria spreading a check- ered cloth and Sandy holding a wicker basket in one hand and a pitcher tinkling with ice in the other.

"Where have you been?" Miss Sanderson demanded.

"Lost my way and had to ask directions. Mrs. Potter and I had a little chat."

"Potty?" Taking the basket, Honoria set it down and started to unpack it. "She must have taken a fancy to you. Seldom Potty speaks to anyone but Potter and me."

"She wasn't exactly talkative. How are you feeling, Miss Farquson?"

She lifted her face and that face was composed, with no sign of swollen eyes or tears. But the cornflower eyes looked

246 E. X. Giroux

older, immeasurably saddened. "I'm coping, Mr. Forsythe. Life must go on and I have guests to look after. Unfortunately I'm losing the maids and if Abigail hadn't offered to help out I don't know what I would do. You've both been very kind."

"The chief inspector has agreed the girls may go?"

"He was far from eager to send them back to the village but Chief Inspector Kepesake realized Edie couldn't be kept on. That child has always been a timid, flighty girl and she's convinced she's in danger here. Sarah was willing to remain but I feel her place is with her sister. Now do eat, Mr. Forsythe, we must keep up our strength."

Nothing loath, Forsythe helped himself generously to cold roast beef, vegetable salad, and accepted a glass of lemonade from Miss Sanderson. Honoria extended a plate of rolls. "Do have one. They're freshly baked. What did you and Potty find to talk about?"

"This and that. The villagers down at the gates and your father."

A wan smile touched the woman's lips. "Did she tell you about her prayers? Ah, she did. Potty fancies herself as a devout Christian. Both she and Potter come from chapel families, yet she sees nothing wrong in asking for the poor colonel's soul to burn for eternity."

"Poor?" Miss Sanderson asked sharply.

"A bare recital of the colonel's life is not fair to the man. You must remember he was a professional soldier, accustomed to command, and he retired too early. He was miffed at being passed over for promotion. The colonel had private means and he was financially secure but here he was on this estate with only his two children. I'm afraid he did treat us as soldiers and demanded absolute obedience. Yes, he had a sad life. The colonel was quite incapable of loving and as a result he never knew what it was to be loved."

Miss Sanderson looked far from convinced and Forsythe hastened to say, "Mrs. Potter had a low opinion of Marcia Mather too."

One capable hand waved. "That was because of me. Marcia was a mischievous little girl and she did tend to get the musketeers in trouble. I remember once…" Her mouth softened and the cornflower eyes glinted with memory. "Marcia stole a bottle of liquor from Doctor Mather's cabinet. Gin, I believe. Your mother, Abigail, was having a garden party at the vicarage and Marcia poured the gin into the punch. It was some women's group being entertained, one connected with the church, of course. The ladies pronounced the punch delicious and drained the bowl. I understand Mrs. Jenkins, she was the butcher's wife, had to be carried home. That took a little doing as Mrs. Jenkins was a stout lady."

"Marcia blamed this on you?" Miss Sanderson asked.

"On your sister and me. The vicar was a man who believed in not sparing the rod—"

"I remember," Miss Sanderson said feelingly and touched her lean bottom.

"Teresa had to sit on a pillow for a week."

Forsythe pulled out his pipe and tobacco pouch. "Were you spanked?"

"The colonel didn't believe in corporal punishment. He watched and carefully decided what Charles and I were most fond of. In this case it was my pony. I called him Butterscotch and I adored him. The morning after the garden party debacle I went to the stable to take him his carrot and Butterscotch's stall was empty. The colonel had arranged to sell him. He told me bad girls could not have ponies."

Forsythe neglected his pipe. He found he was hoping the cook's stern God was listening to her prayers. "So, Marcia was a troublemaker."

"In a way. But she was such a high-spirited girl and so pretty, much prettier than Teresa or I. I remember her hair. Her mother trained it into ringlets and it was thick and such a lovely chestnut color. How Teresa and I envied those ringlets. Teresa had barely a wave in her hair and mine was as straight as a string." She touched fine, silver-gilt hair and sighed. "Such dreamers the three of us were. Teresa called us the dream makers, but Marcia always insisted we must work to make our dreams come true."

Miss Sanderson propped her elbow on the table and turned toward the other woman. "What were the dreams?"

"You were never close to your sister as children, were you? And you spent so much time with your Aunt Rose. Well, Teresa dreamed of a life of wealth and ease."

"She certainly has that."

"Yes, and Marcia got her dream too. She wanted to be a beautiful, famous actress."

"And your dream?" Miss Sanderson asked softly.

"For a time I wanted to be an actress too. But I was greedy and wanted a husband as well, who would love me devotedly, and we'd have a large family. At times I had the number up to eight children and found names for all of them. Both Marcia and Teresa obtained their dreams. I never did."

"I wonder how happy it made them," Miss Sanderson mused. "Teresa seems terribly discontent."

"The only contentment the poor girl ever had was with her first husband, but then she left him. Teresa went looking for Howard later, you know. After she lost her second husband…or was it the third? No matter. Teresa was heartbroken to find Howard had remarried, quite happily, and had children. As for Marcia, I think her life was as unhappy. When I met her again I found her cynical and rather callous." Honoria stared down at her plate. "Perhaps I was most fortunate. I never achieved my dream but for many years I still had it."

Forsythe asked gently, "You no longer do?"

Her mouth trembled. "My dreams died with Marcia, Mr. Forsythe. It's very hard to lose a childhood friend. One feels as though a part of one's past has also died." She glanced over his shoulder. "Mr. Cochrane, how nice of you to join us. Have you had lunch?"

The cameraman mounted the steps with his ponderous tread and lowered his bulk onto a bench facing the barrister.

"Not yet. I came from another session with the police and it ruined my appetite."

Honoria set a plate in front of him and told him firmly, "You must have something." She helped him liberally to meat and salad and placed a bun on the side of the plate. "Abigail and I have to get back to work, Mr. Cochrane, but this plate had better be emptied. Did Chief Inspector Kepesake give you a bad time?"

"Same questions as the other chief inspector asked last night but worded differently." Heavy shoulders moved in a shrug. "He got the same answers. Just came from the gates and all hell is breaking loose down there."

Honoria shook her shining head. "The public is so horribly morbid, isn't it?"

"Got a taste for blood all right." Cochrane's face split in a wide grin. "Looks like that mastiff of yours is better at crowd control than the constables are. He caught a reporter trying to climb over the wall and had at him."

"I do hope Heathcliff didn't injure him."

"Only his pride and one pant leg but my guess is it'll be a while before anyone else tries."

Honoria had finished repacking the basket and Miss Sanderson tipped the pitcher over Cochrane's glass. "Bit weak, Sam, the ice has melted down."

"It's wet and that's all that matters." Cochrane drank thirstily. Over the rim of the glass he watched the women making their way toward the double line of limes. "For their age those two move pretty spryly."

Forsythe had also been watching them. Sandy walked along with her easy loping stride and Honoria took shorter, running steps, but they both covered ground rapidly. "They're not exactly ancient. Miss Farquson is on the sunny side of fifty."

"And Abigail?"

"Anyone's guess and knowing Sandy that's all it ever will be."

The cameraman seemed to have recovered his appetite. He was devouring his lunch. "Didn't mention it in front of

250 E. X. Giroux

Honoria but those villagers are having a time down there. Seem
to be split into two factions. One group, led by a man who
says he's a pig farmer and looks the part, is declaring in front
of cameras that this estate is Sodom and Gomorrah and those
scarlet sinners—that's our film group—are up to every imagin-
able orgy. The other bunch has appointed the local grocer as
spokesman and he's refuting the pig farmer. According to the
grocer Miss Farquson is an angel and nothing sinful would ever
go on around her. The only point they appear to agree on is that
the colonel was the devil incarnate."

"Amen to that," Forsythe said, thinking of a pony named
Butterscotch. "Any idea how Dowling is making out?"

"As far as I know he's still barricaded in the late devil's
room with Erika trotting trays back and forth to him."
Cochrane grinned again but this time there was no humor in
it. "Knowing Mickey I'd imagine she's also acting as royal food
taster. Mickey would put anyone's neck but his on the chopping
block and Erika's going right along with it. Playing a new role—
this one of mother protecting her young."

At the man's tone Forsythe's eyes fastened on him. "I
thought you liked Erika."

"Like her? I guess you'd say I love her, in a fatherly way of
course. And, as you probably know by now, that's one role I'm
not qualified to play. I remember the first time I saw the little
girl. In Hollywood, of course, I've done most of my work there.
Erika was about nine and Mel and I were both working on her
second film. Queer little kid. Those were the days when child
actresses had a lot of blonde curls and did cute little songs and
dances. Not Erika. Went straight into dramatic roles and could
she portray genuine childhood. All the fears and doubts and
frustrations...sad little kid."

"Why do you call her sad?"

Leaning back on the bench, Cochrane searched in a pocket.
Sunlight fell across his face and displayed fine lines the barrister
hadn't noticed previously. "Do you have cigarettes, Robert? Oh,
I forgot, you stick to a pipe. Not to worry, I smoke too much

anyway. Yes, sad Erika. You'd have to know her mother to understand. Mind, I liked Von Farquson, but Lord, what a driver that
woman was! Lousy actress but she knew talent when she saw it.
Von used to talk a lot about her brother and what a loss it was to
the stage when Erik Larsen died. Anyway, she spotted the same
talent in her young daughter and the kid never had a chance.
Came straight out of diapers into drama school and that was it."

He'd finally found a crumpled package and a lone cigarette. Forsythe lit it for him and he leaned back. "Little girl grew
up lopsided. Never had a normal childhood, no time for games
or being young. Von took good care of her. Looked after Erika
like a valuable racehorse—proper diet, proper grooming, that
sort of thing. When Erika should have been playing with dolls
and looking forward to boyfriends, she was learning lines and
working like a pint-sized demon. I blame that childhood for her
falling for Mickey Darling."

"I've followed her career with a great deal of interest and
through the years her name has been linked romantically with
a number of her leading men and also that professional tennis
player."

"Publicity. Nothing more. Von was careful that her
daughter didn't get involved with a man. Might have felt it
would weaken her hold on the girl. Von died about three years
ago. Had hypertension, a woman like that is a candidate for that
sort of thing. I've always thought her death was...fitting."

"How did she die?"

"In the middle of a furious fight over contracts with a
studio head. Von's eyes rolled up and she keeled over, heart
attack. For the first time in her life Erika was on her own and
she wasted no time. Fell head over heels for Dowling. Couldn't
have made a worse choice."

Forsythe was frowning. "That certainly doesn't sound
lopsided."

"What I omitted to say is Erika's playing the role of a
woman with her first love. Like the role she played when her
aunt came to London—dutiful loving niece."

"Aren't you being unnecessarily harsh?"

"Told you I love the girl. It's not her fault she can only counterfeit emotions. Erika's like a—" He broke off, his wide forehead furrowed with thought. "Like a mirror. Reflects what it sees but feels nothing itself. Still, she's a dangerous woman. Men always pounding themselves against her, trying to crack that exterior. Maybe it's a good thing she picked on Mickey. At least she can't hurt him." Cochrane glanced at his companion's frowning face and added, "Only my opinion, Robert, and I could be wrong. God knows I've been before."

His daughter Jenny, Forsythe thought, and that's what I'd better get him talking about. "I think you're being unnecessarily harsh with yourself too, Sam."

Bitter lines were etched at the corners of the big man's mouth. For a time he was silent and Forsythe was beginning to think he was to have no more luck with Cochrane than Chief Inspector Parker had had. Then Cochrane said slowly, "I can never be harsh enough with myself. Since Jenny's death I've tried blaming Marcia for not looking after her better, the house-keeper for being slack, even the police for not finding the man who did it. In the end, I'm the one to blame."

"The police. Did they never get any leads?"

"None. Whoever did it covered his tracks."

"What about those friends of your daughter, the ones who helped alibi her?"

"They couldn't give the police any help. I had a go at them myself thinking they'd talk to me. Found out they had nothing to tell. All Jenny told the other girls was that the man she'd fallen for was 'an older guy' and 'thrilling.' To a girl of sixteen any man over twenty is an older man. Thrilling? Who knows how a little girl would mean that?" Cochrane shifted on the wooden bench and pushed his plate away. "My wife was killed the day before Jenny's fourth birthday. Hit-and-run driver. Never found him either. There I was, left with a little kid. Marcia had been Meg's best friend and she thought the world of little Jenny so between us we tried to raise the kid. Pretty

little thing, fair, with eyes like her mother. Used to tease Jenny
about looking like her mother. Told her it was a good thing she
didn't take after me. Never gave a lick of trouble. Quiet and
well-behaved."

The cameraman stopped and buried his face in his hands.
His voice was muffled as he said, "Couldn't believe it when I
got that wire. I thought some horrible mistake had been made.
Always thought of Jenny as a child. Wasn't until I saw her
on the slab in the morgue that I realized she had developed a
woman's body."

Forsythe regarded the man with compassion and, hating
himself for it, asked a question. "You didn't believe the rumors
that Michael Dowling was implicated?"

"Didn't believe or disbelieve. Didn't know. Rumors came
mainly from Marcia and she wasn't above lying about him.
Couldn't see how it *could* be him. Sure, Jenny tagged around
after him but a lot of girls do. Dowling treated Jenny the same
as the others, teased her and kidded with her. For God's sake,
Robert, he'd known her since she was ten!"

Cochrane lumbered to his feet and Forsythe said, "Have
you stopped looking for the man?"

"Never will. Only thing keeping me alive."

The barrister watched him move slowly toward the lime
trees. Before Cochrane reached them another man, this one
quick-moving, darted out of the shadow into the sunny glade.
Sun glinted dazzlingly from Melvin Borthwick's naked skull.
He paused to speak to his friend, and then made for the summer
house. Before he reached Forsythe he was talking. "Damn
wretches! Wrung me dry. Feel like I've been put through a meat
grinder. Told them the same things over and over."

Forsythe grinned. "I take it you've been interviewed by the
men from London."

"You take it right and that was no interview. More of an
endurance test. Stupid questions. Was I on the first floor after
we came back from Koster's greenhouse? Told the ruddy fools
of course I was. Only bathroom in the house is up there. Did

I see anyone else? Anyone acting suspiciously?" Flopping down in Cochrane's place, the little man pulled out a silver flask. He picked up Cochrane's glass, threw a few drops of liquid over his shoulder, and poured from the flask. He shoved it over to Forsythe. "My own stock. Cross my heart I haven't poisoned it." As though to demonstrate his point he tipped up the flask and took a long swallow. Then he grudgingly added, "Shouldn't blame the police. Be glad to see them get to the bottom of this. Any idea when they'll let us go, Robert?"

"After the inquest, but I've no idea when that will be."

"Damnation! We've got to get back to London. Murder or no murder this film has got to be kept on schedule."

"You are going on with it?"

"Why not?"

"Well, Marcia..."

"Marcia only had a small part. Can get another actress or write the part out." Borthwick stretched and said expansively, "Believe it or not but Marcia dead is going to give it a boost she never could in life. May sound callous but that's show biz. Mickey has the most incredible *luck*. This murder is going to bring the public out in droves. The film will be a blockbuster." Borthwick gazed at his companion and said, "Come on now, old boy, don't look so disapproving."

"Not disapproving, simply stunned. I knew the woman for a couple of days and I *feel* something. You knew her for years and—"

"—feel like hell about her death. We'll go to her funeral and send flowers and do some mourning for her—when we have time. Now we've got a picture to film. Marcia would have acted the same way. We're professionals." The director looked around discontentedly. "Had a dandy scene slated for this spot and now we can't use the place. Have to find somewhere else and keep the location quiet. Sightseers will run all over us if we don't."

"Does Miss Farquson know about the change in location?"

"Told her before I came out and you know what she offered? To give me my advance back. Said it might take a while to come up with the money because she'd used it for the maids' salaries and extra food. What a lady!"

"Are you going to take her money?"

"I said we're professionals, not Shylocks. Of course I'm not taking the poor lady's money. I told Honoria that advance was in the nature of an option and she'd done her part. I wish for her sake we were filming here. Honoria could certainly use the money. That maid, the little one who threw screaming meemies, told me they'd heard in the village that Honoria and the Potters spent last winter living in the kitchen and a couple of other rooms. Couldn't afford the fuel to keep the rest of the place heated. She said the villagers figured the colonel had made bad investments on purpose just to impoverish his daughter."

"I heard something about that myself." Forsythe added casually, "Sam Cochrane was telling me about Erika."

Although his voice was casual he couldn't have schooled his expression as successfully. Borthwick's bright little eyes, under the beetling brows, swung shrewdly toward the barrister. "Told you something you didn't care for, eh?"

"Sam said she's lopsided. Do you agree?"

"With the term, no. With what old Sam's trying to say, yes. I've always thought of Erika as a series of roles, one on top of the other. You peel them off and underneath is…emptiness, a vacuum. Tell you what, you want an authority on Erika Von Farr, check it out with Giles."

"He's in love with her," Forsythe said dully.

"And knows he's a damn fool but can't help himself." Borthwick hopped up. "Better get in and stir things up. Try to pin that Kepesake down on when he'll let us go. He had Giles on the griddle when I left the house. Next one in line is Mickey." A broad smile twitched at the bushy mustache. "Want to make any bets on whether the chief inspector goes up to Mickey or Mickey comes down to him?"

"Not interested."

Forsythe didn't bother lifting his head as the director left. He stared morosely down into his untouched drink. What did

men who considered a friend's death good publicity know about
an intense, sensitive girl like Erika Von Farr? Couldn't see the
forest for the trees, too close to her to realize her emotions were
genuine. Erika *did* care for her aunt, *did* love Michael Dowling.
Good Lord, Forsythe thought, I'm half in love with her.

He sat brooding, unaware of time passing. When he lifted
his head the shadows were lengthening. He checked his watch.
Tea time. To his surprise he found he was hungry again. Tossing
Borthwick's liquor on the grass, he gathered together the plates
and cutlery used by Cochrane and piled them up. Carrying
them, he headed down the double row of limes.

Chapter Nine

As Forsythe entered the front door he spotted the detectives from London coming down the staircase. Kepesake was in the lead and not only was his hair mussed but he looked choleric. Behind him Sergeant Brummell wore a wide grin. Over his superior's shoulder he winked at the barrister. The chief inspector glared at Forsythe and pointed at the plates in his hands. "Acting as a domestic, Forsythe?"

"Doing my bit to help out," Forsythe told him amiably.

Keeping his voice low, Kepesake broke into a stream of curses, all of them directed at the film industry in general and actors in particular. "Wouldn't set a foot out of that room," he sputtered. "Only way I could have got him down here was have a couple of constables carry him. Of all the jackasses!"

"You've interviewed Michael Dowling?"

"Now I'm certain he *was* the intended victim and I can see why. Much more of him and I'd start sympathizing with the murderer."

Chief Inspector Parker had joined them and was trying, unsuccessfully, to hide a grin. "Tsk, tsk, unprofessional conduct."

Kepesake turned the glare on his colleague. "Thought you'd left for Elleston."

258 E. X. Giroux

"On my way, but I waited to hear if you'd picked up anything new from Dowling."

"Same thing he gave you last night. Appears to put undue attention on the most ridiculous trifles. Kept harping away because he broke that glass—" Breaking off, Kepesake looked suddenly thoughtful. "A trifle. Your field, Forsythe. Think there could be anything in it?"

The barrister didn't bother hiding his grin. "I hardly think it pertinent."

"Wanted me to leave bodyguards for him," Kepesake raged on. "Two! One man to sit beside his bed, the other posted with his back against the door."

Sergeant Brummell spoke to Forsythe, "Told the chief it wasn't a bad idea. Someone might have another go at Dowling."

"And how are they going to reach him, Beau?" Kepesake demanded. "He's locked behind two inches of solid oak with Miss Farr on guard. Dowling's safe enough.

"Of course I'm taking reasonable precautions. There'll be constables on the gates and a couple of others on the grounds. Parker's man, Summer, will be in the house until six and he'll be relieved by another man. Did you pick a good one, Chief Inspector Parker?"

"My best. Constable Jenkins."

Forsythe raised his brows. "This constable wouldn't by any chance be related to the people who ran the butcher shop at one time?"

"Still do. At least Constable Jenkins's brother has it now. They're grandsons of the original owners." Parker gave the barrister an admiring look. "You really do pick up on trifles, don't you?"

"Heard the name earlier today. Seems Grandmother Jenkins was carried home in her cups from a garden party at the vicarage."

Parker laughed. "Hardly sounds like the Jenkins family. They're chapel and teetotalers."

"Mrs. Jenkins had no idea she was swilling gin with the punch."

Parker was still smiling but Kepesake pushed past them, one hand smoothing down his ruffled locks. "We'll be in Bury-Sutton at the inn there. Hear it's not bad. What's the name, Beau?"

"The Unicorn, chief."

"Right. Don't hesitate to ring us up, Forsythe, if you think of anything."

"Don't bank on it. I'm as much at sea as you are."

The chief inspector took Beau's arm. "Come on. Speaking of sea we're going to be breasting a rough tide at the gates with the media."

"Issuing a statement, Chief?"

"Guess we'll have to." Kepesake struck a pose. "We have several promising leads and are following them up. Developments expected momentarily."

"Hogwash," Parker muttered in Forsythe's ear and followed the other two officers.

The barrister realized he was still balancing the plates. He looked around, shrugged, and deposited them on the telephone table. Then, wanting his tea, he headed hopefully toward the closed doors of the drawing room. Behind those doors was a peaceful tableau. Honoria Farquson presided over the tea table; Giles leaned nonchalantly against the mantel; and Miss Sanderson was stretching her long legs out to the circle of warmth cast by a crackling wood fire.

Forsythe sniffed the pleasant odor permeating the room. "Smells like apple wood."

"How discerning," his hostess said. "I thought it would make a nice touch. It was a windfall from last autumn I had our boy from the village split the tree up. At one time there was quite a nice orchard near the gatehouse. Perhaps you noticed the trees." She sighed. "They're all very old now and haven't been tended properly. I suppose they should come down but I rather dread to have it done. Do sit and have your tea, Mr, Forsythe. Have the police left yet?"

Taking a chair beside his secretary, Forsythe stretched out his bad leg toward the warmth of the apple wood fire. "They were leaving when I came in. Chief Inspector Kepesake and his sergeant are staying at the Unicorn in Bury-Sutton."

"They'll be comfortable there. Lydia Preston is a good cook and the rooms, though small, are clean. I do hope they're leaving the policemen at the gates. Heaven knows what those curiosity seekers will get up to if no one is there."

"The chief inspector told me the gates will be guarded, the grounds patrolled, and one man will be left in the house. The name of the constable on night duty is Jenkins. Perhaps you know him."

"Indeed I do. He was in my Sunday school class at one time. A nice little boy but shy. I've often thought it was that unfortunate name his mother Arabella wished on him that made him bashful. Absolem! The other boys teased him about it unmercifully."

Forsythe accepted his cup and examined the bountiful tea spread out before him. It was as lavish as the one provided the day before at the Koster cottage. "Are Borthwick and Cochrane joining us?"

Giles smiled. "Sam is upstairs now and I guess Mel has probably joined him. Mel's been ringing up London with a constable hanging over him listening to every word. Putting the pressure on at the studio to have the legal department get us out of here. We are supposed to be back at the studio tomorrow morning. Did the police give you any idea, Robert, when we're being released from bondage?"

"I've no more idea than the rest of you."

"Come now, I'm sure you do."

"Exactly what do you mean by that?"

"You and Kepesake are buddies. He was the officer in charge on that moor murder you solved last year. Come on, open up."

It was Miss Sanderson who said tartly, "Even if Robby has been taken into the chief inspector's confidence do you think he'd be free to tell us anything?"

"Sorry. Guess I'm a bit edgy." The young man's freckled face turned toward their hostess. "Mickey and Erika coming down for dinner?"

"I'm afraid not, Mr. Eady. I did try to persuade them this afternoon to join us. Mickey says he'll be more comfortable in the colonel's quarters. Why I can't understand. It's a gloomy place. Mickey is being such a silly boy."

"This time I don't blame our golden boy. Someone did try to knock him off, you know."

"Nonsense! I'm certain the police will find it was simply a tragic accident."

Giles had been swallowing his tea and now he choked. *"Accident.* My dear lady, you think the cyanide got into Mickey's bottle by accident?"

She considered this and then said slowly, "That is a little difficult to accept, isn't it? Perhaps an absolute stranger crept into the house and put poison into the whiskey. After all, there are many demented people with grudges against public personages."

The writer was regarding her with something approaching admiration. "That theory would get us all off the hook and I'm rather taken with it. But how was this stranger, demented or otherwise, going to get past the noble Heathcliff? That brute would have had him in several pieces."

"Heathcliff could have been drugged by one of those tranquilizing guns one sees on television."

"I'm beginning to think you have the makings of a writer. All right, Heathcliff is drugged. The demented stranger sneaks into the house, goes immediately to the right bedroom, and does the foul deed. Does that sound reasonable?"

Honoria was admitting there could be flaws in her reasoning, but at that moment she examined the Georgian teapot and jumped to her feet. "Dear me, quite dry. Excuse me a moment and I'll get hot water."

Forsythe glanced up. "I haven't seen Potter around today."

"I ordered him to bed, Mr. Forsythe. His back is giving him trouble again. He was reluctant to go, he's so conscientious, but Potty and I insisted."

Giles followed her with his eyes and when the door closed he said, "Know who she reminds me of?"

"A maiden aunt?" Miss Sanderson guessed.

"That woman in the old film, the one made during the war. Can't remember the actress's name..."

"Greer Garson," Forsythe said.

"That's it. Honoria Farquson is much like Mrs. Miniver, keeping an upper lip so stiff you'd think it starched. Carrying on magnificently while her world tumbles around her. Know what she told us about Mickey before you came in, Robert?"

Miss Sanderson chuckled. "Honoria said tomorrow that silly boy is joining us for dinner. She won't stand his foolishness any longer. Giles pointed out that two police forces couldn't budge him, but Honoria told us gently they weren't going about it the right way."

"This I'll have to see," Giles said. "The only way I can think of moving Mickey is by torching the house. Ah, here is fresh tea."

Honoria bustled in and set the pot down. "Your cup, Mr. Forsythe. Do have some of this quince preserve with your scone. I made it last fall and it did turn out well. I'm hoping we have a good crop of raspberries this year. I have a recipe for raspberry cordial, my grandmother's, that's quite tasty..."

The conversation turned to recipes and then, quite naturally, to gardening. Giles admitted he wouldn't know a turnip plant from a carrot but Forsythe was fairly knowledgeable. His grandmother, who Honoria reminded him of slightly, had insisted he help her with her beds. As a small boy his idol had been their brawny gardener and he'd tagged along behind the man. It was a peaceful time, and Forsythe found that with the crackling of the fire, Honoria's gentle voice, the play of light and shadow across the walls, tension drained from him. Finally, their hostess sent them upstairs to rest before dinner. Miss Sanderson didn't argue. "I'll be down to lay the table," she promised and leaned on the barrister's arm.

"Tired, Sandy?"

"Exhausted. Housework doesn't agree with me."

"With Aggie fussing over you I don't suppose you know much about that sort of thing."

"Dear old Aggie. I wish I had her fussing over me now. She has a sharp tongue but no one can complain about her cooking." They paused by Forsythe's door and Miss Sanderson asked, "Mind if I come in for a few minutes?"

In answer he swung the door wide. The room was dim and he reached for a lamp. Miss Sanderson shook her head. "No. It's peaceful this way." She curled up in an easy chair, her legs tucked up under her. "Tea time was peaceful too. I kept thinking all the rest of this had been a bad dream and we'd finally woken up. It doesn't seem possible a woman was murdered last evening."

Forsythe stretched out on the bed and stared up at the ceiling. "In the words of Adam Kepesake, who certainly is not our buddy, have you any ideas?"

"If Marcia Mather wasn't dead, I'd pin it on her. She's my idea of the typical poisoner."

"Beau Brummell was playing with the thought that she might have killed herself to have Dowling brought up on a murder charge."

"Uh uh. She thought as much of her skin as Mickey Darling does. But I've narrowed the list of suspects down."

"Discarded Cochrane and Borthwick?"

"Robby, you can be infuriating! Always one jump ahead of me. I can't work either of those men in as suspects. Mel is so…shallow. There's hate connected with this crime and I don't think Mel could sustain hate or any other emotion for long."

"He could have had another motive."

"Erika Von Farr? Doesn't work. If he couldn't avenge his wife he's not going to kill for Erika. Sam is more difficult. Let's say he's lying about not being sure Mickey was involved in his daughter's death. That would give him a gold-plated motive but I simply can't imagine him using poison. Sam would use his hands or perhaps a gun. Poison is so…so feminine."

"I suppose that eliminates Giles Eady too."

"Giles is still in the running. He has a feminine streak. I don't mean he's effeminate, and on the surface he's bright and glib and amusing but there's a touch of female spite in some of the things he says. And I've seen him looking at Erika. Yes, I think for her Giles could kill. My next suspect is Honoria—"

"Now you have surprised me, Sandy. I should have thought Honoria would be the first person you'd cross off the suspect list."

"I have taken the Potters off it. Honoria would have had to urge them on and she's far too fine and honorable to do that. Yet, oddly enough, I can see her doing it. Where I fall down is motive."

"Erika is her niece and Dowling...well, he's Dowling."

In her shadowed corner Miss Sanderson stirred. It was too dark to see her face but Forsythe had a feeling she was frowning. Then he heard a tiny click and smiled. Sandy must be deep in thought. She was clicking her thumbnail against her front teeth. After a moment she said, "Honoria saw her niece for the first time in thirty years barely a month ago. She may have loved baby Erika but I've the impression she feels little for the adult Erika. As I said, we're dealing with hate. To hate that much there has to be strong emotion. I simply don't feel Honoria loves her niece enough to kill for her. And she did give her consent to the marriage and promised the estate as a wedding present. Honoria would keep a promise."

"That leaves Erika Von Farr."

His secretary made no answer and he propped himself up on an elbow and switched on the bedside lamp. The bulb cast a circle of light on his face but Miss Sanderson's was still obscure. He switched it off. "That verse from Coleridge, Sandy, was that aimed at Erika?"

"Anything I say will sound foolish. And I'm not foolish. I know I have a tendency to mother you, after all I did act as kind of a mother after your own died, but—"

"And did a good job, Sandy."

"Well, I'm not one of those maternal women who get all jealous and upset when their son looks at a woman. It's just... Robby, I don't want you hurt again."

Forsythe winced and closed his eyes. In his mind a picture formed, a girl's face, fine-featured, rather angelic. Virginia, he thought, who had proved the opposite of an angel. "That's all in the past," he said brusquely.

"Not that far in the past. Robby, I don't want you torn apart again."

"Be sensible, old girl. Erika Von Farr is simply an actress I happen to admire."

"More than admire. I blame this whole ungodly business on myself. I thought I was so clever bringing you together. Then I saw the look on your face."

"You make her sound like La Belle Dame sans Merci."

"No, not that."

"'Life-in-death was she, Who thicks a man's blood with cold,'" he quoted.

"That's right, throw up a few lines I quoted at random. I didn't mean that either. It's simply that a woman can see Erika clearer than a man. She has an unfortunate effect on men. Turns them into gibbering idiots—"

"I am *not* a gibbering idiot."

"You feel something for her. Don't deny it. And she's bad news, Robby. Maybe because she seems unattainable. I feel she'd suck everything from a man, give nothing in return…"

"Now you're casting her as Countess Dracula."

"Will you shut up! Robby, Erika could well have put that poison in that bottle!"

"Give me one reason why."

"Very well." A muted click came from the shadows around his companion's chair. "Both Sam and Mel say Erika never looked at a man before Mickey Dowling hove into view. Devoted her entire life to her career. Nothing left over for romance. Out of the blue, she falls for a cad like Mickey. Why the sudden change?"

"Did they also tell you that her mother kept the girl away from males? Erika met Dowling after Von Farquson's death."

Sandy gave an unladylike snort. "Show me the red-blooded girl who a mother, domineering or otherwise, can keep away from men. And when Von died Erika was what—over twenty-seven? In a pig's eye! No, Erika has no interest in men. I don't think she loves Mickey; I think she's acting a part."

The barrister winced again and was glad his secretary couldn't see it. "Then why are they engaged, my wise old friend?"

"I think Mickey's holding something over her head, forcing her to marry him. He wouldn't be above a spot of blackmail, you know."

"What could there be in Erika's past to warrant blackmail? From the time she was a toddler she's been in the public domain. Her life is an open book."

"It could concern her mother."

"Same thing goes there too. And remember, Sandy, this is a permissive society we live in. There has to be something serious to warrant blackmail today. What could it be?"

"Murder? Perhaps Erika...no, that's too farfetched. Maybe something else. How about a hit-and-run and Mickey has proof Erika or her mother did it?" There was movement from Miss Sanderson's corner and a light went on bright enough to make the barrister blink. She was checking her watch. "Enough of crime, domestic duty calls. I have to whip around and dress and then I'll lay the table. Only be six of us tonight. Should make the washing up simpler."

She moved to the door and swung it open. As usual she had the last word. "Mark my word, Robby, when we get to the bottom of this we'll find Erika Von Farr right there."

Chapter Ten

The next morning Forsythe rose late. As he grunted his way to the window and pulled back the curtains his traveling clock said ten after ten. The day looked as gray and cheerless as he felt and when he lifted the sash a chill wind with the promise of rain made him thump down the pane. He knew he was too late for breakfast but he sought the breakfast room hoping for coffee. There he found not only coffee on the hotplate but Potter puttering around. "Back better?" he asked.

"Quite recovered, sir. Mrs. Potter used liniment and Miss Honoria brought down her heating pad. Would you care for breakfast, sir?"

"Toast will be fine. I don't want to put Mrs. Potter to too much trouble."

"No trouble, sir." Potter paused beside the door and one eyelid flickered in something remarkably like a wink. "Mrs. Potter has taken a fancy to you, sir. London papers on the table if you'd care to look at them."

Forsythe pulled the papers over, wondering whether Potter *had* winked at him. He decided it must be a nervous tic. He glanced down at a front page, saw the lurid headlines, a row of photographs of Erika, Marcia, and Michael Dowling, and pushed them away. In a remarkably short time Potter trotted in bearing a platter. Looking down at the platter, Forsythe thought perhaps the cook *had* taken a fancy to him.

"Ah," the butler said, "Mrs. Potter thought you might care for blueberry waffles, sir."

"My favorite," Forsythe said and started to demolish not only waffles but scrambled eggs, tiny sausages, and rashers of bacon. He'd only made a start when Giles Eady lounged in.

"You look like I feel," the writer told him. "Bad night?"

"Rotten. Twisted and turned until after three and when I did get to sleep I had the worst nightmares in years."

"Hell of a day. Looks like rain." He glanced down at Forsythe's breakfast and his face brightened. "Hey, Potter, think your good wife could rustle up the same?"

"I doubt it, sir. Mrs. Potter's put away the waffle iron. I'll see what she can offer."

Giles stretched a hand out to the pile of newspapers. "Je-sus! Well, I suppose you can't expect anything else. Listen to this. 'Police are searching for the fiend who slew the beautiful actress Marcia Mather.' Make it sound like a sex crime. Ah, honorable mention for you and Abigail. 'Robert Forsythe, barrister and private detective, is working with the police on this horrible crime. His secretary, Miss Abigail Sanderson, is also assisting. A breakthrough is expected at any moment.' No picture of Giles Eady, famous writer. Let's see, more photographs on page four. Here I am, and so is Mel, and Sam Cochrane, looking remarkably like a water buffalo. They've got a good shot of this house and a blurry one of Honoria where she looks about fifteen." He threw the papers on the floor. "Wish that breakthrough would happen and we could get out of here. Know what our boys in blue are up to now?"

"Didn't see any of them when I came down."

"Searching the bedrooms. Practically yanked me out of mine and I'd swear the constable went through the pockets of my jeans before he handed them over. Of all the—" Breaking off, he smiled. "Breakfast." His smile disappeared. "An egg and a slice of toast!"

"It is late, sir," Potter told him frigidly and made his departure.

Giles cast a disconsolate glance at Forsythe. He was spearing a bit of waffle. "Teacher's pet. Been buttering up the cook, eh?"

"Not guilty."

"That old world charm of yours."

Forsythe cut into a sausage. "Should cultivate some yourself. You'd eat better. Did the police say what they're looking for?"

"Thought you could tell me that but I guess you won't squeal on your buddies. Can't be large. They shook out the books on my bedtable."

Small enough, Forsythe thought, to be hidden under Marcia Mather's handkerchiefs. "Any sign of Mickey this morning?"

"I suppose he's still locked in. Saw Erika in the hall. She looks like a ghost and I tried to get her to come out for a breath of air but she brushed me off."

Forsythe rose to refill his coffee cup. Giles's prediction was coming true; drops of rain pattered against the window. He said casually, "When we were reading characters from faces the other evening you said Erika was the simplest of all."

"She's an actress."

"What does that signify?"

"Exactly what I said. First, last, and in the middle, the girl is an actress." The writer shoved his plate away and looked moodily at the wet panes. "Take my advice, Robert, and don't get any yearnings for the lass. I keep following her about knowing I'm mad to do it and can't help myself. Falling in love with Erika is like having the seven-year itch and both hands tied."

"You knew her mother?"

"Von? Certainly. She trailed after Erika like a bloodhound. Why?"

"Were either of them in London twelve years ago?"

The other man's face was perplexed. "How would I know?"

"Someone—I think it was Dowling—said this is the first time Erika's been in England. What about her mother?"

"As far as I know Erika's never been in England before. Von was all over the place; she acted as her daughter's agent, you know. She could have been here. What has twelve years ago got to do with this murder?"

"Possibly nothing. But you're a writer. Figure it out."

Giles thought, drumming his freckled fingers on the table. "Murder...roots in the past. But Erika and Von? Robert, Von's dead."

"Erika isn't."

"What could have happened that long ago? Something still important to one of us. Give me a hint."

Silently, Forsythe debated. He needed this man's help. Coming to a decision he said, "Sam Cochrane."

"Sam." The other man chewed his lower lip. "Got it! Meg Cochrane was killed twelve years ago by a hit-and-run driver. She was thrown against a curb and her neck snapped. The bastard didn't even stop. But Von or Erika had nothing to do with that."

"Are you certain?"

"By now you have me so confused I'm not certain of my own name. Okay, you win. I'll ask around. Find out where they were on the exact date. Better not ask Sam. I'll have a go at Mel and see whether he remembers." Getting up, he clapped Forsythe's shoulder. "Just joined your club. Now I'm a detective."

Or a murderer, Forsythe thought dourly. The door opened again and this time Constable Summer's ruddy face poked around the panel. "Chief Inspector Kepesake would like to speak to you when you have a moment, sir."

Both chief inspectors were in the library. The room looked smaller. The bookcases were bare and their contents were piled helter-skelter over the carpet. From the wall over the fireplace Colonel Farquson seemed to glower at this desecration. Behind the desk Kepesake was also glowering. He greeted the barrister with an impatient, "Sit down and take a look at the autopsy report."

Forsythe picked his way through the tumble of books, took a seat, and accepted the report. "Any luck with the search?"

"Not so far. Would help if the lads knew what they were looking for."

Bending his head, Forsythe scanned the pathologist's findings. Cause of death…probable time of death…woman of forty-nine in good condition…organs healthy…slight anemic condition…congestion in the nasal passages. He passed it back to Kepesake. "No help there."

"No help here either." Kepesake thumped a fist on the piles of paper scattered untidily in front of him. "Backgrounds on everyone in the house. Not much here we haven't already got."

Chief Inspector Parker brushed at his thin mustache. "One interesting item about Michael Dowling. The teacher who financed his trip to Los Angeles doesn't seem to have done it willingly. Miss Pike's dead but one of Dowling's school friends says he remembers the man—or boy as he was then—bragging about squeezing money from the woman. This chap said Dowling and Miss Pike were having a hot affair and Dowling managed to get a snapshot of her in the altogether. Threatened to show it to the school board if she didn't hand over her savings."

"Nasty piece of goods," Kepesake said. "But it doesn't have any bearing on Miss Mather's death."

"It does prove he's capable of blackmail," Forsythe mentioned.

"If he's capable of drug dealing he's capable of anything," Kepesake said dourly. "Slippery devil. Narcotics is positive he's bringing the stuff in but can't pin him down. Smarter than he acts."

"He *is* an actor," Parker pointed out.

"Don't belabor the obvious." Kepesake picked up a sheet and frowned at it. "This is the report on Melvin Borthwick. I can see why his wife's affair with Dowling didn't bother him very much. That director is a great man for the ladies. Had one affair after another, before his marriage, during it, and after his wife's suicide. His latest girl friend is a young fashion model who appears to think she'll be the next Mrs. Borthwick. If I were her I wouldn't hold my breath."

Forsythe leaned forward. "Nothing else on Borthwick?"

Parker grinned. "This group of people are really tangled up. At one time Veronica Larsen Farquson was Borthwick's mistress. Years ago, of course."

"Erika's mother," Forsythe muttered. "What about Samuel Cochrane?"

"Not a single black mark. Only women in his life were his wife and daughter. Margaret Cochrane was his childhood sweetheart; they married young, and Cochrane never seems to have even looked at another woman."

Kepesake was still frowning. "Same goes for Honoria Farquson. Life's an open book. The only time she's been away from this estate is for about five weeks when she was—"

"Eighteen," Forsythe said.

"And for about seven months when she was abroad with her sister-in-law. In Colonel Farquson's lifetime the farthest afield she went was to Elleston to shop. Five weeks ago she went to London to meet her niece but she was only there for three days. She had no prior connection with any of these people except Marcia Mather in her childhood and, of course, Erika and Abigail Sanderson." Kepesake transferred his frown to the other chief inspector. "I'm willing to admit Miss Farquson is out of it and—" He broke off and asked brusquely, "What is it now, Summer?"

Summer, wearing a smile, was in the doorway. "MacDonald and Barry have run into trouble in the kitchen, sir. The cook is objecting to them searching her cupboards. Mrs. Potter has both of them backed into a corner."

"Dear Lord." Kepesake gazed at the ceiling as though for help and then waved his jade holder at the grinning constable. "Surely two good-sized men can handle a frail old lady."

"The frail old lady is brandishing a meat cleaver, sir."

Kepesake seemed speechless but Parker, grinning as widely as the constable, told him, "Better have Miss Farquson speak to the old girl."

Kepesake inserted a fresh cigarette in his holder. "This ruddy case! A cook attacking my men with cleavers, an actor locked in a bedroom, that Eady quoting Shakespeare, the police commissioner on my back…"

"You've many problems," Forsythe observed without the slightest trace of sympathy.

Kepesake continued with his litany of woes. "Lawyers from the legal department of the studio swarming all over, Dowling's fan clubs sending wires threatening mayhem if one hair of their idol's head is hurt, the media demanding a quick solution. We damn well are having our problems, Forsythe, and you're not raising a finger to be of help." Sighing heavily, he searched through the disorder on the desk. "Erika Von Farr. Until she met Michael Dowling not a hint about men in her life. Those romances in the gossip columns appear to be straight fabrications cooked up by publicity departments."

"Any information about the finances of these people?" Forsythe asked.

"Yes, a complete rundown. Now who the hell is it this time? Oh, Beau. Thank God you've rustled up some food. Set it down, man. I'm starved."

Sergeant Brummell jerked a nod at Forsythe and put down the tray. "Couldn't manage much, chief. Sandwiches and beer. Kitchen's been in an uproar."

Parker opened a bottle of beer and poured it foaming into a glass. "Did Summer bring Miss Farquson in on it?"

"Few minutes ago. Miss Farquson herded the old girl into her bedroom. Hope she's locked in. All quiet on the kitchen front now, but that cook's a terror. Mrs. Potter doesn't reach MacDonald's shoulder and she had him quaking. Care for a sandwich, Mr. Forsythe?"

The barrister declined and turned back to Kepesake. "What about the finances?"

Kepesake spoke thickly around a mouthful of sandwich. "Tell him, Beau."

"Most of them in good shape. Mr. Borthwick lives above his means and has debts but nothing horrific. Miss Farr has a bundle, most of it invested in property in the Los Angeles area. Michael Dowling is loaded. Among other things he has a controlling interest in a soft drink concern and in one of those fast food chains. Seems to have an obsession with money. Can't get enough. Rumor is he's trying to get Miss Farr to come in with him on some hotel deal."

Wiping off his mustache, Parker asked, "Any luck with the search, sergeant?"

"Not so far and I doubt the lads will turn anything up. Figure whatever it was is long gone. There's a fireplace in nearly every room in this house. Could have been burned or flushed down the w.c." Brummell scrubbed at his shaggy hair. "Good chance it has nothing to do with Miss Mather's death."

Kepesake stared at his sergeant. "What are you getting at?"

"Figure one of these people here knew Miss Mather had something with her he didn't want found when they went through her belongings. Could have been…maybe love letters."

Kepesake gave an undignified snort. "With these weirdies I'm willing to wager any love letters would be read by them in Hyde Park to as large an audience as possible."

"Maybe so, chief. Hey, could have been a snapshot."

"In that case they'd be willing to publish it in a paper. I think you're reaching, Beau. The search of the dead woman's room is definitely tied up with the crime." Daintily wiping his finger tips, Kepesake reached for his cigarette holder. "Any ideas yet, Forsythe?"

"Let's get back to Cochrane. Are you certain he wasn't involved with another woman? I'm thinking of Von Farquson."

"If he was it was kept very quiet." Kepesake leaned forward and looked hopefully at the barrister. "What are you thinking?"

"It was Miss Sanderson's idea. She mentioned a hit-and-run accident and I thought immediately of Meg Cochrane.

Could you find out when the accident happened and where Von Farquson and Erika Von Farr were on that date?"

Eagerly the chief inspector scrabbled through the papers on the desk. The room was blue with cigarette smoke and Brummell coughed and opened a window a crack. A frosty gust of wind blew in and rustled the papers. Kepesake said irritably. "Will you shut that damned window? All I need now is pneumonia. Hmm, the death of Cochrane's wife occurred in…let's see—"

"Twelve years ago," Forsythe told him.

"Right. May the twelfth. You're figuring Veronica Farquson could have eliminated a rival. Well, I can find out where she was at the time. But her daughter…Miss Farr was definitely in Hollywood working on a film. I don't get the tie with her."

"Miss Sanderson found it odd that an actress so devoted to her career would suddenly lose her head over a man like Dowling and put that career in jeopardy."

Kepesake bit his lip and Brummell said, "I've seen level-headed women lose their head over worthless men before this, Mr. Forsythe."

Kepesake looked hopeful, "You think Dowling might be blackmailing Miss Farr about her mother? He blackmailed before, when he was only a boy. It's possible. We'll check it out. Anything further?"

"A couple of points puzzle me. But first I'd like to ask *you* a question. Is the date for the inquest set yet?"

Brummell chuckled and Parker asked, "Using a spot of blackmail yourself, counselor?"

"If he is, he's too late. Someone got there before you, Forsythe," Kepesake told him. "The studio head happens to be a member of the same club as the police commissioner. Orders have come down to let these film people get back to work. So…the inquest is slated for tomorrow afternoon at three. It will be held in Elleston and transportation will be laid on for all of you. Afterward you can go back to your vacation."

"Any objection if I go to Scotland?"

"Not as long as you leave the address and a number where you can be reached. Now give."

Templing his fingers, Forsythe gazed at them. "Miss Sanderson said she didn't believe Honoria Farquson thought highly of Michael Dowling. The first day I arrived I sensed nothing but dislike for the man from her. Yet, she swings right around, starts calling him Mickey, gives her consent to her niece's marriage, and is going to deed over this estate to Dowling. Something fishy there."

"Blackmail," Parker said hotly. "Miss Farquson has nothing to hide."

"But maybe Miss Farr has," Brummell said. "And it could be tied in with her mother like Mr. Forsythe said." He turned to Chief Inspector Parker. "You know Miss Farquson. Is she the kind of lady to protect a dead friend from scandal?"

Parker mulled it over and finally said slowly, "She's a fine person. Yes...she is the type. After all, this Von was her brother's widow. Has a great feeling for family, Miss Farquson."

Kepesake rubbed his hands together. "You said a couple of items, Forsythe."

"The other point that puzzles me is Marcia Mather's manner when she came down that evening to get Dowling. She didn't beg him to go with her; she practically ordered him. Even Dowling remarked on her manner. He said she was like 'a cat full of cream.' Yet, according to his statement, a few moments afterwards Marcia was begging for a larger part."

"Something fishy there, too," Kepesake agreed. "I'd better have another word with Dowling. Beau, you get on to this Veronica Farquson lead. Find out exactly where she was twelve years ago on May the twelfth. Where are you going, Forsythe?"

"Anywhere but here." Forsythe coughed. "Much more of this smoke and my lungs will be destroyed. Why don't you switch to a pipe?"

Brummell winked at the barrister. "Now where would the chief find a jade pipe?"

Kepesake paid no attention to his sergeant. "Anything more, Forsythe?"

"You've drained me dry," the barrister said.

"If anything else occurs to you I'll be at the—"

"Unicorn in Bury-Sutton," Forsythe said and thankfully closed the door behind him.

He headed across the entrance hall and pulled the door open. Stepping out on the portico he inhaled deeply. The air was fresh, a bit too fresh. The wind, driving icy rain ahead of it, beat against the front of the house. Regretfully, he stepped back into the hall. He looked around, shrugged his shoulders, and mounted the staircase. At least the rotten weather had doubtless driven the media and gawkers away from the gates. He pitied the constables still on duty there. Perhaps they'd sought shelter in the remains of the gatehouse. When he reached the landing he found Miss Sanderson, her arms piled high with linen, scurrying along the hall. "How about lending a hand?" she called.

"I know less about housework than you do."

"No matter, I'm desperate. These bedrooms are a shambles. Clothes thrown willy nilly and the beds must be changed. Honoria's downstairs trying to cope and—"

"All right, Sandy. Tell me what to do."

She told him, and Robert Forsythe, eminent barrister and sometime detective, found himself acting as a chambermaid. He changed linen, aired rooms, hung up clothes, and dusted bureaus. As he carried soiled sheets out of Cochrane's room he spotted his secretary pounding at a door at the far end of the hall. "I'll leave the sheets here, Mickey," she yelled. "If you don't put them on you can sleep in dirty ones." Pushing her hair off her forehead, she bellowed at Forsythe. "How are you coming?"

"I'm thinking of complaining to my union. That is, if housemaids have a union." She came closer and he lowered his voice. "Having problems with Mickey Darling?"

"He flatly refuses to let me in. Seems to think I'm going to put a poisonous snake in his bed." She added darkly, "If I could locate one I might do it."

"As a matter of interest, how does he make it back and forth to the bathroom?"

"The Mickeys of this world have always landed soft, Robby. There's not only a study connected to the colonel's bedroom but also a large cupboard converted into a lavatory."

"And the rest of us have to line up for the main one."

"Speaking of bathrooms, have you cleaned it up yet?"

"No, and I'm not about to."

For a moment it seemed Miss Sanderson would let out another bellow. But she reconsidered. "You do look fagged so I'll let you off. You've done a smashing job and if you ever need a recommendation for domestic work come to me. Did you have lunch?"

"No, and I'm not coming down for tea. I'm going to try to get a couple of hours of sleep."

He settled eagerly on his freshly made bed, pulled a blanket over himself, and closed his eyes. A soft tap sounded on his door and he groaned and called, "Come in, Sandy."

It was Giles's voice that said, "Settling down for a nap, eh?"

"Trying to," Forsythe told him ungraciously.

Giles was balancing a bottle and two stacked glasses. He put them on the bureau and proceeded to pour. "Not for me," Forsythe said. "I've had rather too much brandy lately."

"So have I, so I had the good sergeant smuggle in some double malt. Not a bad chap but Brummell has a touch of gallows humor. Advised me not to leave the bottle standing around where someone could drop cyanide into it." Handing the other man a glass, the writer sank down onto the easy chair.

Forsythe lifted the glass and inhaled. After a moment he realized with grim amusement that he was trying to distinguish the telltale scent of bitter almond from the odor of whiskey. He glanced across at Giles and found the man's nostrils quivering. "Well," Giles said defensively, "I suppose it's only natural." Their eyes met and both men laughed. "Cheers, Robert. By the by, this drink is in the nature of a consolation prize. Your sleuth has come up empty-handed."

"Wouldn't Mel cooperate?"

"He tried. Said he was in London and attended Meg's funeral. He did remember at the time Erika was in Los Angeles working. He couldn't remember Von being at the service, so he figures she was probably hovering over her daughter as usual. Want me to have a try at Sam?"

"Not necessary. Chief Inspector Kepesake is taking it in hand." Forsythe drained his glass, looking crossly at his companion, hoping Giles would drink up and leave. But the writer was settling himself comfortably.

"If it doesn't conflict with your vow of secrecy I was wondering if you could tell me which one is the dummy and which the ventriloquist."

Forsythe lifted his head. "I don't follow you."

"Kepesake and Brummell. Which one is the brains of that outfit?"

"Adam Kepesake does happen to be the chief inspector."

"A typical lawyer's answer." In a gesture of wicked mimicry Giles made a waving motion and the barrister could almost see a jade holder in the writer's long fingers. He also mimicked Kepesake's voice perfectly. "Tell him, Beau," he said airily.

Forsythe smiled. "I see you've tumbled. Kepesake is fairly competent but Brummell is far out in front with ability."

"Then why is Brummell sergeant?"

"It's still rather common to find the man with the birth, the breeding, the education, receiving the promotions."

"And poor Beau looks like he tumbled out of a haystack. Think he resents Kepesake?"

"I've the impression he's rather fond of his chief. He certainly does his best to make Kepesake look good. You know, Giles, you're a man of many parts. That imitation of the chief inspector was good. Sure you're not an actor?"

Pulling his rangy frame up, Giles gathered up the glasses and the bottle. "The Lord forbid! But when you hang around with actors long enough some of it is bound to rub off. I'll leave you to your nap. See you at dinner. Wonder if Honoria will be able to rout Mickey out."

"I doubt it," Forsythe said and rolled over, burying his face in the pillow.

When he stepped from his room freshly shaved and impeccably dressed he found he'd underestimated his hostess's power of persuasion. A short procession was making its way toward the staircase. In the lead was his secretary and Erika Von Farr. Forsythe didn't spare a glance for Miss Sanderson but feasted his eyes on the actress. Erika certainly didn't look like a ghost. She was a vision in jade silk with gold bangles on her wrists and more gold glinting from her ears. Behind them Giles, wearing a dumbfounded expression, was walking at Michael Dowling's side.

"What an ordeal this has been," Dowling told Forsythe with no preliminaries. "How I've suffered."

He showed no signs of suffering. His skin was glowing with health and his curls were glossy. He was dressed nattily in a yellow cashmere sweater and white duck pants. Forsythe lifted his brows at Giles and the younger man grinned back. "Found out how Honoria did it. Hit our boy where it hurts. Told Mickey she was cutting off his kitchen privileges. Said he could starve if he didn't come down for dinner."

"I'd got sick of that room anyway," Dowling told them. "And the food! For two days I've existed on tinned soup and sandwiches."

"Think the danger is over, old boy?" Giles asked.

"Erika tells me the chief inspector did leave a man here. He let me think there wouldn't be a policeman within miles of the house. We didn't hit it off, you know. Kepesake's so thin-skinned. I called him 'my man' a couple of times and he fairly flew at me. But I stood right up to him. Told him as a policeman he was a public servant and—"

"Adam Kepesake is the son of a baronet," Forsythe said quietly.

"I don't care if his father's an earl. He's only a dumb cop."

Giles shook a baffled head. "By any chance did you mention that as a taxpayer you are paying his salary?"

"I might have mentioned it. Why?"

"Mickey, promise if you ever decide to change professions you won't go into the diplomatic corps."

"I've no intention of being anything but an actor. I'll tell you why."

All the way down the stairs, Dowling told them why. When they entered the dining room he greeted Honoria and the other two men casually and headed directly to his chair. Forsythe took a place opposite the actor and watched him covertly. Under other circumstances it might have been funny. With hawklike intensity, Dowling followed the old butler's every move. When his plate was set before him he leaned back and waited until the other diners had sampled the course before falling on his ravenously. Waiting for someone to sprawl on the floor and start having a fit, Forsythe decided. Michael Dowling inspired him with amused contempt. A dangerous way of thinking, he decided, so easy to throw a person off whatever the actor actually was. If this man had managed to outwit a bright bunch of lads in the Narcotics Division he must be cunning indeed.

Forsythe transferred his attention to the other diners. Hardly a word was being exchanged. He'd thought Mel Borthwick would be jubilant at hearing about the inquest, but he proved as taciturn as Cochrane. Erika and Miss Sanderson were quiet and Mickey Darling was engrossed in his food. With some concern, Forsythe eyed their hostess. Honoria appeared withdrawn and abstracted, attending to her guests' needs in a perfunctory manner. The only spasm of conversation came as Potter shakily carved the ham.

"Where's the man Kepesake left here?" Dowling asked.

With a visible effort Honoria aroused herself from her thoughts. "Constable Jenkins is having his meal in the kitchen."

"Think I'll speak to him after dinner. See whether we can strike a bargain."

Borthwick examined his star warily. "What kind of bargain?"

"I don't imagine the rate of pay is high for a constable."

"Mickey, are you thinking of offering him money?"

Dowling shrugged. "If he'd keep an eye on me tonight I might make it worth his while."

"For God's sake!" The director clawed at his naked skull as though wishing for a thick head of hair to tear off. "The man will have you on charge for trying to bribe an officer."

Dowling looked sulky and for moments ate in silence. Then he lifted his glossy head and stared across at Forsythe. "Hey, I forgot. You're sort of a detective, aren't you? You bodyguard me until after the inquest and I'll pay handsomely."

"Robby," Miss Sanderson said icily, "is not a bodyguard."

"Keep out of this, Abigail. Well, Robert, what about it?"

An eerie chuckle from Giles Eady swung Dowling's head in that direction. "Have you ever thought, Mickey, Robert might have been the one to slide that poison in your booze?"

"I trust Robert. We only met a few days ago."

"With you that's quite enough time to want to murder. Right, Mel?"

Honoria Farquson brought the flat of her hand down on the table with such force the plates jumped. "That's quite enough, Mr. Eady! Your attempt at humor is in the worst possible taste. Have you forgotten that Marcia died in this house two evenings ago? Your friend, my friend...she died an agonizing death."

Lowering his head, the writer mumbled an apology. Honoria turned her attention to Dowling. "As for you, Mickey, you've been shut in that room too long. What you need is exercise and fresh air. Directly after dinner you're going for a walk."

"It's pouring and it's cold, Aunt Honoria."

"The rain stopped an hour ago. As for being cold, bundle up well. I'm going to."

"You're going to walk with me?"

"Yes, Mickey." She smiled at him. "I'm going to bodyguard you."

Something about that smile disturbed Forsythe. He brooded about it until dinner was finished. Dowling and Honoria disappeared for a few moments and when they returned their hostess was wearing a shabby knitted coat that made her look shorter and heavier. Dowling's expensive doeskin jacket was buttoned to the throat. The others headed across the hall to the drawing room but Potter stopped Forsythe. "A telephone call for you, sir. Chief Inspector Kepesake ringing up from the village."

Kepesake said rapidly, "I know you can't say much at your end but Brummell's had a report on Erika Von Farr and her mother. At the time of Margaret's Cochrane's accident they were both in Hollywood. Shoots your theory full of holes, doesn't it?"

"Looks that way."

"I rather liked it. Would have explained a lot of things. I've been wondering whether Dowling could have anything else on Miss Farr. Think about it, will you?"

"I'll do that," Forsythe told him, and with a smile added, "my man."

Kepesake gave a howl and Forsythe rang off.

In the drawing room the barrister paused to gaze down at the woman they'd been discussing. She was stretched on a divan with jade silk mounding gracefully over her thin body. Her eyes were closed and her face wiped so clean of expression that she appeared to be sleeping. As he watched, thick lashes lifted and he looked down into her eyes. Those eyes had no more expression than her face. Then a trace of animation flickered and Erika said softly, "I feel exhausted, Robert."

"We all do," he told her and wandered over to the hearth. Taking the chair across the hearth rug from the wing chair where Cochrane appeared to be sleeping, he stretched out his bad leg and put his head back. In another wing chair the director's small form was engulfed and he was not only sleeping but gently snoring. Near Borthwick, Miss Sanderson and the writer had set up a jigsaw puzzle and had their heads bent over it. The heat from the fire was making Forsythe drowsy. His nap before dinner had merely been an uneasy doze and he felt unbelievably weary. I'll close my eyes for a few moments, he told himself. He closed his eyes, a thick dark curtain seemed to fall, and Forsythe fell with it.

Chapter Eleven

For moments after Forsythe roused from deep sleep he had no inkling where he was. He was conscious of being comfortable, softness under him and some wooly warmth over him, but whether he was in bed in his flat in London or in the wider bed in Sussex, he couldn't tell. Then he found his feet were resting on an object that felt like a hassock, his back braced against a chair. The Farquson drawing room, he thought, and opened his eyes.

There was little light, only that flickering from a dying fire and one shaded table lamp across the room. Enough light for him to see that except for the figure in the wing chair across the hearth rug the room was deserted. "How long have I slept?" he asked.

"Hours, Mr. Forsythe, it's well after midnight." Honoria turned her head and a log crashed down on the grate. Flames shot up, their light ruddily outlining the curve of a cheekbone, burnishing the long line of her jaw. "Abigail was intent on sending you to bed but I persuaded her to leave you where you are. We did put the hassock under your legs and an afghan over you."

"You haven't waited up on my account?"

"No, after the day I've had it's been pleasant just to sit idly and watch pictures in the flames. Do you ever do that?"

"Many times. What did you see in the flames?"

"My youth. I suppose that's what we look for. Happy times." She looked again into the rekindled fire and the reflected light reddened her pale hair, cast a rosy glow across the high bridge of her nose. "Abigail tells me your father was not only a barrister but a judge."

"As was my grandfather. Forsythes have always been drawn toward the legal profession."

"Then perhaps you will give me your opinion of justice."

"Our judicial system or in the abstract sense?"

"Both."

"Well, in the practical sense our system of justice is imperfect. I suppose one could expect little else of something created by imperfect man. It's a huge, creaking machine that sometimes spews out the guilty and lets them go free. At times, and thankfully this is rarer, it gobbles up the innocent. But on the whole...it does serve a useful purpose and is certainly much superior to vigilante justice."

"And the abstract?"

"The blindfolded figure of a woman holding scales?" Pushing away the hassock, he lowered his feet. "Throughout my life I've noticed rather an odd and at times satisfactory phenomenon. I'll give you one example. A number of years ago a friend of mine—a superintendent of the C.I.D.—had a case that obsessed him. Grantham was investigating a number of murders of prostitutes in the East End—"

"Similar to Jack the Ripper?"

"Along those lines. Grantham had his eye on a young man from a good family who always seemed to be turning up on the case. This man—let's call him John—had a deformity, a club foot. In time John admitted to Grantham that his father had lived a wild life in his youth and at the time he—John—was conceived was suffering from a social disease. John blamed his deformity on this and had a paranoiac hatred of prostitutes.

"Grantham did everything in his power to prove John was killing the girls. He had him in to assist the police inquiry a number of times; he put detectives on John's every movement; but he couldn't get proof that would stand up in court."

"John was getting away with murder—literally."

"Precisely. The duel went on between Grantham and John until the number of victims reached four. Then abstract justice intervened."

"John slipped," Honoria guessed. "Grantham got proof."

"No. He was far too wily for that. John decided to take a vacation. He went to Brighton. He was a strong swimmer but he got a cramp and in full view of crowds on the beach, he drowned. He went under screaming for help and not one person realized his plight or came to his aid."

She propped her chin on a hand. "Divine intervention, Mr. Forsythe?"

"Perhaps. Perhaps what we call fate, or sometimes justice. But I've often noticed that when our legal system can't touch a criminal something else seems to do our job."

"Tell me, if your friend Grantham had been on that beach...would he have tried to save John?"

"I can't answer that. I've no idea what another person would do."

"Would you have tried?"

Folding the afghan, Forsythe placed it across the hassock. "I would never interfere with fate."

He stood up and so did his hostess. She reached for a side table and he noticed a tray bearing a thermos jug, a fine china cup, a dish of biscuits. He took it up and followed her into the entrance hall. In the dim light he could see an easy chair had been moved into it and a young constable hopped up. He was a stocky young man with sandy hair. Honoria passed and wished him a pleasant good night. "Potter has left coffee and sandwiches in the morning room, Constable Jenkins. Do help yourself."

"Thank you, Miss Farquson," Jenkins said and gave her a look of respect blended with affection. This man, Forsythe recalled, had once been in Miss Farquson's Sunday school class.

When they reached Honoria's room the door stood ajar and the terrier scampered to greet its mistress. She scooped up the dog and replaced it in the basket. In the strong light from the lamps her face was drawn, the skin grayish. "I hesitate to ask another favor, Mr. Forsythe, but will you be good enough to take Ciara down to Potty? I'm going to close my door and she is such a silly thing, she'll be quite upset."

Forsythe took the basket and looked searchingly down at her. "Is there…Miss Farquson, do you want to talk?"

"No. I'm talked out. Tomorrow will be soon enough."

She was holding open the door and Forsythe stepped into the hall. After the door closed he stood clutching the basket. Then he retraced his steps. Jenkins was at the foot of the stairs, gazing up. "Something amiss, sir?"

"No, constable. Would you be kind enough to take this little animal to the cook's quarters? Tell Mrs. Potter that Miss Farquson is closing her door tonight."

On his way to his own room the barrister stopped outside Honoria's door and listened. As Kepesake had mentioned, the doors in this house were two-inch oak. He couldn't hear a sound. In his own room the bed, fresh sheets turned down over a down comforter, beckoned. He took off his jacket and vest, loosened his tie, and opened the wardrobe. He'd brought two robes. One, a fanciful silken affair, had been a birthday gift from his secretary, and the other was an old friend—shabby, woolen, warm. Pulling the woolen robe on, he pulled the easy chair away from the wall, opened the door a crack, and turned off the lamp. Sinking into the chair he could see dim light shining against Honoria's door. I'm being a fool, he thought, deserting a warm bed for this cold vigil. But his sense of unease would prevent him from sleeping soundly anyway. Something was amiss with Honoria Farquson. Her preoccupation during the dinner hour, that enigmatic smile she'd turned on Dowling, the recent conversation about justice…

Through the night hours Forsythe kept his lonely vigil. At times he would doze, then jerk up at a sound from the hall. Twice he leaped to his feet at the thud of footsteps. Both times it was Constable Jenkins, moving down the hall to the far end and then returning.

A third time the noise that disturbed him was softer, the creak of a door. This time he looked around his own door and saw Cochrane, attired in striped pajamas, padding into the bathroom. Forsythe stayed at his post until the huge man, carrying what looked like a glass of water, returned to his room.

Later exhaustion overwhelmed the barrister and he was drifting off to sleep when a hand descended on his shoulder. He jerked awake. Potter was bending over him. "You've not been to bed, sir?"

Forsythe stretched and glanced at the window. Pale fingers of dawn showed in a crack between the curtains. "No, but I think I may crawl in for a couple of hours." He looked at the face close to his own. "Something bothering you?"

"Miss Honoria, sir. It's twenty after seven and unless she's ill she's never been in bed after seven."

"Probably sleeping in. She was worn out last night."

"Perhaps, sir." Potter didn't sound reassured. "I think I'd better knock and see if she's unwell."

As Forsythe drew back the curtains he could hear the mutter of Potter's voice in the hall. His unease of the previous night returned and he found himself drawn to the butler's side. A door further down the hall creaked open and Miss Sanderson, her hair mussed and pulling a robe over her flannel gown, joined them. "What's up, Robby?"

"Potter's a bit concerned. Miss Farquson seems to be sleeping in."

Miss Sanderson yawned. "She could have taken something to help her sleep."

"Never!" Potter declared. "Miss Honoria doesn't like drugs. All she has is hot chocolate to relax her."

Forsythe rubbed his bristly chin and stepped closer to the door. "I'll have a go." He rapped sharply and called, "Miss Farquson."

The butler's rheumy eyes turned pleadingly up to Forsythe. "Something is wrong, sir."

Forsythe now believed there was. He was about to send Potter in search of the constable when that worthy appeared on the landing. Forsythe explained and Jenkins took over. The strong fist of the law rang out against the oaken panel and several doors opened and heads popped out. "Back in your rooms," Jenkins ordered. "And stay there!" He tried the knob. "Locked." He turned to the barrister. "Think we'd better have that door down, sir."

"I agree. But how? No use putting our shoulders against it. When this house was built they didn't fool around. This is solid wood and the hinges are strong."

Jenkins swung on the butler. "Got a pry bar around?"

"In the pantry. I'll get it."

The old man took a couple of tottering steps and Jenkins told him, "I'll get it. Tell me its location."

He went to get it. Miss Sanderson was supporting Potter, speaking to him in the soothing voice one uses for frightened animals and small children. Jenkins was soon back, taking the stairs two at a time. "Stand back," he ordered and positioned the tapered end between the frame and the lock. Even with the leverage of his youthful strength, it took time before the wood around the lock splintered and the door gave. He stepped into the room and then called, "Mr. Forsythe!"

The barrister took a deep breath and followed the young man. The curtains were drawn over the window but the room was brilliant with lamplight. The tray sat on the Sheraton desk but now the top of the thermos was off and the china cup was on the desk blotter. Also on the blotter was a sheet of writing paper. Jenkins was on his knees beside a huddled form near the desk. Honoria had collapsed on her face, one arm bent under her body, the other thrown above her head. The fingers of that hand had clawed at the nap of the carpet and were locked in that position. A robe of cornflower blue twisted around the still form. It was hiked up over one leg displaying an inch of pink flannelette and a shapely white calf. Without thinking he bent to twitch the robe down. Jenkins told him sharply, "Don't touch anything!" Then he raised his head and for a minute his training deserted him. There was grief in his face, the grief of a young boy who had affection for a onetime teacher. "She's cold, Mr. Forsythe. Rigid. Must have died hours ago."

Forsythe nodded, stepped over to the desk, noticed a ballpoint pen on the floor near it, and bent over the notepaper. Both men read the flowing writing. "Not suicide," Jenkins breathed in Forsythe's ear.

Forsythe bent lower and sniffed at the cup. It was half full and a scum had formed on the milk. "Murder, constable. Better get on to Chief Inspector Kepesake."

Jenkins opened the door. Miss Sanderson had her arms around the butler. Her face was frightened. Potter looked directly at Forsythe. The barrister flinched at the depths of anguish in those eyes. "Is she…"

"Yes," Forsythe told him gently. He didn't feel gentle. He felt wild with rage. Here was one of the few mourners for Honoria Farquson, not Erika, who had known her aunt for only a short time; not the villagers, who had known her charity for a lifetime and could still gossip about her to the media. An old couple who had never had a child and had taken a lonely little girl into their hearts had been dealt a fatal blow.

Potter put Miss Sanderson aside firmly but with dignity. He straightened his shoulders. "What can I do to help?"

Forsythe stepped out into the hall. "Go to your wife, Potter. Take care of her. A moment, constable. Sandy, did your sister leave a forwarding address with you?"

"Yes, and a number in case of emergency."

"As soon as the constable has finished with the telephone you ring through to Teresa. Don't let her put you off. Tell her she's the last of the musketeers. This is what I want you to find out."

He told her concisely. Then he said to the constable, "Stay with Miss Sanderson. When she leaves the house go with her. I'll take the responsibility."

They left, Sandy and Jenkins flanking Potter. Potter was moving more quickly than was his wont. Forsythe took a quick look down the hall at the row of blank doors and then returned to the room. Like a sentinel he stood over the body, angry eyes raking the room. He looked at the desk, at the table crowded with memorabilia, at the corner where Ciara's basket had sat.

After a time he said aloud, "Justice *will* be served. *Requiescat in pace.*"

Chapter Twelve

Chief Inspector Kepesake and Sergeant Brummell broke something of a record getting from the Unicorn in Bury-Sutton to the Farquson estate. They found Robert Forsythe still standing over the body. As they entered the bedroom Forsythe left his post and backed against a wall. Brummell examined the tray on the desk while his superior knelt beside the body. Kepesake got up, dusted off his knees, and scanned the letter on the desk. "Does this mean anything to you, Forsythe?"

"Yes, I've sent Miss Sanderson to find it. I told Constable Jenkins to stay with her."

"Same modus operandi as Miss Mather," Brummell said. "Only this time the cyanide was put in chocolate. I'd say in the thermos."

Swinging around, Kepesake eyed the barrister's shabby robe, his unshaven chin. "Chief Inspector Parker and the lads should be here soon. Want to take time to freshen up?"

"No, we'd better get to work. Did you leave men to patrol the grounds last night?"

"Williams and Stevenson. You want them?" Brummell asked.

"Yes, and Mrs. Potter, and Jenkins when he gets back."

Brummell's untidy head swung around toward the chief inspector. "The lab boys will be going over this room. Want to talk down in the library, chief?"

"I suppose we'd better." Kepesake stepped out of the room and beckoned Constable Summer. "Stay here until Chief Inspector Parker arrives. Then get Williams, Stevenson, and the cook and bring them to the library."

"What about the other people? They're poking their heads out and complaining."

"Tell them to remain in their rooms. I'll speak with them later."

The library had been restored to order. The books had been replaced on the shelves. Forsythe wondered if the police had done it or if it had been Honoria's capable hands. He stepped to the bookcase and saw the volumes about the Crimean War in their usual place, the Second World War to the right, Napoleonic history directly above. Honoria Farquson, he thought, putting her house in order, and he felt hot rage congealing into icy fury. Touching his arm, Brummell said with awkward gentleness, "You were fond of the lady, Mr. Forsythe?"

"She was a fine woman, warm and generous and courageous. Yes, I was fond of her." Forsythe sat down opposite Kepesake and started, without prompting, to speak. There were many interruptions. Miss Sanderson, tailed by Constable Jenkins, came into the room. She'd slipped a raincoat over her robe and it was glistening with moisture. The bottom of her robe was sodden and streaked with grass stains. She put down a black plastic bundle in front of the barrister. Using a pencil, he pushed it over to the chief inspector. "Get up and change those wet clothes," he told her. "Jenkins, you stay. We've a question to ask you."

Forsythe asked the question, the constable replied, and Kepesake told Jenkins, "Get up to the murder room. As soon as that letter is dusted for prints, bring it down here."

Shortly afterwards Williams and Stevenson entered the library. Rain dripped from their slickers over the gleaming parquet. Mrs. Potter, shepherded by Constable Summer, was the next person who answered questions. She seemed to be bearing up better than her husband had. Brummell questioned her but she pointedly looked at Forsythe as she answered. Kepesake was busily extracting an envelope from the black plastic wrapping. Without looking at his sergeant he extended a hand. Brummell searched in a sagging pocket, found a pair of tweezers, and handed them to his superior.

Forsythe got up to escort the cook from the room. At the door he placed a comforting hand on her shoulder. "It will soon be over, Mrs. Potter."

She looked up and her composure cracked. Behind it he could see his own icy rage. "It *is* over. She's dead. Nothing can bring her back."

Men came and went. The pathologist, whom Forsythe had met briefly at the time of Marcia Mather's death, spoke briskly and told them nothing they didn't already know. A technician brought down Honoria's letter and gingerly picked up the one on the black plastic. "There'll only be three sets of prints on that," Forsythe told him. "One will be Miss Mather's, another Miss Farquson's."

"The third?"

"That will probably be on file with Central Bureau."

"Any idea of the name?"

It was Sergeant Brummell who told the technician the name. Kepesake was leaning back in his chair, lighting a cigarette, glowing with satisfaction. "Well, that certainly wraps this one up fast!"

"At a price," Forsythe said harshly. "Let's get it over with."

"You seem to be calling the shots, Forsythe. Who do you want and where?"

"Dowling, Miss Farr, and Cochrane. In the drawing room. I couldn't care less about the rest."

"You'd better, Robby," Miss Sanderson said from the door. "Borthwick is threatening lawyers and Giles general mayhem if they aren't allowed out of their rooms."

"Jenkins, Summer," Brummell called. "Jenkins, bring Mr. Dowling, Mr. Cochrane, and Miss Farr, down to the drawing room. Summer, you bring Mr. Borthwick and Mr. Eady down to the morning room. And stay right with them, both of you. Where's Chief Inspector Parker?"

"In the victim's room, sergeant."

"Ask him to step down to the drawing room." Brummell looked at Forsythe. "Anything else?"

"Miss Sanderson comes with me."

"Very well," Kepesake said. "Do you want to handle it from here in?"

Forsythe took Miss Sanderson's arm. "Now it's your case, chief inspector. Sandy and I are only spectators."

They took spectators' seats. Forsythe sank down on a chair against the wall; Sandy nudged over a hassock and positioned herself beside his knee. She leaned against him and asked in a whisper, "What *was* in that package, Robby?"

He patted her shoulder. "You'll know soon enough."

Kepesake strode into the room followed by his sergeant. On their heels was Constable Jenkins, herding three people. Michael Dowling was as well groomed as ever and Erika wore a floor-length Chinese gown. Serpents and exotic flowers glowed in silken splendor against white satin. Her hair was loose and fell around a bewildered face. They perched on a loveseat, close together, Erika clasping one of Dowling's hands in both of hers. Cochrane crossed the room and claimed his favorite chair near the hearth. The fireplace in which Honoria Farquson had watched pictures the night before was cold with a tumble of gray ashes. The room seemed as cold and Erika shivered. Chief Inspector Parker was the last to arrive. He turned a grim face to Kepesake and the other inspector jerked his head. Parker circled the loveseat and stood behind it, one hand resting on its back.

"Just what in hell is going on here?" Dowling demanded. "Keeping us shut in like prisoners."

Erika squeezed his hand. "Is something…has something happened to my aunt?"

"Your aunt is dead," Kepesake said.

"Oh my God!" Dowling looked terror-stricken. "Another attempt to murder me!"

"No, Mr. Dowling. The murderer got the intended victim." Kepesake looked at his sergeant and Brummell lounged across the room and halted a couple of feet from Cochrane. After a moment Jenkins strolled over casually and stood on Cochrane's other side.

Only then did Kepesake move. He pulled the tea table out a few inches and sat down behind it, facing Erika and Dowling. On the table he placed an envelope and a sheet of paper covered with Brummell's scrawl.

"You'd better tell us something right now," Dowling blustered. "I'm sick and tired of your high-handedness—"

"Patience, Mr. Dowling," Kepesake told him calmly. "In a short time you'll know what we do."

"I think," Erika said with the same calm, "it's time to make a charge or let us go. Our nerves, particularly Mickey's, can't take much more of this."

"I am making a charge. Mr. Dowling, I am formally charging you with the murders of Miss Marcia Mather and Miss Honoria Farquson."

The muscles in Dowling's handsome face went slack and his mouth trembled. It was Erika who jumped up, her eyes flashing. "You're out of your mind! Someone tried to kill *Mickey*."

"Sit down, Miss Farr. You're only present on sufferance. Mr. Dowling's life was never in danger."

"I want my lawyer," Dowling muttered.

"In good time. When we reach the station house in Elleston you may call for legal aid."

Dowling's mouth firmed. "Let's see you try to prove this." He was suddenly cool, his expression calculating.

Picking up the sheet of writing paper, Kepesake cleared his throat. "This is a copy of an unfinished letter found in Miss Farquson's room. Mr. Forsythe escorted her to her room last evening and it would seem as soon as he'd left her she started to write this. It runs as follows." He started to read in an expressionless voice.

"My dear Mr. Forsythe. If ever you read this you will wonder why I refused your kind offer to talk. At the moment I was so weary and heartsick I simply couldn't discuss it. But now I feel I won't rest until I put it down. I should imagine I will destroy this and speak to you and Chief Inspector Kepesake before Marcia's inquest tomorrow. Our conversation about justice made up my mind. All day I've been pondering, wondering whether to expose this evil or not. If I do someone I care for dearly will suffer, but at times one must speak out and help that divine intervention we mentioned. I shall try to be brief. When I met Marcia in London after all these years I was appalled. She had turned into rather a terrible person and bore no resemblance to the childhood friend I once loved. She told me dreadful things about Michael Dowling's past, hoping to influence me against him. At the time I didn't believe what she said.

Marcia came down to this house two days before Abigail and the other guests arrived. She was getting a cold and was most irritable. The second evening she had rather a lot to drink and first became maudlin about the wreckage of her life. This soon passed and Marcia started boasting about changing all that with something she had brought with her. She kept referring to this thing as her "treasure" and sometimes her "weapon." She said she not only would be able to rebuild her career but also recoup the financial losses she'd made on the film she produced starring Mr. Dowling. I'll admit my curiosity was stirred. I questioned her about it but she would tell me no more. Finally I told her if this was indeed a treasure she might better let me put it in the safe in the colonel's library. Marcia laughed and told me where she had it was "safer than any safe."

My other guests arrived the following morning and in the excitement I completely forgot about Marcia's words. It wasn't until after her death that I began to think about it. If she did have a weapon I decided it could have a bearing on her murder. It didn't take me long to come to the realization of where the hiding place was. I walked down to it and examined Marcia's treasure. Mr. Forsythe, I have always thought I was a gentle person, a woman of peace. But faced with that outrage I found myself not only horrified and sickened but consumed with a feeling of revenge. I replaced the treasure because I knew where it is *is* safe. Tomorrow I will lead the police to it and let justice take its course. I am sorry about Erika but—"

Kepesake looked up and said, "At that point Miss Farquson must have poured chocolate from the thermos and taken a swallow. The pen dug so sharply into the paper that it tore." Kepesake fastened his eyes on Dowling. Under the tan his skin had gone a sickly green shade. Cochrane was no longer lounging back in his chair, he was leaning forward. His darting eyes were locked on the actor's face as though at long last they had found what they sought.

"Chief Inspector Kepesake," Cochrane's voice resounded like a drum beat, "what was Marcia's treasure?"

Kepesake pointed to the envelope. "This, Mr. Cochrane. Would you step over and see if you can identify the handwriting?"

Cochrane approached the table and bent over it. "Jenny's. Addressed to Marcia in Switzerland. She was there when… The postmark is the day of my daughter's death." His face was filled with agony. "Why didn't Marcia show me this?"

"Perhaps she was going to," Kepesake told him, "but she must have decided to hold on to it. She used it to blackmail Mr. Dowling."

"I think I deserve to read it."

"I think you do." Kepesake took a single sheet of paper from the envelope and spread it out. "Don't touch it Mr. Cochrane. It's evidence."

Cochrane didn't touch it. He read it slowly. Then he straightened and, moving incredibly fast for his size, sprang at Dowling. One arm swept Erika aside and his hands fastened on the smaller man's throat. Jenkins and Brummell were almost as fast. They landed on Cochrane's huge back. Parker leaped to their aid and they wrestled Cochrane away. Miss Sanderson turned and hid her face against Forsythe's shoulder. "Did you have to do *that*?"

He smoothed her hair. "Yes, Sandy, we did."

Jenkins, Brummell, and Parker were still restraining Cochrane and Kepesake moved in front of the man, looking up at him. "Our case against Mr. Dowling is airtight. Leave him to us. Let the law take its course."

"Sure! Let the bastard get a battery of lawyers and—"

"Mr. Cochrane, we'll have a conviction."

"And what will he get? Ten years? Maybe five? He *killed* Jenny. As surely as if he'd cut my little girl's throat, he killed her."

"Summer," Kepesake called. "Will you escort Mr. Cochrane to the morning room? Stay with him."

He waited until Cochrane lumbered out with Summer on his heels and then he returned to the table and sat down. Parker, still panting from the tussle, circled the loveseat and stood behind Dowling. Dowling was holding his throat in both hands. "Why did you let him read that letter?" he croaked.

"You do know what was in it, Mr. Dowling?"

"I know the lies the little fool told!"

"Jenny Cochrane told her godmother you were the man who secretly put her on heroin, who secretly seduced her. She adored you and when she found she was to have your child she went to you, expecting marriage. You laughed at her, told her she was a loose little slut and had no proof it *was* your child. She was sixteen. She couldn't face her father. She took an overdose. Do you deny this?"

"You're not getting me on a drug rap! Sure I screwed her. Why not? The little slut threw herself at me." He looked around for support from Erika but she got up, walked over to the wing chair where Cochrane had recently been sitting, and leaned against the back of it. Her face was as expressionless as it had been the evening before when Forsythe had watched her on the divan.

Kepesake was trying to conceal an expression of satisfaction and not managing it. "So, Mr. Dowling, we now have a good idea what happened the evening of Miss Mather's death. She confronted you with Jenny Cochrane's letter or, I imagine, a copy of it. You distracted her attention, slipped the poison in the bottle—"

"If this was the first time I knew about the letter how did I have the poison on hand?"

Kepesake rubbed his chin. "You're a clever man, Mr. Dowling, much smarter than you let on. I should imagine that's easily explained. Miss Mather must have mentioned something about it to you earlier. So, at the greenhouse that day you scooped up the cyanide just in case."

"All right, you win. I'll tell you exactly what happened."

"Is this in the nature of a confession?"

"No. A simple statement of fact. I didn't know anything about that damn letter until Marcia and I got up to my room. She gave me a copy and told me she had the original in a safe place. Marcia said unless I gave in to her demands she'd show it to Sam. You saw him! He'd have torn me apart! I didn't know whether to believe Marcia or not. She was such a conniving devil. I figured maybe she'd made the letter up herself and there was no original. You know what she wanted? The lead part in this film. God, can you imagine her as Catherine! It would have *ruined* me. She also wanted all the money she'd spent on that dog of a Trojan Wars, *plus interest!*"

"So you poisoned the whiskey?"

"Like hell I did." Dowling massaged the red marks on his throat. "To calm her down I offered her a drink. She poured some out and started to down it. Then she grabbed at her mouth, her eyes rolled up, and she fell on the floor. She was twitching all over and I figured she was having a convulsion or a heart attack. I was going to get help and then I thought maybe I should look in her room in case she *did* have the original of that letter. I ran down the hall and looked through her drawers and under the mattress. Nothing was there so I figured she *had* been bluffing. When I came out I noticed the row of glasses on a shelf in the bathroom so I picked one up, broke it on the floor inside my door, and then called down the stairs. That is exactly what happened. I did *not* have any poison."

Brummell was looking at the actor as though the man was from another planet. "You left a woman dying to search her room?"

"Nothing I could do for Marcia and I had to think of my own skin. If she wasn't lying about that letter and Sam got his hands on it—you saw him, for God's sake! Erika, you don't believe this rot, do you?"

Her voice was expressionless as the oval of her face. "I don't know what to believe."

"Look, darling, it's a mass of circumstantial evidence. They haven't got a thing on me!"

Kepesake lit a cigarette. He waved the holder. "Tell him, Beau."

Brummell fished in a sagging pocket and brought out a notebook. He flipped it open. "Miss Farquson insisted at the dinner table, Mr. Dowling, that you walk with her."

"So? We took a walk. Damn cold it was too."

"What you may not have known is there were two constables patrolling the grounds. Constable Stevenson saw you and Miss Farquson come out the front door and start to pace up and down on the driveway. He kept an eye on you but didn't go close enough to hear what you were saying. Stevenson says Miss Farquson was doing most of the talking. You kept shaking your head and then you turned on her. You grabbed her by the shoulders and shook her. Miss Farquson broke loose and ran into the house. According to Constable Stevenson she acted frightened out of her wits."

"So?" Dowling said again. He ran his hand over his curls. "We took a walk and talked. It had nothing to do with murder or Marcia."

"It had everything to do with it. After Miss Farquson read Jenny Cochrane's letter she didn't know what to do. She was torn two ways. Any decent person would be sick at what that child said. Miss Farquson was a gentle lady, never had anything to do with violence before. You are her niece's fiancé. I think the lady wanted to give you a chance to tell your side."

"Bosh! We had a private conversation. Nothing to do with that letter."

"Then suppose you tell us what you talked about."

Dowling glanced at Erika, appeared undecided, and then shook his head stubbornly. "That, my man, is none of your business."

Brummell wasn't taking "my man" any better than his superior had. His face reddened. Curtly, he continued, "Constable Jenkins was on duty inside the house. He was in the entrance hall when Miss Farquson came running in. You were right behind her. Jenkins, tell Mr. Dowling what you heard."

Jenkins said stolidly, "Mr. Dowling yelled at Miss Farquson. His words were, 'If it's the last thing I do I'll get you!'"

"This is a frame-up!" Dowling said wildly.

"Do you deny you said those words?"

"I said them but..."

Brummell flipped over a page. "Jenkins says Miss Farquson went into the drawing room but you continued down the hall and entered the kitchen. According to Mrs. Potter's testimony you asked her to cut you a piece of the cake that had been served at dinner. Mrs. Potter went into the pantry, sliced the cake, and brought back a plate. When she entered the kitchen Mrs. Potter says you, Mr. Dowling, were bending over the stove. On that stove was Miss Farquson's chocolate, heating in an open saucepan."

"I was thinking of taking a cup to drink with the cake. Mrs. Potter ordered me away from it. She said it was for her mistress and if I wanted any I could make it myself. I grabbed the cake and went up to my room. For God's sake check out that saucepan. I didn't put anything into it."

"Mrs. Potter never leaves dirty pans overnight, Mr. Dowling. She washed that pan up before she retired. She poured the chocolate into the thermos, arranged the tray, and took it to Miss Farquson in the drawing room. Miss Farquson drank some chocolate and died. What you hadn't counted on was the letter she left for Mr. Forsythe."

"Where had Marcia hidden that letter of Jenny's, sergeant?" Erika asked.

Brummell glanced at the corner where Forsythe sat silently. The barrister said, "In the secret mail drop the Three Musketeers used when they were children. Miss Sanderson rang up her sister Teresa, the third musketeer, and she told us its location. The three little girls used a hollow in an apple tree near the remains of the gatehouse."

Kepesake rose from behind the table. "And now, Mr. Dowling, I think you'd better come with us."

"I want a lawyer! I want him right now! Erika, get on to London and...for God's sake what's wrong with you?" Dowling had leaped to his feet and approached the girl. His hand was outstretched and she cringed away from him. "I've been framed! Can't you see that?"

"Don't touch me," she whimpered. Making a wide circle around him, she moved toward the door. On the back of the robe a serpent undulated its silken coils.

Dowling followed her and Kepesake, Brummell, and Parker were right behind. Pulling himself wearily to his feet, Forsythe stretched a hand out to Miss Sanderson. "Let's get packed and get out of here, Sandy."

She leaned against him and he led her into the hall. Her blue eyes were shining with tears. Brummell and the two chief inspectors were standing by the door. At the foot of the steps Dowling stretched an imploring arm upward. Erika was partway up the stairs. Her back was toward them and she was clinging to the banister.

"Erika," Dowling cried. "I swear I didn't kill anyone."

She spoke only two words. *"Jenny Cochrane."*

"Forgive me, darling. Erika, forgive me."

Forsythe had a strange sense of déjà vu. He watched Erika straighten, remove her hand from the banister, and turn until she was in three-quarter profile. She wasn't crying but every line of her body showed grief and outrage. Her dark hair fell in a single fluid line down her back. Before she spoke, Forsythe, with terrible certainty, knew exactly what she would say.

"Forgiveness is impossible," said that unforgettable voice, silver swish of steel under black velvet, "but I promise I'll do my best to forget you."

"Dark Decision," Forsythe muttered. "The final scene."

"Robby," Miss Sanderson said gently, "she's a great actress."

"Yes. And that is all Erika Von Farr will ever be," Forsythe said sadly.

Chapter Thirteen

Elleston, normally a quiet market town, in the days following Michael Dowling's arrest assumed an air of Mardi Gras. Buses, trains, cars, and motor bikes delivered streams of people. Among them were contingents of the Mickey Darling fan clubs, young women clad lightly and brandishing placards proclaiming their idol's innocence. Another band of young women, these more modestly dressed, had arrived to urge nuclear disarmament and wave their own banners urging Yankee go home. Mistaking these sentiments as ones directed against Mickey Darling, the fan club members gave battle. Trying to urge peace upon them and getting mauled in the process was a gaunt old man of tremendous height with a wispy beard and bare feet. Finally he lost patience and used his own placard indiscriminately against both sides.

From the vantage point of the window of their hotel sitting room, Miss Sanderson watched the melee. "That placard the old goat with the beard is beating with says 'Peace and Love.' Robby, that man can certainly fight. I feel rather glad Chief Inspector Parker smuggled us in here under fictitious names."

Forsythe looked up from his book. "So do I. I suppose we should also be glad Marcia Mather's cousin whipped away her body for decent Christian burial at some undisclosed location."

"Anyway the inquest is over and the verdict should put Dowling away for some time."

"We'll have to wait for the trial to see, Sandy. Cochrane was right. Dowling has a high-powered legal staff working for him."

She leaned closer to the windowpane. "The police are breaking the cat fight up. Look at that! A couple of sidewalk vendors peddling Mickey Darling souvenirs! Photos and T-shirts and pennants. I'd swear if they could they'd be selling locks of his curly hair!" She turned away in disgust. "You think the prosecution will get a conviction?"

"Certainly. But the sentence? Again I agree with Sam Cochrane. A few years. Perhaps long enough to demolish Dowling's career. Let's hope so."

"And his chance of marrying Erika Von Farr. Speaking of Erika, Robby. Parker told me that Sam, Mel, Giles, and Erika are still barricaded on the estate. Wonder what role she's playing now?"

Forsythe stared steadily down at a page. "No doubt woman betrayed, with Giles Eady dancing attendance on her."

"Do you suppose she'll marry him?"

He shrugged. "Never can tell but I don't think there'd be enough chance for practicing drama with a man like Giles." He looked bleakly at his secretary. "I'm tempted to fold our tent and slip quietly away."

"We can't. Honoria is being buried at Bury-Sutton tomorrow. We simply have to be there, Robby."

"Yes. But if you think that's rough out there—" he waved at the window "—wait until you see the funeral."

"People wouldn't...not at a funeral, Robby."

"It will be a three-ring circus."

It was worse. Rain fell steadily but that didn't dampen the air of carnival. Around the gray stone church and ancient grave-yard crowds surged, restrained by a ring of sweating constables. In the church itself were only a handful of mourners but the vicar's words were inaudible amid the din of those outside. Several choral groups seemed to be competing. At one particu-larly loud bray of "We Shall Overcome" Miss Sanderson dug a sharp elbow into Forsythe's ribs. That was soon drowned out by "Onward Christian Soldiers." No doubt the militant peace marchers, Forsythe thought. Over all thundered the howl of the gray-haired prophet. "Repent" alternated with "Peace" and "Love."

Amid all this the mourners sat quietly. A black-veiled Erika was in the front pew supported by Giles Eady. Behind them were Sam Cochrane and Mel Borthwick. On the other side of the aisle were the old servants. Mrs. Potter, with her sweeping black dress, hadn't needed to don mourning but she had added a thatch of stiff black crepe pinned to her white topknot. Potter's frail shoulders were bowed and occasionally those shoulders shuddered with grief. Poor old devils, Forsythe mused, so little life left for them and now no earthly reason to continue it. The coffin had silver handles and was almost concealed beneath a blanket of orchids. Inappropriate for gentle Honoria, but what did it matter?

The burial service was mercifully brief and Miss Sanderson turned away to dry tears streaming down her cheeks. Her voice was muffled. "Let's make tracks, Robby."

"We have a gauntlet to run. Bear up, Sandy."

Even with the police forming a double line to the funeral cars it was indeed a gauntlet. The line was breached and a howling throng descended on them. Forsythe had a glimpse of a husky man, who looked remarkably like the pig farmer Cochrane had described, fighting his way toward Erika. In one hand he waved a scarlet A and seemed intent on pinning it to her black suit. Giles raised a fist and the pig farmer sprawled back into the crowd. Cochrane appeared to be breaking a photographer's camera and Borthwick was fending off a group of girls attired in shorts and T-shirts. They disappeared from view and Forsythe found he had his own hands full. A middle-aged woman, her hat tipped over one eye, seemed intent on ripping off one of his lapels, presumably for a souvenir. Miss Sanderson had already lost a scarf and was squealing with fury.

Blue-clad help arrived. Jenkins and MacDonald drove the mob back from them and pulled them behind the barricade of police ringing the cars. The big Scot was panting and his face was almost as red as his hair. "Ever see anything as daft as this?" MacDonald growled.

Jenkins had lost his helmet and had a bruise on one cheek. "I'd rather be up against a gang of terrorists. Least we'd be able to use our sticks."

Miss Sanderson tugged at Forsythe's arm and pointed. "Oh God! Do something!" Forsythe looked. Summer and Williams had gotten the film people clear but he caught a glimpse of bobbing black crepe. "Come on!" he yelled at the constables and charged back into the fray.

Mrs. Potter was herding her husband in front of her and managing at the same time to fight a rear-guard action. She turned and pounded the bearded prophet over the head with her umbrella. But she was tiring. By the time the barrister reached her the crepe had been yanked off. MacDonald, harboring no ill will for the meat-cleaver incident, scooped the old woman up in his arms. Forsythe and Jenkins dragged Potter along. Forsythe threw out a fist and felt savage satisfaction when it connected with a fat red face under a Tyrol hat. When they got back to the cars MacDonald had already deposited Mrs. Potter's plump figure in the back of one. Jenkins swung Potter in beside her and stood back panting.

"We should," Mrs. Potter was declaring, "have brought Heathcliff. He'd have settled this lot down. Disgraceful!"

Forsythe braced his back against the open door and struggled to catch his breath. "It's the people involved, Mrs. Potter. Public figures. You must expect a display."

"Film people. Scarlet sinners!"

"Come now, my dear," Potter chided. "Miss Erika's an actress and she's been most kind."

"I suppose so. Give us a cottage in Bury-Sutton, Mr. Forsythe, and says she'll see to us."

I wonder, Forsythe thought, how Erika likes playing the role of Lady Bountiful. Aloud he asked, "Has she any plans for the estate?"

"Don't know and don't rightly care," the cook snapped.

"What my wife is trying to say is that with Miss Honoria gone it really makes no difference to us."

Whatever defenses Mrs. Potter had erected against emotion broke. She broke into a storm of weeping. Wordlessly she held out her hand and her husband, making soothing sounds, touched the crisp white points protruding from the breast pocket of his suit coat. He pulled out a handkerchief, shook out its immaculate square, and tenderly put it into his wife's hand. Forsythe stood, his back to the crowd, and watched these moves. Then the howls behind him seemed to fade and so did the Potters.

Robert Forsythe had a marvelous memory. In argument with friends he always insisted that the human memory is more reliable than any tape, than any computer. Tapes and computers, he was wont to say, can only transmit voices and data. The human memory is capable of playing back entire scenes at will, not only with voices and intonations, but with body language.

Now that memory clicked into place and the result caused him to sag against the car door. A hand on his arm jerked him back to the roar of the sightseers, the hoarse shouts of policemen, the faces of the Potters turned up to him. "Robby," Miss Sanderson scolded, "you're soaked. We can't do any more here. Let's go."

He mumbled goodbyes to the cook and butler and allowed Miss Sanderson to guide him to the Rover. She slid behind the wheel. "I'd better drive, Sandy," he told her. "At least until we get clear of these maniacs."

"The only way to handle maniacs is to act like one."

She proceeded to demonstrate her point. A mob of scantily clad girls lunged out in front of the Rover, waving arms and placards. Instead of hitting the brake Miss Sanderson set her jaw and brought her foot down on the gas. The girls scattered pell-mell, firm little bottoms joggling, high voices shrieking. "That," Miss Sanderson said smugly, "is how you do it."

Forsythe not only snapped on his seat belt but clung to the dashboard. It wasn't until they were clear of Elleston that he relaxed and put his head back against the seat. He was conscious of his rain-soaked coat, a dull pain in his bad knee, a soreness in his right hand. He lifted his hand and discovered the knuckles were discolored. He wondered what the fat face under the Tyrol hat looked like.

Miss Sanderson slackened speed and spared a glance in his direction. "You look as though someone bopped you over the skull, Robby."

"Someone should." He closed his eyes. "Sandy, you're looking at the world's worst ass."

"What are you raving about?"

"I'm a blind fool. I've been led right up the garden path."

"Look, old boy, that scene back there was harrowing. But give you a few days with your trout stream and the MacDougal and—"

"I'm not going to Scotland. I'm going to pursue a ghost so far in the past it will be a miracle if I catch it. Sandy, *don't* ask any questions—just answer one. If I don't make it back to work on time will you hold down the fort?"

"Don't I always?" She laughed and said, "Whatever you're up to—break a leg. That's show biz talk and means—"

"—good luck. Sandy, please, no more show biz. I've had quite enough."

"I," she said grandly, "will never have enough."

Chapter Fourteen

Once Miss Sanderson was back in London she found she too had had enough of show biz for the time. After two days in her cozy flat with Aggie alternately coddling her and scolding her she sallied forth to find some enjoyment in the remaining days of her vacation. She visited with a school friend in Oxford, accepted invitations for lunches and dinners, gave a small dinner for intimates, but flatly refused three invitations for the cinema, one for the theater, and another for the opera.

When she went back to work she found, as she always did after an absence, the cluttered rooms in the centuries-old building a trial. Why, she wondered, didn't they take chambers in one of the spacious new office buildings mushrooming all over the city? Tradition, Robby had said, but tradition came with smoky hearths and dripping faucets and rooms not large enough to swing a cat in.

The stolid Vincent greeted her with restrained enthusiasm and young Peters made no effort to conceal his relief. She regarded Peters with little affection and some trepidation. He was a brilliant young chap but nervous. Did he have the nervous system and the stamina required for his chosen profession?

"Trouble?" she asked.

"None," Vincent told her, "until yesterday."

"We don't know what to do!" Peters was actually wringing his hands. "When will Mr. Forsythe be back?"

"I'm not certain. Tell me about it."

Peters told her about it. "We have to have an answer for the man's solicitor. And this case...it's insane! I've made up a preliminary folder. Would you like to go over it?"

"Did you ring up Eugene Emory?"

"Not as yet. We thought Mr. Forsythe would be back today."

She patted his thin shoulder. "Give me the solicitor's number and I'll handle it, Peters."

She escaped from the boy and opened the door to her cubicle. Pushing the visitor's chair out of the way, she reached her desk. The walls looked even more splotched than usual. Was that a water stain? They really must find other chambers. Pushing the solicitor's number to one side she rang through to Emory.

"Gene," she said, "Have you heard about the case involving Sir Amyas Dancer?"

He chuckled. "It's nearly wiped the Farquson murders off the London front pages. Weird! But the Dancers have always been a rum lot and this Amyas seems the oddest of the lot. Have you been approached?"

"According to Nervy Nellie, yesterday. Any idea what line I should take?"

"Where's Robert?"

"Anyone's guess."

"Poor Miss Sanderson. Holding young Peters's trembling hand. My advice is to stall Dancer's solicitor. Let Robert make the decision. I wouldn't touch the case but it might be something he'd take on. The boy has a taste for murder impossible, you know."

Taking Emory's advice she rang through to the solicitor and firmly put him off a couple of days. As she replaced the receiver she silently begged, Get back, Robby, the defense of your fort is weakening.

He didn't return the next day and by the third she was becoming worried. Could he have had an accident, she wondered; could he be in a hospital somewhere suffering from amnesia? Miss Sanderson didn't share her worry. By the evening of that third day Vincent had become infected with Peters's nerves and the rest of the staff was reacting. Miss Sanderson sent them all home early, shooing the last clerk out of the office and locking the reception door. She stopped at a stenographer's desk to stub a smoldering cigarette. That's all we need in this firetrap, she thought, and went back to her desk to deal with a mound of paperwork.

After a time she thought of going home but something held her back. Maybe, she thought, my wandering boy will turn up. Eventually her patience was rewarded. A key grated in the lock and she jumped up from her desk, tripped over the visitor's chair, and lunged into the reception area just as Forsythe was putting his pigskin case down. "Robby! Where in the devil have you been?"

"Simmer down, Sandy. What's wrong?"

"Everything. New case. File on your desk. Peters has been having hysterics and it's like the measles. The whole staff out of kilter. Robby, we simply must find other chambers. This place is driving me bonkers—"

He put a calming hand on her shoulder. "We'd better both have a drink. Break out the bottle."

"Drained the last into young Peters before I sent him home."

"Well, make it coffee. Bring it into my office."

Forsythe's office was not large but in contrast to his secretary's cubicle it seemed spacious. He was sitting behind his desk. The Dancer file had been pushed to one side. Setting the cup at his elbow Miss Sanderson took a good look at him. He was wearing a lightweight suit and had a deep tan. "You're looking fit. Where have you been?"

"On the Continent, soaking up the sun."

She took an armchair and stretched her long legs. "Soaking up the sun while I've been going bonkers. I hope you found your ghost."

"I did. Took a little doing but when I opened the cupboard it came tumbling out."

"Skeletons, Robby, that's what tumbles out of cupboards. Tell me your ghost story."

"In time. Now I'd like to hear about Dowling. Have they set trial date yet?"

Her eyes widened. "Haven't you been reading the papers?"

"I kept right away from television, radio, and papers. Why?"

"There won't be a trial. Dowling's dead. Cochrane shot him, Robby!"

He slumped in his chair, both hands over his face. His elbow caught the cup and Miss Sanderson rescued it in the nick of time. "Better tell me," he muttered.

She told him. When Michael Dowling had been moved from Elleston to London the police hadn't expected any real trouble. Mobs of people were swarming around but there were also mobs of police on crowd control. This time they'd used dogs and the crowd was held well back from the cars. When Dowling was helped out of the lead car, Cochrane loomed over a constable in front of him, leveled a revolver, and shot the actor twice. "Then Sam turned the gun on himself, Robby. Stuck it into his mouth and blew half his head off. Dowling died two hours later. There was a note in Sam's pocket. He said justice wouldn't be served by the light sentence his daughter's killer would get. Sam said he'd lived only to find the man and he was glad to die. He said from the moment he read Jenny's letter Michael Dowling was a dead man."

"Michael Dowling was a dead man from the moment he interfered with Jenny Cochrane. Sooner or later, Sam Cochrane would have caught up with him."

"I think Sam was only working on that film to stay close to Dowling. Robby, I don't think Sam was doing it for Erika.

But what's wrong with you? I know it's a shock but if anyone deserved it Dowling did. He killed Marcia and Honoria."

His hands fell away from his face. The color had drained from his skin and the tan looked muddy. "Brace yourself, Sandy. Dowling did *not* kill either Marcia or Honoria."

"Robby, you've had too much sun. As Adam Kepesake said, the case against Dowling was airtight."

"The frame was airtight. Dowling was supposed to die. First the murderer tried to poison him and when that failed decided to let the law handle him."

"This murderer…is he running around loose?"

"No. Now, be quiet, Sandy, and listen. You're not going to like this any more than I do but you must know. After you understand I'm going to leave it to you to pronounce sentence—"

"You mean to tell the police?"

"Or not to." Forsythe templed his fingers. "We both have excellent memories. If anything, yours is better than mine. Cast your mind back—"

"One moment. Something tipped you the day of Honoria's funeral. I think I should know what."

"A very simple act. Potter took a handkerchief from his breast pocket, shook it out, handed it to his wife. That triggered my own memory. Now, back to the evening I arrived at the Farquson house. Dinner time. Candles and dim light. What was Michael Dowling wearing at dinner?"

"How would I know? So much has happened. All right, don't push." Miss Sanderson's thumbnail drummed against her front teeth. "Blue…blue jeans, a lighter shirt…a scarf at his throat…lashings of gold jewelry."

"The breast pocket of his shirt?"

"Something blue to match his outfit. Darker…a handkerchief."

"We went from the table to the drawing room in a group. Dowling insisted Honoria go out with him for a turn on the grounds. They returned. Dowling announced his forthcoming marriage. Erika broke into tears. Take it from there, Sandy."

"She put her hand out and Dowling didn't...Robby! He had no handkerchief."

"Then what?"

"Giles—no; first Dowling asked Honoria for hers. She put her hand in the pocket of her cardigan and paper crinkled. Honoria laughed and said all she had was a shopping list. Then Giles—"

"We have all we need. It wasn't a handkerchief in his pocket, Sandy, it was a slip of paper." He flipped back the front of his jacket and showed her blue points sticking out of his shirt pocket. "Exactly like this one. When Honoria and Dowling returned to the drawing room she had changed her attitude towards him, was busily welcoming him into the family."

"He blackmailed her," Miss Sanderson said. "In exchange for her promise about the estate he gave her that piece of paper." She held out an imperious hand. "Give it to me!"

"Patience. Dowling blackmailed our hostess. Now, your memory again. Next morning. Picnic planned but rain teeming down. Morning room. You arrived for breakfast before I did. What was Honoria doing?"

"Looking out of the window. She was rather sad and upset. Her picnic plans had been ruined."

"Honoria wasn't sad because of the picnic. She was sickened and despairing. The evening before, Erika's lover had blackmailed her into consenting to his marriage, among other things. At that point Honoria remembered Marcia's treasure. She didn't read Jenny Cochrane's letter *after* Marcia's death; she read it that morning when she took the walk in the rain."

"Mrs. Potter scolded Honoria about that walk. Said she'd been out in the rain before the sun was up."

"Then Honoria Farquson realized fully what Dowling was. He would have ruined Erika. Honoria had lived a life of quiet desperation; she wasn't going to let Erika's life be destroyed. She maneuvered the entire group to the greenhouse, took the cyanide, and when we returned put some of it in Dowling's whiskey."

"When Marcia died in his stead Honoria was shattered, Robby, simply shattered!" The secretary's pale eyes locked with Forsythe's. "How could she have fooled us? Robby, Honoria was such a *simple* woman."

"A natural actress, Sandy, one of the best. And she had no instincts towards murder. She did what she thought she must but afterwards…her childhood friend had died agonizingly. Honoria still had the rest of the cyanide but she couldn't bring herself to use it on Dowling. So, she changed course and decided to have him indicted on two counts of murder. To do this she set all of us up as witnesses. The constable on the grounds, Jenkins in the hall, Mrs. Potter in the kitchen. And me. Particularly me. Sandy, that simple lady of yours played me like a trout going after live bait. That hint in her letter…she knew I'd follow it up and find the musketeers' mail drop. And I went for it. As though Honoria were pulling me about like a puppet, I helped frame Michael Dowling for murders he didn't commit."

"Incredible! What courage she had! She put the cyanide in her thermos, probably burned its container on her hearth, wrote the letter, and drank the chocolate. Robby, I don't think she wanted to live, not after Marcia…"

"Nor do I. Any questions?"

"Two. How did she make Dowling so angry that night on the driveway that he laid hands on her and shouted threats?" She hesitated and then said, "Oh!"

"I can see you've tumbled. I imagine Honoria simply told Dowling she'd changed her mind and was breaking her promise. The estate would never be his. Dowling saw red. He was already counting his profit. Your other question?"

"Motive. I told you I thought Honoria was capable of the crime but the motive wasn't strong enough. Robby, I'd swear she didn't even like her niece."

He flipped open his jacket and handed her the folded sheet of dark blue notepaper. "I've been in Italy, in a village in the Apennines called Santa Vittoria. As Dowling mentioned, he was there last year. He didn't spend any time looking for souvenirs. Instead he visited a doctor. Salvatore Valenti is very old now but his memory is clear. He remembered Michael Dowling and he clearly remembered the young English girls he'd taken in thirty years ago. I think the good doctor was half in love with Honoria Farquson. He called her a Viking princess. He also says he was hoping her baby would look like her. But instead of having fair hair and blue eyes her child was dark. Doctor Valenti didn't care as much for Von Farquson."

Miss Sanderson read the crabbed writing. "Not Honoria's niece. Her daughter!"

"Dowling was a cunning chap. He carefully filed this fact away just in case it might be useful to him later. When he realized there was money to be made on Honoria's property he used it. Dowling had no honor but he realized that as Chief Inspector Parker said, Honoria's word was 'inviolate.' So…Honoria got Doctor Valenti's letter and Dowling got her promise."

Miss Sanderson laid the blue paper on the desk as though it were somehow fragile. "That's why the colonel consented to Honoria and her sister-in-law going to the Continent. He sent them away so that the baby could be born and his precious family name not be sullied. They must have switched passports and Erika was registered as Mrs. Charles Farquson's child. But this was Honoria's dream—to have children. Why didn't she take the child and run for it?"

"We can only surmise. Knowing Honoria I imagine her father extracted a promise she would return. Also knowing Honoria she couldn't stand the stigma of illegitimacy to be attached to her daughter. Also, knowing your ogre, I imagine the colonel would have allowed her to bring the baby home as her nephew if it had been a boy. It was a girl and he didn't want it. He forced Honoria to let Von Farquson take the child to the States. Remember Butterscotch, Sandy?"

"He punished by taking away a love object," Miss Sanderson said wrathfully. "Honoria loved her daughter, and he made her give up the child. I hope he's burning in hell!"

"You and Mrs. Potter. If there is any afterlife I imagine that's where he is. And amen to it."

Miss Sanderson was tapping her teeth again. "I can make a guess about Erika's father."

"I should have tumbled to that sooner. Honoria let it slip the first night I carried her tray up for her. I was examining her table of memorabilia and—"

"And thinking of nothing but Erika Von Farr."

"Yes," he said ruefully. "But Honoria said that Erika was 'so much like her father.' She covered by saying 'not in looks, but in nature.' Charles Farquson was vacillating and not brainy. But Erik Larsen had, as Honoria told us, 'passion, depth, courage.' Erik Larsen was Erika's father."

"A country mouse thrown into bohemia," Miss Sanderson mused. "Eighteen years old and in a tiny flat with a glamorous young man. If Erik hadn't died, maybe they might have married."

"Perhaps."

"And three people are dead because of Honoria's mother love."

"More of a mother guilt. When Erika and her mother met after all those years I believe Honoria knew what her daughter had become. Sam Cochrane called Erika lopsided; Borthwick said she's a series of roles with a core of emptiness. And Honoria was the one who handed her baby over to an ambitious, driving woman. All Erika has is her acting career and her mother did her best to protect that career. Now, your honor, the verdict."

She glanced down at the slip of blue paper. "You think Doctor Valenti's statement and the other points you've made might be enough to clear Dowling's name?"

"Possibly."

"And in doing so we'd brand Honoria a murderer?"

"Yes."

"Take me out to dinner, Robby. Ply me with that double you owe me and several others and when I'm properly befuddled I'll hand down my decision."

"Not good enough. Now, Sandy."

Her eyes searched his face. "There's no way you could have kept Sam Cochrane from killing Dowling."

"The verdict."

"Michael Dowling versus Honoria Farquson. Dowling... selling drugs...corrupting a mere child...driving a woman to suicide. Honoria...living her life in a hell devised by the colonel...honorable...dying to keep her daughter, who certainly isn't worth it, from ruin. No contest."

Miss Sanderson stood, reached for the blue paper, shredded it. She threw the pieces in the air and they fluttered down like blue confetti. A few scraps caught in Forsythe's hair. "Justice *has* been served. May you rest in peace, Honoria Farquson."